Running Through the Tall Grass

Running Through

the Tall Grass

a novel

Thomas Givon

ReganBooks
An Imprint of HarperCollins*Publishers*

RUNNING THROUGH THE TALL GRASS. Copyright © 1997 by Thomas Givon. All rights reserved. Printed in the United States of America. No part of this book may be used or reproduced in any manner whatsoever without written permission except in the case of brief quotations embodied in critical articles and reviews. For information address HarperCollins Publishers, Inc., 10 East 53rd Street, New York, NY 10022.

HarperCollins books may be purchased for educational, business, or sales promotional use. For information please write: Special Markets Department, HarperCollins Publishers, Inc., 10 East 53rd Street, New York, NY 10022.

FIRST EDITION

Designed by Ruth Lee

Library of Congress Cataloging-in-Publication Data

Givon, Thomas.
    Running through the tall grass : a novel / Thomas Givon.—1st ed.
      p.   cm.
    ISBN 0-06-039200-2
    I. Title.
PS3557.I87R86   1997
813'.54—dc21   97-2033

97 98 99 00 01 ❖/RRD 10 9 8 7 6 5 4 3 2 1

To *mamacita*,
who taught me the song

And to the *pieds noirs* of this world,
wherever you are,
brothers and sisters

ACKNOWLEDGMENTS

This book has been a long time coming, and consequently owes much to many. But especially to: the late Nathan Yalin-Mor, for help with my research in France; the Foreign Area Fellowship Program, for inadvertently supporting my work in Katanga; Judith Regan, for taking a gamble on me; Kristin Kiser, for being a wonderful, perceptive, generous editor; my friend Charles Li, who brought me together with ReganBooks and put up with my temper tantrums; and Linda Cruz Givon, for living through the endless retracing of the journey (part of it in cramped quarters), and for insisting on integrity above all else.

Contents

AUTHOR'S NOTE

xi

ONE

THE CITY BURNING

Marie

1

TWO

THE OTHER SIDE

Jojo

73

THREE

RUNNING THROUGH THE TALL GRASS

Robert

193

FOUR

EPILOGUE

Marie

271

Author's Note

While fictional, the story of Robert Aron—French-Algerian of mixed origins, Foreign Legion veteran of Indochina and the Battle of Algiers, AWOL ex-paratrooper and underground demolition expert and, in the end, reluctant Congo mercenary—is set in a definite historical context.

France took possession of Algeria in the early 1800s, declaring it a province of France in 1830. Settlers were enticed to the new province with promises of free land, a fresh start, and instant French identity. Most of the land-hungry colonists who answered the call were not French, but rather an assorted mélange of political, economic, religious, and cultural refugees from all around the western Mediterranean basin—Corsicans, Italians, Spaniards, Greeks, Jews, and stray victims of France's long succession of losing wars. France invited these would-be Frenchmen to secure for it the crown jewel on the North African coast. But from the very start it condescended to them as marginal Frenchmen, *pieds noirs*—black feet.

Early in the Second World War, the *pieds noirs* succeeded in maintaining an ambiguous semblance of Free France in alliance with "free" units of the French Army. Arab sympathies in Algeria tended toward Germany, viewed as a potential liberator from the French colonial yoke. Together with other Free French forces in Africa, who remained outside the control of the collaborationist government on the mainland, the *pieds noirs* soon came to see themselves as the true French patriots in the mortal struggle against Nazi oppression.

After the war, decolonialization spread like wildfire all over the far-flung French empire. A festering early war to retain control of Indochina—later Vietnam—ended in the crushing 1954 defeat at Dien Bien Phu. For their disgraced withdrawal from Indochina, the French expeditionary forces and the French military establishment blamed the liberal politicians and leftist traitors in Paris.

Many of the French colonial troops, especially the Foreign Legion, were withdrawn to bases in North Africa, most centrally Sidi-bel-Abbès at the foothills of the Kabylia Mountains of Algeria. Two years later, in 1956, the National Liberation Front (*Front Liberation National*, FLN), a group of Arab nationalists, launched its own war of independence against the French. The new conflict quickly cemented the natural alliance between the French military, many of them embittered veterans of Indochina, and the *pieds noirs*. The natural common enemy was clear to both—ten million Arabs clamoring for political takeover of the jewel of Mediterranean France, and the cowardly French politicians and leftist public opinion-makers, by now sick and tired of extended colonial wars.

In 1958, facing dwindling support from the revolving-door governments in Paris, the army rose against the central government, taking over Algeria and precipitating total chaos in France. Within a few months, the chaos was resolved by the return to power of the famed liberator of World War II, General Charles de Gaulle. In his latter incarnation as the nation's savior, *le General* went to Algeria and made some rash promises to both the army and the *pieds noirs*: Algeria would remain French; *Algérie Française* forever.

International and internal political realities soon caught up with the wily general. By 1960, he was secretly negotiating with the Arab FLN, a negotiation culminating in the Evian peace accord of early 1962.

The incensed *pieds noirs* and the French Army in Algeria reacted with shock and then fury. Whole units deserted the Legion and went underground. Generals and colonels denounced de Gaulle as a traitor and put a price on his head. The Secret Army Organization (*Organization Armée Secrete*, OAS) was formed as an underground network to fight both the Arab FLN and the French military units still loyal to de Gaulle. The Battle of Algiers was joined.

By May 1962, the dwindling OAS cells were losing the war. Outmanned and outgunned, they resorted to desperate acts of terrorism against the French government, Arab civilians, and "liberal" local intellectuals. The OAS was now being hunted relentlessly by a new hush-hush outfit, *les barbouzes* (the bearded ones).

The last rebellious fires of *Algérie Française* were slowly being extinguished. The victorious ex-terrorists of the Arab FLN had just signed the Evian peace accord with General de Gaulle. In collaboration with loyal French troops brought in from the mainland, *les barbouzes* and the FLN now closed in on the last active cells of the OAS. *Algérie Française* was done for.

With bitter reality staring them in the face, the one million boisterous, ultrapatriotic *pieds noirs* finally gave up and quit their homes, trekking down to the harbor to sign up for repatriation and passage to France, a country most of them had never known. One hundred and thirty years of French colonial rule in Algeria was coming to a bitter end. The city of Algiers, once the jewel of the Mediterranean coast, was going up in smoke.

The waves of *pieds noirs* refugees hitting French shore were met with scorn and disdain. There was neither work nor housing for them. Their invasion of the warm Midi was resented by the local populace. The government tried to retrain and reeducate them, and to resettle them in remote corners to the north. The mainland French were convinced these marginal Frenchmen brought their bad fortune upon themselves.

To add insult to injury, one million Algerian Arabs, some former French allies, others opportunistic economic refugees, were now flooding the Midi. To the incensed *pieds noirs*, it seemed that mainland France welcomed the Arabs warmly while rejecting her own sons, the ardent patriots of *Algérie Française*.

As the loss of Algeria became inevitable, the OAS shifted its dwindling cells back into metropolitan France where, submerged among the hordes of repatriated *pieds noirs*, they pursued a murderous terrorist campaign against de Gaulle and the French political establishment. Marseilles and the entire Midi soon became a steaming cauldron of antigovernment agitation and conspiracy.

The government reacted with ferocity, mounting heavy pressure on the OAS in an attempt to prevent its resurgence on French soil. The assault intensified after a botched attempt on the life of General de Gaulle. Under relentless pressure, the surviving OAS cells dispersed, some going underground in France, others crossing over to Spain, Portugal, or Italy.

A few diehards joined mercenary bands that fought rear-guard battles against the emerging postcolonial regimes in Africa. One of those bands operated in the former Belgian Congo (Zaire), where the copper-rich Katanga province had just seceded and declared its independence under the nominal leadership of the Lunda tribal politician Moises Tshombé.

The Katanga rebellion quickly degenerated into a nasty free-for-all, pitting several African political and tribal factions against one another; against a United Nations expeditionary force; and against the diehard Belgian colonists, who were supported, clandestinely, by the big mining companies and, one suspects, by the Belgian government itself.

The OAS remnants alighted upon the lush, murderous Katanga scene only to find themselves fighting for one more lost cause. Frustrated and trapped, they were once again the manipulated puppets of forces they neither controlled nor comprehended.

ONE

THE CITY BURNING

∽

MARIE

Algiers, May 1962

All I know is what he's told me. Not that he's been all that forthcoming. I prise them out of him bit by recalcitrant bit, the jigsawed pieces of his dark puzzle. Haphazard, here and there, between bouts of blank silence and stretches of unaccounted-for absence. Neither excusing nor explaining, forever on the prowl, my very own reluctant errant knight, silent like a boarded-up house, wary like an orphaned kitten, nimble like the crows on the road at dawn after a car bomb.

Not that I pry all that hard, mind you. Mostly I am just there, holding on to the brief morsels of our hurried time together, hanging in there, trying to make sense. I wait. He is bound to let go sometime when he just can't help it, and for a brief moment his battlements will be breached. I swoop down then and grab for prized nuggets of clarity, a whiff here, an echo there. I scoop and store and brood over them, sift and rehash them like Mama's two-month old stock that won't be allowed to spoil. I've got time on my hands, gobs of it hanging. Again and again I pick over the shards of his inadvertent confidences, fragile and random like our furtive love.

Still I know, because he tells me, tells me enough so that the rest clicks into place then, my delicate tower of gossamer and guesswork propped up on the scaffolds of his dark silence. Faithfully, methodically, I fill in the blanks of his reluctant life. He is mine to decipher, mine to indulge, mine to forgive and love as the city burns.

* * *

As the small squad files out in silence, the bistro's regulars broadcast genuine disinterest. A decimated band of diehards, their thirst too vast to forego, they have braved the roadblocks and stray bullets to alight upon their low-beamed haven. And, having reached it and debarked, and having then embarked immediately upon the urgent business of slaking the unslakable, they are not in the mood for bar talk.

They are far from oblivious though, and their indifference is studied, feigned, eloquent, as they saunter to the back door, casually, caps pulled low over brow. The gawky old geezer near the cash register is the only one to acknowledge their small procession, beating out on the bar with his gnarled, worn knuckles three quick raps, two steady, *Al-gé-rie Fran-çaise*. What remains of his shriveled brain is mercifully pickled in the cheap anisette that is clouding the bottom of his rough-cut green glass. Things are decidedly not what they used to be, so his gross indiscretion is greeted with a silence that says "What of it?" That says "Who cares?" They've seen it all and then some, the desperadoes of this dimly lit haven, and are only too willing to let the poor slob drown in his brew.

Besides, nothing hangs on it anymore. Only the proprietor, from his station of the cross near the cash register, comments without enthusiasm: "Idiot."

Jojo, in the lead, turns back: "See you, *patron*." A gesture whose feeble ghost of normality has long ceased to mean what it used to. The proprietor, his bulk spilling liberally over the counter, eyes Jojo coldly as he slaps his wet dish rag on the bar to punctuate his parting shot: *"Merde."*

Jojo nods, his sentiments exactly, as the rest of the small band follow him out into the back alley.

Since they got Jaquinot, ten days before in a back alley behind his sister's house—someone talked, again—Jojo is the boss. Their dwindling squad now stands at five. Michel got his the day before yesterday, a sniper at the crossroads, just before dark.

Poor lamb, at seventeen their youngest. Pietro and Jean-Marie got nabbed with Jaquinot. Eugène hasn't shown up since Saturday. Bailed out, Robert says. I know they must be all wondering who's next. Some of the guys used to come over to the house after dark to get Robert. No more.

Jojo is carrying nothing but his handgun. Martel, right behind him, carries the machine-gun and ammo box. Minot, Armand, and Robert are panting under forty kilos each. He is the last one out, my reluctant plastique artist, magus of high explosives and bright thunders. It has just turned nine and the air is still oppressively muggy.

Once they are all outside, Jojo stops and they gather around him, leaning their backpacks against the bullet-pitted wall behind the bar, where the masonry wore away long ago to expose the red brickwork. The sky is glowing deep purple through the thick curtain of smoke. The moon will not come out till three o'clock, but the old commercial school on Rue Mizon is keeping the entire quarters illuminated. The school has been burning for three days now, we can see it from the house too, on the hillside. The gendarmes converge on it in the morning with their screaming engine and hose the fire down. Our boys come back at night to rekindle the charcoal and thick roofing timber. A fresh squirt of petrol and up she goes again with the inevitability of a well-rehearsed script. The gendarmes won't stay after dark, our boys melt away with sunrise. Both sides are sworn to reenact this charade, bone tired and ill fed, their lungs seared with gray smoke, locked in their precise, complex minuet. Like the rest of us.

Most public buildings have gone up in smoke long ago, as have countless Arab homes on the fringes of the Casbah and Climat de France—nothing personal, they were the most accessible. As have the homes of progressive pinko traitors out in Belcourt and Telemley. Our guys have long lists, growing daily, an endless parade of traitors and would-be traitors in our very midst who must be unmasked. So if you are not one of us, watch out, most likely you are one of them, and you better pull stakes and run before we burn your house on top of you and yours, plant your charred memorial in this vast graveyard that used to be our city. We are, so it seems, all doomed to find our names on one list or another, traitors the lot of us, *pieds noirs*.

Am I imagining all this? He tells me it's only natural; we are all under siege, confused, stressed out. The weak snap first. But I know he has become uneasy himself, and even more quiet than before.

Still, he and his buddies are as busy as ever. More houses go up in smoke, the ranks of the traitors, charred to a crisp or in desperate flight, keep swelling. And, what with the other side being just as busy, a pall of thick smoke hangs over the place.

The last few days, most of the smoke is coming from the *quartier* itself, Bab-el-Oued, and our own guys are behind this. It all started with a bulletin over Radio OAS two weeks ago, telling the people to burn their own houses before they took off, to leave the Arabs nothing but charred rubble. At first, nobody paid heed. But now it seems to have picked up. Houses already empty have gone up first, the block committees took care of that.

Nobody left behind to scream. Now, as the exodus gathers momentum, people do their own homes. Always at night. First they finish packing and pull their baggage out into the street. A can of gasoline then, sprinkled over the old couch, the kitchen table, the musty bedding upstairs, and up she goes spewing like a firecracker—doors, beams, drapes, Daddy's stained overalls, and Grandmama's embroidered tablecloth.

Nobody stays to watch. Too numb, they grab their bags and hurry down to the Promenade, where their trickles combine into a swollen river of silent feet and sullen faces. They sneak past the roadblock at the Pelissier barracks and march to the harbor. Nobody bothers to stop them anymore. Robert and the guys are busy elsewhere, dodging the gendarmes and switching from one blown hideout to another on short notice. Someone must have talked, he tells me, someone always talks, and *les barbouzes* are right there on your heels, sniffing for your blood. The OAS is leaking like a rusted sieve, he says. God only knows where he'll sleep tonight. Or if.

The fires of Bab-el-Oued now bloom as summer squash; the gendarmes are busy elsewhere, they're not about to invade our smoking turf where some mad *plastiqueur* with time on his hands would love to torch their few surviving fire engines. And since last month, nobody comes out on the porch at night to drum their pots and pans, the frantic beat of our withered hope: three quick raps, two slow ones—*Al-gé-rie Fran-çaise!* Our tribal drums are silent.

So it is a quiet night as their squad lines up at the wall behind the bistro, silent and bright in spite of the smoke drifting slowly from Bab-el-Oued toward the Casbah and the port, our quarters spewing its ashes into the gathering volcanic gloom.

Into which Jojo now speaks: "It's getting late," he tells them, "we better get going. So first a few items I didn't want to broadcast in there." He gestures toward the back door and there's no need to say more: they all understand, the few of them that are still with him in the glowing dark. Besides, Jojo never tells them much, never tells anybody, not even Robert, who's been with him since Indochina.

"You might as well know," he concedes, shrugging, "though I'm not supposed to tell you. Headquarters is off the air as of this afternoon. Maybe *les barbouzes* got them, maybe the transmitter is down, maybe they're running. Your guess's as good as mine."

The guys remain silent, each one computing his separate odds. They wait. Jojo is just as tired as they are and it is getting late. And, as always, he will tell them only what he thinks they need to know.

"It's not going to change our plans though," he goes on. "We're going to keep busy. We still got the cache. I didn't pass the new address to headquarters after Jaquinot got nabbed. They're leaking worse than us, no use in telling them what they don't need to know. How many more weeks of plastique do we have left, Robert?"

The cache is Robert's department, only he and Jojo know where it is and they dole it out nightly as needed, carefully rationed, as precious as flour, sugar, and oil. Most of the military depots willing to look the other way have been cleaned out. The rest are under tight security now, no special deals, not even for cash. The boys have been cast adrift; they are on their own.

"Two weeks, three tops," Robert tells him, "depending on how fast we go at it."

"Faster," Jojo says, "starting tonight we go every night. So figure it'll last a week, eh? No need to skimp now, we give it to them double shot, use it all up. No point in leaving any of it behind."

There is an awkward silence during which the full implications of what Jojo has just said are allowed to sink in. Is this the end? What then? Jojo lets it linger, and it is not like him, linger long enough for Minot to finally pop out loud: "And then what?"

Which might have echoed for a while had not Jojo stepped in to reassert control: "Never mind now," he tells them, "I'll let you know when the time comes. Headquarters may come alive, who knows? And anyway, we've got standing orders for everything, so it doesn't really matter. We just keep going on our own, no liaison, no support, no nothing. We go out alone; we come back alone; we keep our mouths shut. We meet here tomorrow at seven. If the window on the right is shut, skip and go on to Rue Charles Fourrier at eight. If you see no light there, skip again and come to the Sunflower at ten. If there are tables on the sidewalk, skip that too and go home. Come to my sister's backyard the following evening at seven. Any questions?"

But as things stand, nobody asks the most obvious question, the one that is on everybody's mind. They would rather reckon in private, later. Each of them is reluctant to show his hand.

"He's gone nuts," Robert tells me later, "plum crazy, howling, bonko, like I don't know the guy. What the fuck does he expect them to do? Line up and follow like bleating sheep? He should have left them an out, something to look forward to, a false hope. Instead he has just about gone and told them it's over; we're finished; you guys better start making plans. What does he expect? What else could they make of it?"

But nobody asks the question aloud, so it is back to the task at hand.

"Yes," says Robert, "I've got a couple. For starters, where do we go back to tonight? And how do we get there?"

"No need to worry," Jojo reassures him, "we got a special deal tonight. You'll love it, just wait and see."

They don't always knows when Jojo is joking, not for sure, not even Robert. What he says might strike you as funny, but whether Jojo meant it that way under his deadpan is anybody's guess. The two of them, Robert and Jojo, have been on the dodge since they deserted together in 1960, long enough to make a person grim. Though Robert says Jojo's been that way as far back as he's known him, which goes all the way back and then some.

I sometimes wonder what men mean when they call someone a friend, and how exactly they mean it. Do they mean being with someone years and years, comfortable, relaxed, inseparable, and still knowing nothing about them?

"Good thing you asked though," Jojo says, "because after this one, we don't reassemble any more. We make it home each on his own, and we get together only once a day before going out. You guys stay away from each other—don't visit, don't talk to friends, just find yourself a hole and crawl in and hide."

He lets them digest the news; it adds up to nothing more than he's already told them. Again, nobody needs it spelled out.

"Robert," says Jojo, "if you've got no place to go I'll put you up." The offer is in line with Jojo's normal concern for him. But is there more to it tonight? He wonders. Perhaps Jojo just wants to talk. Can he read his mind? Can he hear the slow corroding drip-drop of doubt? Robert is pretty sure he cannot, but not absolutely sure. In his best matter-of-fact voice he says: "Thanks, I'm okay for tonight."

He can only hope it works, that all Jojo will conclude is that he has a place to stay.

"Good. Let's get cracking then."

They are gliding like mute ghosts down the narrow alley, hugging the low wall, casting but scant gray shadows. Every now and then an explosion from somewhere to the south punctuates the monotony of their slow progress. Distant flames flicker on the low ceiling of smoke. It is still early in the evening or would have been in the now distant gone-by days they all remember. The city is awake and watchful, cautiously clawing at the dark, wary of its own shadows. Like the squad creeping single file along the wall, the city is once again resigned to another night of lost sleep.

In a few minutes they cross Avenue de la Bouzarea. A short time later they stop in front of a nondescript one-story house.

"Keep next to the wall," Jojo tells them. "Won't be a minute." He opens an iron gate to the left of the house. It squeaks plaintively as Jojo plunges into the shadow beyond. A backyard, Robert guesses. In a minute they hear an engine coughing into a start, then a vehicle lurches toward them in the dark. When it comes to a stop, they are peering at an old ambulance, its Red Sickle marks clearly visible in the dim glow. Jojo is at the wheel, he leans over and throws the right door open: "Hop in," he says, "we're late."

"Now how about that," says Martel, "say, Jojo—"

"Never mind, just hop in."

They scramble in. The ambulance is rolling down the dark alley when Jojo resumes his matter-of-fact instructions: "Martel, come sit next to me with the machine." The car lurches and bumps, must have hit the curb. "Crank the window open . . . good. The rest of you guys, unload the stuff, pack it up on the stretcher back in there . . . Cover it with blankets, make it look real."

The ambulance bounces on the cobblestones and the three of them get busy. Real what? Eventually, he tells me later, it blooms into perfect, if perfectly grim, sense.

"That's the way we've come to do things now," he says, his head on my lap, his eyes probing the ceiling. "Never mind why, just hurry up and get it done. Keep it snappy, keep it moving. Soon it won't need to make sense, because if it ever does you're in trouble. Just like we used to do in the *para*. You got to give it to Jojo, he knows the drill."

And so, in the dark swaying hull of the ambulance, the three of them, Armand, Minot, and Robert, fashion a prone figure out of the plastic bricks, under the blankets, with a suggestion of a narrow head wrapped in soiled bedsheets.

"I'm going to turn the lights and siren on once we cross the bridge," Jojo tells them, "at the corner of the cemetery. Robert?"

"Yes?"

In spite of his unease he is swept up in the excitement of the moment, wondering what the adrenaline is doing to his voice, wondering whether Jojo knows how uncomfortable he is.

"Screw the deto into a brick," Jojo tells him, "leave room for it right in the middle."

"Okay."

His fingers, bless them, will get busy on their own in the dark, expert with years of practice.

"Set it for two minutes. Never mind, make it one and a half."

"That's cutting it a mite short," Robert tells Jojo, not expecting a reply. They used to plan things together, in advance. Not any more.

"Not tonight," says Jojo, "this one's got to be timed real tight. We can't leave them time to foul it up. You squeeze when I tell you and we scoot, no margins."

"You sure?" he asks him.

"Sure. We pull out faster tonight, got this sweet baby to truck us back." Jojo slaps the dashboard. It makes a hollow sound. Armand and Minot are putting the final touches on the pile under the blanket.

"Like it?" Minot asks Robert.

"Looks fine. Let me have one."

Minot places the smooth plastic brick in his palm, where it is sweating out the final dissipation of today's heat. Robert wipes one side distractedly with the sleeve of his trenchcoat. Concentrate, he tells himself, pay attention, *mijico*. He presses the cool metal plug through the oily membrane, snug into the tight hole of the primer. The sexual connotations hit him once again, as they always have.

We have had a running battle over this. I tell him it's obscene. He says yes, but he can't help it.

"Do you blush?" I ask him. He says he doesn't think so, but who knows in the dark?

"Do you feel embarrassed?" I insist. He says always, if it makes you happy. We wind up going for the real thing and there is nothing obscene about the way he makes love like a lost boy.

They have all gotten Jojo's drift. Once again Robert wonders if the strain has finally got to Jojo, who pats the dashboard again in the dark and turns to the other two: "Armand, Minot, put on those white robes . . . the caps too. You carry the stretcher. Robert, you done?"

"Yes."

He can only hope Jojo knows what he is doing: a ninety-second fuse is not exactly comfortable at his end of the business. In his business, you don't live to a ripe old age by skimping on margins. He is not about to argue the point though.

"Good," Jojo tells him, "for now keep the deto brick handy, don't slip it into the pile until I tell you. Then let the cord hang out on the right side . . . walk next to the stretcher and make it like you're holding the plasma bag. If they stop us before we've gotten all the way there, don't wait for orders, just slip it under the blanket and squeeze. Say 'now' so we all know. Got it?"

"I think so." When it comes to keeping it simple and plausible, Jojo is tops, he admits to me later grudgingly, margins or no margins.

By now they are rolling down Avenue de Sufrennes, heading toward the Moslem cemetery, with the Casbah looming across the valley. Fragments of Arabic conversation drift toward them, the Casbah is just as nocturnal now as Bab-el-Oued, the two of them immersed together in an ecumenical smoke-and-fire Ramadan.

"Heck, we're supposed to be fighting them," he tells me later, "and look how alike we've become."

The guys are quiet, until Martel asks: "How'd you get her, Jojo?"

To which the response is first a grunt, then, in quick bursts: "Lucked out on this one. They crossed over by mistake last night, from Climat de France. Tried to turn back, too late . . . got in a cul-de-sac . . . The driver lost his cool, jumped out and ran for it. There were two more in there with the wounded one. We got them all right there, dropped them in the alley for the gendarmes . . . stripped the gowns off them. Sorry about the stains, guys."

Minot and Armand must be wincing in the dark.

Jojo negotiates a sharp turn, still driving slow, lights and siren switched off. The ambulance is gliding along the cemetery wall like a runaway ghost. They have left Bab-el-Oued's warm security behind for good. Muffled explosions drift over in rapid succession, must be coming from Climat de France, he suspects, where the comrades seem as busy as ever.

"We've got company," Martel says, echoing everybody's private thoughts.

"The more the merrier," says Jojo. "Keeps the gendarmes busy, keeps the Arabs busy, *les barbouzes* too . . . Now watch it, we start flying the other side of the bridge . . . Hang on to the bars in there. Robert, watch the deto."

"Yes." He doesn't take offense; it is all part of the routine of talking it out loud, walking through it again and again till it has worked its way under your skin like reflex. He and Jojo have been at it together seemingly forever.

They are nearing the flat bottom of the valley now where, in the dry river bed, Boulevard Guillemin and the Marengo Gardens stretch out in parallel like breeding snakes. More explosions, then more. Then the ambulance is on the bridge.

"Here goes," says Jojo. The siren lets loose, a shrill wail erupting out of nowhere and climbing. The headlights are on, bathing the bridge span ahead in bright yellow. The ambulance gathers speed, Jojo is really stepping on it now. He brakes abruptly and takes the sharp turn into Rue du Dr. Bentami. The right-side wheels are both dancing off the pavement. More explosions punctuate the wail of the siren. They seem to come from Belcourt and Mustafa this time. Ours? Theirs?

Up until last December, our guys used to hook the charges up in clusters of five with two short cords then two long ones—*Al-gé-rie Fran-çaise* spelled out in thunder and smoke like a calling card. You could sometime tell the plastiquer by his expertly rigged beat. No one bothers any more, it takes too long. Or is it that they too know what he knows, share his doubts? He says he sometimes wonders.

Jojo maneuvers the ambulance into Boulevard de la Victoire; the Casbah is now directly above them on the left. At the roadblock the gendarmes let the ambulance speed right through and by God it's worked, it's really worked.

"Hang on to the stretcher," Jojo barks, "we're pulling in."

Barely slowing down, he hurtles the ambulance into Rue Porte Neuve. They are now in the upper Casbah, heading down. Another sharp turn, then another, another. Everybody is hoping Jojo knows what he's doing because the streets have gotten narrow and turning back is not much of an option, even at the slower pace Jojo is holding now. They can only hope he's memorized the route.

The streets are teeming with people, who scurry off the narrow roadway to flatten themselves against the walls as the ambulance shrieks its way into their very midst. The little cafés are open, brightly lit, jam-packed. The festive music that wafts out into the street is momentarily drowned out by the siren but reemerges in its wake, as do the people, closing ranks. Jojo is going as fast as he dares, steering the ambulance with an abrupt hand. An accident now would be a disaster. The guys are all holding their breath. This night's mission is brazen even for them, the audacity of what they've gotten themselves into is slowly sinking in. It'd be good if we knew how to pray, Robert is thinking.

The hospital has taken over the old school building on Rue Sidi Abdalla. The gate is open, the guards scurry to pull back, making way. The ambulance has cleared the booth and is sailing full steam into the large paved courtyard. Jojo cuts the siren and brings the ambulance to a stop in front of the main door. People are rushing about their business, ignoring the ambulance. This is apparently routine.

Jojo flings his door open and turns: "Robert, the deto. Martel, stay at the wheel, keep the engine running and the back door open. Put the machine-gun in the back in case someone gets curious . . . and no talking."

Robert gets busy as Jojo leaps out and runs back to open the door. Armand, incongruous in his soiled gown and white cap, slides down and grabs the stretcher, Minot and Robert are pushing it out from inside. Then Minot jumps down and grabs the other end and they are off in a tight cluster. Jojo is leading the way; Robert is on the right side of the stretcher, his left hand under the blanket nursing the soft lead of the starter tube, his head bowed down.

"We must have been a sight," he tells me later, "and of course it was too late to worry about it, but I should have been gowned in whites like the rest of them."

They rush through the gaping main door into a wide corridor. A single kerosene lamp is hanging from the low ceiling, low enough to make them swerve and duck.

"Watch out for the damn casualty," Jojo mutters to them over his shoulder.

A group of white-robed orderlies have just rounded the corner and are approaching. It is a tense moment and Robert is feeling for his revolver before they pass them, hurrying off, wrapped up in their own hushed emergency.

"Shit," says Jojo. "Hang a right."

They turn into a narrow corridor where it's pitch dark.

"Perfect," says Jojo. He guides them on slowly till they are about twenty yards from the corner, in a cul-de-sac of thick stale air. Armand and Minot ease the stretcher down to the floor. Minot lets out his breath: "Sure heavy, your bloody Arab."

"Shut up," Jojo tells him. "Robert?"

"Now?"

He is kneeling next to the stretcher, making sure the deto has not dislodged from the primer, his left hand still nursing the metal foil. His ears are screaming in the silence with the rush of blood.

"God knows how many times," he tells me later, back in my room, "and I still choke, you figure it out." I hug him after the fact.

"A minute and a half?" says Jojo.

"Yes."

"Good, let her go and start counting . . . aloud after thirty."

He crushes the thin tube between his thumb and two fingers, feeling the glass container inside crack like a small skull, the juicy pulp gushing out.

"Up and running," he tells them as he rises. "One . . . two . . ." They all rush back to the main corridor, turn left, and run for the main door. As they reach it Jojo calls out a warning: "Slow down now . . . walk." Then to Robert: "The count?"

"Fifteen . . . sixteen . . ."

They clear the main door in a businesslike trot, giddy and exposed in the open courtyard.

"And so bloody incongruous," he tells me later, "can you see us there? All they had to do was take one good look."

But of course they don't, they're just as busy. And so the four of them make it back to the ambulance, where Martel is waiting with the engine running. They scramble in, Jojo up front and the rest of them in the back.

"Get going," Jojo tells Martel. "Once we clear the gate, turn the siren on. Robert?"

"Thirty-two . . . thirty-three . . ."

He is trying to block out everything else—the gate, the guards drawing back, the ambulance bumping through, the astonishing fact that they are out now and still going. He counts.

"Martel, the siren."

Jojo has the machine-gun now, its muzzle sticking out of the window.

"Minot, cover Martel's side. Armand, kick out the rear window; look sharp." And, as the glass shards scatter behind them, "Robert?"

"Seventy-nine . . . eighty . . . eighty-one . . ."

They are rolling along once again at breakneck speed, lights flashing, siren shrieking, a speeding wailing requiem that makes it hard for him to concentrate. It's getting close, he's seldom been more than four seconds off either way. Here she comes, he tells himself. Then aloud: "Better open your mouths now. Ninety-one . . . ninety-two . . ."

They must be all praying for release.

Then Jojo tells Martel: "Cut left here!" The ambulance lists and screeches as it cuts into an alley. Robert has stopped counting; it better be coming right now, he thinks. His jaws are masticating rhythmically, left to right, to keep the tubes unplugged. He knows what seventy-five kilos can do to your eardrums even at half a mile.

When it finally comes, from somewhere behind, the loud roar hits first, followed by the kick of compressed air, then shrill ringing as the windows shatter all around them and the glass crashes to the pavement. People peer out of the darkened frames, timid as deer in the meadow. Robert lets out his breath.

"Must have held it in for a small eternity," he says to me. "Can you imagine what it would've felt like if it had failed to detonate? I know it sounds strange, but what a relief, like everything finally going slack. Does that make sense?"

"Sure," I tell him.

What else could I say? How could I possibly know? I've never been there with him have I, where the guys all go, both ours and theirs, to snuff out lives they've never known in order to spare those they know. I suppose I will never know what it is all about. And sometime I wonder if they do, as they go grimly about their deadly games. I know he wonders too, and maybe that's why I put up with his plunging back into the dark chaos out there, his shuttling back and forth.

He takes a greedy deep breath, letting the tension wash out slowly.

He hears Jojo say: "Done." The others make no comment. "Turn the siren off, Martel, make a right here." The center of the Casbah is behind them now, the streets are once again deserted. The dark around them absorbs the sudden silence like soft gauze stanching a wound. They still have to get out; they're hardly through. Slowly, faintly, the ululating laments of Arab women begin to drift over the rooftops. The ambulance is gathering speed.

"Where the fuck are we?" asks Martel, who seems to enjoy shaking their guts over the potholes.

"Hang a right the next corner," Jojo tells him. "They should have just about figured out who did it, about now . . . Robert, how do we get out of here?"

He is the only one who knows the Casbah, having grown up there. And of course, he doesn't know if he is more pissed off at Jojo's lousy timing or at himself for not paying attention.

He makes a desperate guess: "The other way. Make a left." He can only pray he's right.

"*Merde*," says Jojo, "where does it take us?"

"South."

"Can we get out that way?" A long interval follows. They all know what getting trapped inside the Casbah would mean. All eyes are on him.

"Not with the car," he tells them. "There's a roadblock just before Place d'Isly." Jojo lets the information sink in.

"They're not going to stop us if we come at them with the siren and lights," he says. He does not sound convinced.

It would be dumb indeed to blow it at this point. The ambulance's description is no doubt making the rounds on the shortwaves by now.

"You could try turning off before that," he tells Jojo, "on Debussy or Joinville." Then, as an afterthought, "Say Jojo?"

"Yeah?"

"Why that one?"

"Why what one?"

"The hospital. Why?"

He is still surprised by the total matter-of-fact ring of Jojo's voice: "It was next on the list."

"A hospital?"

"They must've run out of better targets."

"How do you know?"

Jojo has been scanning the dark street as he talks. Now he turns to face him: "They called."

"I thought they were off the air?"

"Just before they went off."

It sounds plausible enough. Still he presses: "Did they say why?"

"Do they ever?" Jojo waits for his answer, which is not forthcoming. He's got a good point there. After a while he shrugs and offers: "Got a better idea? We'll do yours next."

He is getting nowhere with Jojo, he knows; the others are bound to get jittery. They are cruising in the dark together, slowly, past the shuttered shops of a wide commercial avenue. In the silence each is weaving his own cocoon, pulling the thin thread of private reckoning. Martel had joined them from off the street the year before, having known Jojo since childhood in Bab-el-Oued. Minot and Armand are both new. Minot moved in from Oran in March, Armand from somewhere on the mainland that he never talks about for reasons better left alone. Not much of a talker, but then nobody is anymore. Once again, he is missing Jaquinot, the only one of them who'd never forgot how to smile.

"Though by now *les barbouzes* have probably knocked his teeth out, if he's still alive . . ." he tells me. He pauses. There's more to it, I know, gory stuff he'd rather spare me, stuff you don't tell a girl, though the stories go around. "*Les barbouzes* are wasting their time though," he says. "Whatever poor Jaquinot knows won't help them. We've switched routines twice since. They ought to know better." Still, he misses Jaquinot's optimism.

They are nearing the line. Maybe they've lucked out again, maybe his hunch has paid off. That's when he makes a snap decision, its timing hanging on a taut thread: "Jojo."

"Yes?"

"Could you let me off at the next corner?"

There is a pause, Jojo didn't expect it. Robert knows it is going to sound odd, but he can't help that.

"You're not coming back with us?" Jojo says. "I've got room for you, you know."

"No. Thanks though," he tells him. "I'll crash at the old man's place, it's just around the corner."

Which, although he does not expect Jojo to swallow that, is true, and is what he intends to do.

"You see," he tells me later, "Jojo is not the only one who holds some back. I've never told him about the old man." He is smoking, lying next to me on the narrow bed, and it is perhaps not the best of times to mention that he never tells me all that much either. Though of course I know more than he thinks. I've made it my business. But riding in the back of the ambulance there, he only tells Jojo what he thinks Jojo needs to know, and Jojo does not press him, beyond: "You sure? It's no sweat."

"Sure I'm sure, thanks," he tell him. "See you tomorrow at seven." Then to Martel: "This spot'll do."

Martel is slowing down. Jojo, shrugging, has moved to the rear and is groping for the back door: "Jump when we hit the curve," he tells Robert, "we're not making a full stop."

"Fair enough," he tells him. "See you guys tomorrow."

The four of them are grunting their good-byes. He leans out, peers to both sides to orient himself, shoves the door open, and leaps. His feet hit the ground and the momentum will pull him back toward the car. Instinct and a hundred jumps take over as he crouches and rolls over his left shoulder to cushion the impact.

He is back on his feet, standing in the middle of the street and watching the retreating shadow gather speed on its way back toward the center. He wonders briefly if they will put the siren back on, if they'll make it, if he'll see them again. He feels nothing besides a vague sense of relief at being alone.

Belatedly, he ducks for the cover of the walls and turns into Rue Medée. It finally hits him how tired he is, and how little he cares whether he sees them the next day or not. Not a comforting thought, it follows him as he ghosts his way along the deserted streets, scanning for sounds that could bode trouble. It has been years since he has had the luxury of picking his own friends. For that matter, since he has had the leisure of friendship.

This leaves Jojo, with whom he has spent the bulk of the last ten years. Jojo is another one of his blank pages, where I know better than to intrude. I give the subject of Jojo a respectful wide berth. Some day I might learn more. Though for the moment I am not asking.

He glides alone in the protective dark, relieved. If there's one thing he's sure of, it is that nobody will bother him at the old man's house, neither his comrades nor *les barbouzes*. It is the last patch of private space he can count on. The storefront has been boarded up since last September, which suits just him fine as it blends with the hundreds of deserted homes all over the Old Town. In days gone by, they'd be snapped up by fresh squatters in a matter of days. In Bab-el-Oued, they'd be long gone up in smoke. Nobody has bothered the old man's house yet, though whether out of superstition or shame he's not sure.

Which is his good fortune, since it allows him to come and go as he pleases, once or twice a week when he cannot stay with me and would rather not crowd Jojo; slip into the yard from the back alley where garbage has not been collected in months and where hordes of emaciated rats now scavenge nightly, step inside through the back door whose hinges have been yanked loose, and sleep upstairs in what used to be the old man's room.

His fingers trace gingerly along the rough-plastered surface of the garden wall that rises a foot or so above his own height. The cracked masonry is damp. From here on, if he felt like it, he could keep his eyes shut, he knows his way around intimately, exhaustively, like a hermit in his cramped desert cave. Slowly, he rises to his toes, a light push and his fingers grab the upper rim of the wall, where he had cleared off a span, just wide enough, in the jagged glass shards.

He pulls himself up slowly, flexing his legs for purchase, slipping one elbow over the top, then the other, then pausing to listen. The yard is quiet, the way it always is. The old man's apricot trees are rustling their new leaf in the nearly imperceptible predawn breeze. He swings one leg over the wall, straddling it, bends down and again pausing to monitor the texture of the silence. All seems in order. Slowly, he lowers himself down on the inside, hangs by his fingers for a brief moment, then lets go and lands in the dry weeds. He rolls over cautiously and lies on his back in the dark next to the wall. He pulls out his gun and listens and rests, taking in the cool air in leisurely gulps, exhaling in a soft hiss. Then he becomes conscious of the smell, simultaneously familiar and discordant, of burned cordite and plaster dust.

For a man of his occupation, it is a habituated, intimate smell. It is also clearly, starkly out of place, and all of a sudden his alarm bells are buzzing, his chest is shot with adrenaline, his breath is caught. Could it be the hospital? All the way here? His mind is busy reckoning the distance, as the crow flies no more than half a mile from where he's lying. He hardly needs to strain to hear the faint cries that are still coming over from that direction. But there is virtually no wind, so the smell shouldn't have carried that far, nor this strong. A short surge of relief shoots through him, he is aching to let go and just rest. Perhaps it's just the city, all of it now soaking in his signature aroma, his professional calling card. Or could it be his clothes, or just his frayed imagination? Has it become indelibly etched in his clothing, his nostrils? His conscience? A bit too farfetched, the last one, he suspects.

He is lying in the dry grass and is slowly getting cold, the dew is setting in, the air has finally cooled off a bit. God, what an unholy mess, he tells himself and opens his eyes. The yard is bright, the moonlight must be filtering in through the thick haze. A bunch of apricots are hanging down from a loaded bough just above him. They'll ripen early this year, with nobody irrigating. He gets up and immediately freezes. There's something different about the yard; the birds should be up by now but he can't hear them. He moves cautiously toward the house but can't see it. Tentatively, he leans forward and peers out through the unpruned growth. The smell has definitely grown stronger. He moves on cautiously, gun in hand, then pauses under a tree. There's no need to go further.

Where the old man's house used to stand there rises a pile of rubble. A lone girder beam skewers the sky.

*M*ost of this I have only learned in the last two days, with him sequestered in my room upstairs, waiting, smoking and pacing up and down, growling like a caged bear. I got it piecemeal on the installment plan, and for all I know the bulk of it is sheer imagination, my own faltering attempt to understand. Understand in the only way you ever understand anything in Algiers, because here, where you come from is who you are. Forever.

"*Abuelico*," he says, "my grandfather. He came across from Italy at the turn of the century." His father had moved to Modena from Istanbul, where the family had resided since the early 1500s. "Since the expulsion," he adds.

"What expulsion?"

He sneers at my ignorance and I blush. Still, I will pay my dues if pay my dues I must.

"Tell me," I plead. He looks at me and relents, the ghost of a smile crossing his face.

"Spain," he says, "the Inquisition, the Jews." He chooses the insult term deliberately, pitching it at me like the curse I've always known it to be, *les Juives*. I have known all along he was different, but nevertheless find it hard to understand why it is such a huge deal.

"The old man came alone," he says, "like his father before him." He is more patient with me now as he launches into the tale of a restless young man saddled with nothing but his dreams and a threadbare carpetbag, a windblown seed of an ancient clan of curb-side goldsmiths and frustrated petty scholars. He bought the lot on Rue Dr. Aboulker and built the house slowly with his own hands, brick by brick. The rough stone wall encircling the yard went up first, shielding the young orchard of apricots and olives and cedonias and tangerines and the lone palm tree. The store in front went up next, the back room serving as his bachelor quarters.

'"I lie there in the early morning, after we hit the hospital, shivering in the damp grass," he tells me, "and all I can think of is the old man and his orchard."

Later, having courted and married a local girl of unimpeachable virtue but mysteriously—if allegedly—tainted lineage, he added the second-floor family quarters. Robert's father was born there in 1910. He himself was born there in 1933.

"I never knew my mother," he says.

My poor orphaned lamb! I cannot contain the pity welling in my breast, though I know better than to say it out loud. He acquiesces to my hug and returns my kiss. But soon he disengages and resumes his restless pacing.

"She died when I was three," he says. He remembers his father better, if vicariously, in part from the photographs on the old man's bedroom wall, mostly from the long procession of the old man's stories.

"I know how it must feel," he says. He is smiling at me, for the first time acknowledging my frustrations. "Stories . . . that's all I'd ever had to go on. Just like you, my love, stories wrapped up in more stories."

As near as he can tell, his father took the boat to Marseilles in 1939 and signed up for military service. He thinks he can remember the day he brought him over to the old man's house, just before he left. The old man was living alone by then, having been widowed a few years before. A photo of his late wife, the smiling carefree face of her youth framed in dark teak, was hanging in the store above the cash register.

"It's been hanging there ever since I can remember," he says. He and his father were living in Telemley at the time, with a Spanish maid named Pilar in a large house with many empty rooms. The old man would visit them regularly but, just as regularly, would decline to move in.

He is looking out of the window, his wiry frame all of a sudden stooped, letting the memories flood over.

"'I've got to leave, Papa,' that's what my father told him," he says. "I may have been standing right there though I don't remember a thing, only what the old man told me . . . maybe they sent me out to play." Of course, the old man had told him this a hundred times, later. "So for all I know I was right there," he muses. He must have been out in the backyard climbing the old olive tree when his father said to the old man: "Take care of Robert for me, Papa."

To which the old man retorted: "Marcelico."

This name he used only rarely, mindful of his son's professed Frenchness.

"Don't worry about the boy, he's safe with me. But this war you're in such a rush to join, it isn't ours. Isn't yours either. It's *their* war."

It was an old bone of contention between them, an argument that outlived them both.

"You know, my father loved the old man," he tells me. He is looking out of my bedroom window, carefully keeping himself in the shadow, his eyes scanning the Casbah across the valley. "And he did respect his judgment, even when they disagreed." Still, it was another place and another time. And the old clan's received wisdom—stay out of *their* wars—seemed to have finally exhausted its long reach, leaving on the outside a son who had made up his mind to be French, and a France once again marching to war. This, however reluctantly and in words that sounded hollow even to him, is what he told his father.

"*La France*," sneered the old man.

"Indeed," retorted the son. "They've let us be French. Now the least we can do is pitch in when *la France* is on her knees. I'd feel rotten if I didn't."

I ask him if that's how he felt when *he* joined, and he looks at me as if I've said something weird.

"I don't know how I felt," he says, "it was never an issue." I find this hard to understand, and I wait for more. I think maybe it's coming; it's bound to. Instead, he resumes where I had stopped him.

"My father had gone to the Law Faculty in Algiers," he says. Before Marcel went to fight and die for *la France*, as the old man would later remind Robert, he had already made a name for himself as a trial lawyer, was even asked to come back and teach. The old man, as ever adept at subtleties and contradictions, took an immense pride in that too. *La France* was something else, however. He must have known he had a losing battle on his hands. Still, he was duty bound to persist.

"'Marcelico, you listen now,'" he told him, "'your mother was born in Algiers and her mother in Casablanca. Your father was born in Modena and his father in Istanbul. You'll never be French no matter how hard you try. No matter how well you play their game, it's still *their* game and you're still spilling your blood for *them* and it isn't *their* blood and they won't let you forget it, ever.'"

But of course the son wouldn't listen, what son ever does? My brother never did either. War must be in their blood, the lot of them. They all go, they find the call irresistible, leaving us behind. And we acquiesce, we are glad when they come back. If they do.

"We're French now, Papa," Marcel told the old man. "This is the time to show it."

The old man kept shaking his head. "However many times you say this, Marcelico," he told him, "you'll never talk yourself into believing it. You'll never talk *them* into believing it either. They've tricked you into enlisting in their war, your fancy neighbors, your Bar committee, your pampered magistrates . . ."

The old man turned suddenly and took his son by the shoulders. He kissed him on both cheeks, twice.

"Still, if you must you must, who am I to tell you? I'm just an old man. But for God's sake hurry back."

Robert's father left that night.

"That's the last we saw of him," he tells me, "the old man and I were on our own from then on."

Over their years together, the old man would often talk to Robert about his father.

"Your papa," he would tell him, "was an exceptional man. Anything he wanted he could have done, could have gotten . . . Pig-headed too, he was. A dreamer."

He would pause, after all those years still outraged by the injustice of it all. Bad luck was something he understood well. You learned to live with it, it was as unavoidable as the dry desert wind in May. But the loss of his only son rankled all the more for its total senselessness, having been, so far as he could see, utterly avoidable.

"He would get progressively more enraged," Robert tells me.

This loss was the crowning insult of a harsh life studded with injuries large and small, all of which the old man was inclined to neither forgive nor forget.

"There!" He would gesture at the wall, where his late son's service medals occupied a prominent spot on a dark square of velvet directly under the dark-framed photo that had joined the one of his late wife.

"This is all I've got left of Marcel, not a grave, not even a marker—*Souvenirs de la France* . . ."

The last word would trail off then into a loud hiss.

"This is all *la France* has ever given Marcel, the right to die for her, to lie in an unmarked ditch with the rest of her *goyím*."

The old man would pause, overcome by freshly rekindled grief. The matter of the unmarked—indeed unaccounted for—grave remained a live sore for which there was no succor. If he had only had a patch of hallowed ground to visit, a marker upon which to place a wreath, recite a belated *Cadísh*. For someone with his vast tolerance in everyday life and even vaster indifference to organized worship, the old man turned out to be inexplicably pious when it came to his son's grave, or rather the lack thereof.

"And why?" he'd ask, "For who? For the anti-Semites in *l'Élysée*?"

What Robert remembers of his father, what he told me in those brief hours, comes deeply flavored with the old man's bitter regrets, spiced with his stubborn grudges, seared in the crucible of his quiet despair. Deeply devout, he nevertheless consigned his only son to the state's schools, to be inducted in short order into the mysteries of being properly French. There was something defiant, recalcitrant in his estrangement from the community and its synagogues, an invisible chasm. An outsider who married into their midst, married into reputedly tainted blood to boot, he seemed to relish his otherness, seemed to love his wife all the more for her reputed taint.

"I once asked him, years later, why he left Modena," he tells me. "What he said was a bit oracular, way over the head of an eleven-year-old. Near as I can remember, it went like this—between the black robes, the rabbis, and the rabble rousers, you had nowhere to go but out. Leastwise that's what I think he said. You figure it out."

I am good at riddles, have always been, but this one is his to solve. All I know, suspect really, is that if he ever solved the old man's riddle he might also solve his own. His dad's too, maybe. But who am I to pass judgment, having never been one of them, as he sometimes, however inadvertently, reminds me? Having hardly known one of them, if indeed I am ever to know this one? Knowing about *them* only from what the nuns have taught in catechism—killers of Christ . . .

The old man was not much help either, I am told. He would crack his rare smile, eternally the puzzle, proud, obscure.

"One day I insisted," Robert tells me, "mad in my perplexity, driven to know. He told me this, he said: 'Some things you'll have to find out for yourself, *mijico*. Not from me, not from anyone else. Don't listen to them if they ever say they know. Marcel, may God rest his soul, never found out, never had a chance to. Maybe someday you will.'"

As dubious as the old man was about his son's Frenchness, he took great pride in his school marks, the Law Faculty, his legal career. Even the medals, which he would append to his own threadbare lapel on Bastille day, ambling down with the multitude to watch the parade, his everlasting grudge against *La France* notwithstanding.

"It's for Marcel," he would tell him, "he believed in all this nonsense."

Robert glides through the Lycée effortlessly, matriculating in 1950 with a thoroughly undistinguished record and few prospects, and without a compelling reason for launching himself into anything resembling a career. I know, or rather used to know, boys just like he must have been then, sly and quick and restless, blowing like seagulls across the lemon groves and sandstone hills that gird the city and its sleepy boulevards, their young lives like the city itself, scented in the morning with the salty sea breeze, in the evening with the sagebrush of the desert wind from the south. The boys, like the city, a shifting blend of the sweet coast and harsh interior.

"I was a disappointment to the old man," he tells me later, "not that he'd ever say so. I was welcome to stay on and help out at the store. Though I knew he must have been thinking of my dad."

"You mean, the Faculty, the law?" I ask.

"That. And strange thing, even the service. My dad's sense of purpose, I guess, my lack thereof." He pauses and frowns at me but not really at me. And I wonder, not for the first time, how the shadow of the missing and missed looms larger than their real presence could ever have.

They drifted together like a dog pack, he and his buddies, cruising the boulevards in search of boisterous fun. He hardly remembers, he tells me later, it all seems to him like one long blurred, procrastinous September, with but a hint of impending Armageddon. They had places to go and friends to see, the whole city their private sandlot, suspended from its invisible hook, its last allotted happy days quietly ticking away. With them in tow, the city was savoring this precarious equilibrium, waiting for its overdue day of reckoning, for its scented bubble to snap, for the proverbial other shoe to finally drop. For two years he simply marked time.

In May 1952, having had enough of waiting, he and a whole pack of his buddies went downtown together and signed up for the Foreign Legion.

"And please don't ask me why," he says, "because to this day I don't really know. For all I remember I had been toying with the idea of enrolling at the Faculty . . . Got the old man's blessing too, even a promise of support. He sure was relieved to see me off dead center."

But somehow, given the times and the company he was keeping, the prospect of going back to a crowded classroom seemed unenticing.

"I'm not like my father," he tells me, recalling, almost apologetically, that ten-year-old summer that now seems to him, even more so to me, a lifetime away. "Not much like the old man either. But of course he knew that." Not much like the rest of the would-be scholars that gnarled the emaciated family tree for generations before him, for that matter, he says. "Never found books anything to get all that passionate about . . . couldn't quite see the point." No wonder the Faculty didn't seem like much of a prospect.

Besides, there was a quaint little war going on in *l'Indochine*. Exotic, obscure, just faraway enough to be both enticing and unreal. It never ceases to amaze me, the things men find enticing. But neither he nor his buddies gave much thought to the matter as they hiked downtown together to present themselves at the recruitment office. It was to be a change of pace, a change of scene.

"You chalk it up to youth," he tells me later. He is caressing my hair distractedly, having taken leave of the here and now and of me, having gone to God only knows where it is he goes on such occasions. "Dumb, careless, blissful youth." I don't take it personally, being all of nineteen myself. The boys I've known all my life, those my age or my brother's, have yet to grow up. My brother never did and now never will. I wonder if men ever do.

"I came home that evening and told him," he resumes, "hadn't given him any warning before; hardly had a clue myself. Spur of a moment is what it really was, a lark."

By dinner time he had deep forebodings about the whole affair. He had become convinced, was probably hoping, that the old man would try to dissuade him. It was an uncharted territory for both. The old man was reading upstairs. After he told him, blurting it out in one long jumble, the old man sat for a long time saying nothing.

His back had been bothering him for some time and his posture was beginning to show it. Robert waited, apprehensive, knowing there was still time to pull back, dreading the loss of face if he did, dreading even more the old man's silence.

"*Va bene, mijico*," the old man said at last. "It was bound to happen." His voice carried no reproach, only resignation. Robert had expected him to put up more of a fight.

"I'll be back, *abuelico*," he told him, "you can bet on it."

I listen, I file it away. Some day it may all make sense, though for the moment I cannot judge. I love him, but that doesn't make me blind. Maybe, just maybe, I will come to understand him, now that he's talking to me, come to know his how's and why's. So when he shrugs it off again with: "And there you got it, in a nutshell, the dumb optimism of youth," I know there's more, there's always more. Though will he ever share it?

The old man was being easy on him: "Yes, maybe you will," he observed, "but then maybe you won't. The Legion, huh? Well, if you die for *la France* there, at least you'll die like the foreigner you are."

A whiff of the old bitterness still carried through, the old man must have been visited by the ghost of his departed son.

"Don't count me out so fast, *abuelico*." He waited for more. None came.

"I had a feeling he somehow knew a heck of a lot more than I did about why I did it," he tells me. "I wanted him to either comfort me or cuss me out. Does that make sense?"

"Sure," I say, anxious to reassure, bursting with love for him. Truth is, I don't really know. It's all so strange, so very remote.

The old man, his love notwithstanding, did neither.

"I see," he said, "I see."

"I'll be back," he told him again. The old man shrugged and kept looking at him. After a while he sighed and turned back to his book. The matter was, as far as he was concerned, closed.

He spends the bulk of the next two years in Indochina.

"Hated every minute of it too," he says, "so much for the follies of youth. Never told the old man how bad it really was. Never told anybody."

Is he telling me now? Should I feel honored? I am prepared to, though how long before he clams up again?

"Not that it would have made any difference," he goes on, "he was so happy to have me back alive."

In Indochina, they kept shifting bivouacs from one forlorn patch of sniper-infested marsh to another. At a moment's notice a deafening downpour would pounce upon them, transforming the fine red dust into thick mud that caked into one's hair and skin and toes until the contours of one's very soul were encrusted in dark goo.

"You and Jojo were there together, no?" I say.

There is more to what goes on between these two, not just comrades, more than just army buddies, not quite friends. Jojo has had his hook into him for as long as I have known them, it is not like Robert to just go along meekly. Yet go along he does and I have no clue what the hold is that Jojo has on him. If I am ever to find out, it will not be now, though I have given him an opening as wide as the sea.

"Yeah," he says, "we did boot camp together, and then some."

Once again, stymied.

"Our officers," he says, "were all French, from the *Métropole*. Made no secret of how it was all for nothing."

There was a conspiracy, the officers intimated, a dark pact between the liberal politicians in Paris and the Red gooks in black pajamas. We were to lose the war, deliberately, treasonously, shamelessly. The boys in the rice paddies were being sacrificed, surrounded, isolated, left to their own devices.

Slowly it all sank in. They learned to trust nobody but themselves. You turned your back on someone, dubious friend or certain foe, you were as good as dead. They banded together, sprouting scruffy beards, cultivating graveyard humor and an uncanny sense for lone snipers and plastic mines.

"You learned to second guess them," he says, "they seldom gave you another chance."

They never discovered what it was they were fighting for, nor who they were fighting against. After a while it didn't seem to matter. They fought to stay alive, contemplating desertion though there was nowhere to go.

"And Jojo?" I ask.

"Oh, he was there, we were in the same platoon."

Nothing more.

They shipped them out, those who survived the carnage, back to bases in Algeria two months after Dien Bien Phu.

"We celebrated by getting plastered for a week," he says.

On his first pass he went to see the old man.

"See, *abuelico*," he announced at the door, "I told you. I'm back."

The old man hugged him for a long time, and Robert couldn't help but notice how frail he had become.

"*Mijico*," was all he said.

He disengaged himself from the long embrace and was dabbing his eyes slowly with his sleeve.

"Someone must have been listening to my prayers. At least you're close to home now."

He couldn't help but notice how the old man had aged. He must have been nearing seventy-five and beginning to show it. His back was stooped, the skin under his stubborn chin hung in loose folds. Only the dark eyes were as fierce as ever.

From then on he came home frequently, showing up late Friday nights, knowing the old man would be waiting. On Saturday and Sunday morning, weather permitting, they would sit together under a tree in the backyard, saying little, content with each other's company.

"Another lull before another storm," he tells me, "not that I knew then. Though the old man probably did."

He shrugs, dismissing an older self. Or skin, as he sometime puts it. "I'm like an onion, my love," he tells me, "if you insist on peeling me, you may find nothing inside."

But of course I know better, or think I do, and aim to get to that elusive core of his, past the skins and obfuscations, where I know the real Robert must reside.

They were camped in what seemed the lap of luxury by comparison near Sidi-bel-Abbès in the foothills, where a deceptive calm lasted for most of the year. Then they were yanked out without warning and shipped into the Kabylia Mountains, where the Arab rebellion, just as nasty in its own way as Indochina, was brewing hotter. There was a difference though, leastwise for the local boys. They were fighting to save their homes now, not just for the glory of *la France*.

"This new mess started real small and just kept growing," I can hear his matter-of-fact voice telling me. "Before you knew it, it was big enough to catch everybody's attention. The FLN raids were sporadic first, we'd actually be let to go home on furlough every other week."

Of this I know a bit more, I used to see them coming back to Bab-el-Oued, our young heroes descending from the mountains, the knight defenders of our homes and gardens and cherished French way of life. I was one of the kids who hung around them, patted their dusty fatigues, touched their submachine guns and basked in their burnished auras.

Soon things turned nasty. The FLN guerrillas were resupplied with modern weapons from abroad, and soon it was back to ambushes and plastic mines and elusive snipers and deadly booby traps. Once again the boys in fatigues were straining to protect their backs, to kill and survive and kill again. Except that now it didn't take an officer to remind them that their back was to the not-quite-proverbial wall, to the dusty back gardens of Bab-el-Oued. Nowhere to ship out to this time. And fewer furloughs.

"The old man would never ask," he tells me, "but he must have known what was going on."

"And Jojo?" I ask.

"We were still together," he replies. "He was my squad leader by then, all the way to the end."

Again no more. I'll keep trying.

By the end of 1957 the mountains were given up for a lost cause and the troops pulled out, back down to the outskirts of the city, for what soon bloomed into the Battle of Algiers. For the boys, it was a surprisingly welcome defeat.

"At least we were back home," he says.

He could see the old man often if irregularly, just drop in whenever he could. Drop in, sit with him for a few hours, share a simple dinner laced with the old man's growing if seldom articulated air of gloom. The few men he had counted as friends were all dead by then. The old man kept the store open out of sheer habit, limping down the narrow stairs every morning to open the door, kept sitting there all day surrounded by his books and memorabilia and empty shelves, reading, alone.

"He'd been living off my father's pension by then," he tells me. "He didn't really need the business."

As the city boiled over around him, a steaming cauldron of violence he chose to ignore, he just sat there, brooding.

"I'd tell him what was going on, how the guys in the Legion saw it, my own doubts . . ."

He would listen, his eyes half closed, lips pinched, taking it all in, saying little beyond the occasional grunt. He seemed to have somehow anticipated it all along. He was neither surprised nor shocked, just resigned.

In April 1961, after the generals' putsch against de Gaulle had collapsed, he left the Legion for good.

"The whole company quit together . . . deserted, if you prefer," he tells me. Officers and men together, walked out with their weapons and supplies and, most of them, joined the OAS. As soon as he could, he came home, sneaking in after dark and, for once, catching the old man in a rare expansive mood.

"He was genuinely pleased," he tells me. "Of course, I spared him the gory details."

"We'll drink to that," he announced and went to the back to rummage for his medicinal brandy. "As far as he was concerned I was back home, out of uniform for the first time in nine years."

"Here's to coming home," he told his grandson over raised glasses, his sinewy hand shaking visibly. "I'm getting old, *mijico*, lonely too. You better stick around, let *la France* fight her own war, you've done enough."

What Robert told him next quickly dampened the old man's festive mood.

"Grandpa," he told him, "it's not for France anymore. She's betrayed us, sold us out to the Arabs. It's for Algeria now; it's us."

Too late. The old man's smile had dissipated. He eyed Robert sadly across the narrow table, sitting together as they had done for years.

"Still fighting," he sighed, "one would think you've had enough. You're not growing younger, *mijico*."

"It's not the same this time, *abuelico*."

He did try to explain, though he knew it must have sounded all wrong: "It's for us now. I was born in this house, remember? I don't want to leave. This is my country too."

The old man listened without nodding, and it was no use.

"Robert," he said, "listen just this once. You've never had a country. You never will."

"And that was that, that was all I could get out of him," he tells me as he lies in my narrow bed frowning at the ceiling.

Sometimes, he confesses, just the last two days, he thinks he is beginning to understand what the old man had in mind. That's when he launches into those dark pronouncements that I have grown to resent, that I find so utterly incomprehensible. They take him away from me and make him that much more of a stranger. Not to mention that much older. I am only nineteen, but I know we are all better off leaving alone what is futile and scary and can't be helped. It crowds out of our life the last bits of joy we still have left.

From then on he kept coming back, always at night, following an increasingly elaborate route and even more elaborate feigns, sometimes absent for a day, sometimes for a whole week. But always coming back to the house and the old man. The OAS was keeping them exceedingly busy.

After two months it finally dawned on him that the old man's position had become untenable.

"He was trapped there," he says, "alone, exposed. And my coming and going was not helping either. Someone would notice, someone would find out . . ."

Someone finally did. He had told the old man it was time to clear out.

"I tried to reason with him but he would just brush me off."

No use. They kept going at it for days.

"It wasn't exactly a surprise when it finally happened."

He pauses, and I know what is coming. I have already heard about it, right after it happened. One piece I did not need to pull out of him. I still remember, I dread it, but am nonetheless transfixed.

"They slipped a hand grenade through the back door," was how he told me last November, "at noon, while he was taking his nap. Must have been someone who knew his routine. He was eighty-four . . . They wanted to get my attention; they knew I wasn't in that time of the day."

It was four days before he found out, coming back at night to find the front boarded up with planks. The gendarmes had done it, he was told. The congregation, the one the old man had so steadfastly shunned, passed up a collection plate and buried him in the old hallowed grounds north of St. Eugene.

"I haven't been to see the grave yet," he tells me. "Someday I hope to be able . . . Though I can't say the *Cadísh* for him, wouldn't know how . . ."

I can tell the note of profound regret that has crept into his voice.

"He must have known why they came for him," he almost whispers, "must have anticipated it. Nothing personal, it was only about me."

One more thing he will have to live with for the rest of eternity. How many more are there, silent regrets piled up one on top of the other? I wonder how it must feel living with so many ghosts. If I hang onto him, which I am determined to do, I may yet find out. Sometimes just the thought of it gives me the shivers.

No one had tried to take over the house since. The neighbors were ashamed, no doubt, though most likely they had nothing to do with the outrage. The other side has its own crazies, its own enforcers and goons, hot heads and zealots, sworn defenders of the faith each and every one. Much like ours. He had known all that, of course, and had been trapped there, in the middle, unable to budge one way or the other.

And so, in the midst of the growing carnage, with nobody the wiser, he kept coming back, at night, once or twice a week, slipping over the back wall into the untended yard, across the old man's orchard and on through the back door whose rusty lock still accepts his key with nary a squeak. Sneaking like a faithful spook up the creaky old stairs to sleep in the old man's narrow bed. Not his own across the corridor, but the old man's, in penance for a debt that will never be repaid. It was only a matter of time, sooner or later someone would notice, it hardly seems to matter. Since the old man died, he has become even busier.

*I*t has been ages since he has last been on this beach. No matter, he can still count on the breeze blowing inland from the northeast, the way it always does this time of the day in the spring. The winds over the city are forever predictable in their daily seesaw between the desert and the sea. We all take this for granted like we do the sun's daily trek across the faded blue sky.

"It's still the same," he tells me. "You look straight out across the water and you can't see the smoke . . . no dust either; it's all blown out inland, toward the Mitidja."

As he makes his way along the sand, he can, like the rest of us, count on the wind to keep blowing that way till late afternoon. Then he can count on it just as assuredly to shift the other way and start blowing the smoke back across the harbor and out to sea. Out there, a mile or so from the edge of the sand, he can see the Arab fishing boats strung out like white linen on a clothesline, scouring the green water for the stray fish that might, hope springs eternal, have survived the years of high-explosives fishing. Closer in, just outside the harbor, is the reason why the fishermen feel all of a sudden so emboldened— four gray destroyers at anchor, sedate and formal like beached turtles. They have been brought in only last week.

"Our doing too, come to think," he chuckles. "The OAS had threatened to blow up the refugee boats. Now they've called our bluff."

He and his buddies used to spend their summers on this strip of sand and rock, roaming wide and doing all those incomprehensible things that gangs of boys have always done. I wonder if they dream aloud sometimes like girls do. They must, though what about God only knows. I don't expect he'd ever tell me. He would probably blush if I asked, the same endearing way he blushes when I probe, ever so delicately, about other girls in his past. I suppose he thinks whatever they dreamed about was all very silly. Though while he disavows whatever youthful fantasies he and his buddies may have entertained those faraway summers, he can still remember every crevasse in the crumbling rock face further north, where the beach reconstitutes itself into small strips and shaded nooks, divided by salients of eroded sandstone. That is where he winds up in the early afternoon, like a homing seal, beached face-down on his shirt in the shade of the low cliff.

"The sun was going full blast once the wind had died down," he says.

The tired surf keeps thumping on the sand in delicate small ruffles. It is so quiet you could almost forget the ugly mess we have all gotten ourselves into. Except for the smell of cordite soaked indelibly into his clothes.

"Can you smell it?" he asks me, now concerned.

What can I say? To me he smells like he's always smelled, sweat mingled with smoke. But of course, he has been with that stuff since long before I met him.

He winds up sleeping for over an hour, waking up only when the shadow of the cliff has reached down to touch the surf at five o'clock.

Suddenly chilled, he puts on his shirt and threads his way through the fallen rock back to the promenade, then slowly back to Bab-el-Oued. He must, he knows only too well, come up with a plan. Soon.

At ten minutes to seven, still without a plan, he strolls past the café. Nobody he knows is out there, and the window on the right is shuttered tight. He passes by unhurriedly, turns right at the corner, then right again, then left at the next corner. Nobody seems to follow, though as he knows well that may mean nothing. He spends the next hour walking the *quartier* till it finally gets dark.

"That felt much better," he tells me. He is beginning to relax a bit. Just before eight he turns from the Avenue des Consulats into Rue

Charles Fournier. Keeping to the left side all the way to the next corner, he can scan the second-floor window. It is sepia dark. He hurries on past. Two more hours to kill.

Emerging on Avenue de Bouzarea, he meanders toward Boulevard Guillemin, where few people are likely to recognize him in the milling crowd. He buys the evening paper and ducks into a café, selecting a table at the far end, near the back door. He sips his anisette slowly as he watches the crowd and scans the paper. It is there all right, a cryptic note tucked in at the bottom of the third page.

"Censored," he tells me, "just the bare gist of it . . . A whole wing down, twenty-three people still missing in the rubble, mostly patients." And further below: "The explosion is tentatively attributed to a commando coming and leaving in a Red Sickle ambulance." It is taken for granted that the OAS is behind it. An official investigation is ongoing.

"Nothing else about the ambulance," he tells me. "Which means Jojo and the others must have made it back."

Which also means, as he knows, that he must keep his next appointment, or at least go through the motions.

At nine-thirty he begins heading back. If it is a consolation, he knows it is too late for another job tonight. He will have to tell Jojo about the old man's house, though on second thought maybe not right away. He is an untouchable now, branded, an exposed pariah, a status he must reconcile himself to. Before, it was just *les barbouzes*. Now he knows the FLN must also be after his hide. The bombing of the old man's house makes it crystal clear. Whoever he gets in touch with might become a target as well.

"Not a comforting thought, in case you're wondering what I'm doing here," he tells me later as he darts to the window once more to peer outside, a gesture that is rapidly becoming reflexive. "You should have slammed the door in my face."

"Oh hush," I tell him.

I'd rather not hear this, though of course I know exactly how things stand. We have been circumspect, sneaky, to be precise, if only because of my parents. But the guys gunning for him are a harsh lot. Two lots now. All the same, I've got him all to myself, right here, alive and warm, if increasingly restless.

As he goes up the street toward his rendezvous, people are trooping the other way with their scant luggage, eyes fixed straight ahead as they march in shamed silence toward the harbor. The wind is again blowing from inland, the smoke is back. Machine-gun fire flares up from the direction of Isly. At exactly ten he cruises past the Sunflower, nonchalant, eyes averted. No tables on the sidewalk, the place is deserted. Momentarily he is flooded with the acute relief of twenty-four more hours to play with. First he's got to find a place to sleep though, and he can't think of any. Except for the one he knows he must resolutely avoid. He keeps walking, trying to come up with a plan. He is approaching Rue Lavoisier, still with nothing tangible at hand. Which is when he finally gives up and, to my eternal relief, knocks on our door.

We met last year in April, right here at the door. He was on a short leave from the Legion, just before deserting. He came to tell us about Antoine, my brother, who was killed a week earlier.

"Bloody waste," he tells me later, after I have gotten to know him, "a lousy night ambush in Kabilya. No rhyme, no reason, just go take a walk in the dark and see what happens . . . A training mission, we call it . . . Kids, the whole bunch of them, just came in as replacements."

Antoine is, was, only two years older than me, and Mother didn't want him to go, screamed at him, screamed at my dad. I could hear them having a loud go at it all the way from the shop. But nothing would deflect Antoine from his appointment with a land mine in the sand.

"He was just like you ten years before," I remind him.

"I guess so," he concedes. "He must have known . . . made me promise, just in case, to call on you. What could I say? I was his sergeant. The guys were having weird premonitions all the time over there. Sometimes they were wrong; sometimes they were right. He died in my arms. We had to stuff him piece by piece in a plastic bag, what was left of him . . . if you really must know."

I assure him I do, though the image is not exactly comfortable. He brought back Antoine's St. Christopher's medallion.

"Could have been St. Jude's for all you'd know," he says. "The captain gave it to me when I told him I'd stop by."

He has the medallion in his pocket when my dad opens door.

"Yes?"

My dad is unshaven and disheveled, and has been drinking for days. But even in his stupor he must recognize the uniform.

"Monsieur Laforge?"

I can hear them from the living room where I am sitting with Mother helping her with her cross-stitching.

"Yes."

"Robert Aron," he says, "I served with Antoine . . ."

Even from inside I can tell how uncomfortable he is. My dad does not make it easier.

"He'd asked me to stop by, just before . . ."

His voice is a deep baritone, I feel drawn to it already. His inflection is neutral, guarded. I can tell he is from Algiers, but little else.

He pauses again. There follows an awkward silence before I finally hear my dad: "Come in."

My father is large and thick and fills the door frame snugly, as befits a butcher. What with his present state, it takes him a while to shift his bulk and let Robert through. When I see him for the first time now, I get up immediately. He is shorter than I have imagined from his voice, only slightly taller than me, wiry, with deep set dark eyes. His face is thin and angular, you would expect it to be darting about. Which makes the controlled calm of his bearing all the more striking. He is dark complexioned, must have been spending most his days outdoors.

I am dressed to the hilt with rouge and lipstick because of the constant flow of condolence bearers we have been receiving. I can only hope he won't notice how young I am.

"Marie," my father says by way of introduction, "the sergeant was a friend of Antoine's."

I offer my hand. He takes it, gingerly, and I notice the thick calluses on his hand.

"Robert Aron," he says.

"*Enchantée.*"

I know I am blushing profusely as we stand there holding hands and inspecting each other, rather shamelessly though my dad acts as if he doesn't notice, and probably hasn't.

"It was funny," Robert tells me later, "good thing he was so stewed. Truth is, Antoine had never mentioned a kid sister. I don't think your mom missed much though."

"She seldom does," I assure him.

Consequently, she's right on her feet now as my dad motions Robert toward the couch: "Sit down. Adéle!"

He doesn't look at my mom as he again addresses Robert, who is still standing: "Sit down for God's sake. The sergeant was a friend of Antoine," he tells my mom as if she hasn't been sitting right there all along. She's still wearing her black funeral robe, her silver-streaked auburn hair pulled up tightly in a bun.

Robert steps forward and offers his hand: "*Enchanté, Madame.*"

She barely touches the proffered palm as she gives him a quick once-over.

"Nice of you to come," she tells him. "Robert Aron, is it?"

She seems to mull it over briefly, until my father cuts in: "Adéle, anisette!"

Which she professes to ignore, keeping her eyes on Robert: "Would you have a drink with us?"

"Sure, thanks."

He sneaks a quick look at me. As our eyes meet I shrug to let him know he can ignore whatever is going on between my parents, that it is all right in the sense that nothing can be done. Though of course it is hard to imagine how my shrug could convey all that.

"Good," my mom says as she retreats to the kitchen, though not before stopping me in my tracks as I make out to join her: "You stay, Marie, I'm sure the sergeant could use some company."

Which is as far as she is prepared to go in castigating my dad in public. She's back in a minute with the bottle on a tray with two glasses and pastries. She sets them in front of Robert on the small coffee table, then withdraws to stand behind me.

My father pours two glasses and hands one to Robert.

"Here. Drink up."

"Antoine?" Robert raises his glass.

"Antoine," my dad echoes, "*Algérie Française*. You're going back?"

"Yes."

"Soon?"

"A couple of days."

"Well, my house is your house."

The old formula tumbles out somewhat rough.

"You kill as many of them as . . . "

His voice catches, he clears his throat unsuccessfully, resuming in a hoarse whisper: "Antoine was worth the lot, the whole ten-million lot."

"Yes, he was," Robert agrees.

He must feel just as awkward as the two of us.

"For all I could tell, he was," he confesses later, "though I hardly knew him."

What he doesn't say is of course what I know for fact, namely that he feels responsible anyway, since he was in front and somehow missed the mine that got Antoine.

The two of them drain their glasses and my dad refills both.

"Drink up," he urges Robert. "*Algérie Française!* What did you say your name was, sergeant?"

"Robert Aron."

They drain their glasses in unison. My mom is still standing behind me, monitoring them just as I do, though for different reasons. Robert darts a quick look at me and I raise my eyebrows and keep my eyes on him, which for some reason I cannot resist. Neither can he, it seems.

An hour and a bottle later he finally gets up to take his leave, with the rest of us rising with him. Neither he nor my dad are exactly steady on their feet, and it is Mom who takes charge, bless her quick wits: "Watch out for yourself, Robert," she tells him, using the familiar form now while extending him a formal embrace. "Come see us again soon."

I could have kissed her on both cheeks too, the way he does.

"I will, *Madame*," he says, "and thanks again."

"You do that," my dad says. "Marie, see the sergeant out."

It could have ended right there with me holding the door for him. We stroll down the narrow stoop and across the yard, and of course we both make sure it didn't. The evening outside is cool in spite of the smoke. When we stop at the gate he says abruptly: "Hey . . . " and digs into his pocket.

"What?"

"This."

He comes up with the medallion.

"I almost forgot, it's Antoine's."

I take it from him and hold it up with both hands, lingering over the familiar features, before he says: "May I?"

I nod and hand it back to him and lean forward so that he can slip it over my head and around my neck. By now our faces are real close and my eyes are locked into his and my voice is a whisper: "Yes . . . Mother gave it to him when he signed up. Didn't help all that much, did it? How well did you know him?"

We are both determined not to break contact, that much is settled.

"Not all that well," he says. "He came in with the last batch . . . hardly had time to train . . . much too young to be there."

"You don't look all that old yourself," I say, daring him to contradict me.

"You must be kidding," he says. But his thin, drawn face breaks up in a smile for the first time. "I'm ancient, one foot in the grave . . . practically."

To which we both respond with a laugh and I admonish him, my hand on his sleeve: "Don't ever say that!"

I am taking unprecedented liberties with him, I know, but will worry about it later.

"And please don't mind my father," I add. "It's been a terrible blow. Antoine was everything to him, he had such grand plans . . . He's got nothing now."

"He's got you and your mother," he reminds me.

"It's not the same."

He is looking at me quizzically, so I add: "You know how fathers are."

"I guess," he says, "though I really don't remember much of mine."

"When are you going back?" I ask him, stirring us back to the present and the task at hand. It's good that it is so dark, I have never been that forward before and I know I am blushing.

"Day after tomorrow."

"For how long?"

He pauses. I know now he already knew then his days in the Legion were coming to an abrupt end, but he is still prudent: "Not for very long this time." Then, finally: "Can I come see you again?"

After which we play our lines like well-rehearsed troupers: "I thought you'd never ask."

"Okay then?"

"Of course."

"When?"

"Any time."

"How about tomorrow?"

"Sure."

"Where?"

"Right here."

"Seven?"

"That'll be fine."

After all this, he doesn't act surprised when I let him kiss me. Though I myself am still dazed as I watch him leave. Then I run back up, skipping steps.

And so, since April of last year, he has been coming to visit us—that is to say, me—with great regularity. Mother fusses over him like he was her own son resurrected. And on nights he doesn't take me out, he sits with my dad, drinking and talking politics, sometimes well into the night.

After which I see him out, ostensibly, then rush back to my bedroom upstairs. There I wait for him to double up on his tracks and make his way cautiously back across the garden. Whereby I sneak him into my room through the rear window. He is delicious. I am delirious. The way I figure it, Antoine has sent him to me, so it must be all right. And he is mine.

*P*apa is there to open the door, still in his pajamas. He has taken to wearing them all day long, now that the shop is closed and he has no pressing reason to go outside. His face is sprouting weeks-old gray whiskers and his eyes are permanently bloodshot. My mom and I do a credible job of ignoring him most of the time. But we can't avoid hearing Robert's voice from the door: "Marie home?"

My heart thumps, I haven't seen him in over a week. My dad must be going through his routine of inspecting Robert, after which his voice rises derisively: "Where the fuck would you expect her to be this hour of the night?"

My mother winces, but stops me from going to the door.

"Who is it, Papa?" I ask instead.

"Your lover boy," he says, as he turns and walks back into the room, leaving the door open. He is dragging his left leg noticeably and has developed a stoop for reasons that have little to do with his health.

"*Georges!*" my mom says.

He ignores her and goes to sit at the table.

As Robert comes into the room I go up to meet him.

"What happened?" I ask.

He usually comes over much earlier, just after dark.

"Nothing," he says, "got a free evening, that's all."

"Sit down, Robert," says my mom.

"*Merci, Madame.*"

He walks past the table, where my dad has staked his silent vigil next to the radio, and joins me on the couch. I take his hand in mine.

"How are you?" I ask.

We are both a bit formal because of my parents, though by now everybody is wise to our charade.

"Fine," he says, "just fine."

But his eyes avoid mine and I know something must be seriously askew. For the moment though I let it be.

"Will you have some coffee?" my mother offers.

"Sure he will," my dad says, "ever heard him say no?"

As my mom rises and departs toward the kitchen, he proceeds to grill Robert: "So," he says, "what's new?"

"Nothing much."

"Just like that?"

"Well..."

My dad is doing his best to precipitate a scene. Robert is doing *his* best to deflect him.

"You know how it is..." he says lamely.

My dad considers that for a minute.

"Yes, reckon I do," he says. "And Radio OAS, what is it saying? Been kinda quiet, eh?"

"Oh, they off the air again?"

I can tell Robert's ignorance is feigned, as can my dad, who won't let him off the hook.

"Off the air and quiet as mice," he says. "You'd think they'd moved down to the port, wouldn't you?"

Robert shrugs.

"Papa, let him be," I finally intervene.

"Shut up, child," he tells me, then turns back to Robert. "*L'Algérie Française*," he tells him, "she's dying. Finished. Nothing left, just a carcass. The Reds and the Jews, they're selling us out to the Arabs, the dirty bastards . . ."

Robert gets up and I get up with him. Now my mom, who must have been standing at the kitchen door, intervenes: "*Georges*, hush!"

"Oh, I don't mean him," he tells her. "He's all right, we all know that. He's still fighting, isn't he? It's the others . . . " He stops, at last deflated. "I'm going to bed," he announces.

We are all silent as he drags his game leg toward the stairs. His climb is slow and laborious. He stops halfway up: "Marie."

"Yes, Papa?"

"You can spare him the detour through the yard, he might hurt himself bumping into something nasty in the dark."

After which he resumes his climb. A moment later we hear the door slam upstairs.

I don't know where to look. Robert's eyes are planted firmly at his feet. My mother is bringing out the coffee tray.

"I'm sorry, Madame," Robert tells her.

"Not your fault," she says. "Not his either. Here, sit down and have some coffee."

I sit next to him and hold on to his arm as she pours and he sips his coffee slowly. I am content to just have him there, as my mother withdraws back into the kitchen, leaving us alone. Presently he says: "Marie."

"Yes?"

"I need a place to stay."

"What do you mean?"

He looks toward the kitchen, then back to me: "They blew up the old man's house," he says.

My breath is caught.

"When?" I ask him.

"A couple of days ago, I'm not quite sure when."

"Where were you?"

"Out, working."

His euphemism carries its own irony, though it remains serviceable.

"You didn't sleep at all," I say.

He shakes his head: "I did . . . in the backyard. That's when I found out."

My God, I am thinking, staying out there all by himself *after* . . . What I learn later does not extinguish my fear for him. Will I ever be able to imagine the totality of his night in the damp grass under the curved moon? Once again, I find myself on the outside of his hermetic circle, looking inside in search of a flicker of light, a clue, some commonality—and gazing into an opaque core.

"You shouldn't have stayed there," I tell him, "you could have come here."

"I know," he says, "but it was late and I was too tired. Besides, it was quite safe. They probably thought they'd got me there, buried in the rubble."

Just the thought makes me shiver. He senses that and pulls me to him, brushing his lips to my temple.

"Shall I ask Mother?" I say.

Neither of us can think of an alternative.

"Might as well," he agrees. Though I can see he is not exactly comfortable with the thought.

Almost immediately, her voice comes from the kitchen: "Marie?"

"Yes?"

"Put clean sheets on Antoine's bed. He can stay there."

"Oh, Mother . . ."

Neither of us says more. I am overwhelmed with gratitude and would like to jump up and hug her. Except that she is carrying the coffee pot as she rejoins us.

"It's all right, dear," she tells me as she refills Robert's cup.

"*Merci, Madame,*" he says, rather stiffly.

"Oh, don't mention it," she tells him. And a while later: "You must forgive Georges, he doesn't really mean it. He's been depressed, everything's falling apart. It's tough on him, what with Antoine and all . . . He'll learn to cope, just give him time."

She skips over how tough it must be on her.

"Oh, *c'est rien, Madame*," Robert assures her, "no need to mention it. I know he's doing his best."

"So is everybody else," she retorts. "So are you. No call to insult people . . . " She pauses, weighing her words carefully. "Well, it'll be over soon enough. For me it was over with Antoine . . . They burned five houses up the street, did you notice, Marie? Didn't wait for night-time either, come to think . . . "

"Yes, Mother."

I am shocked to hear her say that much out loud.

"I think I'll go to bed now," she announces. "See you two in the morning."

"Good night Madame," Robert tells her, in near unison with my "Good night Mother."

"Good night loves."

*W*e are lying in bed, my head propped up on his arm, his head casting a dark shadow on the moon-bleached pillow we are sharing in my narrow bed. I will send him back to Antoine's room before we fall asleep, but for the moment I am running my fingers through the thick hair on the back of his neck. It could use some barbering, definitely, which I will do tomorrow if he lets me. His face is shaded and too near for me to see, but it must be relaxed and peaceful, for once. I know this from the slow circular patterns his finger draws around my left breast. The room is brightly lit through my thin muslin curtains, everything is peaceful, hard to believe. I let out an involuntary sigh.

"What is it, my love?" he says.

"Mmm . . . nothing, just being with you."

"So why the sigh?"

"I don't know. Just."

Though of course I know, we both do. In the meantime, I shift over and gain hold of his nipple, which I lick slowly, again and again.

"Mmm, what do you know . . . " I tell him.

"Not much," he concedes.

"You love me?"

"Sure do."

"How much?" I insist.

"A whole bunch."

"Why?"

"Beats me. You're the one who's supposed to tell me, remember?"

He pulls me closer to him and the bed creaks ominously.

"Shhh . . . not so loud," I tell him, "you'll wake them up."

"Sorry, you better remind me of that too."

"I will," I tell him.

We are both tired out. He has stopped circling my nipple and has fallen silent. I cannot tell from his breathing whether he is drifting into sleep already. The night is for once quiet, we haven't heard a single blast in the last hour or so. Were it not for the smoke you couldn't tell the city is still out there self-destructing.

"What are you thinking about, *chéri*?" I ask him.

"Mmm . . . " he says.

He doesn't sound a wee bit sleepy.

In a minute he gets up on his knees and pulls the thin curtains apart. My window faces east, and from where he crouches you can see the lower end of Bab-el-Oued, down Boulevard Guillemin and all the way down to the lurching mass of the Casbah. I wonder if he is doing what I think he is doing, locking in on where the old man's house used to be. But when I join him there, I see he is looking in the direction of a burning house, much closer, in front of Hospital Maillot.

We are both stark naked, the cool breeze blows in my face as I press my belly tight against his back. We listen together to the early roosters crowing over from the small farms on the outskirts, the other side of Bouzarea. Their peaceful exuberance is punctuated a minute later by the thud of a distant explosion. Someone is still busy. His buddies? The others? All I know is I am glad he's in here with me. I dig my face into the back of his neck and breathe in his dark fragrance.

"Marie," he says.

"Yes, love."

"I've had it."

"What?"

In the ensuing silence the echo of my question reverberates for a long moment.

"This whole fuckin' mess," he says, "it's no use. I've been an idiot not to see this before. I've got to get out."

My antennas are propped up. I've been waiting for us to have this conversation for a long time. But now that it is upon me, I'm not sure how to proceed.

"What do you mean?"

My voice comes out muffled. Am I finally to be let in? Slowly, I struggle for more evidence: "But how?"

"I don't know," he tells me. "I haven't had time to think."

Strictly speaking, we both know, this could not be true. He has been brooding about this for months, though I have not been made privy to the deliberations. He has finally told me about the hospital, just an hour ago, before we made love. So what else could he have been doing since last night except thinking?

I wait for him to proceed.

"All I know is, I'm not going back," he says. "There's nothing left to go back to, just more of the same . . . Another house down, another traitor trashed . . . ours, theirs, who cares? We're all a bunch of butchers."

"You sure?" I ask him.

It is all out in the open, finally, he's talking to me. I can hardly believe my ears.

"Sure I'm sure," he says. "We're finished. Headquarters is gone, no more orders, no more chain of command, no OAS, all gone. All that's left is a bunch of mad goons running wild, dragging us down with them till we're all dead and buried."

"I know," I tell him. He is watching me from the corner of his eyes. "I've been wondering how long it'd take you."

He smiles.

"I'm kinda slow," he tells me.

"I've noticed."

"Smarty-pants."

I accept his hug, then bring us back to the present: "What will you do?"

A long silence ensues. I am not about to press him; I have no idea what to expect. All I know is he's finally talking to me, my heart swells with gratitude. I also know there is absolutely nothing he can do without me now. He knows it too. Don't push, girl, I tell myself.

"I don't know," he confesses.

"How about the rest?" I ask him.

"What rest?"

"Well, the rest of us, you know..."

The way it comes out I may be asking about *l'Algérie Française* or the whole *pieds noirs*, or Bab-el-Oued. Those are not my real worry, however. They are too big and way out there for me. My real worry is my mom and dad, and us.

"I don't know."

He is reluctant to say what is obvious to us both.

"It's finished, right?" I press him.

"Probably."

"It was all for nothing? Antoine too?"

"He knew it."

I find this somehow farfetched about Antoine, my happy-go-lucky brother.

"Did he tell you?" I ask.

"He didn't have to. A month in Kabylia is a long time... no glory, just a bloody mess. Lots of learning time there."

"You kept going," I remind him.

"That's different."

"How come?"

"I signed up. Antoine and the rest of the kids didn't, they were draftees. Besides..."

He hesitates.

"Yes?" I prod.

"Well..." he says.

I can see he is treading on delicate ground.

"There's the name," he says.

"What do you mean?"

"Aron, Laforge... It's not the same."

"Why?"

I know I am being obstinate, but I am determined to get to the bottom of this. So this is where I finally get the story about the old man and Robert's father. I listen, it all makes sense, but only up to a point. Beyond which I am still mystified.

"I still don't see how the name should make such a big difference," I tell him.

"A whole world of difference," he tells me. "It marks you, you're under the gun, forever. You try harder, you keep hanging in there. No use, you'll never pass. Like they've got your number and you're stuck." He stops. "Marie," he says, "you mind if we change the subject?"

It is time I relented.

"Of course not," I tell him.

I've got enough to mull over, an earful.

"How about your friends? Will they ever quit?" I ask.

"I doubt it."

"You mean, they'll keep going?"

"For a while."

"How can they?"

"You don't know them," he says. "Some of them've been fighting and losing ever since Dunkirk. They're not about to quit just because one more battle is lost. They're mad, *chérie*, mad at the perfidious General, mad at the stinking Arabs, mad at the traitors right here at home, mad at the whole wide world."

"I see."

There is one more thing I need, not a question, a favor: "Robert?"

"Yes, love."

"Please don't tell Papa."

"Tell him what?"

"About Antoine, and the rest."

"All right, I won't." Then, as an afterthought: "Don't you think he already knows?"

"He does," I tell him, "but just the same don't tell him."

"I won't."

"I love you," I tell him.

I am about to show him again how much.

*T*here is not much left of the night and we are still wide awake. I am forever amazed how gentle he is when he makes love, how, for those brief moments, I can almost crack his shell. At such moments I am almost convinced we might somehow wind up together at some place where one can live and love and breathe without ducking and looking over one's shoulder. I know I am going to do my utmost best for him, for us, but will it be enough, ever?

He is smoking now, and although his eyes brush over me, his mind is elsewhere. I ask him again: "What now?"

He looks at me pensively.

"I don't know," he says. "I should really clear out of here. The guys'll start looking for me once they realize I skipped the rendezvous tomorrow."

"That'll make it three lots chasing you," I remind him. First *les barbouzes*, then the FLN, now the OAS.

"You got it," he says. "But our guys are the worst. They're lifers, nothing left to lose. And you don't quit the OAS, you only go out feet first. They'll come after me, you'll see."

"But they don't know you're here," I protest.

"They're quite capable of putting two and two together. Especially Jojo."

That one again, can't get around him.

"How long do you think we've got?" I ask.

"A day, two at most. I'm more worried about you though."

"Never mind," I tell him, "you're staying here."

His dark eyes appraise me. I have staked my claim, this is my move.

"How about your parents?"

"Don't worry," I brush him aside, "I'll talk to my mom."

"I see," he says. "But I won't stay more than a day. Truth is, I've got to get out of Algiers."

I was afraid it was coming to that, and cannot claim surprise.

"Where will you go?" I ask.

"The mainland."

"Marseilles?"

"For starters."

As much as I try to control myself, my heart plunges all the way to the bottom.

"I'll never see you again, right?" I whimper.

He grabs me by both shoulders and shakes me gently. His voice is stern as he chides me: "Don't ever say that."

"I just don't want you to lie to me," I tell him. "I'm a big girl, remember? Whatever happens, I can take it."

I myself am not quite convinced, but he seems to agree: "I know you can," he says, "so let's not make it harder on you. Now listen."

His eyes assume that determined, opaque look they have every time he goes out at night.

"We can do it together. You can come with me."

He waits, I look at him. This is precisely what I have been longing to hear, but also what I now dread.

"I can't," I tell him.

"Why?"

"You know why."

"You mean your mom and dad?"

"Just my dad, he's not going to leave till the very end."

We are facing each other, both crouching on my bed.

"The end is here, Marie," he tells me.

"I know," I tell him, "but you go tell him."

We both contemplate a task neither of us is anxious to undertake.

"Why don't you come alone then?" he finally says, "just you and me."

"I can't leave Mom here," I tell him, "and she won't leave him no matter what."

It is as simple as that. We know there is nothing to argue about. I know exactly what he must do, he knows what I must do. Though I can tell he doesn't like it and is feeling rejected.

"I'm cold, *chéri*," I tell him. "Let's crawl back under the covers."

He seems reluctant, but I am not about to relent, and eventually I get him under the blanket and wrap myself tightly around him. "Come now . . ." I coax him, "come . . ."

"Marie," he says.

"Shush . . . later."

"I love you."

"Show me."

And I close my eyes and we slide down together and soon I melt his reluctance and he is all mine once again.

"Here," I tell him, "now . . . now . . . now . . ."

I try to wake him up late in the morning and at first I'm having a devil of a time at it. He squirms and moans and holds his arms defensively in front of his face as if trying to fend me off. I finally get him to open his eyes, after which his body slowly relaxes.

"Good morning," I tell him.

"Uh . . . oh, it's you . . . "

He sounds immensely relieved.

"Who else did you expect?" I chide him. "You sure looked like you were ready to whack me. Did you sleep well?"

"I'm not sure," he says. "Thanks for waking me up though."

"Another bad one?"

"Yeah."

"You want to tell me?"

"I don't know," he says, "it's always the same one."

"I don't mind."

"Well," he says, "you've just rescued me in the nick of time. They were coming after me again . . . three of them this time . . . getting closer and closer, no matter what I try . . . I ran out of bullets, as usual. I throw my gun at the one closest, he's coming at me with a raised machine-gun. I'm waiting for the end, paralyzed."

He stops and shakes his head.

"You think it'll ever go away?" I tell him.

"I hope so," he says, "I'm getting sick of it. If I could only shake loose, maybe then I'll only dream of you."

He has regained some of his normal composure, his eyes have their playful spark now. I lean over and kiss him lightly, or at least that is my intent before he drags me back on top of him and we wind up tangled in the bedsheets where the kiss gets drawn to the point of imminent danger. When we finally disengage, both out of breath, he shifts back to business.

"Did you talk to your parents?"

"I talked to Mother," I tell him. "She says she'll talk to Papa, says she'll try to talk him into leaving."

"You think she can?"

I have to be candid with him.

"I doubt it," I tell him.

We both sit and contemplate the situation. It is rather simple, really.

He cannot be seen outside, and he cannot stay with us much longer. We know what that means.

"You'll have to help me set it up," he tells me.

"Go ahead," I say to him.

"First you've got to get your parents to swear, I mean it, not to tell anybody I'm here. Nobody . . . We can only pray nobody saw me coming last night—"

"They won't," I reassure him.

"Good," he says. "Now, go to the Governor General's building down in the city, you know where that is?"

"Sure."

"Find the Bureau of Evacuees. Tell them you've got a friend—don't mention names, ever—who's got to get out in a hurry. You can tell them my story, it's all right, they've heard it before. Just remember, no name. I think the amnesty offer is still on, they won't bother you too much, they're glad to get rid of any of us, don't worry. Tell them my friends are after me, that I've skipped the OAS for good. They know what that means. Tell them it's urgent, that I can't stay in Algiers another day. Make sure they put me on a boat leaving at night. You think you can remember all that?"

"Sure."

"You're a doll," he tells me. "Oh, one more thing?"

"Yes."

"Don't let them have your name or address, give them a fake one if they insist. We've got guys on the inside there, they tell us everything."

"I see."

I haven't expected it to be simple.

"Anything else?" I ask.

"Yes . . . When you get out, make sure nobody's following you. Don't come back until you're sure. Switch busses, cut through stores, but just make sure they're not tailing you. Think you can manage?"

He has let me into his world. For the first time I am to be trusted. But as happy as I am at being there on the inside, I don't know I really like what I have gotten myself into. Still, everything is up to me now. Our roles have fully reversed. He is the one who must wait, anxious, helpless, while I weave and dodge in his harsh world of action on the outside. I don't know that I can manage, but no matter, I hasten to reassure him: "Oh sure," I say, "I'll take care of everything."

"Good girl. Better get going."

"Right now?"

I cannot help but sound a bit miffed at his haste, as much as I know he is right.

"Not before I feed you breakfast," I tell him.

"Better be a quick one."

"Coming . . . Anything in particular?"

"The maid," he says and sneaks his arm toward me.

I dart back.

"Only at night," I tell him.

And, as I turn to leave: "You better move back to Antoine's room while I'm downstairs. I've mussed up the sheets for you."

And I serve him his breakfast there, in the small room my mom had left unchanged, with Antoine's clothes and books and records the way he left them. And the old poster of Marina Vlady to keep him company, as he restlessly paces the floor between the window and the desk, adjusting the drapes every time he peers outside, and drawing and reholstering the gun he tries so diligently to make inconspicuous in my presence. I know he feels trapped. Like all the men I know, he hates prolonged inaction, hates waiting. It makes them feel helpless, for once like us.

At one o'clock my mother brings him lunch.

"She was so sweet about it," he tells me later. "We were both embarrassed, without you there to mediate."

"Marie told me," she says to him.

"Oh."

He is not quite sure of his grounds with her.

"I'm glad you've finally decided," she says. "There's nothing left to do here except to die, that's the only thing Algiers is good for anymore . . . I'd be leaving too but for Georges."

"He might change his mind," he tells her.

"Not before it's too late," she says. "A year ago . . . I talked to him then . . . he could have sold the store. Now we can't give the house away. Everybody's leaving. The Arabs won't buy it either. Why pay today for what you can get for free tomorrow?"

"She seemed resigned," he tells me later.

"Everything I've ever owned is right here," she says to Robert.

"We'll have to burn it like the rest of them. They don't let you carry much to the boat. Well . . . "

There is nothing he can say to reassure her. She goes on: "You and Marie, you're good together."

"Yes."

"She loves you, you've been good to her. You're both still young. You seem to know much already . . . " She is groping for words. "Take her with you," she says, "there's nothing for either of you here. I can manage without her."

"She doesn't want to leave," he tells her, "I've asked her."

I am not sure I like the way they barter over me, trying to arrange my life between the two of them. People who love you seem to take such liberties over your destiny as if you were incompetent. We have words afterwards, when she tries to reason with me. The truth is, she cannot manage without me, and she knows it. Not with Papa the way he is and things falling to pieces all around us. She just doesn't want me to know, but of course I know, I have been around them for nineteen years now. I am not blind, though they have done their best to shield me.

"I figured she'd give it a try," he explains later. I assure him she did, and that it made no difference whatsoever. I know she will talk to my father again, and I know what he will say. I cannot leave because she can't; she cannot leave because my father won't.

We play out our lives, like puppets, each trapped in our own set of imperatives, our own private center stage. If we could only merge those spotlights into one. But we can't, or won't.

"She'll talk to Papa again," I tell Robert. And again. And again. "He'll give in eventually."

Just not soon enough for me to leave now, not before it is much too late.

"He will," he assures me, "she said so too, said we have to be patient with him."

Then she excuses herself and hurries downstairs before my father comes back from the bar. Though not before he thanks her for the food. What he really means is to thank her for being so sweet about it all. She apologizes for the food being so dull. What she really means is, she is sorry she can't do more for him. The rest of the afternoon is just as frustrating.

He waits, jittery, despondent, for me to come home, pacing the floor and cussing himself.

When I come back at six I hurry upstairs to deliver my report.

"Well?" he demands.

"Well what?" I stall.

The truth is, I've got everything arranged the way he had asked me. It all went just like he said, though it took time. And the longer I stall, the longer I've got him.

"Out with it, Marie. What happened?"

"Nothing," I tell him, "it's all set."

"How?"

"You're leaving," I tell him, "I've got your reservations."

"When?"

"Tonight."

"What time?"

"One in the morning."

"Oh, Marie."

He takes me in his arms: "You're an angel," he says into my hair.

In his relief he fails to detect my mood, though eventually he stops: "I'm sorry," he says, "my sweet darling."

I avoid his eyes, I am desperately trying to fight back my tears, which I know are coming.

"You can still come," he says, "you mother says so too, I've talked to her . . . Marie?"

I am torn between the gratification of knowing he really wants me with him and the frustration of not being able to accept. A perfect backdrop for tears. I will talk to my mother in a few minutes. I have a good idea of what she's going to say. I also know what I must do.

"I can't," I tell him, "you know I can't."

And I love him all the more for not pressing me further. For recognizing—like the good *pied noir* he is in spite of all that is different about him—that things are bound to follow their course, that nothing much can be done while our collective reason is suspended and other matters press into the fore. We are all alike here, however different our little clans may seem to the outsider. Live or die, we persist in being who we are, playing out our assigned destinies.

We hug each other, standing at the window. Antoine's room is submerged in shadows now and no one is likely to see us from the outside. In spite of myself I begin to sniffle, claiming my privilege as a woman, just like he claims his as a man to offer me his crumpled handkerchief, smoothing my hair as I blow my nose and dry my cheeks. Just as it is his privilege to reassure me, ever so lamely: "I'll be waiting for you in Marseilles."

"Yes."

Which is all I can say. I know he will too, though for the moment I cannot draw much comfort from such knowledge.

"Your dad will change his mind soon," he says. "He can't stay here much longer. The FLN are taking over in a few months, they've signed a pact with de Gaulle . . . "

His voice tails off, his chin is grazing my temple. His eyes, when I look up, are once again detached and probing, scanning away through the gathering gloom, homing in on where his grandfather's house used to be. I don't want him to leave, I know he doesn't want to leave either.

"Let's make love," I tell him.

After a while he says: "Yes, let's."

We come out into the street well after dark. Inside, before we depart, my mother gets hold of Robert and hugs him tightly.

"You take care of yourself," she says. "And don't worry about Marie, it won't be long now before we all follow."

"Shut up, woman," my father growls from behind her.

His rudeness comes out somehow deflated, and when he shakes Robert's hand he sounds almost friendly: "All packed?"

"Yes."

My father seems to echo this: "Yes . . . " Then, conceding, "Guess I can't blame you. Why should you stay? When all is said and done, this is not really your country, is it?"

"Beg your pardon?"

Robert is taken aback.

"Oh, you know," my father says, "your people just move on. They do well wherever they go. It's different with us, you know."

It takes no great feat of logic for Robert to know exactly what my father means, so his dogged attempt at equanimity is all the more admirable: "If you say so, sir."

My father is far from done, though: "*Et l'Algérie Française?*" he demands, "and all that blood . . ."

He pauses, then proceeds to deliver what he takes to be his coup de grace: "Well, I guess it isn't your blood . . ."

The irony of this gratuitous insult escapes nobody, least of all my mother, who at this point cannot contain herself any longer and launches into my dad with rare ferocity: "Georges Laforge, *tais-toi!*"

"Oh lay off, woman," he retorts. "You don't need to protect him, he's pretty good at taking care of himself."

"It's all right, *Madame*," Robert tells her. "Let him have his say, it's nothing I haven't heard before."

Nothing his father hasn't heard before either, if his bleached bones could only be queried from their unmarked grave in the Ardennes. Nor is it anything his grandfather hasn't heard either. I marvel at how utterly detached he seems, as he turns and extends his hand: "I'll be seeing you, sir."

"I doubt it," my father retorts.

After which he turns to me: "Marie, see him out."

*U*nder the canopy of white smoke the two of us are standing in the dark. I have pleaded to be allowed to walk him down to the port but have been rebuffed, as I had expected. Robert is wearing one of Antoine's suits, which is one size too large for him. All he's got with him is a small suitcase, and since I packed it for him myself I know exactly how little it contains. We are entwined in a long embrace. I wish I could find a way to keep him with me, but my visit with the authorities has made me realize how tenuous his existence has become.

"You can still come with me," he says.

"You know I can't," I tell him. "But I will soon."

"I guess so," he says.

"You'll wait for me, right?" I ask him.

"You know I will."

"Please, please watch over yourself," I plead.

"I promise. Will you be all right?"

"Sure."

What else could I say? I have not the foggiest idea how things will turn out. Our mutual assurances are brave rituals, delivered and accepted as such.

"Good-bye, my love," he tells me.

He leans over and hugs me. One brief kiss.

"I love you," I tell him as I let him go.

The route he follows next, his final descent from Bab-el-Oued, I know by heart, to the last meaningless detail. The bare skeleton of it has been woven into the instructions I received earlier, in that dingy gray-walled room, from an officer—clearly a military man, conspicuous out of uniform—who had interrogated me for hours and then, apparently satisfied with my story, made me repeat his instructions again and again until they had become etched into the folds of my frightened brain. The rest is not hard to imagine, and as he goes down I follow along with him, hovering above and tracing his steps from my bedroom perch, on the bed where we made love only this morning. I lose sight of him soon, when he rounds the corner. But as he drifts down the narrow alleys of Bab-el-Oued, my worn old valise dangling half empty in his hand, I am still there.

A familiar distant thud of muted explosions reaches over from across the harbor. He must be thinking of Jojo and the others now, of the skipped rendezvous, if there was one, of how they must be wondering about him, maybe already looking for him. Once he turns into Rue Rochambeau, past a house that has just been set on fire, he has company. Others like him are emerging ghostlike from the smoke, silent and resolute as they scurry along together, their meager possessions dangling as silently as their tired thoughts. More join them below, as they trudge the length of Boulevard Guillemin and turn into Rue Borley la Sapie.

He is submerged among a multitude of *pieds noirs* now, and I know he is safer that way. But I have lost track of him in the thickening human flow that is cascading out of Bab-el-Oued. The Casbah is looming above them to the right as their determined descent gathers momentum, a silent herd stampeded by the sporadic bursts of faraway gunfire. There are scores of them now marching in the dark as they approach the harbor gates.

They process them in the cavernous old customs depot, crowded and brightly lit. The line moves at a snail's pace. When his turn comes at last, the gendarme takes the proffered card, scans it, inspects him briefly and hands it back to him: "Room eleven, over that way. Show the card when you get there; they'll take care of you."

At the door to room eleven, an armed guard examines his card again, then invites him to step inside. He is following my instructions faithfully, producing his real passport now. An officer reads it slowly, ticking items off an invisible list on his desk. Robert is given the appropriate forms, he fills and signs them as he is told. It all seems to be happening to someone else.

Another officer reads him the terms of the amnesty and asks him if he understands. He nods and signs again. It is nearly one in the morning when he receives his temporary travel documents, issued to one Bernard Dupont. For a fleeting moment he wishes they had shown a bit more imagination. His own passport is also returned to him, stamped with a red "invalid."

"Dock seven," the officer tells him, "get on board right away. She's leaving at six."

"Thanks."

"Never mind. You must be someone special, Monsieur Dupont. Somebody must want you out of here real bad or you'd be waiting for days."

"Thanks all the same."

"*Bon voyage.*"

*H*e wanders back across the customs shed, checks through the controls, and is out on the open pier. In the cool of the early morning, the port is mercifully quiet. He pulls up his collar and glides along the pier, alone in the dense fog, my gaunt knight on his precarious errand. I see him with my mind's eye as the ship emerges just ahead of him, from the looks of her a converted freighter. A narrow plank leads up to the mid-deck. The two guards at the bottom check his papers once again and wave him through.

The main hold is overflowing with people, the newly constructed bunks laid out four deep and double-decked. The stagnant air reeks of urine and chemicals. In the thin light of the lone hurricane lamp, it is impossible to tell which cots are already taken. He must thread his way slowly toward number sixty-three, the one assigned to him on his card. The bunk is second from the rear, on top and far away from the door. He knows, as I know, he could not spend the night there, not even the short fragment of it still left. He hoists his suitcase on top of the bunk, turns, and makes his way back down the aisle. He climbs an interminable winding iron-grill stairway, at last emerging on the upper deck. The smell of salt and dead fish cleanses his nostrils. So far his plan has worked out by the book. The water below is dark and immobile, reflecting nothing.

I imagine him circling the deck along the rail, taking stock of his surroundings. Lone human silhouettes are leaning to the rail as he passes midship, the red cigarette flares reveal their position. Leaving them behind, he reaches the bow and then turns around, leaning his back into the curved metal rail.

The city above the port is still dark, except for the fires in Bab-el-Oued. From his vantage point he must be observing more passengers struggling with their packs down the pier. They clear the guard post as he has and come on board. At some point he must feel for the reassuring gun metal in his right pocket.

Sooner or later, restless as I know he is, he must resume his sweep of the upper deck. He passes under the bridge and ducks into a narrow gangway that opens into the stern. The deck is littered with crates large and small, all strewn around in great disarray like boulders in a god-forsaken wasteland. He threads his way cautiously among them to the very tip of the curved aft. In the shadow of the last crate he must stumble upon a damp coil of rope and lowers himself to a crouch, his back to the rail. I imagine him pulling his coat over himself and slipping his hand, once again, into the right-hand pocket for the reassuring touch of the cold metal. He must be both surprised and relieved that no one has bothered to search him. I know he is doing his best to stay awake.

The one called Martel stands guard over me behind, near the starboard railing. The other two glide forward slowly, pausing every few steps to peer into the waning dark. They have woken us up at three and made me dress quickly and come downstairs. There, I see my father first, sitting on the couch, his head bloody, his face buried in his hands. One of the others is in the kitchen holding a gun to my mother's head. I need no further prompting, I go ahead and tell them all they want to know. Although from their questions I can tell they already know everything.

It is the one called Jojo, the one I'd like to know more about, who administers the final stern warning to my mother, just before the three of them depart. I watch him from the corner of my eyes, following his every move, hoping he won't notice. He means every word of it, I can tell.

He is not that much taller than Robert, a bit heavier, all muscle. A strange fire burns in his light hazel eyes, his sun-bleached brown curls are cropped close to his scalp. A touch of the African? A pinch of Berber? Incongruously, his face is strewn with freckles like a child's, though there is nothing playful in the voice that instructs my mother in graphic detail about what would happen if we called the police.

His two companions now grab and usher me rudely outside, and onward into the battered taxicab waiting at the curb. At the port we are whisked inside the restricted zone through a side gate, no questions asked.

I am led by the elbow, shivering, though whether from the cold or my paralyzing fear I cannot tell. I can only pray he is awake and vigilant. They have no trouble finding the boat.

*H*e wakes up with a start just in the nick of time to see the two shadows stalking closer in the waning dark. They are criss-crossing the aft slowly, systematically, taking their time as they creep from one crate to the next. He flattens himself to the crate. In its protective shadow, he raises himself slowly to a crouch. He can see the two of them more clearly now, searching for him in the chaotic jumble of the stern. He sees them pause and listen. A moment later a hushed voice says: "Must be all the way at the end."

They know where he is and are so cocky they don't bother to hide. He pulls his gun out, steadies it in both hands and draws a bead on the one closer to him: "That's close enough," he calls.

A moment of complete silence follows. He can hear their whispered consultation next: "That's him."

"You sure?"

"Sure I'm sure."

Another pause, then the first voice: "Robert?"

Unmistakable.

"That you Jojo?"

"Yes."

"What are you doing here?"

"Looking for you."

"How'd you find me?"

"Does it matter?"

It obviously does. The answer, too, is obvious: "You got Marie, right?"

"Right."

"I see," he says.

They both wait. Finally Jojo says: "Can we talk?"

He ponders. They've got him trapped. But their silhouettes are etched clearly against the skyline while he is submerged in the deep shadow.

"Raise your hands where I can see them," he says. "Real slow, I've got you in my sights."

"Take it easy," Jojo says as his hands go up slowly. "I just want to talk."

As far as Robert can see, Jojo is holding nothing in his hands.

"Send your friend back," he tells him, "then come over, real slow."

A hushed exchange follows, then the other one with Jojo creeps back to join us. Alone, Jojo now approaches Robert.

"Close enough," Robert tells him. "Now turn around."

Jojo is no more than ten paces from him now. I can see him turning around slowly, hands still held high. The three of us are further to the fore, silent witnesses, peering intently from behind a crate. The brute they call Martel's got his gun pressed into the small of my back.

"Where is she?" Robert asks.

I suppress the urge to call out "I'm here," to rush to him.

"Back there."

Jojo gestures with his head toward our crate. There is a pause as Robert digests the information.

"Let me see her," he says.

Jojo shrugs. "As you wish," and calls: "Martel?"

"Yes?"

"Bring her out." A pause. "Go ahead, Martel."

"Okay."

His gun prods me harshly as I step out from behind the crate. The two of them are flanking me now.

"Enough," says Jojo.

We stop.

"Marie?" Robert calls.

"Yes."

"You all right?"

"Yes."

I can only hope my voice does not betray my utter desperation. He trusted his life to me and I am an abysmal failure.

"Your mom and dad all right?" he asks.

"Yes."

An awkward pause, then Jojo's voice: "All right, Martel, pull her back."

The three of us retreat behind the crate. After a while Robert breaks the silence: "Okay," he tells Jojo, "I'm listening, go ahead."

"Can I turn around?"

"Real slow."

They are facing each other now. Jojo in the open with his hands raised, Robert in the protective shadow of the crate.

"Drop your gun," Robert tells him.

Jojo shrugs and reaches for his waistband. His gun makes a loud metallic clank as it hits the deck.

"Can we sit down?" he asks.

"Go ahead," Robert tells him, "sorry I can't join you, I don't trust your gorilla."

"Martel? Oh, he's harmless."

"He better be. Well, go ahead, talk."

Jojo lowers himself to the deck.

"Take it easy, Roberto," he says. "We're still friends."

"Friends don't creep on each other in the dark," Robert reminds him. "What do you want, Jojo?"

"I want you to come back with us."

"Anything else?"

"Nope. Just that. No questions asked, we all forget about tonight."

"Just like that?"

"Yes."

He looks at Jojo and it occurs to him he probably means it, that no questions will be asked, at least not to Jojo's face. That as far as Jojo is concerned, everything remains the same, frozen, suspended. Can he be made to see?

"Why should I?" he asks Jojo.

Why indeed? Except for the most obvious fact that I am standing there with Martel's gun grinding into my back.

"Listen," Jojo tells him, "we go way back, you and I . . . how long?"

"Plenty."

"*Bon.* So I won't bother you with the big words."

"Gee thanks, Jojo."

"No need to be sarcastic."

Jojo sounds totally matter-of-fact about what he says next, but the finality of his words belies his crisp manner.

"Nobody leaves the OAS. That's all there is to it."

"I just did."

"You only think you have. Besides," his voice becomes more intimate now, "I need you, I've got nobody who can handle the plastique."

"You can," Robert reminds him.

"Not as good as you."

Which is true, he must admit. But still not much of a reason, not any more.

"Nice to be needed," he tells Jojo.

"This is not a joke, Roberto."

"Whatever."

The truth is, he is not sure how to proceed. He tries stalling for time.

"Look, Jojo," he says. "I appreciate your position, honest I do."

He waits. For a while no one talks. Finally he breaks the silence.

"How long has it been, Jojo?"

"Twelve years."

"That long?"

They have been together almost constantly since the early days in

Indochina. Neither of them really needs the reminder. They seldom need to talk any more, each can predict the other's next move, almost every move.

"It's been quite a time, Jojo."

Is he trying to reach and maybe reassure Jojo? Can he? From Jojo's silence there is no telling.

"While it lasted," Robert goes on. "But it's lasted long enough for me. So I'm getting off. Nothing personal, can't you see? Nothing to do with you. So you've got to let me out."

He pauses. Jojo says nothing.

"So, good luck if you're staying," he tells him. "I respect that. Still, if you had any sense, you'd quit right now with me."

Still no response.

"How about it?"

Jojo sighs. Will he even consider? "It's not that simple," he says.

"Nothing ever is."

Another long pause ensues. There is much more that can be said, but really very little. Both can see the obvious, which is what Jojo is stating next: "We got her."

"You do."

"Well, what are you going to do about it?"

"You know damn well what, Jojo," he tells him. "I'm holding a gun on you, and you know exactly what I'll do if she's harmed."

As if to amplify, Martel's gun bores harder into the small of my back. I let out an involuntary moan.

"Take it easy, Martel," Jojo calls over, then turns back to Robert.

"Nobody's going to harm her," he says, as much to Martel as to Robert.

"Good," says Robert.

They eye each other.

"Just think about it, Jojo," he tells him. "I won't be too far, you know where to find me."

"You're coming back with us."

"You can't make me, Jojo."

"I've got her."

"I've got you."

Robert looks at his old companion. In the dim glow of the predawn,

Jojo's face is drawn, unfathomable. He couldn't have gotten much sleep the last two nights, has probably been on the dodge like Robert.

"Let go, Jojo," he tells him. "Don't you see? It's done, *fini* . . . You want to stay on, fine. But let the rest of the guys make their own choices, they're not kids."

Jojo is silent, the seconds tick by. In the dark, I am straining not to miss any of it. Next to me, Martel is getting restless. The barrel of his gun is grinding harder into my back, but I am determined not to cry. Instead, I begin to shiver uncontrollably. Finally Jojo says: "Can't do that."

"Why?"

"Just can't. You don't quit just like that."

"Don't be ridiculous, Jojo."

"Well, you just don't."

Next to me Martel has finally lost his patience: "You're wasting your time, Jojo," he calls. "He isn't worth it. Let's split, we can take care of him later. We got her."

"Shut up, Martel," Jojo tells him.

"Oh *merde*," Martel says, and before anybody notices he grabs me roughly with his other hand and jams my arm behind my back, twisting the elbow until I cry in agony.

"You hear that, *petit Juif*!" he calls out to Robert, "I've got your woman right here. Now what are you going to do about it?"

What happens next is a blur. I struggle to stay on my feet as the pain shoots through my shoulder, then give up and crash to the deck, taking Martel with me. My head hits the deck and everything explodes in a sharp burst of light, then nothing.

When I come to, Martel is crouched next to me, his gun pointed at my head. Jojo is looking on from five paces away. Robert is right behind him with the gun. A stalemate if I have ever seen one.

I have done my utmost and have wound up a liability. I don't know which hurts more, my throbbing elbow or knowing how useless I am. Ignoring Martel, I prop myself up from the deck on my good arm: "I'm all right," I call out to Robert. "Please, don't shoot."

In the stunned silence that follows, the three of them watch me in disbelief.

"You guys lay off each other," I tell them. "There's always the next time."

I address myself to Jojo: "You know where he's going," I tell him. "You can always find him. And you've got me. Please let him go, just for now."

"The fuck!" hisses Martel next to me.

"Shut the fuck up, Martel!" Jojo barks at him.

He turns to Robert, who is still holding his gun on him: "You can still change your mind," he says.

"No way, Jojo. I've had it. Someday you will too."

It is almost light now, enough for me to see his thin unshaven face, see his gun pointing at Jojo, see Jojo shake his head. He seems almost sad.

"We've got to split," he says. "One more thing."

"Yes?"

"The money from the last bank job. I want it back."

My ears prick up. Another item no one has bothered to share with me. I wonder where he had the money stashed, probably the old man's house.

"Sorry," I hear him tell Jojo, "I need it. Relocation expenses, if you will."

"It's OAS money," says Jojo.

"I've worked just as hard for it as the rest of you guys. Besides, there isn't much left. Call it my cut."

"Not any more."

"Fuck it, Jojo!"

He has finally lost his temper.

"Go hit another bank," he tells him. "You guys are still in business. I'm not. Write it off as a loss if you like, headquarters won't audit your books."

Right next to me Martel again cannot resist: "Try and squeeze money out of a *Juif*..."

A sharp look from Jojo reins him in, after which Jojo turns back to Robert: "Is this how you want to leave it?"

"I suppose."

Jojo shakes his head. "Too bad," he says. "It doesn't end here, you know."

"I know."

"I'll be seeing you then."

They watch each other, God only knows what they are thinking. Nothing ever ends where these two come from, everything is just the prelude to what comes next. There is always more, forever.

"Reckon you will," Robert tells Jojo. "Better get going before they find out you're here."

"They know."

He turns, then reconsiders: "We'll be watching her."

"I'll hold you to it."

In the last remnant of the waning night I look to him for the last time as they whisk me away. He is leaning to the crate, watching us depart, a lone figure barely discernible as they rush me back toward the gaping mouth of the gangway. The horizon above him is a murky blend of coal and crimson. I crane my neck, straining to see the last of him. I know he won't go back to sleep.

*I*t is almost an hour since they cleared the tip of the northern jetty. The boat is pointing now toward the rising sun. He has finally relaxed his vigil, though he is still maintaining his position at the tip of the aft, leaning back to the rail. More and more of the skyline is rising into view as the boat pulls further to sea. The city is stretched in front of him across the low hills, from Nôtre Dame d'Afrique to Bouzarea and el Biar, through Bir Mandrais and onward to Clos Salambis. From the crest of the hills the city slopes down to the Agha, Belcourt and Hamma, from whence everything funnels in toward the lower basin and the port. Thick clouds of smoke are suspended above it all, waiting for the morning breeze to pick up and blow them in toward the interior and Blida.

In the lower basin, the Casbah and Bab-el-Oued squat together like Siamese twins, bound and bounded by their shared placenta, the dry river-bed and the Marengo gardens. As the boat prowls further out to sea, the two old quarters come slowly together, their smoke commingling in a single ascending plume. The city is slowly waking up to the new day, though it is too far now to hear the morning traffic. As the boat slowly shifts course from east through northeast to north, the city is growing smaller, muted, smoking away.

He stands at the rail, watching the lower basin sink behind the horizon. After a while only the rim of the hills protrudes above the shimmering white surf. At last she is but a receding smudge between the sea and the sky. He walks back slowly, threading his way toward the overstructure in search of breakfast.

TWO

THE OTHER SIDE

※

JOJO

Marseilles, July 1962

I *need not follow him across the seven seas to know where he is, what he does, whose company he keeps.* If he thinks he can hide, he is just being naive. I have known him so long now, seems like a lifetime, long enough to know this is just a passing phase with him, a rare ripple, an aberration. Sooner or later he will come to his senses. Trust me, it is just a matter of time.

Wherever he goes, we are right there behind him, our patient eyes glued to his stubborn sinewy back. Martel says fuck, man, burn him; be done with it now; he's poison. Martel is a punk, a street-corner bully, a trash-talking braggart and anti-Semite to boot. We've got those hair-trigger zealots among us. The other guys have them too, I notice. These crazies have their use, granted. But you better keep your eyes on them constantly, lest they drag you down with them, drag all of us down to flaming hell with their rabid, purgatorious, exterminatory passion.

I can handle Martel though, no big hassle. I tell him not now; no hurry; we better wait a while; never mind about the slippery Jew; we will settle our accounts with him in good time; he's going nowhere. In the meantime, while Martel is straining his leash, I get weekly updates over the short-wave set, written reports too from the Marseilles network whenever the mails work. My files are bulging, not only on him but on everybody else who has dared to skip. When the time comes, all scores will be settled. Down to the last startled gasp, if need be. Though I hope not with him; I hope he can be made to see reason; I am counting on it.

When he eats, I can taste the steaming couscous. I am with him at the bar daily to share his anisette. I can smell his sweat, hear his anguished moans as he thrashes about his lonely bed, straining to break loose of his nightmares.

If he ever picked up a stray whore, I would be right there under her cheap rented bed, listening to his dispirited loveless tussles. Marie, he would be moaning soundlessly, Marie. I wish I could remind him then, whisper in his ear, how a soldier is much better off with the whores, who give him no sass and thank him for his largess and won't mourn him when he is gone. Like the skinny pair we used to mount in tandem off the main drag in Hanoi, tired warriors in search of temporary amnesia.

Though I can't begrudge him his love. And young as she is, she has turned out to be quite a woman. The way she kept her cool that morning on the boat, saved us all from a real mess. What is more, she gives me a wonderful lever over him. Not that I am in a hurry to pull it, but in a pinch, if all else fails, who knows. Beggars cannot be choosers.

In the end we will reel him back in. We of the OAS indulge no strays, brook no defection, abide by no loose ends. We tolerate no resistance but our own. *L'Algérie Française* may be dying on its fiery cross in Algiers, but is alive and well in the Métropole. Like the phoenix, she is rising from her ashes across the water, no longer a state, forever a state of mind.

We've got our cells in place all over the mainland now. The colonels are gone to ground, proselytizing, plotting, planning. We are prepared to wait out the traitors, for whom we have spilled our blood from Dien Bien Phu to Dakar to Kabylia. The mainlanders may call themselves French. We know better, being the last of the true French. We are coming home at last for our transcendent day of reckoning. Last time around, our sniper barely missed the Great Impostor, *le General* hiding out his *Élysée*. No matter, we will get him next time, or the next, or the next. Or the next.

Our bond has been forged in the festering rubber plantation, etched in the hot sands, sealed in blood. First his, then mine. We are chained to each other forever, each both captor and captive. Whether he knows it or not, no one will dare do him harm or they must reckon with me. If his blood is to be on anyone's hand, let it be on mine alone.

The gendarmes think they can turn him. They're going to try, they will huff and puff, promise and insinuate, cajole and threaten. Let them. I know better; I know him inside out, down to his jealously guarded dark core. He will spit in their face. Or rather, sly one that he is, he will lead them on a merry chase, prevaricate, hedge, stall, feign, promise. This is more his style. In the end, he will come about, back to us, to me.

Whether he knows it or not, he's got nowhere else to go.

*H*e has been to Marseilles many times before, used to talk about it in our early days in Indochina. First with his father, the year before the father left for the war. He was six then and doesn't remember all that much, except for the lone elephant in the zoo and the cruise to Château d'If, where the Count de Monte Cristo had spent his years of hopeless solitary confinement. It is one of the few memories of his father he hangs on to for dear life, a trinket made precious by loss.

He came over again, he told me, must have been 1947, with the old man on one of his rare ventures out of Algiers. Someone had tipped the old man off to a shipload of Persian rugs impounded from a Lebanese boat and about to be auctioned, the owner having run afoul with Customs. The auction was being delayed, if he understood correctly, to let the in crowd skim the rare Bukhara pieces off the top. The rumor may have been correct; he still remembers being present at the auction. Although he could never imagine the old man indulging in such a deal.

Much later, during the hazy hiatus between the lycée and the Legion, he used to cross over with his buddies, like I used to with mine. For all I know, we could have taken the same boat, traveling deck class, spending the weekend in Marseilles and catching the Monday morning ferry back to Algiers. They, just as we, would stagger aboard supporting each other, sated, drunk to the gills and immensely pleased with themselves. We used to compare notes in the early days in Indochina, during those interminable nights in the mud, used to marvel how we had never bumped into each other, growing up half a mile apart. That was before we had to grow up in a hurry.

He visited the city a few more times while on leave from the Legion's jungle warfare school in Arles. I was there with him on many of those occasions, and have always assumed his memories of the city were as pleasant as mine—the railroad station, the peeling walls of the cheap hotels around the Vieux Port, the bars swarming with garishly painted ladies of the night, our stupored slumber till early afternoon, barely catching the last train back to camp.

It must be all different this time around. The trip over the water lasts an interminable day and a night, with the overladen freighter lumbering its way slowly across the glassy blue sea. He spends the day out on deck, studiously avoiding other passengers. Our last encounter should be still vivid in his mind. Of course, what he doesn't know won't hurt him. Among the aged lonely men and the worried mothers desperately trying to keep their children from falling overboard, an OAS courier who later reports to me has his eyes firmly if discreetly planted on him. He is as safe and as closely monitored on board this crowded tub as he would be in a barred cell.

The kids are a world of their own, the only ones aboard utterly unperturbed. They tear up and down the gangways from early morning on, and only threats of bodily harm will get them to bed late at night. Their carefree chatter stands out against the general backdrop of stunned, brooding silence.

After nightfall, he enacts the superfluous maneuver of sneaking back to the aft, piling a few empty fertilizer sacks together, and spending the night out in the open once again. Our guy has clear instructions to leave him alone.

At five in the morning he is awakened by angry bickering among the crew and the creaking cargo doors. They are unbattening the hatches in preparation for docking, and the commotion persists for the duration. He must be soaking wet from the dew, his body aching all over. He gets up, stretches, and makes his way slowly down to the dormitory hall. He gropes his way among the bunks, finds his own, pulls down Marie's worn-out suitcase and makes his way back out and up to the bow, onto the open cargo deck, where, for all he knows, he is alone.

* * *

The boat is pushing through dense fog, the horns blowing every few seconds. Other boats are honking all around them, they must be close to port and creeping onward gingerly, to judge from the reduced vibrations. At seven, when the sun breaks out through the clouds, Château d'If looms to the right, the white-washed walls floating over the mist. The passengers are beginning to assemble on deck. Soon the boat slows down to a crawl, then stops altogether one mile from the Batteries du Pharo.

The line of vessels awaiting their turn to dock stretches far in front and behind them. The tall coastline rises to the right, picturesque villas are lining the hillside. The gothic spires of Notre Dame de la Guard thrust up above the scene through shards of mist, with the sun reflecting brightly in the Virgin's gilded robe.

All passengers are now on deck and silent, their meager luggage stacked up around them. At ten o'clock the boat is directly under the Batteries. At noon it crosses the narrow strip of water into Porte Sainte Marie. Soon it is roped to Quai de la Joliette, and at three o'clock the passengers begin their slow descent ashore.

He stands and watches the others being cleared slowly at the makeshift checkpoint on the pier below. He is not in a great hurry; nobody is waiting for him down there. As far as he knows. So it is almost five when he finally comes down the narrow plank and stops in front of the control desk. Two officers are sitting behind it. He hands over his papers to the one in charge. The man unfolds them slowly.

"Bernard Dupont?"

"Yes."

"You know these documents are invalid, don't you?"

"I know."

"Do you have your real passport with you?"

"Just a minute," he says, "they promised me back in Algiers . . ."

The officer cuts him short: "Yes, Monsieur Dupont," he says, his voice flat, tired, "we know. But that was back in Algiers, and this is here in Marseilles. Now, can I see your real passport?"

The officer hands the temporary travel documents over to his companion, who unfolds them, scans them briefly, and puts them aside. The inference is sufficiently clear—Bernard Dupont, guarantor of his anonymity, has been retired.

He shrugs, digs into his coat pocket, pulls out his passport, and gives it to the first officer. There is no use arguing; they have their orders. He would like to clear out of the harbor as soon as possible.

The officer leafs slowly through his papers. The routine there seldom varies; they know all about him and want him to appreciate that.

"Robert Aron?"

"Yes."

"Born in Algiers, 1932?"

"Right."

"Residence Rue Dr. Aboulker 28, Algiers?"

"Formerly."

"Volunteered for the Legion in 1952?"

"That's correct."

"You still have your discharge papers?"

He is about to fumble for an answer when the other officer interrupts and beckons to his companion, who excuses himself and turns to look at the defunct travel documents. The two of them exchange knowing looks, then the one who was interrogating him turns back.

"You were saying, Monsieur Aron? Your discharge papers?"

"I haven't got them on me."

"You haven't got them?"

"No," he tells him.

He stops. They are watching him coolly. What the heck, he thinks; they surely know.

"You see, Monsieur l'Agent," he says, "I was discharged under special circumstances, if one may say so. April of last year, you may recall. I wasn't the only one, you know."

"I see."

The officer raises an eyebrow. It is all done for the sake of appearance. He knows exactly what Robert is talking about. There were thousands of us that quit together in April of 1961, including the captains and colonels.

The officer and Robert eye each other like two weary roosters in the ring. Both know the score; it is a matter of who will move first. Robert waits patiently.

"So," the officer says finally, "one of those?"

"Well . . . "

"Well indeed. When did you quit?"

"Four days ago."

"Waited till the last minute?"

He shrugs. He knows it is only a game to them, but maybe the orders they've got are different from what he agreed to. He is beginning to feel a bit worried.

"I quit," he tells the two of them. "Isn't that what you wanted me to do?"

"Sure is, Monsieur Aron."

A pause ensues, then the officer goes on. "What are you planning to do in Marseilles?"

"I don't know yet."

"How long are you planning to stay?"

"That depends."

"Got a place to live?"

"*Nom de Dieu*," he explodes, "have a heart, I've just arrived."

The officer now becomes apologetic.

"We know," he says, "we know. Still, we've got to ask these questions, that's the law. Here's your passport."

He hands it over to him.

"Please don't lose it, keep it on you at all times. That's the law too."

The officer takes a small green card and turns to his comrade, who hands him Robert's temporary papers. They copy details from the paper into the card, which they then stamp and hand over to him.

"Go find yourself a place to sleep, Monsieur Aron," the first officer says, "then come tomorrow at eleven to register at the prefecture. The address is right there on the card. Don't leave town without notifying us first. All right?"

"All right," he says. "Now, can I ask something?"

This is when the man next in line, an unshaven thin type in worn-out workman's clothes waiting discreetly a few steps back, must earn his keep, feigned nonchalance notwithstanding. Neither Robert nor the officer pay much heed to him, but what I get two days later is near verbatim.

"Sure," says the officer.

"Where do most of the evacuees live?"

"You looking for someone?"

"Not exactly."

"Someone's looking for you?"

"Maybe, people I'd rather avoid."

"Your old friends? You think they're after you?"

"Could be."

The officer eyes him thoughtfully.

"I see," he says. "Well, the whole town's full of your *pieds noirs*. There's a whole bunch of them in Sainte Marguerite . . . Then, there are all the new arrivals right here in La Joliette and Hotel de Ville. They stick together pretty much; you couldn't miss them if you tried."

"That bad?"

"Getting worse."

The officer's smile carries a sad, sarcastic tag that says "Welcome to Marseilles, sucker." Robert smiles back. It will soon dawn on him how daunting, how foolish this escapade really is. He can't avoid "them" and thus can't avoid us, since "they" are the sea in which we swim, the forest that shades us. By the same token, we, the OAS, are but the shadow they cast, the anguished cry piercing their *pieds noirs* nightmare. He cannot avoid us more than he can avoid himself. But all in due course.

"How do I go about finding a place to live?" he asks the officer.

"How . . ."

The officer turns to his companion.

"How's that for an original?"

"Very," says the other.

The first officer turns back to Robert. His face is lined, drained, he has been at it since early morning and is no doubt aching to shuck his stale uniform and soak his feet in a warm salt bath.

"Monsieur Aron," he says, "we've had four thousand people debarking today right on this pier, two more boats are still waiting offshore, God only knows how many more by tomorrow. How do you go about finding a place to live? How would I know? Here, go over there . . . "

The officer points toward the end of the pier.

"The charity organizations have their desks over there, in front of the cathedral. Pick out the one that suits you best, and if they can, they'll try to do something for you. Just don't hope for miracles."

He picks up his battered suitcase.

"I see," he tells the officer, "thanks."

"Oh, never mind," the officer tells him, "good luck."

He starts down the pier, heading over toward the crowd of refugees milling in front of the cathedral. The huge Roman dome rises incongruously between two coal depots. He joins the crowd and elbows his way toward the center, where bodies are particularly thick. He skips the *Secoures Catholiques* and keeps pushing on slowly. *Service Social de la Communauté Arménienne* . . . Corsican Committee for Mutual Aid . . .

He keeps on moving. In front of the next sign he hesitates for a brief moment. *Fond Social Juif Unifié* . . . He almost stops; he is tempted and could certainly give them a try. Then he remembers the old man. He decides to save them for a real emergency. He suspects the old man would have approved.

ANFANOMA, reads the next sign—National Association of French Patriots of North Africa and Their Friends. The name is a bit long-winded, but the bombast ought to be familiar; it has our ring to it, the rhetoric of the fringe. He stops. There are two of them sitting there behind the table, both middle-aged, both tired, both sympathizers who have been prompted and will report. The taller one looks up.

"Monsieur for us?"

"Yes, I suppose."

"Here."

The man hands him a stack of mimeographed sheets.

"You'll find it all there," he tells him. "Information about your right as a *rapartrié*, the various social aid agencies and all the rest. Monsieur was an activist?"

He hesitates, then shrugs: "Yes, I suppose."

"Here then."

The man hands him more papers.

"Read," he tells him, "you might find it interesting. And this one, and this, and this . . . There's a meeting in two weeks, why don't you come?"

"Thanks," he says.

He is about to move on when it occurs to him. "Excuse me," he says, "would you know where could I find a place to sleep tonight?"

"Where . . . ?" says the man, looking him over. "Are you alone?"

"Yes."

"Got any money?"

"A little bit."

"Wait."

The man turns to leaf through a thick card-file on the table in front of him.

"No . . . " he mutters to himself, "no . . . no . . . no . . . perhaps this one." He scribbles a note on a slip of paper and hands it over to Robert.

"Go try this one," he says, "quick, right away. She might still have a room."

The convoluted scribble reads "Hotel du Coq, Rue du Coq." He reads the words aloud.

"Where is it?" he asks.

"Near Gare Saint Charles," the man tells him. "You go up Rue Panier, into Rue Colbert, and straight up Rue Nationale. When you hit Place Capucines keep going on Boulevard Gambetta all the way to the church, then turn left and ask. It's right around the corner from there."

He is straining to remember, St. Charles . . . Capucines . . . Gambetta . . .

"Thank you so much," he tells the man.

"Oh, it's nothing," the man tells him. "Come to the meeting, don't forget."

"I won't," he promises.

He pulls out of the crowd, crosses the Old Port square and circles to the right around the cathedral. It is getting late; the warehouses are casting their long shadows across the road. As he walks up Rue Colbert, the shopkeepers are pulling down the shutters. The corner of Cours Belsunce looks familiar, with people milling around, crowding the cafés. He waits for the light to change, crosses the street, and proceeds into Place des Capucines. The streets are feeling more and more familiar, he can see the spires of St. Vincent de Paul towering above the busy avenue. As he pauses to drink from the old fountain, the whores at the corner of Rue Petit St. Jean spot him and begin to drift in his direction. He resumes his walk before they reach him.

Rue du Coq is narrow and surprisingly quiet. A faded copper plaque at the entrance announces HOTEL DU COQ. He steps into the hallway and, failing to find the knocker, tries the door. A bell chimes inside. He waits in the dark hallway. In a minute the inner door opens and a woman steps into the hall.

"Monsieur?"

She takes in his clothes, his lone suitcase. She is pert, about fifty-five, he guesses.

"I'm looking for a room, madame."

"For who?"

"Myself."

"Monsieur is alone?"

"Yes."

"Got a passport?"

"Sure."

"Mind if I take a look?"

He digs his passport out and hands it to her. She turns the pages slowly.

"I have to insist, you know," she says. "Monsieur is from down there?"

He nods.

"Aron . . . *C'est pas un nom israélite?*"

"That a problem?"

"Not at all."

She hands back his passport.

"My daughter's husband is Jewish. They lived three years in Oran. You know Oran?"

"A little bit. I'm from Algiers."

"Oh, really?"

She warms up to him, she becomes almost friendly.

"He's an engineer," she says. "They live in Paris now."

She eyes him speculatively. "Well, we're just about full at the moment. Who was it that referred you?"

"The people from ANFANOMA . . . you know, down at the port."

"You know them?"

"No. I've just arrived. They were rather helpful."

She is quite good at lying; she has been expecting him ever since the ANFANOMA man called. She may not be a dyed-in-the-wool sympathizer, but she knows what is good for her, and for that husband with the bad ticker.

"Are you in trouble?" she asks.

"What do you mean?"

"With the law."

"Oh, no, I'm clean."

"How long do you plan to stay in Marseilles?"

"I'm not sure. It all depends."

"You drink?"

"No."

She examines him, plainly skeptical.

"We are very quiet people here," she says. "My husband has a heart condition. We don't like trouble. You all cleared up with the police?"

"As far as I know."

"I could find out soon enough. I'll have to report your presence here, you know."

"That's fine."

"Well . . . I'll tell you what. I've got this small room, number thirteen B, top of the fourth floor. It's not much, but monsieur should consider himself lucky to have found even that, the town is overrun by your *pieds noirs*, you know . . ."

She smiles apologetically. He smiles back.

"Not to mention the Arabs," she says. "All the hotels are full too. You'll have to pay a week in advance, we've had trouble with people from down there."

"That's all right," he tells her and brings out his wallet. "How much?"

"Well," she says, "five hundred a day makes thirty-five hundred a week."

"Here's for two weeks."

He hands her the money and she counts it, visibly impressed with his promptness.

"Fine," she says, "I'll make a receipt for you. Here's the key; you go up yourself, too many stairs for me . . . Take a look and see how you like it. Leave your passport here, I'll have it ready for you when you come down next."

"That's fine. *Merci,* madame."

"Lechar, Madelaine Lechar," she says. *"Je vous en prie, monsieur."*

While he is making his way upstairs, she will retire to her private quarters where she keeps her office in a cramped kitchen cabinet. Though not before dialing a number. Discreetly waiting for him to disappear up the narrow stairs, she will listen to the impersonal voice grunting *oui* at the other end, then without identifying herself, report his arrival. We have made sure room thirteen B remained vacant, and the guys at ANFANOMA were most helpful. It is all a matter of planning, and if plan A had not worked, we have plan B and C and D waiting in the wings.

I am glad it turns out not to be necessary, and old Lechar puts on a rousing show for the zilch she gets in return, a pat on the back. For a true patriot this ought to be plenty.

Though, just in case, she's got a brother in Oran, a postal inspector who is still waiting for his final embarkation clearance.

Room thirteen B is small, the door opens only half the way in before it jams into the bed. There is a small piece of furniture next to the bed, a combination chest of drawers and nightstand. A little sink is crammed into the corner next to that, next to it a narrow closet, then back to the door. No windows except for a little hatch up in the ceiling, no crawling out of that. No back door either. The room is stuffy and smells of stale clothes. Dim light filters down through the dusty pane. Definitely too small, but he is lucky to have gotten even this. And, no need for him to know, the location has been picked for its obvious lack of alternative routes.

He flops down on the bed but doesn't expect to fall asleep. When the ceiling hatch has gotten darker, he hauls himself up, unpacks his suitcase and hangs his few clothes in the closet. Then he takes out his gun and holds it in his hand. The law forbids him to carry one, but he would be foolish to leave it behind. He stuffs it into his belt, pulls his jacket over it, takes a last look at the room and steps out.

Madame Lechar is waiting for him downstairs.

"Here's your passport, Monsieur Aron. No trouble at all. Are you going out for the evening?"

"Just for a walk," he tells her, "maybe get something to eat."

"Don't be too late," she warns him, "I lock the outside door at midnight. We don't like to get up and open it in the middle of the night. My husband, you know, I've got to watch him."

"Sure," he tells her, "I'm not going to be that late. Shall I leave my key with you, madame?"

"You can keep it, I've got a duplicate. Good evening."

"Good evening, madame," he tells her and walks out.

It is cool and humid outside, a typical Marseilles summer night. The fog has begun its nightly trek inland from the harbor. He goes down toward Place des Capucines, slowly recalling the streets from his past visits. No Monday morning ferry this time, no midnight train back to Arles. He has always liked Marseilles. In fact, he prefers it over other mainland cities. It is closest to Algiers.

But he is not here by choice this time, not quite.

"*Merde*," he tells himself as he proceeds down the street, "*merde, merde...*"

He keeps going down Rue Petit St. Jean, cussing and seeing nothing, till he emerges on the wide, busy sidewalk of Cours Belsunce, where the cafés are open and brightly lit, the newspaper stands are still doing a brisk business. He looks around and cannot help but notice the unusually high proportion of blacks, Arabs, and Indochinese on the sidewalk. He buys the evening paper and strolls on past the cafés, scanning slowly as he goes. The first two cafés look too expensive. In the next one, most of the clientele is black. He keeps on walking.

From the next café comes loud conversation in Arabic. He goes past it, steps into the last in the row, next to the pharmacy, and takes a table outside at the left-most corner. He sits down and orders a double cappuccino, short on the foam. When the waiter comes over with it, he leans forward and asks, gesturing discreetly to the right: "Say, how come there's so many of them in there?"

The waiter eyes him with a deadpan expression. "Monsieur is from down there?"

"Yes."

The man leans closer over the table. "The whole *quartier*, over there," he says and nods to the right, "from Rue Colbert to Place Marceau . . . why, all the way down to Rue de la République . . . it's full of them. A few blacks, some of the yellows, but mostly the Arabs. The General, *le salaud*, he's brought them in, swarming all over. He's got even more coming. Monsieur won't believe it, but the General has already signed a pact with the FLN, all hush-hush, letting them all in. Once they have their dirty paws on Algeria, Marseilles is next. They're already here, everywhere, snatching away the few available jobs and pushing true French patriots out into the street. Nothing you or I could do about it, monsieur. They're our allies, if monsieur can imagine. As if we haven't got enough problems with your *pieds noirs*. No offense meant, monsieur understands. We don't serve their kind here. Most of our patrons are *pieds noirs*."

"That so?" he says.

"*Oui monsieur*," says the waiter. "Now, if monsieur will excuse me . . . "

The waiter departs. He turns to look around. The café is packed, people crowding around their tables in twos and threes, talking in subdued voices. Others are sitting alone, contemplating their murky anisettes. No one looks across the low diving rail into the café next door, from which loud Arab music and conversation pours over.

So, he tells himself, what else is new?

He knows he should get up and leave, someone on either side might recognize him. Still, he keeps sitting.

The hell with them, he tells himself. The hell with them on this side and on the other.

He is unlikely to feel any sense of belonging, on either side of the rail. He only feels tired, immensely. And just about now it should begin to dawn on him, what I could have told him all along if he had only been halfway civil, if he hadn't of a sudden turned so goddamned bullheaded. It is not all that easy to just up and leave, jump the crowded old ship and be strictly on your own after all these years.

Sure, people try, people contemplate trying, or they just dream. Mostly dream. Even I do, sometimes, might as well own up to it. Not too often though. Besides, suppose you cut and run, what then? Wherever you go, as he is soon to find out, you are still stuck. Stuck right there, stuck right here, is it ever all that different? Might as well not have bothered.

Of course, his kind are not known for ever giving up. No one would have ever accused them of taking things as they stand. They make a big fuss about their apocalyptic moral dilemmas, make themselves a pain in the butt in the process. As he is doing right now. I have to keep reminding myself that he is worth the trouble, that he is still my friend. He is, regardless.

The dense fog from the waterfront is spreading over the city. He feels for the gun in his belt, then turns to read the paper.

*H*e wakes up late the next morning, gets up and washes, then wanders outside. In the small mama-and-papa cafeteria just across from the hotel, he orders coffee and a croissant. It is ten o'clock, the sun is shining outside, and the young waitress smiles shyly as she swings over to him among the empty tables. Her mother, behind the counter, is a rasp-voiced, thick-waisted bully, who turns back periodically to scold her husband, the cook. The husband, a small man by all evidence, is exiled to the back kitchen, from whence he peers cautiously through the service hatch, his white cap wilting down over his forehead. The wife's garrulous voice must carry all the way out to the sidewalk, punctuating the slow morning.

As far as one can tell, they live upstairs in a crowded small flat.

As he drinks his coffee, he wonders idly whether the husband ever escapes his confinement. Under the withering eyes of the mother, he finds it prudent not to chat with the waitress, obviously their daughter. He pays, crosses the square and ventures into downtown traffic of la Cannebiere.

He passes the big banks, the travel agencies, the chic tourist restaurants. In five minutes he is down at the waterfront on Quai des Belges of the Old Port. He walks past the fishing boats anchored at the wharf, taking in the early rising housewives haggling with cold fury over the price of last night's catch. He listens till he gets bored, then turns back and makes his way slowly to the prefecture on Rue Edmond, just in time for his appointment.

He has been expecting more trouble, but the interview proceeds smoothly. He shows his card to the policeman at the front door, who turns it over a few times before referring him to the information booth on the ground floor. From there he is dispatched through a maze of corridors to the main elevator, which he takes up to the third floor. A policeman at the desk there asks him for his card, inspects it, and phones his chief. The chief apparently says to send him back to the second floor, room 252, where he finds a young inspector in gendarmerie uniform waiting for him with a stenographer. They have his file already spread on the desk in front of them. He is invited to sit down; he thanks them.

The inspector eyes him speculatively. The stenographer is poised waiting, eyes averted. The inspector trusts her implicitly, having brought her over with him from Nice upon his well-deserved promotion. What he doesn't know is that her sister is married to an ex-para from Blida, just resettled in Pyrénées Orientales. A different last name, they will never trace the connection. She writes her sister regularly and stays late most nights to catch up with the paperwork. For the latter, the inspector, acutely short-handed, is eternally in her debt and often contemplates recommending a raise. On occasion he also contemplates staying late with her. Never more than an idle thought, which is just as well. Running an extra copy of the day's transcripts might prove a bit awkward if he did.

"So," says the inspector, "Monsieur Aron."

"Yes."

"Well, well . . . a surprise. You look younger than your file would have me believe."

"You don't look all that old yourself, Monsieur l'Inspecteur."

The inspector smiles wryly. They will be taking each other's measure first, jockeying for position, neither conceding a move. This is part of the procedure and they both know it.

"Flattery will get you nowhere, Monsieur Aron," the inspector observes.

He shifts awkwardly in his metal chair, which does not appear to be too clement to his back.

"Shall we start?" he says.

Robert shrugs and waits.

"Where are you staying at the moment, Monsieur Aron?"

"Hotel du Coq, Rue du Coq."

"Found a place so quickly?"

The inspector sounds surprised, so he tells him he was too.

"What are you planning to do in Marseilles, Monsieur Aron?"

"I don't know," he tells him, "haven't had much time to think. I've just arrived yesterday. I suppose I'll hang around a while and look for something suitable."

"Such as?"

"Anything. Whatever comes along."

"Hmmm," says the inspector, "I see. You're planning to stay then?"

"I don't really know, too early to tell."

"I suppose that makes sense, Monsieur Aron, though of course it doesn't make my job easier."

"Sorry about that, Monsieur l'Inspecteur."

"I bet you are."

They both smile. The inspector resumes: "Let me be frank with you, Monsieur Aron."

Here we go, Robert thinks.

"You're presenting us with a problem, not only you but others in your situation. Take your record—deserted in 1961, joined the OAS, a year of extra-legality doing God knows what . . . I'm not prying, mind you."

He need not pry. The file in front of him is explicit, down to the gory details. We know what is in it and we don't mind, as long as we know what they know and as long as they can do nothing about it. The inspector shrugs.

"A year goes by," he says. "Now you've had enough, you want out. All to your credit, you understand . . . The governor general down in Algiers is naturally ecstatic; he's getting you out of his hair—one less *plastiqueur* to worry about. So he sends you over to us, let Marseilles worry . . . Down there, they don't care if we're swamped here; they don't ask if we can handle it; they don't even let us know—nobody gives a fuck. They march you down to the boat and ship you over to us. You following my drift?"

"Perfectly, Monsieur l'Inspecteur."

"Good, good. I'm merely stating the obvious, right?"

They face off across the narrow table. The early skirmishing is over. Outflanking maneuvers are about to begin.

"Right," he tells him.

"Good..."

The inspector gathers his thoughts.

"Now we've got you here, so what do we do with you?"

He leaves the question hanging in the air. Robert waits patiently.

"We're overextended as it is," the inspector resumes. "We've got trouble up our ass with the FLN on Rue Chapellier. We can't send the bastards away, as much as we would love to; Paris says to leave them alone. Still, we've got to keep an eye on these guys here or they'd be at each other's throats."

The inspector pauses and clears his throat. He is warming up to his subject. Robert waits patiently for the punch line, which is sure to come.

"On top of which," the inspector says, "we've got you people moving in, thousands every day and more coming. Trouble and more trouble. Now how are we supposed to cope, Monsieur Aron?"

"I haven't got the foggiest idea," he tells him. "Don't see much I can do about it, though."

"Well now."

The inspector eyes him speculatively. He is about to come to the point. "You're a potential source of trouble, Monsieur Aron," he tells him. "Nothing personal, you understand, but the record speaks for itself."

He sees the inspector's drift, and he doesn't like what he sees.

"Just a moment, Monsieur l'Inspecteur," he says, "doesn't the record show I left the OAS of my own accord?"

"Four days ago."

The inspector raises his hand in anticipation.

"Yes, I know, I know," he says. "And personally, I'm inclined to take your word for it. Still, you were with them, one of them. They know you, they'll try to rope you back in. Or you might decide to go back on your own. Why, you might get desperate—out of a job, no place to live... You got a job, Monsieur Aron?"

"*Nom de Dieu*, I've just arrived."

"Friends or relatives here?"

"None."

"See what I mean? You're ripe for them, Monsieur Aron. Sooner or later it's bound to happen, willing or unwilling. We won't know the difference, and we won't be able to do much about it. See what I mean?"

The inspector's logic is unassailable, he has to concede that much. What the inspector doesn't know is my friend's boundless obstinacy. This is not in his files. But I know and count on it.

"Perfectly, Inspector," he tells him. "But has it ever occurred to you that I may not want to rejoin them?"

"It has, Monsieur Aron, it has. But then, how could I know? It may not be up to you, you see?"

They are again facing each other in silence, neither conceding. Their relationship will be defined from now on by this initial stalemate.

"Now," the inspector resumes, "here's something I'm authorized to offer you. First, you get out of Marseilles. We'll buy the ticket, anywhere you choose—Altkirch, Peau, Mourenx, Metz, Verdun—you name it. Marseilles is just not for you, Monsieur Aron. Too crowded, if you wish. Once you leave, we'll get the government to help you get started. They've got all those brand new programs; we'll make sure you qualify; get you to the head of the line. How about it?"

The inspector eyes him earnestly. Robert knows he is only doing his duty, doing his best, trying to be fair. All the same, this does not diminish the bitterness he feels about the offer, a bitterness that he now cannot help but let spill over.

"Listen, Monsieur l'Inspecteur," he tells him, "wouldn't it be much cheaper to just lock me up? Solve all your problems. Mine too."

"Now, now," says the inspector, "let's not exaggerate, Monsieur Aron. Suppose we really wanted to do that, how could we? You're a citizen, protected by the law. A deserter, true, but still covered by the terms of a legally declared amnesty that is still in effect, still valid till someone says otherwise. Which they won't very soon, seeing as how it has proven to be quite a lure."

About that the inspector is unfortunately right. The amnesty is draining the OAS, some of the best have taken the offer. It is a sore point yet no one will talk about it. Everybody keeps hoping it will go away. It won't though; we are bleeding. Though with headquarters scattered and the squads on the run, only a few know how badly.

"That so?"

"You'd be surprised how many have come over."

"I would?"

"You would," the inspector assures him. "At any rate, Monsieur Aron, we can't arrest you; our jails are overflowing as it is. Technically, we can't even tell you what to do, as long as you abide by the terms of your amnesty. But for your own good, we'd much prefer if you could get out of our jurisdiction. The Midi is not good for your health, Monsieur Aron. I know you'll find out sooner or later. Take my word for it, move on."

"And rid you of a little headache in the bargain?"

"I've been frank with you. Your presence here is an invitation for trouble. We're way over our heads as it is, can't you see?"

"Sure I can see," he tells him, "you've got a problem. Now, here's mine. I've arrived last night. I don't know a soul on the mainland. I've got nowhere to go and no reason to go anywhere. And I've promised someone to wait right here in Marseilles. It might be a short wait, I hope so. But I can't leave right now. See?"

"And who's that someone, Monsieur Aron?"

"Makes no difference; it's personal. I know you have ways of finding out, so go ahead if you need to. But for the moment you'll have to put up with me here in Marseilles, at least for a while longer. I'll do my best to stay out of your hair."

It is a long speech and he can only hope it will be taken in the same spirit in which it is offered. He is not a free agent, and it is fine with us if the inspector knows that. We don't even mind if the inspector knows who is pulling his strings. Some secrets are not secrets, just part of the game. For the moment we would like him to stay right where he is, where both we and the prefecture can keep an eye on him. This stalemate is only temporary. We will break it when we are good and ready.

"I see," says the inspector, "I see. Well, I suppose we'll just have to keep an eye on you."

"Be my guest."

"Yes... You'll report once a week, Monsieur Aron, every Thursday. Report every change of address immediately. What did you say your address was?"

"Hotel du Coq, Rue du Coq."

The inspector scribbles in his notepad. He is all business now.

"Fine," he says.

And, to the stenographer next to him, "You got it, didn't you?"

She nods dutifully. The inspector turns back to Robert: "You still have your own passport, right?"

"Yes."

"Keep it on you wherever you go, don't leave it behind. If you change your mind about leaving Marseilles, come and talk to me, will you?"

"Sure thing, Monsieur l'Inspecteur."

"Good."

A delicate pause ensues. Their business is clearly at an end, yet the inspector is reluctant to dismiss him. This is where the standard offer should come. The inspector is right on cue: "There's one more thing I could perhaps ask you, Monsieur Aron."

The inspector has all of a sudden found his own fingernails rather fascinating.

"Hmm..." he says, "this is rather... a favor, entirely up to you of course."

"Yes?"

"It concerns your friends."

"Friends?"

"From the OAS."

"Ex-friends, if you please."

"Yes," the inspector hastens to concur, "ex-friends. Who knows about your quitting?"

"Let me see... our squad leader does. The rest of the guys too, the three that are left. The prefecture in Algiers does. Soon there'll be more."

He leaves Marie and her parents out of it, as I would have expected him to. All in good time, no need to spill your guts on the table; what they are determined to learn about him they'll find out soon enough.

"I see," says the inspector.

He pauses.

"There's information coming down to us lately, Monsieur Aron, about the OAS switching its base of operations to the mainland."

"I wouldn't know about that."

"Sure. Still, quite naturally many of your ex-friends will be passing through Marseilles, staying under our jurisdiction, maybe for a while. They will know you're here, might decide to look you up, might be looking for you. You might just bump into them, on the street, in the café . . . see what I mean?"

"I'm not sure I do."

"Well, I wonder if you could let us know if you see them around. I mean, even if you just think you have . . ."

The inspector is still busy with his fingernails. Robert is looking at him directly, and it is clear he has succeeded in embarrassing the inspector. He must surely enjoy the tables being turned and the inspector squirming: "Are you asking me to do something, Monsieur l'Inspecteur?"

"Well, I'm not sure I really should—"

"Then don't," he tells him. "It's a waste of time. I'm not about to turn snitch. I quit, right? That ought to be enough. There's nothing in the papers I signed about singing to the prefecture, so don't even bother. What my old friends do or don't do is their business. I'm out, so keep me out."

"I see."

My old buddy has played it to perfect pitch so far, just the way I had expected. Questions about him have been raised from this end, someone else in the prefecture must be leaking stuff through another channel. Heads will roll when I find out who it is, which I will. In the meantime, I tell the fuckers to pipe down; tell them I can handle it; tell them not to worry. In a few days there'll be no one left here to do any more worrying. For all intents and purposes I am headquarters now, I am still around, and I don't worry. Though I will make damn sure nobody talks out of turn. If anybody is to worry about him, it will be me.

The inspector is not surprised either, he accepts it all stoically.

"How about if they came after you?" he asks. "They might, you know."

"I'll wait and see."

"Will you come to us if you're in trouble?"

"I don't know. Let's hope there won't be any."

"But just in case?"

"We'll see."

"Well," the inspector sighs. "Let's hope nothing turns up. Still..."

"Good," says Robert. "Is that all?"

"I think so, for now."

They both rise and he offers him his hand: "It's been a pleasure, Monsieur l'Inspecteur," he says. "See you next time."

"Thursday, Monsieur Aron. *A bientôt.*"

The inspector and his stenographer both watch him as he opens the door and wanders out into the corridor.

*H*e stands alone near the brackish dark water of Quai des Belges. It is noontime, and the sweating, red-faced tourists from the north crowd the gangways of the motorboats going on the economy excursions to Château d'If, where, for an additional consideration, the guide might be persuaded to let you smell the damp straw in Count de Monte Cristo's solitary dungeon.

The rest of the harbor to his right and left is jam-packed with private pleasure boats, stacked up around the small basin in a thick tangle of masts and rope. The grand hotels on the Corniche rise above the Old Port, giving way at the far end to dilapidated stone mansions, as the pier creeps up on Fort St. Jean. The hotels, the forts and the hills to the left, topped by Nôtre Dame de la Guard, block the wind almost entirely. The lower basin is already stifling hot.

He turns to walk up Quai Rive Neuve, past the pleasure boats on the right. As the road slopes sharply uphill, he passes in front of the gate of Fort St. Nicholas. The guards at the narrow baroque gate are in Legion uniform. For a brief moment he feels a strange, almost nostalgic twinge. He braces himself and hurries on past the gate, past the Pharo, past the Faculty, and on down Rue des Catalans, where he stops above the small public beach. The sand is jammed with people going in and out of the bath houses, the gaudy arcades, the yellow sand. Mixed couples are playing volleyball in the sand. The men are darkly tanned in tight briefs that reveal too much; the girls young and golden in their bikinis. He watches for a while, then turns and resumes his walk.

In a few minutes he finds himself on the curving promenade. The offshore islands are visible above the calm, blue water. Somewhere below he can hear the waves crashing at the bottom of the cliff.

Fifteen minutes later he is in front of the Monument for the Dead. He steps down from the promenade and walks under the small replica of the Arc de Triomphe, this requisite piece of banality mainlanders hold so dear to their hearts. The monument stands erect at the edge of the cliff, its back turned to the water, a tall marble block supporting a woman with a child. At her feet lies a soldier in terminal throes, his rifle held high in valiant supplication. The legend, carved in bold letters into the dark granite, reads:

ARMISTICE DAY, 1919
WE SALUTE THE BRAVE PATRIOTS
WHO GAVE THEIR LIVES FOR PEACE

The lumbering sculpture is flanked on both ends by old iron-cast cannons of Napoleonic vintage.

Those who gave their lives. For peace, to be sure. They and countless others before and since. Peace, a voracious pedophagous Molloch, seems to have over the years sustained a boundless appetite for young lives, feasting on fresh corpses, a silent procession of sacrificial lambs among whom, somewhere toward the discernible end, must stand his own then-young father. It is, he knows, a fruitless train of thought, but he can't help it. By now he has been told countless times, like the rest of us gullible suckers, what one should expect—indeed strive, honor bound—to die for: *la France*, the tricolor, *l'Algérie Française*, Bab-el-Oued. The list stretches on, and for all he knows, peace is just as good an excuse for throwing away one's perfectly serviceable if by now frayed young life. Like him, I have given up on the big words. Except *Algérie Française*, which is not a word.

An old woman is feeding breadcrumbs to the scruffy pigeons. A pregnant young mother with a baby cart sits on the opposite bench. He walks over to inspect the sharply receding edge. His eyes trace down the small promontory of fallen rock protruding a hundred yards or so out into the turquoise water at the bottom of the cliff. The breakers are pounding on it, restless, if for now tamed. On the spur of the moment, he climbs over the low iron grill and hikes down to the rocks.

At the very bottom, just above the water, there is a small lovers' nest, cupped in the bleached rock. He takes off his shirt, lies down and closes his eyes. If he didn't pay too close attention, he might be able to pretend he was somewhere else. The sun is not quite as warm, the wind not quite as dry. The breakers are still angry, rising and falling with repressed menace. He almost falls asleep.

It shouldn't be long now before his stomach starts rumbling; I can practically hear it though he hasn't yet noticed how hungry he is. He has always been this way—possessed by the orphan's desperate passion for food at regular intervals. We used to joke about it in the rubber plantation, where the next meal would often be a tantalizing hundred yards of sniper-infested swamp away. I used to offer him the last of my K-ration, which he would furiously decline, becoming all flustered in the process, enraged at the prospect of having been found out.

He rises, puts his shirt back on, and vaults over the low stone wall, onto the narrow pebble-strewn cove tucked in precariously between the rock and the surf. The promenade is suspended directly above on a curved concrete bridge, spanning the narrow inlet underneath. He follows a narrow flight of stairs that hugs the cliff, passes under the bridge, and emerges at the edge of the water at Vallon des Auffes.

A few fishing boats are moored in the sleepy basin. Residential villas cling to the steep hillside. Most of the buildings at the bottom house assorted waterfront cafés. From the one nearest to him, on the left, the deafening roar of rock-n-roll music is blaring into the otherwise somnolent air.

He climbs down the cracked cement steps and enters. A roomful of teenagers are dancing inside, the music spewing out of a giant chromed jukebox. Every so often, a boy—or is it a girl—steps over and feeds the machine fresh coins.

No one pays any attention to him. He skirts the milling hordes and lowers himself into a stool at the far end of the bar. In a few minutes, the patron comes over, a deeply tanned, finely wrinkled man wearing a thin, neatly trimmed mustache.

"Monsieur?"

The man leans close to him. He leans closer yet. The music is deafening.

"What've you got to eat?" he asks.

The man is almost on top of him.

"Louder!" he says.

"What've you got to eat?"

"Eh?"

"Eat!" he fairly screams.

"Oh . . . sandwiches . . . fish . . . omelets . . ."

The patron's voice is swallowed whole in the uproar.

"What else?"

"Rice pilaf."

"That's it," he tells him, "the rice pilaf!"

"The pilaf?"

It finally occurs to him that gestures will serve him better, and he responds with a vigorous nod.

"Drink?"

"Bordeaux."

"Cheap or fine?"

"Cheap."

"Very well."

The man turns away and goes about his chores. In a few minutes he returns and sets the steaming plate on the bar. The pilaf smells divine, perhaps because he is very hungry. A while later, when the patron comes back, he asks him: "Where did you learn to cook like this?"

The patron leans closer, mercifully, so that their heads almost touch.

"Oran," he says.

"You from down there?"

"No way. I just lived there, five years . . . My wife, God rest her soul, she was from down there . . . left after she died. . . . Just as well, eh?"

"Good timing."

"What?"

"Good timing!"

"Uh..."

He leans closer to the patron, his mouth grazing the man's hair: "How can you stand the noise?" he screams into his ear.

"What noise?"

"Them."

He gestures toward the writhing youths.

"Oh," says the patron. "I don't mind. A bit noisy. Good kids, though."

"Don't they drive you crazy?"

"Take getting used to, yeah. They're all right, really."

The patron is blaring at him full throttle: "Have nothing to do with themselves. Can't just sit around quiet all day long and behave. Hardly blame them. Got to give them something to do. At least here... don't feel so goddamn useless."

"Think so?"

"Just watch them. Sit and watch. Might learn something too..."

They both turn to watch the milling crowd. The boys wear their hair long, the girls have theirs hanging down in loose strands, falling down to their endearing skinny butts. The multitude is swaying in jumbled random unison, couples dispersed in the pack, facing each other, feet planted firmly, neither drawing closer nor pulling apart, rocking, seemingly oblivious to the harsh sound pouring in great riffs out of the jukebox. He scans them slowly. Their eyes are shut, their faces somber, vacant, ascetic. For the life of him he cannot imagine what goes on in their tender brains. They seem so young, but are probably Marie's age. He is trying to picture her in their midst and is having a rough time of it. He is, I suspect, having a rough time imagining her at all.

In a while he cannot take the noise any longer. He turns back to the patron: "You can have them," he tells him over the din. "They're all yours. I can't make any sense out of them. Reckon I'm too old... How much?"

"What?"

"How much?" he bellows.

"Five fifty... You get used to them; they're not all that bad."

"Probably," he tells him. "I'll try harder next time. Very good pilaf you got there."

"What?"

He smiles at the man and threads his way out along the fringe of the swaying melee.

*H*is first day in Marseilles sets the tone for the weeks that follow. He comes back from his long walk, takes a two-hour nap, gets up and showers, dresses, and goes back down to Cours Belsunce. He sits in the same café, reading the evening paper and sipping his anisette. After dark, he goes back to the hotel, walking up Rue Petit St. Jean and doing his best to be as sweet as he can in declining the coarse solicitations of the whores on both sides of the old cobblestone.

The next few days he pays consecutive visits to various offices. His first, to the Office of Veteran's Services, is rather short. He takes his place in line, reaches the window, and is asked for his discharge papers. He explains, or tries to. The young clerk shrugs and tells him he qualifies for nothing. He is lucky, he is told, to have sneaked in under the amnesty clause in the nick of time, lucky not to be further investigated. At any rate, he finds out his rights as a veteran were automatically voided by his desertion.

If he had bothered to listen, back on the boat, I could have told him just that. He is discovering how the mainlanders' word goes only this far; how their loyalty to him—to all of us *pieds noirs*—extends no further than the old borders of their shriveled empire. If he thought he was coming home, he is in for a rude awakening.

His next visit is with the Bureau of Repatriates, where he waits three hours in the crowded dim foyer. He finally gets to the screening desk, his name is taken down and he is given an appointment for the following week. When he comes back then, he is sent up to the second floor, where a tired social worker in her mid-twenties bids him enter.

"Monsieur Aron?"

"Yes?"

"Please sit down."

"Thank you."

He sits across from her in a folding metal chair.

"What can I do for you, Monsieur Aron?"

"Well," he says, "just about everything. To begin with, you can help me find a job."

"I'm glad that's the first thing you asked," she says. "Some people have a different order of priorities. Now, let's see, what's your line of work?"

He thinks for an embarrassingly long minute. The question is simple enough, yet not quite.

"I don't know," he tells her.

"Beg your pardon?"

She leans forward, prepared to concede she hasn't heard him right. The upper regions of her breasts reveal themselves over her modest décolletage.

"Well, it's like this," he tells her, prudently averting his eyes, "after I finished the lycée, I signed up with the Legion. I was a demolition sergeant for eight years, so that's what I know most about . . . Blowing things up, you know, like houses, bridges, things like that. Before that I used to tend the counter at the old man's shop, now and then, selling stuff, giving change."

"I see," she says. "Is there anything else you can do?"

"I can do just about anything," he tells her. "I mean, I would do anything, I'm not choosy."

"Have you tried the Office of Veteran's Services?"

"I have. Seems like I don't rightfully exist, as far as they are concerned. Certain irregularities in my discharge papers, you see . . . "

He stops. She eyes him above her low-perched glasses. He can see she understands, most likely he is not the first one in the same predicament. He is beginning to suspect he could trust her, that she wants to help him, but probably can't. For a while she muses over her files in silence.

"I see," she says. "Well, Monsieur Aron, the best thing we can offer you right now is a place in one of our centers for professional retraining and reorientation. You can choose among quite a variety of programs: industrial design, building technology, drafting, office work if you've had any education. In some instances, we also have openings for aircraft technicians, though I would worry about your security rating."

"The last three you mentioned sound just fine," he tells her. "Where are your schools located?"

"Well," she says, "we've got quite a few. There's one in Altkirch, one near Metz, three in Bordeaux, two in Pyrenees Orientales, one in Mourenx, another one in Pau . . . "

"Hold it right there," he tells her, "those are all pretty far. How about something a bit closer to Marseilles?"

"We've got nothing here."

"Nothing near Marseilles?"

"Not a thing."

"Then it's no use," he tells her.

"What do you mean?"

He knows she is trying to do her job. This is not her fault, but as things stand she cannot help him.

"I can't leave Marseilles," he tells her, "right now. I'm waiting for someone."

"Someone from Algeria?"

"Yes."

"Can't you wait somewhere else while training?"

"No, I've got to stay right here. It's complicated, I'm sure you wouldn't want to hear about it. Are you sure there's nothing available in Marseilles?"

She looks at him, genuinely puzzled.

"Monsieur Aron," she says, "I know how you feel, but this is all we've got. Believe me, you're not the only one who wants to stay in Marseilles. Most of you people do. That's why we've got nothing allocated for anywhere in the Midi. Government policy. If you insist on staying here, you're on your own. All our programs are targeted at other regions."

"I see."

She is sympathetic, and somehow cannot quite hide it.

"Between you and me, Monsieur Aron," she says, "Marseilles has got more than its share of the repatriation burden. I'm sorry I can't be more encouraging."

She leans forward and he catches another, this time more generous, glimpse of her breasts. What the hell, he muses as he gets up to leave.

"I'm sorry too," he says, "I'd like to find some work. I'll try somewhere else, I suppose. Thanks for your help."

"I'm sorry I couldn't do more," she says.

Her eyes follow him to the door.

"If you ever change your mind, Monsieur Aron, don't hesitate to come back. We'll try to place you."

"Thanks," he tells her, "I will."

He wonders fleetingly if she would go out with him. That is, if he asked. He dismisses the thought and steps out.

His next visit, a rather enlightening one, takes him to the ANFANOMA office. He tracks them down to a dingy hole-in-the-wall on top of a shoe repair store in a dilapidated commercial edifice on Rue Vavon, just north of the Old Port. He is let in by a tall, bony woman, leathery and weathered, scanning the world about her with trained bouncer's eyes.

"Is this the ANFANOMA office?" he asks.

"It is. Who're you looking for?"

"Anyone to talk to."

"What about?"

She is not about to take his bona fides for granted, nor concede an inch. With her, he'll have to earn it. He decides to try an outflanking gambit: "I'd like to talk to someone in charge."

"The local secretary is out for the day, he's in court. The regional president, Monsieur Pucciani, is in Paris for the national convention. There's no one here to talk to right now."

"How about you then?"

As an afterthought, he adds, "I'm from Algiers."

Her skepticism does not appear to diminish. If anything, she seems more recalcitrant.

"What is it about?" she asks. "Monsieur is an activist?"

Doing a credible bit of quick thinking, he goes along with the proffered out: "Yes. I wonder if you people have any way of helping me to find a job?"

"A job? Monsieur, ANFANOMA is a political organization, not an employment agency. We don't find jobs, we do other things. Here, read this."

She hands him a bundle of tracts.

"It will give you an idea of what we do. And come to the meeting next week, Colonel Berensac is going to speak."

"Colonel Berensac from . . . ?"

The colonel is not exactly an unknown quantity, having been cashiered out of the paratroopers following the April 1961 disturbances due to repeated intemperate public outbursts directed at the perfidious General. An insufferable windbag, if truth is to be told, but one of ours.

"The one," she tells him. "You know him?"

"Not personally."

"Well, this is your chance. Come and listen."

"I will," he tells her. "But don't you people run any social services for repatriates? I mean, those who used to be . . . "

Apparently she decides he merits another once over. Her eyes inspect him slowly, lingering on the thin white scar under his chin, visible from where she is seated.

"Monsieur's name?"

"Aron," he tells her. "Why?"

"Aron," she says, "*c'est pas un nom israélite?*"

"*Oui.*"

"Why don't you try their bureau of social services? They've got all kinds of special funds for their own people. They're rolling in money, you know, and they take care of their own. We're not a charity here; we are a political organ. You come to the meeting and see for yourself."

He sees little use in pursuing the conversation further.

"I will," he tells her. "Thank you."

"You are most welcome."

She escorts him to the door and follows his descent from the top of the stairs, her eyes clamped on him as he turns to look back up. For as long as he is in her jurisdiction, she won't let him out of her sight. What the hell, he tells himself, he's got enough money for two more months, three if he is frugal, which he has always been. It is only money. His job search is, for the moment, suspended.

Only money indeed, ours to be precise, and some day soon we will be there to collect. He thinks Marie will rejoin him long before that day of reckoning, that the two of them will just pick up and go somewhere else then. But that is yet to be seen.

Given what he has discovered by now, he sees no reason to hit the charities either, not yet. Once again his train of thought must lead him back to Marie, as he walks down the street, alone and feeling dejected and oblivious to the two guys shadowing him at a respectful remove from across the street. One of them soon excuses himself and makes a quick pit stop at the corner phone booth, his low monotone imparting a few laconic phrases into the receiver before rejoining his partner. They report to the prefecture and are good at their stuff. What they don't know, and don't need to know, is that they too are being shadowed and their every move recorded, later recounted. In this game of cat and mouse, all is determined by the need to know. My need outstrips theirs.

Her absence must be hitting him hard now, what with the rapid cumulation of uncertainties and improbabilities to which, he is discovering, he has entrusted his life. It sure must hurt. He goes to the café and writes her a short letter, telling her how much he misses her, that he is all right, and please watch out and come over soon, he is waiting. He tells her to write care of *poste restante*. Which makes things easier on us, we've got our man there. Although Madame Lechar at the hotel would have cooperated too.

The following week he goes to the ANFANOMA meeting at the Odeon theater, on Rue Curiol near the upper end of la Cannebiere. He is more than a little wary about showing up there to begin with. Put plainly, I am astonished he is taking the chance.

He comes in late and finds the place packed and, of course, the air conditioning is out. The thick odor of unwashed bodies must hit him as he enters the foyer. He pushes his way in, elbowing through the dense crowd in the back.

Colonel Berensac is, of course, a familiar name, having been haranguing the mainland circuit on behalf of the cause for over a year. In person, he now discovers, the colonel is a stocky type sporting a shining pate and a hook nose. His well-trimmed mustache is the sole hint of an erstwhile military bearing. It is belied by the distinctive little paunch acquired since his hasty retirement from the para. This last a domestic trait that gives the colonel the incongruous air of a prosperous haberdasher.

The colonel is already at the microphone, surrounded by members of the local presidium.

He ignores the dirty looks as he shoves his way up toward the front. The dark faces around him are glistening with perspiration. Mustaches are dark and thick and curl upward in defiance. The teeming multitudes of Bab-el-Oued seem to be crammed together around him like oxygen-starved sardines.

He parks himself just behind the last row of benches, from where he can observe the proceedings a bit better. When he tunes in to listen, Colonel Berensac is in mid-harangue.

"They are selling Algeria, right this very minute, to the bloody assassin Ben-Bella!" he is intoning. "But, my friends, that is not quite enough! They are chopping the greenest branch off the sacred oak of France—but that is not enough! They are kicking one million French patriots out of their homes! The cream off the top, the very best, the ones who rose to take arms in defense of their beloved France! And still that's not enough, my friends! My brothers, fellow patriots, you who've stood up for your country in her bleakest and most shameful hour in 1939, stood up and lent your hands and hearts and blood while others collaborated or waited out the long struggle across the la Manche! *They* are betraying you today, my brothers! Those who ran away and hid—and that is still not enough! My dear comrades, you've been told in Monsieur Deffere's paper about an invasion of Marseilles by the *pieds noirs*! The same Monsieur Deffere, do not forget, who was bosom friend to Ho Chi Minh, the same Monsieur Deffere who struck the knife at the back of the glorious French Army fighting the yellow hordes in Dien Bien Phu! The same Monsieur Deffere who signed the Red petition demanding the release of the FLN terrorists! The very same Monsieur Deffere who, with colossal impudence, demanded punishment for the men of the First Para Regiment—our own glorious PRP—in the middle of the Battle of Algiers! This Monsieur Deffere is bitching and moaning today about *your* invasion of his private fief, *his* Marseilles!

"What this Monsieur Deffere has forgot to tell you, my brothers, is the story of another invasion, silent yet massive, that is at this very moment pouring into his city of Marseilles—the invasion of Arab so-called labor from Algeria into France!"

The colonel pauses and turns to drink from a glass of water placed on the table in front. His head is glistening with perspiration. One of the people seated next to him refills the glass, as the colonel resumes his harangue.

"So, my brothers, *pieds noirs*, no room for you in Monsieur Deffere's Marseilles! You are being sent, exiled, expelled, to the frozen remote corners of the mainland! No jobs for you here either, no housing, no relief funds, no schools for your children! For you, my brothers, Monsieur Deffere's Marseilles is just too small, not enough room for you! And why should there be? With Monsieur Deffere reserving his entire city for his friends and allies from the FLN, who swarm in by the thousands every day to take your houses, your jobs, your schools ... who come to pitch their smelly tents in the gray shadow of Monsieur Deffere's prefecture! ... Swarming black hordes, protected by the bayonets of French soldiers and French police! Swarming in to the tune of the crying French babies of Algiers, Oran, and Constantine! Swarming in under the auspices of *le General*, the same General you, my brothers, brought into power on May thirteenth, 1958!"

All around him, the sweat is pouring down the dark brows. Most of them are shabbily dressed, many in old military garb. There are no women in the hall. Familiar and faintly familiar faces from the back alleys of Bab-el-Oued and Isly keep turning up in the dim yellow light. They lap it all up in rapture as the colonel, whose thundering operatic voice underscores his diminutive clerical frame and polished bald head, proceeds.

"The very same traitors," he tells them, "have been undermining the Republic since the Soviet government of the *Juif* Leon Blum! Throughout the *Front Populaire* of 1945! Throughout the sellout of the French Army in Dien Bien Phu, this time by the *Juif* Pedro Mendez who calls himself—the irony—Mendez-France! The very same traitors are now abandoning the greatest of all the provinces of France, *l'Algérie Française*, leaving her in the bloody paws of the assassin Ben-Bella! The very same traitors, now led by the arch-traitor himself, *le General*, are busy, scheming and plotting this silent invasion of France!

"And to make more room, they are throwing French patriots into prison by the thousands—generals, colonels, captains, lieutenants—the glory of the Republic, flower of the French Army! Throwing them into prisons and murdering them under the guise of that shameful spectacle, the high court-martial! And why, my brothers, why are these French patriots dragged to the guillotine? What is their crime? My brothers, their one and only crime is their love for France, their refusing to turn coats, to turn their skin the way the arch-traitor *le General* has done!

"Their real crime is refusing to stop being French, rising in support of the blood-stained tricolor! Refusing to extend their own necks to the chopping axe of the murderer Ben-Bella! My brothers, *pieds noirs*, once again now, when France is being sold out to her enemies, her one and only bulwark are the patriots from *Algérie!* You, *pieds noirs* from Oran and Constantine and Blida and the Mitidja and Mostaganem and Bab-el-Oued!

"My brothers, the fate and glory of France is once again in your hands! Your hands and the hands of thousands of patriots on the mainland who refuse to turn their coats despite the brutal terror directed at them by the General and his Jewish hatchet men! To them, to *le General* and his Jewish Gestapo, we have only one answer—there will be ten people replacing each one thrown in jail! Ten heads replacing the one rolled down the guillotine! Ten hands replacing the one chopped off! Ten new tracts distributed for each confiscated by the gendarmes!

"Let them know, my brothers, let them hear, let it ring loud and clear—the battle for Algeria is the battle for France! And, as long as the voice of French Algeria rings true, the voice of France rings true! Wherever the warm heart of French Algeria beats, there beats the heart of France! My brothers, tell the traitors, the assassins, the Jews, the Reds, tell Monsieur Deffere whose Gestapo agents, I assure you, are among you this very moment! Let them all hear the one thing we know—*l'Algérie Française* is not dead! *L'Algérie Française* marches on! *L'Algérie Française* . . ."

The crowd drowns out the colonel's last words in a maelstrom of cheers and whistles and applause. Sunken faces seem revived, dark eyes flash with rekindled light, heads turn round excitedly, friends salute each other, strangers slap one another on the back.

In the ensuing commotion he may have glimpsed a familiar face that shouldn't have been there. Could have been Eugène, who for all he knows had deserted a week before he did. If so, it will have to be dealt with later. Eugène was told in no uncertain terms to wear a disguise and lay low.

No way of really knowing, but someone or something has spooked him. Because he turns round abruptly and shoves his way hurriedly toward the door.

Or is it that he's just had all he could take of the colonel, who—as useful as he is for the cause—is a loud windbag and crushing bore? In the long haul that is sure to come, everyone has their niche, windbags and bores and ascetic scholars, accountants and dentists and *plastiqueurs*. We shall take them all to our bosoms, beggars-not-choosers that we are. It is only natural that Robert should feel depressed though, and sorry for the simple souls inside the theater.

He is almost outside when the colonel resumes his mantra: "*L'Algérie Française* . . ."

When he is finally out on the sidewalk, a nimble hand lands on his shoulder. He turns, his hand sneaking reflexively down to his belt. Then he remembers—he is not carrying the gun. Bloody idiocy too, he should know. How easy it is to be lulled into carelessness, or so it seems. He pulls his useless, naked hand back. The man standing next to him says: "Your papers."

He is wearing the inevitable gray fedora and a soiled light-colored raincoat. Both of his hands are stuffed deep in the coat's pockets.

"Are you the police?"

"Yes."

"How do I know?"

The man pulls his left hand out of his pocket and turns out the lapel of his coat. The small badge flashes briefly in the dark.

"*Bon.*"

He hands over his wallet. The man takes it and goes methodically through the contents.

"Robert Aron?"

"Yes."

"What were you doing in there?"

"Listening."

"Liked it?"

He shrugs.

"I've heard it all before," he tells the guy.

"Is that why you left in the middle?"

"It gets boring, don't you think?"

The guy looks him over skeptically.

"Don't get smart," he says, "I wasn't in there. You belong to their organization?"

"What organization?"

"Don't act stupid. ANFANOMA."

"No."

"We have ways of checking out," the guy reminds him, "so you better be right. You from down there, *l'Algérie*?"

"Yes."

"I see."

The guy is shuffling slowly through the contents of his wallet.

"Hey," he says, "what've we got here?"

He has just pulled out the weekly police report card.

"It says it all there," he tells him.

"It does, doesn't it?"

The man is scribbling in his notebook.

"We'll see."

He gives him back his wallet.

"Is that all?"

"For the moment. Go on, scoot. If I were you I'd stay as far from these jokers as I could. A bunch of rabble-rousers, up to no good, nothing but trouble. Especially for you."

"Yes," he says, "I know. *Merci,* Monsieur l'Agent."

When he turns back to look from across the street, the guy has already melted into the contoured shadow along the theater wall. Others like him are all over. Ours? Theirs? He'll never know for sure. They are his constant companions now as he makes his desultory rounds between relief agencies and the prefecture. He may think he's left us, may protest he has to all who would listen, again and again and again. No matter, they won't believe him. Which is just as well. What they don't know *will* hurt them.

It doesn't hurt, of course, that half of them report to us even before they report to their superiors at the prefecture. They have been made to see the glory of cooperation, what with their extended families scattered all over the place, some still in Algeria.

The guys from the prefectures spy both on us and for us, some help us spy on others. Some die in the process, like our guys do, though most are smart enough to get by. The fuck, we all die. In the meantime we go about criss-crossing each others' paths playing our deadly games. Ostensibly by the same deadly rules, though with a difference. *They* think the rules bind us all. We know different. We know better.

*I*t is early in the afternoon a few days later. He is on his way back to the hotel, this time following Rue St. Basile. He has got up early, has lingered at the café over breakfast and the morning paper, has then spent the rest of the morning walking the streets south of the Old Port. It is a scorching day even for Marseilles, and at three o'clock, threading his way slowly up the street, he is ready for his nap.

His reveries are interrupted by the clamor of loud voices. He looks up and then comes to a halt. There is a deserted empty lot on the right side across the street, bounded by a low mold-streaked limestone wall. From over the wall flows animated male conversation. He can see the heads on the other side and, with nothing else to do, his curiosity is pricked. He turns around and walks back to the corner, where the gate should be, a stone arch of the same molding vintage. Above the arch the sign, painted white in a small irregular hand, reads:

CLUB BOULIST ST. BASILE
ADMISSION AT ONE'S OWN RISK

The gate is open, the hingeless metal door leaning on the wall to the left. He walks into a wide courtyard where a hundred men or so are gathered around, clustered in five or six groups all playing *les boules*.

It has been years since he has seen the game, let alone played it himself. We used to play it at school during intermission, he must have too, even in his fancy lycée. We played it in the backyards of Bab-el-Oued; we played it on the beach where the sand would stop the balls from rolling and make the game somewhat easier to control. There is no working-class neighborhood in Algeria or the Midi where one doesn't find those lots, sandwiched between crumbling old homes and the local dump, where one plays *les boules*.

It is, on the face of it, a disarmingly simple game. You use heavy, cast-iron balls the size of small watermelons, their surface grooved like a fine net for better grip. A golf ball is placed at the end of the field as target, and the players, each with his own set of metal balls, line up at the other end. From there, they pitch their balls, aiming to place them closest to the golf ball at the other end.

You throw four times, the first two each in separate turns, the last pair in the final round, one after the other. When all the balls have been pitched, the player whose ball remains closest to the golf ball is the winner. By the normal consensus, a money pool is collected in advance. It all goes to the winner. Needless to say, complicated side bets can be arranged at any moment, betting on winners, rank order, distance, number of balls, you name it.

There are only men in the yard, some playing, the others chatting, shuffling their feet, slouching with their backs to the wall. Men of all ages, dressed in overalls or cheap casual garb, the older ones wearing peaked *casquettes*, the young sporting the thick trademark mustaches of the coast.

He joins the group of onlookers near the left wall. Five men are playing, throwing from the far corner toward the gate. It pays to keep your eyes on the ball after it lands, the crowd might lend a helping foot, what with the side bets. So each player throws and joins the group, where sideline commentary is rather animated.

"Here she comes," says a squat old man next to him. "See . . . no, too much. She's going to roll all the way to that little mound, see? What a pity, started real good. Hey, you try again! *Vive Mostaganem!*"

The young man joins them, having just overshot the mark by a shameful margin.

"L'amerdeuse!" he comments, "slipped me. I should have rubbed some sand in."

"Watch it . . . " calls someone from behind.

The next ball is coming, thrown by a sun-tanned man somewhere in his forties. The ball arches widely and lands with a dry thump, having forced the onlookers to draw back. The sand has checked most of the ball's momentum. It rolls on slowly and stops four inches from the golf ball.

"Bravo!" come voices from the crowd. *"La-haut Oran!"*

"Nothing to worry about," says the young man, who has wound up next to Robert. "I'll knock him off that spot next time."

"You go there and show them, brother," the little old man tells him.

"How many do you have left?" Robert asks the young man.

"Two."

"Good. Listen, don't try to knock him off; it's a waste of a shot. Just put your first one as close in front of his ball as you can. Touch it if you can. If he tries to bump you off then, you'll stay put. He's not going to bother with his last one."

"You think so?"

"Worth trying."

"You play?"

"Used to."

"Oran?"

"Algiers. Been a while though."

"Want to team up for another one later on?"

"Sure, I'd love to."

"Good," says the young man, "we're trying to teach them a lesson, *les Oranais*. They're getting a touch too cocky around this yard."

"A neighborly fight?"

"The usual."

He cannot help smiling. The fishermen of Mostaganem have been carrying a legendary grudge, as old as time, against those from Oran.

The next player is a wizened old man wearing a dirty gray casquette. He studies his remaining three balls, shifting them thoughtfully from one hand to the other. The crowd is egging him on impatiently.

"Get going, *grandpère!*"

"They all weigh the same, *vieillard.*"

"What's he waiting for, *l'idiot?*"

"Just trying to rub off some weight . . ."

The old man remains oblivious to the provocations. His hand creeps up slowly, reaching to scratch a week-old beard.

"Beat it, *grandpère!*" he is urged.

The old man stoops down slowly and drops two of the balls to the ground. In the same smooth motion he scoops a handful of sand and rubs it into his third ball, bringing himself into position. His concentration is unbroken, the crowd is getting antsy as he continues to ignore them. He bides his time, his arm drawing an wide upward arch at whose apex the ball is finally released. It rises into a low trajectory, spinning counter orbit and coming down half a yard behind the golf ball, where it stops, spins in the sand, and then slowly rolls back. The ball comes to its final rest two inches from target.

"Bravo, *grandpère!*" shouts the crowd.

He turns to the young man next to him: "Where's the old geezer from?"

"Blida. Never teams with anybody. Always plays by himself."

The last two players gun for the leader. The first misses, pitching his number two into a useless roll by the wall. The second hits the old man's ball. The two balls ricochet wide apart, the golf ball gets knocked off, rolls a yard farther and lands near to the wall. All is set for the last round.

"Good," says the young man next to him. It is his turn again.

"Don't rush it," he tells him. "Put both of them against the wall, next to each other."

"Easier said than done."

"I know, try for it anyway."

"Will do."

The young man follows his advice to the letter and leaves both shots bunched together, nearly touching the wall and ten inches from the golf ball.

"Terrific," says the squat old man next to Robert.

"Sure," Robert tells him, "he's got a chance all right, but the game is not over yet. All four could still bounce him off."

"You'll see."

The young man rejoins them.

"Good shots," Robert tells him.

"Not good enough. Thanks all the same."

The sun-tanned man from Oran is throwing again. His first ball grazes one of the two near the wall, which then bounces and hits the other before careening off. The crowd catches their collective breath.

"Still got one left," muses the old man next to him. "He's pushed you even closer."

The next shot is high in the air now. It comes to rest two inches from the golf ball.

"*Merde*," says the young man.

"Game's not over," Robert reminds him. "Watch for the old buzzard."

"He's not going to play my way."

"That depends," he tells him, "if it comes to choosing between you and the other guy, who knows?"

The old man bides his time again. Nobody rushes him this time, the crowd is with him, holding their breath. He pitches his first shot toward the wall. It catches the young man's ball and transports it within four inches of the target.

"See?" Robert says to the young man.

"He'll bounce me off with the next one."

"It's either you or the other guy," he tells him, "and he's closer."

The old man's last shot lands neatly in front of the closer ball, rolls forward, shoves it aside and remains resting at the very same spot. The crowd applauds grudgingly, old age and treachery having once again carried the day. Robert turns to the young man next to him.

"He's good, the old fart, no shame in losing to him. He's a great one, an artist."

"The best around here," says the little old man next to them. He seems resigned now. At least it is not an Oranais.

The band of spectators, their ranks swollen now, wait intently, tan unshaven faces turn round, eager not to miss a single move. He smiles in spite of himself, he ought to. This infectious enthusiasm, the uncontrolled delight in competition. God, he does remember all too well this reckless, bet-crazy spirit, still rife on a deserted back-lot in Marseilles. He sighs, exasperated, for a minute wishing he could be one of them once again.

With patience, it will come back to him. Where else can he go? His persnickety Jews will never accept him, what with his Corsican mother. He may have been too young to know about her, but I do. It is my business to know.

The first of the two young men from Oran is making ready to throw again. Robert turns back and starts toward the gate.

"Hey," says the young man from Mostaganem, "aren't we teamed up for the next one?"

"Make it the next time, my friend," he tells him. "I'll be around. Too tired to be much help now."

"Next time then."

He goes on out through the gate and down the street along the stone wall. The animated voices from the other side trail after him all the way to the hotel.

*H*is nap must have lasted nearly three hours when he is woken up by a knock on his door. He rolls over and pulls himself up to a sitting position on the bed.

"What is it?" he asks.

"It's me, Madame Lechar," her voice filters in from the landing, "you're wanted downstairs."

"Who is it?"

"The police."

He is only half awake but has no choice.

"Tell them I'll be down in a minute," he calls to her, "I'm getting dressed."

Two of them are in the hall next to the phone when he shows up five minutes later. As he comes closer, he recognizes the inspector from the prefecture.

"Monsieur l'Inspecteur," he says, "what a pleasant surprise. Sorry to have kept you waiting. My beauty sleep, you know."

"Monsieur Aron."

The inspector's curt nod is decidedly chilly.

"Will you come out to the car? We need to talk."

"Sure. What is it all about?"

"Let's talk out there."

The three of them walk out, the car is parked right in front, a regulation unmarked olive-green Renault. The other man opens the back door and the inspector motions him in, follows behind, and closes the door. His man then stations himself discreetly at the curb. The inspector turns.

"Monsieur Aron, you're putting me in a rather delicate position."

"Me?"

"Precisely. Now, there's still the possibility, however slim, that you're not fully aware of what you're doing. I'm willing to give you the benefit of the doubt. But you better give me a good reason."

He is racking his brain for an answer. The best he can come up with will do him little good: "You've lost me right there, Monsieur l'Inspecteur. What is it exactly we're talking about?"

The inspector nods sadly.

"You're making it difficult, Monsieur Aron," he says.

"How?"

"To begin with, last Thursday. Where were you?"

It hits him then, and in a way he is relieved.

"*Mon Dieu*," he says, "I forgot all about it . . ."

He had missed his weekly appointment. The inspector nods.

"A man in your position can't afford to skip his appointments," he says, "not with us, Monsieur Aron."

"I'm so sorry, Monsieur l'Inspecteur. It'll never happen again, you've got my word."

"You bet."

The inspector pauses, there's more to come; there always is.

"Then there's this," he says, "you were seen at Ciné Odeon attending the ANFANOMA fund-raiser. Is that correct?"

"I was seen in front," he tells him. "I hope your source also told you I was leaving. Before they passed the hat."

"It was noted," says the inspector. "But then, why should the detail make a difference? I don't really have to tell you, Monsieur Aron, what kind of people you're dealing with in ANFANOMA. Now do I?"

"No, you don't," he tells him, "I recognize the type, same crowd as back home. Same talk too."

"Still you were in there."

The inspector does his best to impress him with his incredulity.

"But why, Monsieur Aron, why? A man in your position, your background, could it be plain stupidity?"

The question hangs in the air between them. The inspector shakes his head.

"Talk to me, Monsieur Aron, make me understand, make me believe you."

"Nothing to understand," he tells him, "not really."

"Really? It never occurred to you you were coming dangerously close to violating the conditions of your amnesty, your signed pledge? Talk to me, Monsieur Aron. Make me see it."

"I did nothing except drop in, listen, leave early."

"Why?"

"Curiosity."

Resentment is finally beginning to well in him. Good and well, I was wondering when he would finally get mad. The madder he is at the inspector, the better. Who could he turn to except back to us?

"I'm not under house arrest, am I?" he blurts out. "So how does this violate my amnesty? I was there for the whole of fifteen minutes. I listened, heard what the man had to say, got bored and left. Same old garbage I've heard before. You don't think I'd fall for it now?"

The inspector dismisses the last words with impatience.

"Who did you talk to in there?"

"Nobody."

"How do I know?"

"You don't. Why ask then?"

"My point, Monsieur Aron, your word is all I got. How much is it worth? Has it ever occurred to you how short a route it is from ANFANOMA back to the OAS? What guarantees do I have you haven't made contact right there with your old friends?"

"You have my word."

"Precisely. You must have known some of them were bound to be there."

"I didn't recognize any."

"Nobody?"

"No one."

While I will never know for sure—Eugène won't tell me if Robert recognized him—I have my doubts, as apparently does the inspector: "Why do I find that hard to believe, Monsieur Aron?"

"You're a born skeptic, Monsieur l'Inspecteur."

"Indeed."

They eye each other wearily.

"You're going to be trouble, Monsieur Aron," says the inspector, "I can tell. I can smell it. Suppose I believed you. Suppose you didn't see anybody there. Do you know who saw you?"

The obvious answer is he doesn't, the inspector has backed him into a corner. He is proving to be a handful, this hotshot inspector. The worst, an idealist, rich, and monogamous to the core, a young bride stashed away in a modest château, right family, provincial holdings, *les Grands Ecoles*, skids greased all the way to heaven. Squeaky clean, might not listen to reason. The wife might though, worth a try.

The inspector goes on; definitely a handful. "Listen, Monsieur Aron, we could have found your body floating face down in the Old Port, red necklace ear to ear. We get three, four a week like that, your friends' signature, or can't you tell? Is that how you'd like to wind up?"

"Not if I can help it."

"*Merde*, why don't you help then? Screw your old friends, to them you're just another traitor."

"I'm not!"

"To them you are."

Silence. But the inspector is not through yet: "Take this afternoon," he says.

"How about it?"

"Where were you?"

"This afternoon? Let me see ... I went for a walk, rather came back from one. Why, you tell me, Monsieur l'Inspecteur, you seem to have gotten me well covered."

"Know anything about the Club Boulist St. Basile?"

"*Cher Dieu*, is *les boules* out of bounds too?"

"Know the kind of people that hang out there?"

"Why sure," he tells him, "*pieds noirs*, lousy *pieds noirs* like me, right?"

"Now now, Monsieur Aron," says the inspector, "you know exactly what I mean. The Club Boulist St. Basile is a major rendezvous point for the ex-Delta from Oran."

"How am I supposed to know that? I'm not from Oran. I don't know any of those guys."

"How do I know?"

"Oh for God's sake!"

The inspector is brimming with genuine disgust.

"You see, Monsieur Aron, I've got no way of knowing one way or another, not for sure. So in the meantime, what have I got? I see you making the rounds, hitting all the wrong spots, one after the other, by the book. If one wouldn't have known different, one would say you were deliberately trying to incriminate yourself. Don't you see?"

He must. And, I must confess, I am not quite sure myself what he is up to. Though his protestations of innocence sound genuine enough: "But *you* know, Monsieur l'Inspecteur," he tells him, "you've got me tailed. If I'm not supposed to move about, why don't you lock me up then?"

"We've already been through that, Monsieur Aron. I don't have the authority. And for all I know you've done nothing wrong, yet. But the way things are shaping up, you're getting to be a pain. So how about it?"

"How about what?"

"Leaving Marseilles. My old offer still stands, a ticket anywhere, you name it. Personally, I don't think you've gone back on your pledge, not so far. But you're a magnet for trouble; something is bound to happen; this city is crawling with ex- and not-so-ex-commandos. Why take a chance? Why should *we*? Why should *you*? Go somewhere else, Monsieur Aron, cool off a spell, make a fresh start. Let us help you. How about it?"

Yes, how about it? He must know the inspector means it. Under other circumstances he would have been more than glad to accept. But he won't. We know why; we know he won't tell the inspector.

"Look, Monsieur l'Inspecteur," he tells him instead, "do you think I like this town all that much? I've told you, I'd leave tonight if I could. But I'm still waiting for someone to come over. As soon as that's settled, I'll be gone in a jiffy; you won't have to ask. I give you my word. Until then, keep me tailed if you must. I don't mind."

The inspector draws a long breath and lets it out slowly. He turns to light a cigarette, then puffs on it as he contemplates the gathering twilight.

"Reckon we'll have to do that, Monsieur Aron," he tells him. "It's a damn nuisance though, you know. We're overextended as it is. Well, from now until further notice you'll report twice a week, Monday and Thursday. You don't have to come up to me, just show your papers downstairs and get them stamped. I'll let you know if I want to see you myself. And if you change your mind about leaving, come up and talk to me, anytime. Or in case there's trouble. Okay?"

"Sure," he tells him, "you'll be the first to know, Monsieur l'Inspecteur."

"I bet."

The inspector leans over and opens the door.

"All for now, Monsieur Aron. Good night."

"Good night, Monsieur l'Inspecteur."

Behind him, as he turns to walk toward Cours Belsunce, the car coughs to a start, makes a U-turn and drives away.

*I*t is one of those mornings when he is feeling exceedingly blue, a malaise which I am sure will plague him more and more now, as his time in Marseilles stretches on into an uncharted, horizonless blur. All of us in this deadly line of work, our chosen predicament if you will, tend to misjudge how utterly alone we have become. In the gathering doom, we hurl ourselves about, fending off the gnawing void with ceaseless motion. Forced into inaction, as he is now, the void reclaims us with a vengeance.

Surely he must be missing Marie in the worst way now, missing her in the farthest recesses of his proud, haunted soul, missing her with every sinew of his loveless taut body. I feel his gnawing hunger; I count on it.

To assuage the pain, he makes his daily trek down to the main post office on Rue Colbert to see if there is any word from Marie.

"Aron . . . Aron . . . Aron . . . here it is."

The clerk at the *poste restante* window hands him a pack of letters bound with a red cord. There are six in all, the first five postmarked Algiers and addressed from no. 36, Rue Lavoisier. He feels warm inside as he hurries out. The sixth letter, also from Algiers, bears neither a postmark nor a return address.

He goes back to Course Belsunce, claims his corner table at the café and starts sorting out the letters by dates. Once they are lined up in order, he opens the first one.

2 June 1962

Mon cher Robert,

 It's only two days since you've left but I've got to write you. When I came back into the house after you left, Papa threw a fit and started screaming and cussing—you, me, Mama, everybody. I've never seen him that bad before, if you can believe this. The things he said. I ran upstairs and locked myself up in my room, I was really scared. My mother must have said something because before you knew it he started beating on her and I ran back downstairs and jumped right in the middle. The neighbors came over too, the shame. We finally had him pinned down on the couch and called the doctor. He gave him a shot and put him to bed. He's a little better now, thank God. But he wouldn't talk, not to me, not to mother. The doctor says he'll get over it. Nerves, he says. But I don't know. He's not supposed to move, his heart is too weak, the doctor says. He needs time to regain his strength. Oh, Robert, I wish I could be with you right now! The doctor says maybe in a few weeks when he's better we can take him and leave. I don't think he'll get better though. Mother doesn't think so either, I know, even though she says nothing. I have to stick around and help her, Robert, I can't leave them now. So please wait for me, I'm coming as soon as I can, please, please wait. And write!
 Your loving Marie.

Much too early for her to have received his letter, he reasons. He opens the next one, dated June 8.

Robert Chéri,

 Everything is still the same. Papa in bed, still not talking. Mama is silent too. The place is like a morgue. I'm always waiting for a letter from you. Only the city is changing, a little bit every day. Though it's really more of the same. People are leaving the *quartier* by the hundreds every day now, in broad daylight, not only at night. They've stopped burning the houses too, they loot the stores instead. Not only those of people who've already left. Yesterday morning at ten they hit three banks at the same time, right here in Bab-el-Oued. People say it was your friends. The radio said General Salan was captured, is that true? Radio OAS is off the air most of the time. Last week they broadcast only once.

I try them every evening. Yesterday they broke through for about three, four minutes, warned against deserting. Said the fight goes on, whatever that means, nobody believes it any more. But I'm scared, Robert. I'm so glad you're out of them, they're becoming desperate. Please watch out, they'll do anything. And please, please write soon. Just a note will do, just to let me know you're safe. Please? And wait for me. Love, Marie.

She still hasn't received it. He opens her next letter, dated the following week. She should have received it by then.

Mon cher Robert,

Why aren't you writing? Are you all right? I'm so worried. I went down to the prefecture yesterday, that place where they fixed your papers, you know. I spent the whole morning there, they finally told me you're still in Marseilles. Are you all right, *chéri*? Please write soonest, please! Your loving Marie.

"*Cher Dieu,*" he hisses in frustration. She hasn't received his note, and, he reasons, something must be wrong with the delivery at her end. Not his side, since he has posted his letter from a public mailbox. His reasoning is of course flawless; it is at this end where we intercepted his note.

He quickly opens the next one, dated a week later.

Cher Robert,

I'm still in dark limbo, waiting to hear from you. It's terrible, all this waiting. I hope you're all right, I can only hope. Here it's still the same only a little bit worse every day. Papa is not mending. The doctor says he doesn't want to get well, that he's given up. Mama knows it must be true. I can't imagine how she can go on like this, but she does. The house is completely isolated now, all the neighbors are gone. I've tried to talk to her again, but she says she won't leave without Papa and he can't be moved the way he is. She says for me to go ahead and leave, but I won't, not without her. I wonder if he's going to die soon. I'm ashamed of myself having such crass thoughts. It's so hard waiting like this. The worst of it is not hearing from you. I wish you'd write, Robert, just to say that you're all right, just a word. Love, Marie.

She still hasn't received it and he assumes it must have gotten lost. Though of course it hasn't. I've got it right here with me, courtesy of our friends at the post office. I've read it, twice, just to make sure there's no clever trickery hidden in there. Seems straight enough, we might let her receive it. When the time is right. If it ever is. In the meantime, let them both squirm.

In mounting gloom he opens Marie's fifth letter, stamped Express. The one we would have pulled had the man at the post office done what he was supposed to. He did steam it open and reported the contents, but then let it go through anyway. Rules and regs. Someone will have to jiggle the fuckin' bureaucrat's chain, get his priorities straightened out for him.

Chéri, watch out!

They're looking for you! Last night two *types* stopped me at the gate, asked if I heard anything from you. I said I hadn't. Then one of them said I'd better not lie, that they knew where you are anyway, that all traitors are going to end up the same way. Before I pulled away and ran inside they tried to put the squeeze on me. They wanted money, said they're going to get you. Please be careful, Robert. They're awful! Please write. Your Marie.

That one was botched, badly, should have never happened that way. The organization is falling apart, time to put my foot down if I still can. Must have been those gorillas Martel brought in, I'll have to talk to him about this before he makes a real mess of everything. Not that I've got much pull with the guys any more, what with all of us hopping from one hideout to the next. I hardly see them between bank heists. Time to pull up stakes, cross to the other side.

In his frustration, he runs out to the *librairie* at the corner, buys an envelope, a notepad, and a stamp, and goes back to the café, where he sits down and writes.

"Dearest Marie," he jots down hurriedly, "I'm all right. I got all your letters. Please don't worry, I'm waiting for you, right here. So please keep writing even if you don't hear from me. I'm still here, I'm still yours. Just come soon. Love, R."

He goes to mail the letter at the corner, a futile gesture. It'll wind up next to its predecessor, right here in my breast pocket. When he comes back from the mailbox, he sits down and slowly opens the last, unmarked, letter. We have debated whether to send this one or not. I was not convinced, but what the hell, he needed a reminder. Or at least that is what I thought before Martel and his gorillas botched it in front of her house. By then, our letter had already been posted.

He reads slowly; it is only a short note written on a slip of paper in a hand he should not recognize. I dictated it myself; I am hardly a master of *belles lettres*.

"You can't escape us, so why bother?" my note says. "Sooner or later we'll catch up with you, one way or another. If you value the life of one dear to you, better stay right where you are; don't even think of leaving."

There is no signature, and none is needed. He folds the note and tears it into little shreds. The guy who watched him from across the rail, dressed like an unkempt Arab, said he was seething, said his hands were shaking.

"*Les salauds,*" is all he was heard say, "*les salauds . . .*" again and again and again. The air is oppressive, a humid August day, no discernible breeze. Maybe the note should have never been written, but then who knows.

"*Garçon!*" he calls.

The waiter saunters over and he pays and leaves. He must be furious, the guy said he left immediately and went straight home. I can see him lying on his back in his airless third-floor cell, sweating and cursing.

The following Thursday he stops by the prefecture to get his papers stamped. The gendarme downstairs sends him up to see the inspector. He goes to room 252, knocks and enters.

"Eh, Monsieur Aron," says the inspector. "This will only take a minute. Please sit down."

"Thanks."

They are facing each other, smiling cautiously.

"So, Monsieur Aron, what's news?"

"Nothing, Monsieur l'Inspecteur."

"Nothing at all?"

"Not a thing."

"Have you heard from your friends?"

"Friends?"

"Ex-friends, if you insist, the OAS."

"Should I expect to?"

"By now you should. Have you?"

"No."

"You sure?"

"Sure."

"No letters?"

"None."

"I just thought I'd check."

"You have."

The inspector clearly doesn't believe him.

"Interesting, don't you think?" he says, "I'm told there was a letter waiting for you at the *poste restante* today. I've been wondering."

"Your people must've forgot how to count, Monsieur l'Inspecteur," he tells him, "there were six."

"So I'm told. I mean one in particular."

"Oh?"

The inspector eyes him thoughtfully. As usual, each of them knows what the other thinks.

"Monsieur Aron," says the inspector, "all I'm trying to do is help you, I'm really trying. So long as you are here under our jurisdiction, you're mine. I wish you'd help. I really wish you would."

"You seem to know everything already, Monsieur l'Inspecteur," he tells him, "I'm not sure there's very much I could add."

The inspector shuffles through the papers on his desk. Had he been a pipe smoker, this would have been the time for him to tinker with his pipe tools.

"I don't know," he says. "What are your plans?"

"I haven't got any."

"We know you're in trouble. Would you let me help?"

"I'll think about it. I appreciate your concern, Monsieur l'Inspecteur."

"We're all trying, that's all we can do. I wish you'd make it easier on us, Monsieur Aron."

"I'll try, Monsieur l'Inspecteur."

"Be careful."

"Thanks, I will."

"Till Monday then."

"Monday."

*H*e is once again on Quai des Belges. It is noontime and the day promises to be a scorcher. The place is fairly reeking of dead and dying fish. Even the housewives are lethargic, bargaining with little of their habitual fury. No movement is discernible in the labyrinthine tangle of masts and rope. The entire Vieux Port seems to have sunk into deep slumber.

Then, further up Quai Rive Neuve, he sees a small crowd, about a hundred people, massing where the wharf meets the promenade. A squad of policemen are straining to keep them away from the low wooden fence that borders the Yacht Club. He has nothing to do, and so, slowly, cautiously, he edges closer in to have a better look. That is when he sees the seventy-foot sloop gliding serenely toward the dock. The gendarmes have thrown a rope across the quai, but the crowd is pressing against it. He joins in from behind as the yacht draws closer.

The crowd is heaving with excitement, straining the barrier. He turns and circles the main body from behind till he is at the left corner of the fence. Once there, he starts to plow his way toward the embattled policeman at the hub of the melee. He absorbs, without acknowledgment, a string of nasty remarks but keeps pushing on. A female voice curses him indignantly as his right elbow is shoved into what must be her well-padded ribs.

"Pardon, madame," he apologizes, but keeps going.

When he finally makes it to the very center, the yacht has reached its intended berth. He turns to look. He is pressed flat against the policeman's shoulder before he can finally catch the boat's name—*Jasmine III*. The crowd is crushing him and the gendarme to the fence.

"Monsieur!" the policeman admonishes him.

"Pardon, Monsieur l'Agent," he explains. "They're pushing me from behind. I'm doing my best."

"They're crazy," the gendarme says.

"Right," he agrees.

Soon the crowd is growing frantic.

"Here!"

"They're coming down . . ."

The cries come from behind him. He can see the plank being lowered down from the yacht. A small group appears on deck. A medium-built balding man with dark glasses is at their hub. A ravishing blonde is appended to his side, sheathed in a luminous crème evening gown. Five dark-clad goons form a tight circle around them.

"Say," he turns to the gendarme next to him, "who are they?"

"Who?"

"Them!"

"The Aba Khan," he tells him.

"And the lady?"

"Mademoiselle Duclos."

"The movie star?"

"You got it."

"Hot damn, that's right!" he says. "She sure looked familiar."

The serene oval face from countless magazines and cosmetic ads peers straight at him, alive and cool, from under an enormous straw hat of Twenties vintage.

"Still looks lovely."

"Doesn't she?" the gendarme agrees. "The lucky stiff, with his kind of money I could get Bardot . . ."

The rest of the gendarme's commentary is not all that flattering, having to do with Mlle Duclos's reputation which, if one were to believe him, is not altogether unblemished.

"That so?" he says, nodding. "How about him? That rich?"

"I wouldn't be standing here trying to keep low life like you from crashing his party if I only had a fraction of what he's got."

"How did he come by all that money?"

"Who knows?" The gendarme shrugs. "Probably born into it. The surest way, still."

Three of the bodyguards are climbing down now, followed by the man in dark glasses. As he steps onto the gangway, the man turns back to extend his arm to Mlle Duclos, who is gliding right behind him. She swishes graciously down the narrow plank.

"Hold it!"

The newsreel people and the paparazzi are on the pier, right in front. The man and the woman freeze, cameras click and buzz furiously. Then the couple, ensconced in their cocoon of bodyguards, mount the red-carpeted walk leading from the Yacht Club enclave to the curb. The newsreel people press closer in clicking-and-buzzing frenzy, the crowd is nearing hysteria.

"Pull back! Pull back!" The gendarmes admonish the crowd.

"Don't block the view!" shouts come back.

The small party makes its passage through a narrow pathway roped open in the middle of the crowd.

"Make room! Make room!" the gendarmes shout. They are helping the bodyguards split the crowd, plowing their way through. The prearranged passageway has by now collapsed, the ropes are pulled down to the pavement, where people are tripping on them, climbing over each other, screaming. The bodyguards muscle their way onward mercilessly, leaving a shrieking pandemonium in their wake.

When the little party passes by him, Robert catches a glimpse of the Aba Khan. The olive-complexioned face is heavy set, a chiseled, frozen mask. The dark glasses are opaque, impenetrable. The man moves slowly, serenely, unperturbed and seemingly oblivious to the pandemonium breaking all around him.

A minute later the small party is inside a black limousine that has materialized at the curb. The limousine then pulls off in a low roar, a huge American monster with tinted windshields. In another minute they round the corner and disappear into Rue Berteuil.

Later in the afternoon he buys the evening paper. On the front page, in the lower right corner, the picture is staring at him again—impassive bronze face shaded by the opaque dark glasses, the shining blonde angel towering over him, her luminescence fairly reflected in the squat man's bare olive pate. The two of them make the most improbable of pairs, but there they are, staring into the camera from the gangplank. The caption reads: "The Aba Khan in Marseilles."

The rest of the legend follows below:

His Holiness the Aba Khan, together with Mlle Duclos, who is currently vacationing with him at his villa on Cap Ferrat, has consented to join the Marchioness de V. for her annual charity ball, slated to take place tonight in Marseilles, for the benefit of North African refugees. His Holiness has been known in recent years to express grave concern for the growing plight of stateless refugees worldwide. His name has been repeatedly mentioned as candidate for the office of U.N. Commissioner on Refugees. He and Mlle Duclos, a well-known animal-rights activist whose name has been linked—some say intimately—with His Holiness' in recent months, are shown here as they debark from His Holiness' luxury yacht, the *Jasmine III*, earlier today at the Vieux Port.

The paper is resting on the table in front of him, His Holiness dead-panning the world from behind his dark glasses. He cannot help but wonder what is so holy about the squat, aging, sun-tanned playboy staring at him from the page. His curiosity is aroused and, with nothing better to do and the rest of the afternoon to kill, he makes his way to the public library on Place A. Carli. He has the place almost to himself; he wanders among the dusty stacks until he locates an encyclopedia. He looks up the entry for the Aba Khan. It makes for fascinating reading.

"The Aba Khan," it says, "absolute ruler and divine guardian of the principality of Andrabad in northern India, pop. 17 million, territory 260,000 sq. miles."

He skips over a few current statistics about the principality, coming back to: "Also considered supreme religious authority to his people, True Prophet, Sword of the Faith, Incarnate of the Living God on earth, Supreme Commander of the Host of the Faithful, who are sometime referred to as Aliites."

More titles follow. His Holiness, it soon becomes apparent, is as good at collecting epithets as a Soviet field marshal. What is more, the True Prophet seems to have gotten himself insured from all angles, leaving no stone unturned in his quest for the ultimate status.

He goes on reading:

> The Aba Khan dynasty established itself early in the eighteenth century during the convulsive upheavals that preceded the collapse of the Mogul Empire, as it was being overtaken by the recently consolidated British viceregal rule. Its beginning may be traced down to Ali the First, a Persian national of obscure extraction, a history of unfortunate entanglements with Persian Imperial law in Iran, and unusual suggestive powers acknowledged by friends and foes alike. He is said to have appeared in Andrabad on the first day of spring draped in the rays of the new sun. Consequently, he was proclaimed True God in the flesh.

Et incarnatus est. Now, he cannot help but think, there rides a dynasty with all the requisite gall if not the originality, a latter-day link in the long chain of desert-bred prophets spewed periodically out of the very same dusty soil, seizing destiny by its succulent balls and giving it an expert tweak. He feels nothing but grudging admiration, as he reads on.

> The dynasty had steadily expanded its sway, secular as well as religious, by maneuvering deftly between the retreating Moguls, the expanding British, and the local Hindu and tribal chieftains. Its present charter was negotiated with the Queen's Viceroy in 1863, following an abortive mutiny—some say British inspired—by tribal chieftains who came as close as taking the Prophet's fifth wife hostage. The uprising was

quelled with extreme ruthlessness after the sequestered consort committed suicide by throwing herself into the Royal snakepit. Her gravely discolored body was consequently enshrined next to the preserved remains of the dynasty's founder, where her martyrdom is acknowledged with yearly jeweled offerings by the faithful. The heads of the conspiring chieftains were presented on sharp stakes to the viceroy upon his return from a conveniently arranged inspection tour of the northeastern provinces.

A parade of the incumbent Sword of the Faith's less illustrious if equally hapless forbears is dutifully listed, the chronology of their accession to the Jewel Throne strongly intimating a penchant for abbreviated reign. He skips over more gruesome chronicles, picking up again with:

The current Aba Khan, the seventh Ali to accede to the throne, is reputed to be paid by his loyal subjects a yearly tribute consisting of the equivalent of his bodily weight in gold and precious stones. Male scions of the Aliite dynasty have been renowned for their excessive corporal heft and extravagant lifestyle, often electing to spend the bulk of their reign in the fleshpots and watering holes of decaying imperial Europe.

More details follow, sounding increasingly incongruous and far-fetched. The Aliite dynasty, it is apparent, has succeeded in pulling the supreme con, catapulting its ornate anachronism into the latter reaches of the twentieth century, not to mention the U.N. Commission on Refugees. The irony ought to cheer him up, but instead he finds himself growing depressed. The story is indeed absurd, he keeps reminding himself, a fairy tale, meaning nothing. But I know all he can see in that tale is the success story of a self-made man, an enterprising hustler, an outcast, a lousy outsider making good, beating the odds.

Which brings him back to his current predicament, back to Marie and to the growing ache he carries inside him like an unwanted child, back to wishing his haphazard life would finally sort itself out one way or another, because he is not sure anymore how long he can hold on without going stark raving mad. He may think he is already, but I know better. He is the most adept survivor I have known, a walking miracle of grit and ingenuity. I count on him to pull through, however downcast he may feel at the moment. Though I will probably have to cross over soon and take a closer look, just to make sure. One's got to protect one's investment.

*H*e goes back to the hotel and, with nothing better to do, takes a long nap. He gets up and washes, which makes him feel a bit better. So it is after dark when he leaves the hotel again, though not before digging the gun out of its hiding place and putting it in his coat pocket. He is half a block away from the hotel before he begins to feel somehow uneasy. He stops and turns back. Nothing seems to be moving. He resumes his walk, though now with frequent turns and twists. By the time he hits Cours Belsunce, he is almost sure he is being followed.

He knows he shouldn't stop now, so he plunges into the crowd in front of the cafés, makes it all the way to the last newsstand, which he circles; then he turns around and hurries back. At the next corner he makes a sharp left, cuts to the right through a narrow alley, jumps into the first dark doorway, crouches, and pulls out his gun.

He waits in there for what seems to be a small eternity, but hears nothing. Presently he peers out. The alley is deserted. He thinks he may have shaken them off. But of course, there may have been nobody following him, only his frayed imagination. He cannot know for sure; the guys have explicit orders to leave him some breathing room. No sense in spooking him unnecessarily.

Finally he leaves his shelter and slides cautiously along the wall. At the next corner he turns right, crosses Cours Belsunce at its deserted commercial end, and keeps walking toward the Old Port. He needs time to collect himself, to think. He keeps on moving.

He comes up to the waterfront and keeps to the northern pier. The air is growing cold now, a damp wind is blowing in from the south, over the water. He makes his way toward the old fort, leaving the bright cafés of Hotel de Ville behind. The breakers are savaging the batteries to the left, the wind's howl grows perceptibly stronger as he circles the fort. He makes it all the way to the bright lights of Quai de la Joliette, then turns and starts heading back.

He walks back slowly on the left side of the road, away from the water. There is a small, dilapidated movie theater on his side of the street, before the row of hotels begins. He is already past the theater when the ad catches his eye:

EDDIE CONSTANTINE IN A NEW RELEASE

He has not been to the movies in years—none of us have; movie theaters were the first terror targets in Algiers, first the FLN's and then ours. The government closed them all two years ago. He still knows, though, that there is no better place to kill a few hours in complete anonymity. The ticket is only 200 francs. He pays and makes his way inside. Our man, third in the relay that is tracking him this evening, follows him after a discreet interval.

The hall is small and narrow, the low ceiling almost oppressive. He feels his way slowly away from the door, along the back row toward the green-lighted exit sign. The seat squeaks under him as he lowers himself in; it keeps squeaking every time he shifts his weight. Once he gets used to the dark, he sees that the theater is almost empty. That suits him just fine; he hopes he can relax now and enjoy Eddie in his latest release.

The movie must be a bitter disappointment. To his horror, he is witnessing the terminal descent of an exalted hero of his—and my—youth. Flashy Eddie—magus with the ladies, fastest arm in town, debonair smoothy par excellence—finally, inexplicably, stumbling upon his comeuppance. Fast Eddie trapped in a low-budget production of unbearable drabness, surrounded by a gauche troupe of sleazy amateurs shuffling painfully across the set in front of a tremulous hand-held camera. All expensive trimmings gone, the adoring dames departed, a balding Eddie presiding over a drag-racing gang of grungy teenagers camped out in a deserted railroad terminal near the racetrack.

The humiliation proves almost too painful to bear. He watches the down-sized Eddie, stooped and obviously tired, going through the act flashing his brave crooked smile, taking it all like a good pro. Of the glamorous past only those two remain—the crooked smile, the fist faster than light. So much for the demise of an erstwhile God. He finds the experience near unbearable, as I would have if I had been there with him. Still, he sits through the ordeal stoically, simultaneously riveted and disgusted. I know it is a point of honor with him. If Eddie could take it, so can he. I can't help but approve.

Without waiting for the second feature to begin he gets up and turns to leave. Our guy is right behind him when, at the exit door, he sees him bumping into a woman. She too has apparently had her fill and like him is trying to beat a hasty retreat. She drops her purse and in the ensuing confusion he fetches it for her. Our guy maintains a discreet distance.

"Pardon, madame," he says.

"But no, no, it was my fault," she insists.

Her accent is strange and hard to peg. He hands the purse back to her. As they come out together on the pavement, he takes a closer look.

She is tall and well-dressed, about forty. Her eyes are blue and clear, her hair light brown, wavy. They walk together toward la Cannebiere.

"You're not from here," he says.

"Canada," she says. "Thanks again, it was my fault, the purse. Dark in there . . . Easy to spot my accent, huh?"

She sounds apologetic.

"Not at all," he reassures her. "Besides, I'm not from here either. How'd you like the movie?"

"I couldn't follow much of it," she admits, smiling at him.

"You're better off," he tells her. "Shall we cross?"

"I was going to."

"Let's then."

He takes her arm in his hand and they cross to the port side.

"Strange," she says.

"What?"

"You sound native to me."

"Not quite."

"Where are you from?"

"Algiers."

"Oh, isn't that the same thing?"

"Not anymore."

They are slowly following the low brick wall, over which they can look down into Old Port basin.

"It is a lovely night," she says.

"It is," he agrees.

"Why don't you invite me for a drink then?"

"I'd love to," he says. "Only thing is, I didn't bring any money."

She ponders.

"If you won't get insulted, I can pay," she offers.

"I don't know."

"Please? I hate to drink alone. Don't worry about the money, it's not mine either."

The way she says it suggests there is a story lurking behind.

"Whose is it then?" he asks.

"George's."

"Who's George?"

"We're traveling together. He's an old friend from back home."

"I see."

She looks at him briefly, then drops her eyes.

"It's not what you think."

"How do you know what I think?"

"I can tell. Shall we go?"

A drink could hurt neither of them, he reasons. He's got all the time in the world, he is not even sure he should go back to the hotel tonight, someone might be watching for him.

Someone indeed is, though the guys have strict orders to cool it. Strictly hands off, as long as they keep track of where he is. They are fast on their feet this time. I hear about the woman the very same night, good details. Sure is a pity about Eddie Constantine, used to be my hero too.

"I guess we could," he tells her.

They walk in silence for a while, slowly threading their way back to the center.

"About George," he says.

"Yes?"

"How come he lets a beautiful woman like you go out alone at night?"

"George?"

She is considering her words with care.

"He was tired," she says, "he likes his sleep."

"*Bon*," he tells her, "we'll drink to that."

She smiles, and seems peculiarly grateful.

He lets her lead the way to one of the tourist hotels on la Cannebiere. They make it to the bar and take a table. After they sit down, she squeezes a few bank notes into his palm.

"Thanks," he says.

"Thank *you*."

He takes a long look at her. In the yellow light, dim as it is, the wrinkles about her eyes show more prominently. Still, there is something childlike about her face, the clear blue eyes perhaps, the eager, self-effacing smile. He wonders.

"What's the matter?" she says.

"Nothing. What would you have?"

"Whiskey and soda."

The waiter is at his elbow, having materialized silently out of seeming nowhere.

"One whiskey and soda, one anisette," he tells him.

"*Oui*, monsieur."

The man floats him an appraising smirk as he departs to fill their order. His retreating shuffle is truly eloquent, insinuating an equal measure of servitude and condescension.

They wait. By way of making conversation, he asks her: "Where are you from, in Canada?"

"Montreal."

"Born there?"

"No. Born in Quebec City."

"The accent is from there?"

"Not anymore," she says. "Once you get to Montreal, you learn it doesn't pay to speak French, soon as you start looking for a job. They let you know real quick."

"I thought Montreal was kind of French?"

"I thought so too, till I got there."

"What are you doing in Marseilles?"

"Nothing, just visiting."

"Like it here?"

"I'm not sure. It all feels so strange."

"Like it better back home?"

"I'm not sure either. Back home where? I haven't been back to Quebec City in years."

"How about your family?"

"All gone. Besides, they wouldn't approve of me now. Never did then either. One reason I left."

The waiter brings their drinks over. She launches into hers eagerly, draining the glass in a few long gulps. He watches her, again wondering.

"Easy now," he tells her.

"Buy me another one?"

"What's the hurry?"

"Please?"

He hails the waiter over.

"Where do you live?" she asks.

He looks at her, but is not about to tell her.

"In a hotel," he finally says, "down near the station."

"Could we go and drink there? I don't like this place, they stare at you like you've done something, makes me feel cheap."

"Ignore them."

"Well, I'm not."

"I know," he assures her.

"Can we?" she persists.

"Not tonight."

"Why?"

"We can't."

She looks at him thoughtfully.

"You've got secrets," she observes.

"Doesn't everybody?"

"*Touché.*"

They are quiet for a moment, each pondering the other. The waiter is eyeing them from the bar. He seems in no hurry to bring them their drinks.

"Where were you going to spend the night then?" she asks.

"Walking around, I suppose, killing time. Haven't thought that far ahead."

She eyes him speculatively.

"It isn't *les flics*, is it?" she asks.

She seems intrigued at finding someone who is also in trouble, as he suspects she imagines she herself is.

"No," he tells her, "not them."

"Who then?"

"Someone else."

"Dark secret?"

"Nothing romantic."

"I read the papers," she says, "I'm not stupid. You want to come up to my room? We can drink there."

He pauses and tries to clear his head. It is not that he doesn't know what she is driving at—she hasn't been all that subtle. And even if she had been, he would have known. Now he is not sure how to handle it, so he decides to stall.

"How about George?"

"We've got separate rooms," she assures him. "Well, shall we go?"

There is a clear note of desperation woven into her voice. Is she offering to help him? Does she mean it? Her baby-blue eyes are set in a mature, intelligent, now tired face. He looks down.

"I don't know," he says.

"Please?"

"Just for a drink?"

"Sure."

"All right," he tells her. "Where to?"

"Nowhere," she says, "we're already there."

After collecting for the drinks, the waiter leans over the bar, his squint follows them as they pass into the hotel corridor. Robert looks the other way, trying to ignore the bastard's cool smirk, hoping the guy will drop dead. But of course he won't. Once they are out of sight, he will pick up the phone and make a discreet call. For the cause.

The small bedside bar in her room is well stocked.

"Make yourself comfortable," she says, "I won't be a minute. You can fix yourself a drink. Another whiskey and soda for me, okay?"

He busies himself with the drinks. There is a small ice chest built into the bar. She comes back barefoot and joins him at the couch. He hands her her drink and, once again, she drains it in a few thirsty gulps.

"That's good," she says.

"You got some stock in here."

"I hate drinking alone in the bar," she says, "they won't leave you be. The men all assume you're there for one thing. Gets tiresome, having to fend them off."

"Well, you don't have to worry about me," he tells her.

"I know. That's why I like you."

She gets up to replenish her drink. Before he knows it they match each other one for one and before long both bottles are half empty. They are both slumped on the floor now, leaning back on the couch. She keeps telling him about her life and he nods and then nods off. He remembers waking up periodically and taking sips out of a glass that is, mysteriously, always full.

She giggles and slides closer to him. They click their glasses in drunken camaraderie. Eventually he loses count and drifts off.

He wakes up with a start. He is in bed, under covers, undressed. The room is flooded with light and his head is throbbing. She's lying next to him in her nightgown. She wiggles.

"Ouch," he says. "Feels like someone's punched me out. How did you get me in bed?"

"Took some doing. Good thing I'm a big girl."

She is eyeing him speculatively, propped on one elbow. He becomes aware of her soft breast pressing at his shoulder.

"Did we . . . ?"

He pauses, embarrassed.

"I don't remember a thing," he confesses.

"Then I won't tell you."

"I doubt I was in any shape."

"You'll never know."

He looks at her. He is almost sure she is pulling his leg, and is somewhat relieved.

"Christ," he says, "you can drink."

She smiles at him; she seems pleased with herself.

"You're sweet," she says and touches his cheek with her finger. "Just lie down and let mama get you some ice."

"Never mind the ice, I'll be all right. I could use some coffee though."

"Coming. We've got our own contraption in the other room."

"What about what's his name?"
"George?"
"Yes."
"Oh." She giggles. "He's asleep."
"Still?"
It must be nine already.
"He loves to sleep."
"How long have you two been together?"
"We're not *together*," she corrects him. "He's just an old friend."
"Faithful."
"Oh, it's not that. Let's not talk about him."
"All right."
Her eyes are dead serious as they search his.

"I know what you think," she says. "You're being silly. You all are silly. George is not interested in women; he's just a friend."

"I don't know," he says, "you travel together like that?"

"Like what? He's been good to me, helped me quite a bit. I was a mess after the divorce. George handled it for me; he's my lawyer."

"I see."

"It's not what you think. He makes no demands."

"I bet."

"Don't."

She frowns. "I think I like you, don't make me change my mind. You're not like that, like the rest of them. I bet we can be good together. I bet I can be good to you."

"Hey, slow down," he tells her, "I haven't even told you my name."

"Does it matter? Besides, I looked it up in your wallet while you were asleep. Only thing is, how do I know it's really you?"

"You don't," he tells her, "that's the whole point."

She will know soon enough, not that it will do her much good. This is not in the cards, not by a long stretch. We can't afford to let her stick around, let the two of them get involved, happily or otherwise. She will distract him, get his mind off Marie, make a mess. Also, she's too unpredictable; we don't know a thing about her and we can't take chances, not at this point. So as soon as he leaves, she'll be getting a visit.

She is snuggling closer to him, and, to his embarrassment, he finds he is beginning to respond. Why should he expect otherwise?

"What time is it?" he asks.

"I don't know. Why? You have to go? Please don't. You can stay here."

"I'm not sure."

"You're running or something," she says.

"Or something."

"You don't need to tell me."

"You're better off not knowing."

"That bad?"

"Some."

"What are you doing in Marseilles?"

"Waiting."

"For what? For who?"

He tries to concentrate, and she is not making it easy. I expect he wonders if he should tell her about Marie.

"Nothing," he says, "nobody. Just waiting."

"Robert, right?" she says.

"Yes."

"You shouldn't stay here, Robert."

"Can't go home either."

She is studying him earnestly, her brow knitted. Her hand is sliding down his chest.

"Cut it out," he tells her.

She doesn't take offense. After a while she says, her voice barely audible: "You could come home with me."

"What?"

He heard her right, he knows he did.

"To Canada," she goes on, "to Montreal. I'll be good to you, I'll take care of you; you wouldn't have to do a thing. I've got a big house; you could come and go as you please."

My God, he thinks, she really means it. This is what I mean by unpredictable. She'll have to go.

"You're crazy," he tells her.

"No, I'm not."

He raises himself on his elbow, looking at her, trying to read some sense into her. He pulls the hair off her forehead. The baby-blue eyes are peering at him intently.

"What's your name?" he asks.

"Margot," she says, "to you, Margie."

"Margie," he tells her, "you're mad, plum crazy."

"No, I'm not," she says. "Here."

She slides off the bed quickly and crouches on the rug in front of him. Her eyes glow earnestly.

"I'll give you my address. You don't have to decide now, just think about it, wait till you need to. If you decide, then you know I've got a place for you. Okay?"

He can't believe his ears, but, somehow, it is clear she really means it. The whole idea sounds farfetched, a fantasy.

"You don't know a thing about me," he tells her.

"I know enough, all I need to," she says.

"Let's talk about it later."

"You are sweet."

"Don't be silly."

She leaves the room and he hears her hushed voice on the phone. Presently she comes back with a breakfast tray. They eat voraciously, facing each other in silence. She keeps looking at him, soon he is beginning to feel uncomfortable.

"How's what's his name this morning?"

"George? I just talked to him. He's fine."

"You sure he's not going to give you a hard time?"

"I can handle it."

They sip their coffee. Presently she asks: "You're going out now?"

"I have to."

"Wouldn't it be safer for you to just stay here?"

He pauses to think. If I know him, he will keep her in the dark, prevaricate, parry. Force of habit. Besides, he can't be sure she is not working for us.

"I'll have to go out sooner or later," he tells her. "I can't hide here forever. Besides, the whole thing might be my imagination."

"You think so?"

He can tell she is not sure. The woman is too smart for her own good.

"Don't worry. I'll be all right."

"Will you come back in the evening?"
"Would you like me to?"
"You know I would."
"All right, if I can."
"I'll wait for you, up here."
"Fine."
"Please take care of yourself."
"I will."
"You won't forget to come back?"
"Don't worry."
"I pressed your jacket for you, while you were asleep."

He takes it from her, feeling for the right-hand pocket to make sure the gun is still there.

"It's there," she says.

"Thanks. You're sweet."

"I know about such toys," she tells him.

Their parting is awkward. Neither of them fully trusts the other, which is just as well. For his sake, I wish I could play cupid, but under the circumstances I will have to settle for playing God.

He bends down to plant a perfunctory kiss on her cheek. Her face smells of baby powder and expensive perfume. He is still undecided whether he'll be back, though it is clear she wants him.

"*A bientôt*," he tells her.

"*A bientôt*."

Though of course, the matter is not up to the two of them anymore, if it ever was. The guys come up to pay her a visit; they're there within minutes. They are firm, maybe a bit too firm, and she tells them everything. Then they get her out, out of the hotel, out of Marseilles, no time wasted. They have been told to put the fear of God into her, just in case she has ideas. They make sure she understands we are not playing games.

She goes along all right; she doesn't have much of a choice. The guys are good at what they do: they show her a gun, a knife, threaten to tell George. That clinches it. We've had access to her file at the prefecture; we know where she comes from, just in case. We've got our friends in Quebec too, patriots, Frenchmen fighting for their country, like us.

* * *

As our men are busy with her, he goes back to the hotel by a circuitous route, stopping frequently to check for tails. Nobody is following him, no need to. He pauses down the street, away from the hotel, and watches the entrance. He doubles back and does the same from up the street. Nobody seems to be loitering around. Not that obviously, though his moves are observed and recorded from the apartment across the street.

Mme Lechar gives him the key without comment. He knows she knows he did not spend the night there, knows she must disapprove. The stairs are deserted; he goes up and into his room, takes a slow shower, and spends the rest of the day right there, lying on top of his bed. Early in the evening he decides to dash out for a minute to get some food before it gets real dark, thinking it would be safer. He pulls on some clothes and a pair of old sneakers left behind by the former tenant.

He is barely out of the hotel and making the first turn down the street, toward the cafés, before he catches on to being followed. As soon as he can, he makes his way into a busier street and forces himself to maintain a leisurely pace. He must be cussing himself for having again left the gun behind. The cafés would not be safe at this hour, he reasons. He keeps on walking.

Nearing the next corner, he dashes across against a red light, then keeps running. A car screeches, barely missing him. He rounds another corner, makes a left and another left, not looking back. Before he knows it, he is deep inside Petite Algérie, on Rue Chapellier.

You cannot mistake the crowd in Petite Algérie, nor the narrow streets, nor the smells of spicy food, nor the loud, undulating music that is pouring out through the open doors of the small coffee joints. He leans against the wall to catch his breath. As he closes his eyes, he must be caught off-guard by bittersweet nostalgia. I know how he must feel, though I did not grow up in the Casbah. Like being back home. The men stand together at narrow café doors, lean idly to the decrepit limestone walls, huddle in the street around low backgammon tables. The familiarity assails him, so must the danger. Whoever chased him there should have shown better sense. Sloppy work again, someone better remind those gorillas.

In a minute he pulls himself together. In a perverse way, he may think, this is a perfect place to hide. He turns around and walks into the first café. The owner, a bent old man wearing a woolen cap and a dirty apron, ambles forward to greet him.

"Welcome," he creaks, "Monsieur . . . ?"

His French is raw and tentative; he is obviously wondering whether to switch to Arabic and would at the first hint, given the dark complexion he sees in front of him.

"*Café et soumsoum, s'il vous plaît*," he tells the man, having managed only a slight hesitation. This instant choice of identity is far from trivial, and must be resolved right there on the spot.

"*Oui monsieur*, in a minute," the man says, retreating into the kitchen.

He sits down and stretches, trying to unwind. In ten minutes he gets his coffee, accompanied by a glass of cold water and the syrup-soaked pastry, all served by a fifteen-year-old boy who speaks lycée French, apparently the owner's son. The boy places his order in front of him, smiles engagingly, and threads his way back to the kitchen, from whence he is watched approvingly by the father.

He tears into the pastry with relish, then sips the coffee slowly, letting the music seep in. The male singer is praising his beloved, recounting the graphic details of her abundant physical attributes.

I asked him once, back in Algiers on a weekend pass, must have been right after we came back from Indochina, how he could stand this primitive sentimental drivel. He said I wouldn't understand, said you had to grow up with the guff. I suppose.

The male chorus joins in for the refrain—my love, my life, my light, my precious mare. The song rambles on and on, seemingly forever. The singer's depiction of his beloved gets bolder, more graphic, more intimate. A climax had better be reached soon, lest the singer, if not the chorus, burst a seam. He listens and sips his coffee, alternating it with sips of cold water.

In a while the owner comes over with a fresh cup: "Good, huh?"

"Terrific."

Their coffee is, indeed, if you could only pry it loose from this infernal music.

"More *soumsoum*?"

"No, thanks."

So as not to offend the man, he adds on the conventional praising gesture, drawing his fingers together to his mouth, then pulling them away as he smacks his lips. Evidently relieved, the man says: "Music—sugar, huh?"

"Music—sweet honey," he reassures him.

"*Aywah.*"

With consensus established, the man again retreats to the kitchen.

Later still he summons the boy and sends him to go out for cigarettes. When the boy comes back, he takes the pack from him and goes over to the kitchen to pay his bill.

"Monsieur happy?" the old man inquires.

"Very," he tells him, "good coffee, good *soumsoum*. Music..."

He repeats the requisite gesture.

The old man is very pleased. "Monsieur come back," he says. "Many thanks."

"I will."

He steps out, scans both sides briefly, then takes off. The guy who trails him must be breathing a sigh of relief.

He meanders up and down the narrow alleys for another hour. A feeling of peace slowly descends upon him, as if he is somehow back home. He listens to the familiar music, the rasping oud, the uneven rhythms, wafts of Arabic conversation. He eavesdrops on curses, spies on hushed transactions, intercepts sly grins. He keeps following the crowded narrow streets until sunset, hoping he looks sufficiently like everyone else.

When he comes out on Rue Colbert, the afternoon in its entirety has become somehow remote. He strolls leisurely up the boulevard, dragging his feet and not thinking. That is when he notices the gendarme with the huge dog, on the sidewalk smack in front of him. The dog's mouth is muzzled. It is an imposing Great Dane. He flashes a bright smile at the dog, then at the gendarme. Bad move, must have been the goddamn music. But it is too late.

"Your papers, monsieur," says the man.

"Beg your pardon?"

He is not quite there yet.

"Your papers."

He plunges his hand into his coat pocket. That sobers him up.

"I'm sorry, Monsieur l'Agent," he says.

"Yes?"

"I left them at home. I live just around the corner, Rue du Coq . . ."

"Come with me."

"But, Monsieur l'Agent . . ."

His protestations are weak, he knows he has no valid excuse.

"Stay right where you are."

The gendarme tugs briefly on the dog's leather leash. The dog rises, comes all the way to Robert, and seats himself at his feet. His razor-thin trimmed ears are propped at attention, dark eyes alert. It makes no sound.

He looks down at the dog, who is watching him attentively. No use. He shrugs and turns back to the gendarme.

"All right."

In five minutes, a blue paddywagon pulls over to the curb. Another gendarme hops out and walks toward them.

"Got another one?"

"Yes."

"What's with him?"

"*Sans papiers.*"

"*Eh bien.* Throw him in."

"Where are you guys taking me?" he asks them.

"To the station," says the one with the dog as he herds him inside.

In the back of the narrow wagon he finds himself crammed together with eight others, all men—five Arabs, two blacks, one Indochinese. The agent with the dog takes a seat next to him, near the door.

The dog is sprawled across the back. The man on his left smells of sweat and dust, garlic, and cheap brandy. In ten minutes the wagon stops. The back door is thrown open and the agent and his Great Dane alight first.

"Get out," the men are told.

They are a sorry, dispirited bunch as they clamber out of the wagon. Three patrolmen march them through a narrow door into the old stone building of the Hotel de Ville police station. Once inside the processing room, they are lined up against the bare wall under a harsh neon light. He is the last in line. The sergeant at the desk surveys them dourly, addressing himself to the agent with the dog.

"What've you got there?"

"*Sans papiers.*"

"All of them?"

"Yes."

"Well. Get them moving."

One by one, the men are taken to the desk, their pockets are emptied, and they are subjected to a cursory body search for hidden weapons. The routine is invariable.

"Name?"

"Huh . . . ?"

"Your name?"

"Huh . . . ?"

"*Merde*. Take him to number seven."

No one protests. These men have been through the grinder before. None speaks French, and the procedure is always the same. The guy who reports to us says they couldn't tell him from the rest, took him for just another dirty Arab.

In ten minutes he is the only one left, having arrived at the head of the line. Two policemen march him to the desk, turn his pockets out, and pile the loose change on the desk in front of the sergeant, who apparently expects no departure from the norm.

"Name?"

"Robert Aron."

The sergeant looks up.

"Nationality?"

"French."

"Where are you from?"

"I was born in Algiers."

"*Pieds noirs.*"

He shrugs. We all hate the name when it comes from others, but use it with grudging pride among ourselves. Under the circumstances, he doesn't protest. The sergeant seems disappointed.

"Where's your passport?"

"Back at the hotel."

"Where's that?"

"Hotel du Coq, Rue du Coq."

"Can you prove it?"

"I've got all my papers there."

The sergeant eyes him knowingly.

"*Bien*," he says, "number . . ."

"Just a moment, sergeant."

"Just a moment what?"

"Why don't you call the proprietress and ask her? Her name is Madame Lechar. She's home; she'll get you the number off my passport. She's got my residency forms too."

"Impossible."

"Why?"

"You're not supposed to ask questions here."

"But . . ."

"That's enough. Number seven."

He is reluctant, but it is hard to blame him for seeing no other alternative. He is damned if he is going to spend time in the can, not with the clientele he is with.

"In that case," he tells the sergeant, "you better call Inspector Mariceau at the prefecture and tell him you've got me locked up. He might be interested to know."

An interesting gambit, a shot in the dark, just like him. Still, it does the job. The sergeant is caught off-guard; he eyes Robert with undisguised resentment. But Robert's got his attention.

"You work for him?"

"Call him and ask."

Slick move. The sergeant stalls.

"We can't do that."

"Fine, if you want to take the responsibility."

The sergeant shuffles the papers in front of him. The others in the room are watching now, keeping a straight face. They know he is damned if he does and damned if he doesn't, and are not all that sympathetic.

"Hey you," the sergeant barks at one of them, "go get Inspector Algazi."

The man departs in a rush. He reappears a minute later followed by a short man, dark and balding, in crisp inspector's uniform.

"What is it?"

The inspector barely bothers to disguise his scorn as he addresses the sergeant.

"Him," the sergeant points.

"What about him?"

"*Sans papiers.*"

"What the fuck do you call me for? Pitch him in."

The sergeant beckons to the inspector, who moves closer with apparent distaste. The sergeant points to the papers on the desk and starts to whisper. The inspector listens, his face blank. Finally he takes the sheet of paper from the sergeant and turns around.

"Robert Aron, that you?"

"Yes."

"From Algeria?"

"Yes."

"How long've you been in Marseilles?"

"A month."

"What are you doing here?"

"I live here."

"Where do you work?"

"I'm not working at the moment."

"What happened to your passport?"

"It's in the hotel, Hotel du Coq, Rue du Coq. Madame Lechar will—"

The inspector cuts him short: "The law says you've got to keep it on you at all times. The law says everybody's got to."

"I know, Monsieur l'Inspecteur," he tells him. "I went out for just a minute to grab something to eat—"

"The law is the law," the inspector lectures him. "Even when you come from Algeria. Even if you have friends at the prefecture."

"But—"

"Shut up. And for your own good, stop trying to impress us with your connections at the prefecture. You understand?"

"Yes sir."

"Good. Now, can you prove your identity?"

"Easy," he tells him, "you call the hotel and ask for Madame Lechar; she's the owner. I've been there for over a month. She's got my passport and residency forms in her file."

Inspector Algazi turns to the sergeant: "Ring them up and check out his story."

He turns back: "It had better check out," he says. "Not that it's going to help you all that much. There's no excuse for breaking the law."

He turns to one of the listening gendarmes: "*Et toi*, march the prisoner to my office."

Then, back to the sergeant: "I'll interrogate him there."

A deft move, that. The inspector no doubt despises the sergeant as much as the sergeant despises him. His room is not exactly soundproof, though no one has bothered to tell him.

Robert is marched out in front of the inspector, through an inner door, then along a narrow corridor, finally into a cluttered small office. The inspector dismisses the gendarme and closes the door behind him. The two of them now wait in silence, finally broken by the inspector.

"Sit down."

He gestures toward a metal chair, then walks around the heavy metal desk and lowers himself into an upholstered armchair.

They eye each other. Finally the inspector speaks: "Robert Aron . . . *un nom israélite, n'est ce pas?*"

"Yes."

"The men in front, the sergeant, they know that too. It's not doing you much good with them, you know. You should have a little more sense than to get mixed up in a stupid idiocy like this. Where the fuck did you leave your brain? On file back in the hotel with your papers?"

All he can do is blush and keep quiet. Which seems to be what is expected of him.

"Listen," the inspector resumes, "you give those goddamn anti-Semites out there a chance to hit you, what do you expect them to do, say no, thank you? Shit, you don't have to ask them twice. Believe me, I've got to deal with them every fuckin' day, *les salauds!*"

The phone on the inspector's desk begins to ring, he snatches it angrily.

"Algazi!" he barks into it. Then a bit more subdued, "Huh . . . uh-huh . . . I see. Thank you, sergeant."

The inspector replaces the receiver and turns to face him.

"The woman at the hotel corroborates your story, Monsieur Aron, so at least we know you didn't lie. This still doesn't make you less of an idiot, which is what you've been all along. You understand? Now, what's the nonsense about the prefecture and Inspector Mariceau? You working for them?"

He tries to keep it vague at first, though not with much hope: "I report to him."

"What about?"

He shrugs.

"I'm under supervision."

The inspector's eyes measure him briefly.

"You were an activist down there?"

"You might say that."

"I see."

The inspector's voice seems to have changed timbre, for the first time imparting a modicum of respect.

"I see," he says. "Yes, I think I can see that. I was born down there myself. Constantine. Ever been there?"

"Once."

"Used to be quite a place. All gone now, just about. I never went back after the war. You from Algiers?"

"Yes."

"Beautiful, the city . . . the best."

"Yes, the best . . . Not much left of it either."

For a while the two of them seem lost in their private reveries. We have checked out Algazi, routine, earlier on. For a while he sounded like a good prospect, a sympathizer. Turns out to be unpredictable. Can't tell which way such guys will hop. They say he is not a tame acolyte of *le General* either. Civil service ever since the war. Like the rest of them up here plays it close to his vest, keeps his face clean, stickler for procedure. Though God only knows he hasn't got much of a career ahead of him without some godfather upstairs, being one of *them*. Pity, we could have used him.

Deep musings seem to have consumed the inspector. Robert waits patiently. Presently the inspector says: "You guys have sure done a number down there." His voice is almost inaudible. "All of you, together. Their side, yours, ours. Whoever you all are . . . "

The inspector's tan, sinewy fingers are scratching absently at his balding scalp. It would have been useless trying to turn him our way. You have to be able to tell the difference between *them* and *us*. This is where I worry most about Robert, who agrees: "We sure have."

"Bloody waste."

They are both quiet again. The inspector finally pulls himself together: "Monsieur Aron," he says, "you've acted like a fool, but I'm letting you get away with it this time. We need to help one another; the fuckin' *goyím* will never bother, believe you me. Now, you let me handle the show out there."

He nods toward the door.

"And be sure not to come back here. I don't think I can pull this for you more than once. So don't make me regret it. They're watching."

He knows the man is right, and is no doubt ashamed to have imposed on him. He ought to appreciate how lucky he is for having landed in Algazi's precinct. They stick together like glue, *les Juives*, tighter than bedbugs, take care of each other, like family. I wish our guys were the same, instead of fucking you over the minute you turned your back on them. The worst thing about this whole mess is I can't afford to sleep.

"Merci, Monsieur l'Inspecteur," he tells him.

"Never mind," the inspector says, "I'm not sure you deserve it. But then, blood is thicker . . . "

He shrugs and flashes a brief smile.

In the presence of the sergeant and his men out front, Inspector Algazi says: "Sergeant, the prisoner's file. I'll take him to Central personally; they'll teach him a lesson or two down there, him and his friends from the prefecture. Throw him in the car."

"Oui, Monsieur l'Inspecteur."

The sergeant hands the inspector a sheaf of papers and the car keys.

"Would you like to take an escort?" he asks.

"No."

The inspector turns and pushes Robert toward the door.

"Get going."

He sits alone in the secured back seat, bobbing and swaying as the inspector tears through the deserted streets. In ten minutes they are in front of the hotel. The inspector comes around and opens the back door: "Here you go."

They stand together on the cobblestone walk.

"Want a cigarette?" the inspector offers.

"Thanks, no. What time is it?"

"Half past ten."

"Sure gets dark fast up here."

"Not like back home, eh?"

"Is anything ever?"

The inspector sighs. "Got a point there."

"Thanks again."

"Forget it. Take care. I don't want to see you back at the station."

"Don't worry, you won't."

"Good luck."

Then, as he turns to walk back around the car, the inspector pauses: "*C'est dommage, l'Algérie.*"

"*Oui, c'est dommage.*"

*H*e knows it was a close call, he must have been chastising himself as they drove back. How many more before his luck runs out? He is not the only one who worries, I worry too. I worry even more when his next move is reported, a move that smacks of irrationality. I had expected him to call the prefecture perhaps, but when he stops at a public phone on la Cannebiere, his call is to the switchboard of Hotel St. Denis.

"Hotel Saint Denis."

"Hello, may I speak to Margot . . ."

He stops, having realized he doesn't know her full name.

"Yes?"

"Could you give me room three thirty-seven please?"

"Very well . . . One moment, sir . . ."

He waits. He is not sure what exactly he should tell her. A minute passes by. Then the voice comes back on line: "Room three thirty-seven is unoccupied at the moment, sir."

"But . . . just a moment, there's a Canadian lady staying there, isn't there?"

"Monsieur and madame left this afternoon," says the voice.

Does he detect a note of glee? Probably his imagination.

"Left?" he echoes. "But how?"

"By taxi, sir. To the airport. At five o'clock."

"Did she leave any message?"

"I'm afraid not, monsieur."

"Did she say where they were going?"

"I'm afraid not, monsieur."

"I see . . . thanks."

"*Je vous en prie, monsieur.*"

For once, the guys did what they were supposed to, no fuck-ups; she cleared out while he was having his misunderstanding with Algazi, sent packing back to Montreal with a stern warning and that weasel of a man, the stuffed shirt in the adjacent room who sounded at first like he was going to throw a fit, said he knew some big-wigs in the mayor's office, but who came back to his senses as soon as the guys showed him some gunmetal.

A close call, too close for comfort. The guys in Marseilles keep blowing it and I am too far away to keep them in line. The way they described her first, I thought she might bloom into an asset. A chance encounter, play her real subtle, make it sound natural. But there was no way to keep control. Right off the bat she starts working her own side deal. Fuckin' bitch had to go, another goddamn freelancer, and a lush to boot. Can't trust them. Can't trust anybody, for that matter.

One good thing came out of it though. It made me see the obvious, what had been staring me in the face for days, ever since the old butcher Laforge up and croaked. We have been holding the girl's letter at this end, where she tells Robert about it, tells him she can leave now, tells him she and her mama've got their papers, are just waiting for their place on a boat.

I have been reading and rereading this letter, trying to make up my mind. Now it is made up for me, thanks to the Canadian tramp. He has become desperate; we better rush the girl across right away, let him see her, before he forgets what she looks like, forgets how much he really loved her, forgets the color of her eyes in mid-ecstasy, the smell of her lush hair in his face, the smooth silk of her young thighs hugging his hips, the rasping slide of her dusky grove. She has been my main lever all along, only I've pulled on her the wrong way. Time to up the ante.

She and her mother are on their way, with Martel as their chaperon. We're working on an apartment for them in a resettlement block north of town. I will be crossing over next.

Things have collapsed here, total chaos, nothing can be done anymore, nobody left to do it, just the smoking ruins. The stinking Arabs can have those. I will go across and bang some heads together, knock some sense into those pea brains in Marseilles before they fuck us all up the way they have down here. The colonels say to go ahead, pick your own time. I think I better.

*T*he phone call is cryptic, a male voice with no regional trace.

"Monsieur Aron?"

"Yes?"

He is groggy, having overslept after the previous day's misadventure.

"There's someone waiting for you, Hotel Saint Denis, room three thirty-seven."

"What?!"

Is someone playing a trick on him? Is Margot back? He can't believe it. Perfect.

"Better come," says the voice. Then a click disconnects him.

He grabs some clothes, splashes water on his face, and gallops downstairs. Whoever came up with the idea was a genius, just the right dash of plausibility, plus we had plenty of time to wire the whole place, clear up the room next door for the chaperons, three guys around the clock as waiters, one chambermaid. The smart-ass desk clerk has been leaned on real hard, knows his lines by heart.

He rushes in and heads for the stairs, the clerk has to stop him.

"Monsieur is looking for someone?"

He retraces his steps.

"Room three thirty-seven," he says, "I'm expected."

"One moment, monsieur."

The clerk dials slowly as Robert watches. Our man inside the room picks up the phone.

"You've got a visitor."

"Send him up."

He takes the steps up two at a time. When he reaches the door the chambermaid is fussing with laundry bags across the hall. She smiles at him shyly; he ignores her and opens the door without knocking.

The room is dark, heavy curtains drawn to keep the bright noon sun out. He stops. Is this a trap? he thinks, have they finally got him? His hand shoots belatedly for the gun in the back of his waistband. He draws and crouches, expecting the worst. Then he hears her voice: "*Chéri?*"

Before he knows it, before he has a chance to make sense, standing there in total incredulity watching the slim shadow darting at him, she is in his arms, her wet lips are all over his face, her fingers locked at the nape of his neck, his own starved hands mauling her cotton dress.

"My God!" is all he can say.

*I*t happened so fast," she says.

She is nestled in the crook of his arm, her auburn hair all over the pillow, her eyes wet with the tears of their crashing, desperate, endless orgasm. Her breathing has calmed down a trifle. She is holding tight to his other hand, kneading his fingers absently, compulsively.

"Papa died in his sleep. You didn't get my letter?"

"What letter?"

"I wrote you the day after he died."

"When was that?"

"A week ago."

"Never got it."

"I posted it at the port when I went to get our repatriation papers."

No reason he should be surprised. Posting the letter at the port is a trick we had expected.

"I see," he says.

"They said there was a long list, but then the adjutant's office called the next morning, said they could give us passage on the next boat, something about priority for widows and orphans . . . We hardly had any time to pack, not that they let you take that much with you—"

"But where's your mother?"

His critical faculties are beginning to come back. I have labored mightily to make the story plausible; she certainly suspects nothing, Martel for once kept out of sight on the boat. Still, it is a tough one to pull off.

"She's at the apartment, another stroke of luck."

"But how did you come here, to the Saint Denis?"

To this room is what he really wants to know but has enough sense to keep to himself. It could hardly be a coincidence, but he couldn't tell her that without explaining the Canadian bitch. And the next thing she says mucks things up further: "The nice sergeant from the prefecture was there to meet us at the boat," she explains. "He told us they had an apartment for us, took us out there . . . Then this morning he came back for me, brought me over here, said you were coming . . . "

Even trickier, that part. He might smell a king-size rat, but whose rat? She ought to make it sound believable, sweet innocence and all, thighs smeared with warm juices. He should suspect a set-up; the room is too much of a coincidence, that was the whole point. But he has no way of telling whose set-up. Could just as well be his inspector; he's got no way of knowing and will not come right out and ask. And the guy who picked them up is a sergeant at the prefecture, another bureau though, but legit.

"Where's the apartment?"

"On the outskirts somewhere, I'm not sure I can find it. A whole bunch of blocks full of people from back home. The sergeant will know. He left his number."

"He did?"

He is on edge, ought to be. But he is also famished, has been pining for her, driven half mad. So it doesn't take her long to pull him back down to where he can't resist, and before you know it they are at it again, thrashing and heaving, and will consume the rest of the afternoon with their rites of reunion.

My old friend is as predictable as he is starved, and she needs no prodding; she sucks him dry and goes for more, then more.

Which is just as well. The more he gets of her, the more he'll remember, the more he'll know what there was to miss when we yank them apart next. Which, as much as I regret his pain, we must, if he is ever to rejoin us.

I rehearsed them in advance ad nauseam, just to make sure they don't blow it this time. Just a pair of local *mecs*, never been to war, dedicated and ignorant; the kind we have to put up with now. They were told to be polite but firm. They are right behind him when he goes out for cigarettes; he never has a chance.

It is late afternoon; he has to cross over to the corner and walk down Rue Petit Jean where the whores are at their battle stations, standing languid and limp at the doors of their hotels. Their blandishments are strictly pro form, they have long tagged him as a non-buyer: "*Chéri, allons chez moi . . .*"

"Want some candy, lover?"

"Where have you been all these years, *mon chou*?"

They giggle in the slow, lazy way they do when the day is just too hot to try hard. Though he knows they are not beyond flipping an early trick if a randy stray john turns up. He rushes past them impatiently, eager to go back to his sugar in the St. Denis, without responding. They know him well from sight and don't really expect his business.

He is drowsy with lovemaking, which is a bonus for the guys behind him, since we know he is packing his gun, tucks it into the back of his belt; I have made sure the guys know.

From where I am ensconced, deep in the shadow of a doorway and up five steps from the narrow landing, I can see nothing. But for once it all goes as planned.

The man's voice comes directly from behind. It is precise and low key: "Pull your hands up slowly and clasp them behind your neck . . . natural like . . . easy. *Don't* look back."

He does, as I had warned them, make as if to turn back. The voice behind him is low, level and strict, one he doesn't recognize. He slows down to a stop and as his left slowly raises up, his right hand slides behind him toward his belt.

"Keep moving," the voice says, "and pull that hand from behind you, quick! No tricks, you're covered."

He pulls both his hands up in tandem and clasps them behind his neck.

"Much better," the voice observes. "Keep moving. The next corner you'll make a left turn, not before I tell you. Don't rush it, slow and easy; it's a hot day and you're just taking a walk . . . Don't look back."

He can hear the footsteps following from behind, he estimates the guy is not more than five yards behind. Must have come out of a doorway. Far enough to disengage if the gendarmes show up, not far enough for him to make a dash for it. I have set it that way; we have rehearsed it to precision. I hate sloppiness.

He keeps walking, hesitating as he comes toward the next corner on the left. The sidewalk is too narrow at that point; he has to step off to the cobblestone. He is desperately looking for a break, his one chance.

"Now turn," says the voice behind him.

He can tell the guy has moved out too, to compensate for the blind spot at the corner. Damn. He turns left into a narrow alley.

"Good."

There is a second man, there must be one, somewhere behind. He can hear the extra set of steps now, just barely, synchronizing with the rhythm of the first. These guys are pros, he can tell. Still, he is looking for his chance.

"The next corner turn left again," the voice tells him. "When I tell you, not before. You're doing well so far, don't blow it."

Two men are walking toward them in the alley, two bums, lean and disheveled, swaying from their first round of booze. He wonders briefly if they are part of it. Good thinking, but one way or another they offer him no real chance. The voice behind warns: "Drop your left hand. Scratch your head with the other one. Act natural, no talk."

The two bums trudge by in silence; if they have noticed anything, they are wise enough to keep it to themselves.

He is looking down at the pavement, still waiting for his chance. Sooner or later, he assumes, they will give him enough of an opening. I have warned them, a little crack is all he needs.

"Pull your hands up higher," the voice behind him says. "That's better. Clasp your fingers tight. That's the way."

The narrow entrance to a dead-end passageway is opening to the left just ahead of him. The voice instructs him: "Turn left now. Slow down."

The cul-de-sac is barely wide enough for two people walking abreast. The far end is blocked with a high brick wall. They have advanced into deep shadow now. Whatever doors that might open into the alley are locked; no doubt barred from the inside.

As they approach in the almost total silence now surrounding them, he ought to see the empty garbage cans rolled on the ground next to the wall. I tossed them; adds a touch. The steps of the other guy cannot be heard anymore; he knows the drill just as well as I do; someone has to stand guard at the mouth of the alley.

The voice behind him is very quiet now as it says: "Stop right there. Good. Now put your hands to the wall. Higher. Keep them there. Don't move."

He does as he is told, leaning over an overturned garbage can out of which emanate ripe smells. The old bricks must feel damp and cool under his fingers. The cul-de-sac is utterly silent, except for the brief intrusion of the creak of rusty door hinges. Then a hand reaches forward and begins to pat him methodically about the waist, first his pockets, then slowly following his belt till it reaches the gun in the back and pulls it out of his waistband. A pause, then the hand returns to feel under his arms and down his legs.

I am watching the proceedings now from the doorway, as the man who brought him in, a local I've met this morning, instructs him: "Close your eyes tight now and put your hands behind your neck. Now turn around, real slow. Sit down."

He does as he is told, he may seem resigned but I know he is still looking for his break. He will get none.

I gesture to the local to join his partner at the corner. They will let me know if anyone approaches. The people who own the apartment are out for the afternoon and the front opens to a street that is not directly connected to the back alley. The place has been chosen with care.

I step out. He looks small, crouching there near the wall. I can't see his face clearly, the shade is too deep. All I can see is his eyes. They are wide open.

"*C'est toi,*" is all he says.

"Yes, it's me."

I sit on the doorstep, facing him. I need not display my gun. He knows where I carry it and he knows how I move. By the same token, I need not remind him to keep his hands where they are. We spent days interrogating prisoners together, first in Indochina, later in Kabylia, later still in Algiers. There is little he does that will surprise me. And vice versa. Though I still don't know what he thinks.

As my eyes adjust further to the shades around his face, I see that he has grown thinner. His hair is longer and is worn somewhat wild. His eyes seem larger, as they are fixed on me. We watch each other in silence, biding our time.

"*Bon,*" I tell him. "How've you been?"

"Fine."

"Been a while, eh?"

"Seems so."

"Surprise, eh?"

"If you say so."

"I'd expected you to put up a fight."

"You got me on an off day."

I know the reason for his carelessness, of course, but am in no hurry to say so.

"Must have," I agree.

We both lapse into silence. This will require some delicacy, not my strongest suit, though I am learning.

"Got our letter?" I ask him.

"I did. Not one of your best efforts."

"We were pressed."

"Not much of an excuse. You didn't bother her again, did you?"

His voice has an edge to it, which is understandable. He knows about that clumsy business. Interesting though, he is not owning up to having just seen her. Which could mean only one thing—he has bought the story about the prefecture; he hasn't yet connected it to us. It is not every day you pull a fast one on an old friend.

"No," I hasten to reassure him. "Sorry about that scene. The boys went beyond their instructions."

"Some gorillas you got there."

"Can't be picky."

"Whatever."

He must expect me to tell him more about her now, but I won't. The guys at the St. Denis have their instructions. All in good time.

He finally says: "You're out for good, I take it?"

"Yes."

"If it's about the money," he says, "forget it. There's little of it left."

"Never mind the money," I tell him. "We've got plenty and the banks this side are loaded, haven't you noticed?"

He shrugs, by which I suppose he means he has no direct knowledge of that.

"No," I assure him, "it's not the money, though some of the guys are still sore about it. Me, I've sort of figured you'd have eaten your way through it by now. Forget the money."

"What then?"

He is on edge, not exactly surprising, what with all the spooking and Marie back at the St. Denis. I don't like to see him down. He is not much use this way.

"You got her letters?" I ask, to make conversation.

"I did."

"Anything I should know about?"

"Leave her out of this, Jojo."

"Can't, she's part of it as long as you are. No fool, that girl. I figured she'd be writing. Still, she's there. And you're here."

He says nothing and I go along, no need to tip my hand, yet.

"You're here too Jojo. Not much later either."

"That's not the same," I remind him. "I'm under orders."

"Whose orders?"

"Headquarters."

"I thought *les barbouzes* got them ages ago."

I see no harm in conceding his point.

"They did. In the end it was down to just me."

"Good for you then. You give the orders, you obey."

We eye each other like a pair of tired boxers with nobody to egg us on. He sounds bitter. We have never been much for big talk, the two of us, except for those rare spurts. I wonder if she ever got him talking, maybe earlier at the hotel. I will find out soon.

Some girls have this way with a quiet guy. Not that I will ever know. My women put out and put up; they ask nothing, like the dumb, good *pieds noirs* they are.

I look at him and shake my head.

"Place must agree with you, Roberto," I tell him. "You're looking good."

"You don't look half bad yourself, Jojo. How's the old haunts?"

"Gone to the dogs," I tell him.

"Congratulations."

"No need to be sarcastic, you did your share. You were quite good at it."

"That was a long time ago, Jojo."

"A month?"

"Feels like eternity."

"Doesn't it? I hear you go to the prefecture. Twice a week, is it?"

"You hear right. I am supposed to. They've got a big dossier on me, probably on you too."

"I know," I tell him. "We've got copies. They asked you to snitch?"

"They did. I refused."

"I know, so far. You haven't told them about our letter. I've been wondering."

"They knew about it already."

"Not from you though."

He shrugs, he must consider it a trivial matter. Here is where it gets tricky. It is not enough that we have the girl. As much as he cares for her, you can bait him only so far. Gets to be counterproductive beyond a point. He is one of those guys who need to believe. As smart as he is, he's still like his father, a sucker for a cause.

And so, I am treading on thin ice here. I have to gamble on him. Which is why I am anxious to point out he hasn't really left the OAS, that he is, the last month notwithstanding, still one of us.

"You didn't run to them for protection when we started following you," I remind him. "And don't tell me you didn't notice. You gave them the slip twice."

"Wasn't difficult."

"Never mind, these locals are amateurs. You didn't tell them about the letter."

"None of their business."

"That's not how they see it. I know you won't tell them about today."

"You got Marie," he reminds me.

Again, I pass: "Is it really just her?"

"What else?"

"Isn't it obvious?"

"You tell me."

So I lay it on him, straight out, as simple as I can put it, and I only hope I am doing the right thing. Because it is going to be messy if I am not.

"You're still one of us," I tell him. "You can't escape that. You really didn't quit. You just left a bit earlier than the rest of us, had a misunderstanding, that's all. We're all back together now. And this is where *l'Algérie Française* is, right here."

He shakes his head slowly and I know what he must be thinking. I feel awkward about it too, preaching to him. Especially since it has always been him who's done the preaching, with me just going along. I could point this out to him but won't. No need to push.

"You got it all wrong, Jojo," he says.

But I don't hear a great conviction there.

"You've been on the mainland long enough, Roberto," I tell him. "You've seen how they treat you here. How they treat all of us. You won't be able to make your peace with them; they won't let you; you'll always be *sale pieds noirs*."

"Yes," he says. "*Juif* too, don't forget."

He is off on his tangent again, the one I find so hard to swallow. It has always been hard to believe he is one of *them*. The few I have known beside him were different, obvious. You wouldn't find any of them in the Legion. Or Indochina, or Kabylia. As far as I can see, this whole *Juif* thing is just his imagination. Especially if what they say is true about your mother having to be one in order for you to be one.

His mother wasn't; I've looked up the records back in Algiers. Though why the fuck should it matter so much? Beats me.

He has always been a tower of strength to me, a rock, the only guy I have ever really admired. Now, sitting there, leaning back to the wall between two battered garbage cans, he looks small and vulnerable and curiously passive. My heart goes out to him, though I can't afford to be sentimental about our situation.

"This *Juif* business is dumb," I tell him, "and you know it."

"Maybe," he says, "but do the others? *Les Juives* are never sure I'm one of them. But I'm not one of you either. Seems like there ought to be some room in the middle."

He looks at me as if his life depended on the answer, but I can't imagine he hasn't figured it out for himself. It is the same one for him as it is for me, for once the same for Jew and Gentile.

"Not this time," I tell him. "This time, anyone in the middle gets shot at from both sides. And the shooting has barely started. You watch out, Roberto, we're going to make the traitors take notice."

I know I haven't answered his question, but it is a matter of priorities, some things must be settled first.

He ponders. I wait.

"For how long, Jojo?" he finally asks.

"For as long as it takes," I tell him. "We've got all the time in the world. We've got the people too."

"So why me?"

We are back thrashing the same old grounds, back where I still don't understand why I can't make him see what is so obvious to me. I am sick and tired of this old barrier he always erects around himself.

Once again, I can't get through to him. Though not for lack of trying, since, for once, I see the glimmer of a winning stroke, my ersatz contribution to social analysis. Not halfway bad for a high school dropout, the son of a railroad mechanic.

"You're one of us," I tell him. "Don't you see? More than ever now that they've kicked us all out together. *L'Algérie Française*, she's nothing but a state of the mind now; we carry her in our hearts wherever we go, like your guys carry their *Sión* in those little *mezuzás* around their neck."

I have never seen him wear one of those. All the same, I am struck by the seductive force of my far-flung analogy.

"We, the *pieds noirs*," I proceed, "are just as stateless now as you guys. We are France's new *Juives*, all of us together. They lured our grandfathers to Algeria, our promised land. Only it turned out to be a false promise. We've shed our blood for them like the bunch of dupes we were. Now they've turned around and thrown us to the Arabs. So you see, you are twice ours!"

I don't know if he buys it; I am not sure how much of it I buy myself. A pinch. Funny thing, being one of them. I am not sure I like it. Probably total crap. What I need to do right now is down to earth though, downright crass.

"I need you back in," I tell him, "you're the best I've got."

"Spare me, Jojo."

He flashes his quick smile, like he is amused. I don't think I am getting through to him. I try another tack: "That night," I tell him, "on the boat. Remember?"

"What about it?"

"You wouldn't have shot me, would you?"

He mulls it over.

"I don't know," he says. "If Martel'd pushed me just a bit further, I might have."

"I don't believe you."

He shakes his head.

"You believe what you like, Jojo."

We are again at a stalemate, but at least we are talking. Maybe it's time to get down to business.

"The OAS needs you," I tell him. "We are regrouping on the mainland. We've lost Algeria, but it's only temporary; we'll take it back. In the meantime, Algeria is right here."

"That's a pipe dream, Jojo," he says, "just like *Sión*. Count me out."

"The other side won't," I tell him. "They've been after you, right? As far as Inspector Mariceau is concerned, you're still one of us. So he'll either find a way of tripping you and locking you up, or he'll press you into snitching. They think they can; I know you won't. But they don't believe in the middle either. They'll hound you; they won't let you be."

"I'll manage."

"Not with them after you, you won't."

"Leave me alone, Jojo," he says. "It's my life, I've paid my dues. Can't you just let me be?"

I shrug. He has earned it if anyone has, but he is too late. No more standing alone, no more room in the middle, if there ever was any; he ought to see that. This conversation could go on forever, like one of those interminable dialogues they made us memorize at school. Time to ratchet up a notch.

"The girl, Marie," I tell him.

He makes a valiant stab at it again: "You leave her out of this, Jojo. How many times do I have to tell you?"

"How could I?" I ask. "She's part of it. You saw for yourself today didn't you? Room three thirty-seven, is it? What if she finds out about your Canadian dish?"

This gets his attention, as I have expected it would. Another coincidence he'll never be sure about.

"What the fuck!"

He is up on his feet, livid, face contorted, looking at me as if he is about to pounce. The whole thing slowly dawns on him.

"You bastard," he says, "you dirty cheap bastard."

"*Alors* . . ."

I let my coup de grace sink in slowly, delicately, probing raw flesh. Truth is, the Canadian wench said nothing happened between them, swore to it on her mother's grave. Still, enough happened for him to want to keep it from Marie. The room at the St. Denis was a genius touch; I ought to congratulate myself. But it is now time for compassion, damage control.

"I only found out about it after the fact," I tell him. A tortured bit of literal truth. Their initial meeting at the cinema was pure chance.

"You don't expect me to believe that," he says.

I shrug. I suppose he won't now, not with Marie at the St. Denis, not with room 337.

The minutes tick by, him at the wall trying to run the odds, me at the doorway waiting, solicitous. The shadows of early evening grow deeper, the cul-de-sac is almost dark.

"What do you want me to do?" he says at last.

Bingo, we are in business.

"For the moment, nothing," I tell him. "Just stay where you are and do what you've been doing. There're all kinds of plans being discussed, nothing decided yet. It would help if they thought you're staying away from us. So we'll give you enough room, though we'll be watching. Just keep reporting to your inspector, wait for orders. And be ready to leave."

"Leave for where?"

"Who knows? Up here I'm just a small potato; they tell me zilch till I absolutely need to know. *Les barbouzes* are thicker than locusts on this side."

"What about Marie?"

"She's all right. Oh, don't bother to go back to the St. Denis; she's not there."

"Where is she?"

"In a safe place, with her mother."

"Would you let me see her?"

"Out of the question. She'll wait for you; we'll make sure."

"Please? Just to tell her."

He almost breaks my heart; he has never said please before, must cost him some. Still, we can't have that.

"We'll tell her, I promise."

We are both quiet. I let the truth sink in, let him get used to it. The girl has obviously been good for him, even a hard-ass *pieds noirs* like myself could see that. For most of our years together, I have kept strictly out of his private affairs. I don't spill my guts to him either, some things a man keeps to himself, even when he wishes he had someone to talk to. Sometimes I think it's a bloomin' shame, but I didn't make this world.

"*Bon*," I tell him, "it's settled then."

I get up and walk to him. He watches me from his low squat at the wall as I take his gun out of my pocket and hand it to him.

"Here," I say, "better take this back."

He is looking at me, and for a while we just wait there. Then he extends his hand and takes the gun. He gets up slowly and stuffs it in his belt, behind his back, where he always carries it.

"Just like that?" he says.

I shrug.

"Sure," I tell him, "you going to shoot me?"

How can he?

And I turn and walk to the doorway and step into its sheltering shadow without looking back. He is just standing there, watching me, I know. After a while he takes off, retracing his steps out of the alley and back through the maze of narrow streets and out to Cours Belsunce. He follows the promenade and, I expect, will follow his evening route up the Corniche, perhaps all the way to that weird café with the long-hair kids and the indulgent *patron*. I leave him be. He's got some thinking to do. But push come to shove, I can count on him to do what's right, do what needs to be done. A delicate business, this. Does he have a choice? Do I?

*H*e waits for a whole week and nothing happens. The corroding uncertainty of waiting is part of the deal. He keeps his daily rounds, going about his business, never trying to skip the tails, never going near the St. Denis. He visits his inspector, and nothing untoward transpires between them.

I expect he is tormented by the knowledge that Marie is right here in Marseilles but he cannot get to her. I don't enjoy seeing him suffer, but under the circumstances, things are as they ought to be.

In the meantime, I am as busy as ever. The last attempt on *le General*'s life has been botched, royally. Seven civilians, five of them schoolchildren on their way to Mass, are among the dead. In the public outrage that follows, we have become pariahs, public enemy number one. We are hunted like jackals; we are all on the run now and have got orders to lay low and, if possible, split.

He seems not to pay attention, having apparently stopped reading the papers. But the prefecture is not going to leave him alone much longer; he is too tempting a prize for them to resist.

He is awakened late in the morning by loud knocks on his door.

"Monsieur Aron, are you up?"

It is Mme Lechar.

"Uh . . . yes."

"There's a phone call for you," she says.

He pulls on some clothes, goes down and picks up the receiver in the hallway.

"Hello?"

His creaking voice must be groggy with sleep.

"That you, Roberto?"

I didn't really need to ask.

"Yes."

"It's me."

"I know."

"Remember the place where we talked last time?"

"I think so."

"Go down there. Make sure you're not followed."

Someone will be there to head them off him in case he is followed. Still, we don't take chances.

"Yes."

"Walk all the way to the wall and wait there."

"When?"

"Right now."

"Jojo, is this—?"

I am not about to say anything on the phone.

"You come down," I tell him, "we'll talk."

I listen to his breathing.

"All right," he says, "I'll be there."

He follows a different route to begin with, weaving and cutting through several cafés with double exits. When he is satisfied he is in the clear, he doubles back and makes his way to the alley. I can hear his footsteps as he approaches and slows down. I don't expect him to play tricks on me, but I am not about to make bets. The whole point is to give him no time, and the Lechar woman would have called if he had tried to use the phone. I wait for the guys to set up their watch at the corner. Then I push the door open and step out into the alley.

"Sit down," I tell him.

He crouches at the foot of the wall. They have been late again collecting the garbage, the stench must be bothering him too. I sit down at the doorway. We eye each other.

"You're leaving tomorrow," I tell him.

"Where to?"

"Leopoldville."

"Where's that?"

"The Congo, formerly Belgian."

"*Merde.*"

"My sentiments."

I wasn't exactly enthusiastic about it myself, though I am going too.

"Why then?" he asks.

"Orders."

"What the fuck am I supposed to do there?"

"Don't get mad at me, Roberto," I tell him, "it wasn't my idea. Once you get there, there'll be orders waiting. I'm not supposed to tell you but—"

I am not surprised when he cuts me short.

"Now you listen to me, Jojo," he says. "I'm not going anywhere, certainly not to the fuckin' end of the world, without being told exactly what I'm going to do there, without first—"

"But," I finally manage to cut in, "just between you and me, we've got a job there. Any of the old timers who can make their way down. Temporary. And the pay is good."

"What kind of a job?"

"Our kind of a job," I tell him, "the only kind we know."

I don't have to explain further: he knows what we are good at, what he is good at.

"Fighting?" he says, "another war?"

His voice is ripe with incredulity.

"Jojo," he says, "you gone crazy?"

"A good one," I tell him, "a just one too. Working for friends of *l'Algérie Française*."

"Shit," he retorts, "shit, shit, shit."

"Relax, Roberto," I tell him. "They're good guys down there. We go help them; they help us. The pay is good. Real good."

"That's it? We fight for money now? And *l'Algérie Française*, all bullshit now? That's it?"

"It's not that simple," I tell him. "And how different is it from the Legion?"

"We quit the Legion, Jojo. Don't you remember?"

I suppose I do, seeing as how we did together.

"There's more to it," I tell him. "It's unhealthy for us to stay up here, for the moment. Haven't you been reading the papers?"

"No."

"Well, maybe you should."

He doesn't respond. Presently he says: "Tell me about it, Jojo."

"Well, there's really not that much to tell."

But of course there always is. Though in this case I better make the long story a bit shorter.

"We're dispersing," I tell him. "The high command has reassembled outside France. Jouhaud is already in Madrid, the rest of the generals are on their way there. We have all been told to pull out. So this little war in the Congo is a godsend, tailor-made for us. We get out, we go down there, as many of us as can make it. We stay together, we make new friends, get paid. We bide our time. Once it's safer up here, we come back. Right now, what with this last foul-up, it's much safer for us down there."

"Safer? In the middle of somebody else's goddamn war? Are you listening to yourself, Jojo?"

"Now, now," I tell him, "this one isn't all that bad. The blacks down there are fighting each other, so one side is paying us to help them fight the other. They're all black down there, no training, no modern weapons, just old carbines and axe handles and wooden spears ... bows and arrows, you know. Not much of a war really, more like a safari. You go around knocking fear into their woolly skulls, keep them in their place, that kind of thing. Plus the money."

"Fuck the money," he tells me, "I'm not interested. You know something, Jojo? This is the fourth time in the last ten years I hear the same line—it's not really a war, only an expedition. So first they're yellow gooks who can't fight. Then they're dirty Arabs who are just a bunch of desert thieves with rusty old daggers. Then it's conscripts from the mainland who have nothing to fight for, and *les barbouzes* who just don't know their ass from a hole in the ground. Now the blacks with their bows and arrows and wooden spears. Do you expect me to buy it again, Jojo?"

He's got a point there, no use denying. We have been together through the last twelve years, been lied to together, jerked around together, dumped with a thud together. Still, somehow, we've survived. Together.

"Fine," I tell him, "don't take my word for it. Come down, see for yourself."

"What if I don't like it?"

"We'll cross that bridge when we get to it."

"Just like that, on faith?"

"If you insist."

"I don't really have a choice, do I?"

"None of us do. You don't have to believe in it if you don't want to, just think survival. Someone's shooting at you, you shoot back, the usual. Follow orders, do the job, keep out of trouble. We've been there before, Roberto. We'll survive this one too and come back."

"Come back to what?"

"To reclaim what's ours, *l'Algérie Française*."

Yes, it sounds hollow too, I know. But what else can I tell him? The truth is, I don't know what I will come back to; at least he's got Marie. All I know is it's going to be another war. Nothing really changes, ever. Indochina, Algeria, the Congo, Angola, Aden. They are all the same, one war really, just different skirmishes. So we can't go back to Bab-el-Oued. For a while, maybe forever. Tough luck. You can't just throw a temper tantrum and quit. Or sing lamentations like *les Juives* do for their *Sión*. You just can't. I don't know what else to tell him. I am tired, but I am not about to whine.

After a while he asks: "Are we going down together?"

"No. Each one by himself, then reassemble in Leopoldville."

"Where's that?"

"Mouth of the river."

"How am I supposed to get there?"

We are in business.

"There's a Belgian freighter taking on grain at pier 32," I tell him. "Quai Wilson. They're leaving tomorrow afternoon. Be there at eleven. The captain knows about you, no questions asked. He'll have to be paid though."

"How much?"

"Fifty thousand."

"Where am I supposed to get such money?"

"Your friend at the prefecture will give it to you."

"Inspector Mariceau? You mean *he's* working for the OAS too?"

"Not quite," I tell him, "that would be asking too much. He's offered you a ticket before, right?"

"Well . . . "

"Twice, right?"

"Well . . . "

The mood he is in, I will have to spell it out to him.

"You're going there this afternoon, right? Ask to go up and see him. Tell him you've decided to accept his offer."

"What if it's not on anymore?"

"It's still on," I tell him, "don't worry. Just be there."

"How do you know?"

"Never mind. He's still just as anxious to get you out of Marseilles. We know his orders."

"You think they don't know about your Congo deal?"

"Who says they don't? Only, it's no skin off their nose. They want us out of here, out of France, all of us. The Congo is far away. They don't give a shit what we do down there: it's somebody else's headache."

He is looking up at me. I don't expect him to swallow everything right off the bat. Still, we both recognize the inexorable logic of our situation. You don't need to buy into all the small print to appreciate how it all makes perfect sense, how it all fits together, smoothly, inevitably.

Not that I expect him to quit bucking. He will try, and we will be watching him. Mind you, I haven't given him much time. And he doesn't know where the girl is.

"You'll see," I tell him, "once you get down there. I'll be there to meet you."

"The Congo," he says, tasting it. "*Merde*."

"Yes, I know."

He digests that. I wait patiently.

"Say, Jojo," he says at last.

"Yes?"

I can sense his mood has shifted, he is more relaxed, almost casual. That's when he is at his most unpredictable, most dangerous.

"How do you know I won't shoot you?" he asks.

The truth is, I don't, but that's another story. We have been in this alley too long; it won't be safe much longer.

"You won't," I tell him.

"How do you know?"

"I do. You can go now."

Again, I don't wait for him to make the first move, I get up, turn my back to him, and step back into the doorway. He is over the hump and on his way. The rest is just details, making sure nobody goofs. Which keeps me busy.

*A*s I have anticipated, he doesn't give up easy, tries to pull something first. The tail follows him to the *Fond Social Juif Unifié* on Rue Grimaldi. Interesting, but still futile, we know all about it before he is even out of their office.

They start out by receiving him like a long-lost prodigal. They pour tea and make him tell his story, letting him keep out the details he figures they don't need to know. He fits the profile, so everything purrs on smoothly, till they mention Palestine. Israel, they call it. He tells them outright that is not what he had in mind, and they are naturally disappointed. They ask if he would reconsider; he says maybe later. That doesn't bother them all that much.

But somehow, in the process, they pick up a note that is a trifle off to their well-trained ear. They go ahead and let him fill out their standard green forms though, where under "mother's maiden name," he puts down, after considerable hesitation, "not known." The old guy who is reviewing his forms looks up when he gets to that point, then asks him point blank. He tells him the truth as far as he knows it, that he doesn't know, that he never has. He also tells him why. There is an awkward shuffling of papers there, then the old guy excuses himself and goes back to consult with someone.

When the old guy comes back, he is visibly embarrassed and profusely apologetic. If Robert had taken the trouble to learn anything about them, his own people, it should have occurred to him by now. In their books, unless he can prove his mother was one of them, certified, he is not one either. They would like to help him, the old guy says, but their hands are tied. Unless he can bring a birth certificate with his mother's maiden name. Perhaps the prefecture might help, the Registry of Births. Monsieur knows where that is?

He walks out of there deflated, equally disgusted with them and with himself. His next stop is the prefecture, where I expect he will follow the drill, do what is expected. But I won't be fooled; I can't relax. I need to make sure he doesn't go after her. I know he'll try.

* * *

*H*e has not been scheduled to see the inspector today, so he stops at the desk and the clerk makes the call and sends him upstairs, where Inspector Mariceau receives him with undisguised pleasure. The inspector still has his hopes. Perhaps, he must be thinking, something has finally changed.

"Sit down, Monsieur Aron, sit down," he motions him to a chair, "a pleasant surprise. What can I do for you?"

"Well . . ."

He pauses. He knows what he has to say yet is reluctant, and will take it one step at a time.

"Yes?"

The inspector waits solicitously.

"Monsieur l'Inspecteur, remember the offer you made me the first time we talked?"

"Well, sure, I remember."

"Is it still good?"

"Certainly. Why, Monsieur Aron—"

"Very well," he tells him, "I'd like to accept, I'd like to get out of Marseilles. I think you were right then, Monsieur l'Inspecteur, this place is not good for me."

"Hey, that's terrific, Monsieur Aron."

"Good, I'm glad you think so, Monsieur l'Inspecteur. Now, I need money for the ticket."

"Where is it you think of going, Monsieur Aron?"

"Leopoldville."

"The Congo? What for? I thought you wanted to stay in the Midi."

"I did. But things have changed."

The inspector smells a rat, or he should by now.

"Tell me about it, Monsieur Aron."

"Well, it's like this, Monsieur l'Inspecteur. It's far away, for one. Things are getting too hectic here. For another, they don't know me there, so maybe I can have a fresh start. They tell me there's a lot of room there and not too many people, lots of room for someone who doesn't mind working hard."

"Working at what, Monsieur Aron?"

"Whatever."

"You got a job offer?"

"Not yet. But they say it's a wide open country. I'm sure I can find something."

The inspector looks dubious, might take some convincing.

"I've got nothing here either," he tells him. "I've got no family, nobody seems to want me here. And as you said, sooner or later I'm bound to get into trouble. So I'll try the Congo for a year or two; get myself started on something; let things cool off a bit here. Then I'll come back. You don't expect you'll miss me, do you?"

"Now, now, Monsieur Aron," says the inspector, "no need to put it quite that bleak. You know there's nothing personal about our wanting you to leave."

"I know, Monsieur l'Inspecteur. No offense taken. Still, you'll be happy to see me out of your hair, right?"

"It's for your own good, Monsieur Aron."

"Right."

The inspector sounds embarrassed. Robert can't help but feeling sorry for him. The guy has been sympathetic on the whole, a decent man trying his best.

"The Congo . . ." he says, "I don't know. You sure you know what you're doing?"

"Sure."

They eye each other across the table. Over the month he has been in Marseilles, he has come to appreciate Inspector Mariceau's perspective, sympathize with his predicament, even wish he could help.

I have been worried about this growing bond between them, about his inclination, at the darnedest times, to go soft. The inspector may sincerely wish to help him, but he may be sharp enough to tag my old companion for who he is, a divided soul who can be manipulated, tripped, taken advantage of. This is where we need to watch out, monitor the inspector, make sure he doesn't muck up our plans. From what he says next, it is again clear he is not a simpleton.

"Is this your own idea, Monsieur Aron?"

"Yes."

"No pressure from you know who?"

"None."

"We've had reports of your friends, Monsieur Aron. Have they been in touch?"

"My ex-friends," he reminds him.

"Well?"

"No, they haven't."

"I see," the inspector says, "I see . . . "

Whatever knowledge he may have, we have reasons to believe the inspector will keep it to himself. He does.

"The Congo . . . " he says again, tasting the sound and not finding it to his liking. "The Congo. I don't know, it's so . . . "

He lets the rest trail off into silence. Finally he shakes his head, as if to rouse himself.

"When would you like to leave?"

"There's a Belgian ship docked at Quai Wilson," Robert tells him, "leaving tomorrow at noon. They've got room for me, if I can come up with the money."

"Tomorrow?"

"Yes."

"A bit sudden, isn't it?"

"I suppose."

"You sure you're telling me the truth, Monsieur Aron?"

"Absolutely, Monsieur l'Inspecteur."

"Still, the Congo . . . "

"You said anywhere I want, no questions asked," he reminds him. "Well, this is your chance."

"I did. I don't intend to renege on that. What time do you have to be on board?"

"Eleven in the morning."

"I see. Well, if you're sure you know what you're doing. I'll send an officer to pick you up at the hotel. Will you be ready for him at ten o'clock, in the lobby downstairs?"

"I will," he tells him. "How about the money? It's fifty thousand."

We have been counting on the inspector to handle this adroitly. We've got a stake in safe delivery to the dock.

"He'll bring the money with him," he says. "You just be ready. I still don't like the idea, Monsieur Aron. You deserve a better break.

You could make things easier on yourself if you'd only let me help. I wish you would."

"You've been a great help already, Monsieur l'Inspecteur," he tells him, "I'm very grateful."

"*Merde*," says the inspector, "I wish I could do more, it's this damn situation, you understand. My hands are tied."

He pauses.

"Truth is," he says, "I've always had great admiration for you people. You've fought for us and got a raw deal in return. We made you our sacrificial lambs for this rotten peace without honor. A bad day for France, for all of us."

Well now, that's something to look into later. I hope his own people don't have his office bugged. Robert doesn't look surprised, and why should he be? Such sentiments on the part of Inspector Mariceau are all too plausible, but could easily be a trap. Like the good soldier he is, my friend keeps silent.

The inspector rises, signaling the end of their conversation. Robert rises with him.

"Monsieur Aron, I wish we could have met under more auspicious circumstances."

"Likewise, Monsieur l'Inspecteur. I know it couldn't be helped. I appreciate all you've done for me."

The inspector offers his hand: "Oh, *c'est rien*."

He takes the proffered hand and shakes it formally.

"Good luck, Monsieur Aron," the inspector says.

"Thank you, Monsieur l'Inspecteur."

He turns and walks to the door. The inspector will watch him with his sad, skeptical eyes whose sympathy, in spite of valiant attempts to hide the fact, is now tempered with relief. They both know they are unlikely to see each other again. They both suspect it is all for the best.

*H*e has less than twenty-four hours left; we have to watch him like a hawk. As soon as he steps out of the prefecture, he goes down to the central post office to check for his mail, for the last time. We have anticipated the trick and intercepted her letter when it reached the *poste restante*.

Smart girl, just not smart enough. It is a short note written in a great hurry, but it could have wreaked havoc. So I keep it. I may tell him about it some day, later, let him appreciate the kind of woman waiting for him, make the ordeal seem worthwhile.

"*Chéri*," she writes in her neat schoolgirl hand, "I hope you get this, they're watching us constantly. Here's the address where they've got us, I've finally managed to find out . . . "

Holy shit, the guys were not supposed to let her out of the bloody door! I better find out how she did it. The rest is inoffensive: "Go to the police if you can," she writes, "but don't come here. If you can't do anything, I'll understand, I know you will have tried. Please don't give up on me, I'll be waiting for you wherever you are and however long it may take. I love you, love you, love you. Please take care of your sweet self for me. Marie."

With us holding her, he is helpless, paralyzed, at the end of his wits, his restless mind grinding out the dwindling options, ruling them out. If my design had any halfway plausible crack in it, he would have spotted it. It is up to me now to make sure all the holes are plugged tight. I expect he will never give up hope though, I expect he will do his best to come back and reclaim her. As soon as he can, as soon as I say so.

The way I see it, I have given him something to live for, a hope, an illusion. Men fight more ferociously and die more readily when they know, or think, they have something to live for. I will give him her letter once it is safe, let him read it again and again, let him brood and pine away. No harm in that, I am not without compassion.

All he can do now is second best. He goes to the drugstore at the corner and buys an envelope and some writing paper. He goes back to the café, addresses the envelope to Mlle Marie Laforge, *Poste Restante*, Marseilles, and settles down to write his note. I will make sure she gets it. I will also make sure there's nothing there to upset my delicate apple cart. No harm in what he writes:

> Dearest Marie, I had to go away before I could find you. It's not for very long. I tried to stay and look for you as long as I could, but I can't any longer, must take off, short notice. Just for a while, I

promise. I'll be back as soon as I can, so please wait for me, right here in Marseilles. And please don't worry, I'm fine. I'll write as soon as I can and explain everything. So please, don't panic, just wait. Don't tell anybody, not even your mother. You can write me *Poste Restante*, Leopoldville, The Congo (formerly Belgian Congo).

This last line will be excised before she gets it, the rest is fine:

Can't tell you more about it now, you're better off not knowing. I'll tell you everything when I come back. I love you, Robert.

After further reflection he adds a postscript:

P.S. Please give my regards to your mother.

Then another:

P.P.S.: Sorry again about your dad, he was an honorable man.

He writes "*je t'aime*" once again, signs again and seals the envelope. Then he gets up, pays, and goes to mail the letter at the corner box.

In the evening he goes down to tell Madame Lechar, who seems genuinely disappointed.
"You're leaving so soon, Monsieur Aron," she says.
"I know," he tells her, "I wish I could stay longer."
"You've still got another week on your rent, you know."
"That's all right, Madame Lechar, it doesn't matter."
"So, you didn't find anything in Marseilles? It is a difficult town, especially now. Maybe you'll come back later on, find it better then."
"I hope so. I'm planning to come back."
"It's getting rougher all the time, maybe you're better off leaving now. Still, I wish you found something here, it's not fair, what you people have been going through."
"*C'est la guerre.*"
"Yes, it is. Where will you go?"

"The Congo."

"So far? You should have been able to find something closer. Things couldn't be that bad here, they've got all those programs, you know. Why, I just read in the paper the other day—"

"Yes," he tells her, "I know. Still, the Congo isn't all that bad. And I won't stay very long, I'll be back soon."

"You've got a job waiting for you there?"

"Yes."

"That's different, I suppose. Still, it's a shame you couldn't find something right here, a real shame. You're going so far away."

"Yes," he agrees, "it is a bit far. Madame Lechar, I'd like to thank you for being so kind."

"Oh, it's nothing," she says, "you've been a wonderful tenant, what with the way the neighborhood is going. I could tell the minute you walked in, I told my husband. You take care of yourself, Robert."

It is the first time she has called him by his first name, a considerable concession to intimacy. She is almost old enough to be his mother and he still knows next to nothing about her, which he now perhaps begins to regret.

"I will, Madame Lechar, thank you again."

"Madelaine," she says, "please. You've known me long enough."

"*Merci*, Madelaine," he tells her.

"*Je t'en prie*, Robert."

And she leans forward and kisses him on both cheeks, rather unexpectedly, and he knows he must be blushing. After which, somewhat awkwardly, he bids her good night and, for the last time, goes up the creaky stairs to room thirteen B.

*H*is escort from the prefecture shows up the next morning at nine. He is already downstairs, pacing, suitcase parked next to the door. The man is wearing civvies but is not fooling anyone, unmistakably a cop.

"Monsieur Aron?"

"Yes."

"You ready?"

"Sure."

"Good, let's go then."

"You got the money?"

"Don't worry."

"Good."

They go out together and get into the car, which the agent has parked across the street. They pull away from the curb and, if he turned to look back now, he could see the small black Peugeot pulling out some fifty yards behind them. I am not taking anymore chances, also won't cede the last rites of escort. No harm in him seeing us; he won't know the driver and I am tucked low in the back.

We follow them down Rue Colbert, Rue de la Republique, then along the curving harbor drive. He may have looked back, maybe once too often, so that the agent may notice and ask him: "Anything wrong?"

"Nothing," he will tell him, looking straight ahead.

They make their way down to Quai Wilson, where the agent slows down.

"Which pier is she docked at?" he asks.

"Thirty-two."

A uniformed guard at the gate salutes them casually, checks the agent's papers, then draws back to let them through. They circle the depot, if he turned back now he would be catching a glimpse of the black Peugeot cruising past the gate.

In another minute they stop at the pier.

"This one?" his escort asks.

"Looks like it," he says.

He must be eyeing the small freighter with apprehension. She is moored thirty yards further down the pier, her freight winches fully extended, her gray paint streaked with rust.

"*La Pèlerine*," he reads aloud, "Antwerp."

He turns back to his escort: "Yes, it's her all right."

Stepping out, he pulls his suitcase with him. The agent comes around to his side.

"Come," he says, "I'll walk you up, make sure you're taken care of."

"All the way?"

"Orders."

"Sure."

They walk up the plank and get hold of a sailor who leads them to the bridge. A balding, heavyset man wearing faded maritime uniform is sitting at the desk. He raises his eyes as they walk in.

"Yes?"

"*Monsieur le Capitain?*" his escort inquires.

"Yes."

"A passenger for you, a Monsieur Aron. Are you expecting him?"

The captain rises slowly. His back must be bothering him.

"Monsieur Aron?"

The narrow gray eyes take him in, unhurried.

"Yes," he says.

The captain turns to the escort.

"Yes," he tells him, "he's expected."

"*Bon.*" The agent pulls a brown envelope out of his pocket.

"Here."

He hands it over to Robert.

"Your money. And Monsieur l'Inspecteur sends his best regards and a pleasant journey."

"Thanks. And thank Monsieur l'Inspecteur for me."

"I will. Good luck."

The agent turns and salutes the captain.

"He's all yours, *mon capitain*," he tells him.

The captain mutters something unintelligible. The agent steps outside.

The two of them are left alone now. He tears the brown envelope open.

"Fifty thousand, was it?" he asks the captain.

"Yes."

"Here."

He hands him the five crisp bills, then counts the rest. It comes to another thirty thousand, which he pockets. He must be making a mental note to thank Inspector Mariceau someday.

The captain rustles the bills in his rough palms, opens a drawer, and puts them inside.

"You're all set, Monsieur Aron," he tells him. "You can leave your suitcase here, the steward will have it sent to your cabin. Number seven, don't forget. Here's the key. You eat with me and the rest of the officers. Lunch is at one, dinner at seven thirty, breakfast from seven to nine. We'll be leaving early this afternoon. I expect to be in Leopoldville in a little over two weeks. We stop once, in Las Palmas, the Canary Islands. Just for a few hours. If you have any problems, you come to me. All right?"

"Yes, captain."

He is about to leave when the captain says: "You've got your passport?"

"Yes."

"Better leave it with me. You'll get it back in Leopoldville."

"Fine."

He digs out his passport and hands it over. The captain drops it on the desk in front of him. A reliable man, this captain, does what he is told, stays out of others' business. Smart too.

"One more thing," he says.

"Yes?"

"I've promised to deliver you safe and sound in Leopoldville. I don't wish to know more about it than I have to. I expect those people have got their reasons for wanting you there. It could be an unpleasant journey if you decided to give me a hard time. It would be much nicer if we understand each other. Let's not make it more difficult than necessary, Monsieur Aron. All right?"

"Don't worry, *mon capitain*," he tells him, "I won't be any problem."

"You understand my position?"

"I understand. You've got a job."

"A family too, back in Antwerp. Need I say more?"

"Not a word," he hastens to assures him.

The captain shrugs. He appears embarrassed.

"I'm glad we understand each other, Monsieur Aron."

"Same here, *mon capitain*."

"You look like a reasonable person, I just wanted to make sure. See you at lunch."

The captain goes back to his desk. Robert steps out of the cluttered bridge and climb down to the main deck. The crew are scurrying about energetically, unloading cargo off the big winches. A gentle breeze is blowing in from the sea. He makes his way to the bow and leans against the rail.

Our black Peugeot is still there in plain view, parked near the depot to the right of the gate. My driver, wearing dark glasses, is leaning casually against the trunk. He should notice. We are still there three hours later when the boat casts off its ropes and toots its brief farewell.

A few minutes after the tugboat has detached them from the pier, the gong sounds for lunch. The boat is picking its way slowly, under her own steam now, negotiating deftly the complex labyrinth of the Marseilles channels. It toots its horn several more times in a mournful salute. He should be looking at the receding city now, for a few more minutes in the gathering dusk. The last I see of him he turns, crosses the deck, and disappears behind one of the bulkheads. No doubt in search of the officers' galley.

THREE

RUNNING THROUGH THE TALL GRASS

∽

ROBERT

Katanga, November 1962

The gelatinous heat stalks you like a tree snake, dark green and hungry, slow and cunning. And deadly, and unpredictable. Half the time I have no clue where I am, and when I close my eyes I can easily imagine being back among the bleeding ficus trees in the delta. My Tho, Qua Nang.

Except for the smells, which are more primal down here, more visceral, infinitely more alarming. So that you cannot help but notice how precariously we hang, by the thinnest filament, over this lush abyss that just barely tolerates us, that just barely acknowledges our existence, let alone our uniqueness.

I have no idea where we are heading, nor even where we really are. The steaming limbo I find myself in seems to have done something to my sense of place and time, to have dissolved them into a turbid continuum that is sucking me deeper and deeper.

My associates, if you wish to call them that, are fast reverting to primal rock-bottom, trigger-happy sociopaths thrashing about in a dense homicidal fog. Some have taken to shooting at their own shadow. Our compound reverberates nightly with their drunken braying and brawling. Mindful of my murky status in between comrade and captive, they manage to both shun and shadow me with equal tenacity and distaste. I communicate with them only to insist they give me a wide berth. For their part, they would no doubt be content to dump me in a ditch and bulldoze me over, together with the weekly quota of dispensable black corpses.

Jojo is really doing his best to keep the crazies off my back. But Jojo himself is slowly being sucked into a vortex of manic kinesis, a whirling dervish in the blur of his own orbit, invisible in the howling dust, remote even when present.

Still, I cannot but notice the wild gleam in his fevered eye, the yellow patina of the near-translucent skin stretched tight over his raw bones, sweating profusely as he battles a recalcitrant malaria. The parasite wanes, but then rebounds in spite of the prodigious doses of chloroquine he consumes daily and that, as far as I can tell, do him little good except to turn his skin sunflower yellow.

In an improbable switch, I now worry about him, as if he were my hostage rather than I his. This bizarre metamorphosis indeed worries me, as it murks up Jojo's role—my nemesis or my charge?

The blacks are the deep sea in which we swim, all about us and worlds apart. They part as we come through, then close ranks again, allowing no ripple in our wake. Some, we presume, are our allies: the ones we fight to defend, for a price. Others we take to be our foes: the ones we stalk and ambush, mow down and burn. The vast mass are stranded mid-carnage, perched to jump whichever way their fortune blows—silent, watchful, opaque, waiting for someone to win, for someone to lose, for someone to die. Waiting for us to give up and depart, or else to rot in the rain-swollen gullies.

The few whites that still hang on by their last colonial threads—in the idle mines, in the rusting government Quonsets where nothing is ever transacted, in the lone hotel and two expat bars that are still open—avoid our company like the plague. Although ostensibly we are here to save their bacon from the searing dark fire. Save their bacon from who? Their black enemies back in Leo? Their black allies here in Eville?

In the midst of the general carnage, I have never been more alone. I cannot think of Marie anymore, except with wrenching regret. I hardly remember what she looks like, hardly know what I look like myself for that matter, having given up shaving. When I hack at my beard with the dull scissors I have managed to acquire, I do so in the dark seclusion of my room, clawing blindly at my own anonymous face. As I strive to hang on to some vestige of order, questions intrude. Who am I and what am I doing in this godforsaken hell hole? How long will I cling to the handy fiction of being a victim, Jojo's reluctant puppet?

If there is a way out of this infernal mess, I will find it, somehow. For the moment, I need to contend with the daily chores of staying sane and alive.

I have gone to sleep early, in utter exhaustion. The evening is unbearably hot; it had been raining for the better part of the afternoon, with squalls beating in rapid succession over the dark water. Afterwards the sky cleared up briefly, long enough to wait the sunset out on deck. I am treated to a lush display of blazing color, and for the first time in my life I see the fabled green flash as the last fleck of sun plunges under the horizon. A violent tug squeezes my heart, I don't know why.

Sleep doesn't leave me quite refreshed. In the eternal night of the lower deck, I toss and turn in the stale humid air, my damp bedsheets crumpled around me. It is almost a relief when a series of knocks rap on my cabin door, followed by a gruff voice: "Monsieur Aron!"

I sit up.

"What is it?"

"The captain wants you on the bridge."

"What for? What time is it?"

"One o'clock. He wants to see you."

"Are we there?"

"Not yet."

"All right. Tell him I'm coming."

I sit on the bunk for a while scratching my flanks. My hair is a dank mess; I splash water from the small enamel basin over my face and pull some clothes on. I am feeling almost awake and have lost the resentment about being yanked out of bed in the middle of the night. I get out of the cabin and feel my way up the dim stairwell to the bridge, two decks above. The narrow gangways are eerily quiet. I find the captain sitting at his desk, poring over navigation charts. I pull out a chair and sit across from him. He ignores me as he continues to plot lines with a pencil. I watch him for a while.

"A man can't get a decent night's sleep on this tub," I tell him.

"Ah, Monsieur Aron."

He raises his eyes. As usual, they are red and puffy. Lack of sleep? Booze? Likely both.

"Thanks for joining me. Sorry about the time. We're getting into port in two hours. You better go down and pack up, be ready."

"Will take me all of five minutes," I tell him. "How close are we?"

"Still ten miles downriver."

"What's the big rush? Couldn't you let me sleep till the morning?"

Over our three weeks together we have arrived at a rather fair modus vivendi, mostly over a chess board after dinner in the galley. I have no reason to assume he doesn't like me.

"Well . . ." He sounds apologetic. "The thing is, we've just received a radio flash about you. Seems like you're getting off before we dock. There's a boat coming by to pick you up."

"That so? They sure take care of their own, don't they?"

"Seems like it. You must be an important man or something, Monsieur Aron."

"Or something. I'll go down and pack."

"Come back up here when you're done, we'll have a drink. Another game maybe?"

"Sounds good," I tell him.

As I leave, it occurs to me the captain is more than a shade reluctant to let me out of his sight. For which I can't fault him.

In fifteen minutes I am all packed; my meager possessions crammed haphazardly into Marie's old suitcase. I hoist it up and make my way back up to the bridge. The captain is still where I left him, though he has taken off his maritime cap.

"Throw the valise over there," he points to a corner. "Sit down. Gin? Cognac? Whiskey? Cointreau?"

"Cognac," I say as I join him. "What are we celebrating, *mon capitain*?"

"A successful journey."

"Getting me off your back?"

"Nonsense. It's been a pleasure."

"Likewise."

He pulls the bottle out of the small cabinet to the right of his desk, together with two crystal glasses, and pours. As he leans over to hand me my glass, the bald spot on top of his head glistens in the yellow light. It is deeply tanned, like the rest of his face, neck and arms.

"Here," he says, "*santé.*"

"*A la vôtre.*"

We sip our drinks in silence for a while. In a minute he will propose one last game. His chess is solid if uninspired. Mine is fickle and erratic. In a month of nightly bouts, we have proven almost evenly matched.

"You know where you're heading, Monsieur Aron?"

"Not a clue," I tell him. "Do you?"

"Well . . . In this business one is better off knowing as little as possible. Must be a weird feeling, going off like this. Can't you guess?"

"Can you?"

The captain examines his fingernails, which are closely trimmed, or bitten, like mine.

"I should say Katanga."

"Where's that?"

"All the way east. Eville used to be a nice place once, they say. Never been there myself; no way going up there with a boat."

"What's there now?"

"Nothing but trouble, I'm told. You're not here on your own, are you?"

"No."

"I didn't think so. You don't look the type, not quite. I've seen some of the others . . . "

The gesture that follows is both eloquent and opaque.

"Got a family?"

"No."

"Makes it easier. Maybe."

"You think so?"

"They say so. Who knows."

"Yes," I agree, "who knows."

I take another sip of the captain's brandy, which is surprisingly good. I go ahead and drain my glass. I think about Marie and her mother; I wonder whether they are still in Marseilles.

"Have another one," the captain says.

He refills both glasses without waiting.

"Good idea," I tell him, "thanks."

We toast each other in silence.

"Is there anything I can do for you, Monsieur Aron?" he asks. "I'll be back in Marseilles in five weeks."

"Oh?"

"Anything. Within reason."

"Well," I tell him, "you can look up someone for me, a girl. Marie Laforge's the name. Trouble is, I'm not sure where she is. Maybe the Ministry for Repatriates will know."

"She from Algeria too?"

"Yes."

"Sure, I'll look her up for you. What shall I tell her?"

"Well . . ." I say.

In the month since I last saw Marie, during which she has been on my mind almost constantly, I have come to appreciate how little I really know her, how much of her may be just a figment of my fevered imagination. What can I tell her? Will she ever understand why I left? How could she, when I hardly understand myself.

The captain is waiting.

"Tell her I've made it down here in one piece," I tell him, "that you saw me. Tell her I'll be back in Marseilles as soon as I can. Tell her I love her. Tell her . . ."

I wish I knew what else to tell Marie. I stop.

"I will," says the captain.

"Thanks."

"Don't mention . . . I wish I could do more. You could have easily given me a lot more trouble, you know."

"I tried not to."

"I appreciate. I wondered why you didn't try."

"What's the use?" I tell him. "They'd have kept after me. Besides, they've got Marie."

"I see. Still, I appreciate."

"Forget it. *A vôtre santé*."

"*A la vôtre*."

We both empty our glasses and the captain refills them again.

"One last game?" he proposes.

"Why not."

I stop him from getting up and rise myself to fetch the set from its customary berth. He draws white and opens with a complex defensive maneuver, which I counter with long sorties of bishops and knights on both flanks. In the protracted game of attrition we settle into, we trade pieces one by one and consume the rest of the cognac. We are well on our way through the captain's Cointreau, when I finally do the honorable thing and surrender, having survived with my lonely king to his king and two pawns.

I lean into the rail, staring into the dark. A languid breeze blows the humid warm air into my face. Some distance further up the river, on what must be the left bank, I can see the lights now. We must be going near enough to the shore, since I can actually hear snatches of music, singing voices. If I were inclined to try for it, this is probably my best chance for jumping and swimming ashore. But I know next to nothing about where I am, and the little I have managed to glean suggests my chances of escaping the crocodiles are zilch. Not to mention the fact that the captain is still in possession of my passport.

We are cruising at reduced speed now, parallel to the river bank. The lights are slowly growing brighter, suggesting a sizable town. Presently I hear, somewhere to our right, the low murmur of an engine. I peer out for a light but see nothing. Nonetheless, the sound is growing stronger. When the boat is about one hundred yards away, I finally see it, a shadow gliding toward us on an interception course from the right. As it draws closer, I can make out the outline of a sizable tugboat.

An exchange of calls takes place, which I take to be an indication that this is indeed my ride. When I thread my way back to the bridge, I find the captain there peering out of the hatch. He turns.

"This one sounds like it," I tell him.

"Sounds like, about the right spot too. No hurry though; they'll pick up some cargo first, will be fifteen minutes or so. Make yourself comfortable; they'll come for you here."

I sit down and stretch my legs. The captain seems restless, switching his vigil from one hatch to the other. He grabs the phone and barks some instructions in a language I don't recognize that must be Flemish. He listens and seems reassured, after which he joins me at the table and offers me another drink. I expect he is relieved to be rid of me and whatever other illicit cargo has been foisted on him.

We are both listening for the steps; we finally hear them approaching the bridge. As I turn to the door, a short stocky man has just materialized there.

"Monsieur le Capitain?"

"You've finished loading off?"

"Yes. The receipts will be cabled off to Antwerp this morning. As usual, your cooperation will be noted."

"I follow orders."

He keeps his voice appropriately neutral. The stocky man nods.

"You do," he says, "you get paid for it."

He turns and, for the first time, acknowledges my presence: "You Aron?"

"Yes."

"Got your stuff?"

I gesture toward the suitcase near the door.

"Good. Let's go."

I get up, turn to the captain and offer my hand: "Thanks for everything," I tell him.

"It's been a pleasure. I'll miss the chess. Good luck."

"Likewise," I assure him.

I turn to my apparent next custodian: "Shall we?"

The captain has the grace to not mention what he promised to do for me, a small omission that, I hope, will not cost him. In the world we inhabit, even the most well-meaning bystander may turn out to be a puppet in someone else's convoluted game plan, strings attached. Much like Mme Lechar, inspectors Mariceau and Algazi, the young social worker, the Canadian lady Margot and the nameless others now slowly receding in my aching memory, the captain has done his best for me, given his strings.

I expect the dour man now leading me onto an uncertain future will turn out to be like the rest of them, an honorable man abiding by his strings. Like him, like the rest of them, I dangle at the end of someone else's rope.

As we turn to leave, it occurs to me that Jojo, my own puppet master, must also be dancing at the end of someone's string. Though for the moment I can't tell whose.

My chaperon leads the way. I follow him down to the cargo deck and through a door into the open hull. A narrow plank with rope railings leads to the boat, bobbing a few yards away, engine spluttering quietly. My custodian displays surprising agility in hopping aboard; I follow him cautiously. In a minute I am led down a flight of stairs into a narrow room where a small kerosene lamp casts more shadows than light. Just as we walk in, the engine's rumble grows perceptibly louder and the boat jerks forward. At the other end of the room a man is hardly discernible, sitting at a narrow table. The room seems a combination mess hall and office. Maps and charts are pasted to the walls.

"You can put your valise down there," my escort gestures toward the near corner. "Bourget here will keep you company. No tricks please. We get there in about forty minutes."

"Get where?"

"Brazzaville."

"Where's that?"

"Across the river from Leo."

"What then?"

"You wait."

"You guys sure keep a body guessing."

"I've got my orders."

Another one.

I settle down to waiting as the engine purrs on and the boat swings on gently. The man at the other end never says a word; in the shadow I cannot even see his face. Presently the boat slows down, and in a minute my first companion is back. I rise.

"We're just about there," he says. "Come on up."

I nod, grab my suitcase and follow him up to the deck.

The boat is inside a small inlet, approaching a wharf. Lights from a settlement the size of which I cannot tell flicker at us from across a strip of water. The wharf we are slowly approaching seems to be a rickety affair of wooden poles extending into the river. At the far end, the hulk of what must be low buildings looms in the dark. As we get closer, I can make out the silhouettes of three men waiting near a truck. A crew member throws a rope toward them, the rope is grabbed and secured, then we are slowly pulled toward the dock. In a minute a plank is drawn out. Next to me, my companion says: "Let's go."

I follow across the precarious gangplank. Once we step onto the wharf, it reveals itself to indeed be jerry-built of rough-hewn boards, now creaking and swaying under our weight. As we close the short distance to the other end, one of the figures near the truck detaches itself and comes forward to meet us. And it is a shock to realize the great sense of relief with which I now welcome the familiar voice: "Roberto?"

"Jojo?"

He stops in front of me and offers his hand, and I take it. In spite of all the resentment I have amassed toward him, I am smiling in the dark. His voice suggests he is too: "Welcome to Brazzaville."

"Wherever the hell it is. I thought you said Leopoldville?"

"I did," he says, "but we had to change plans. They stiffened up their controls over at Leo, got to the point where we couldn't bring anything in after the government kicked out some of the Belgians who used to help us. So we've switched to Brazza. It's just as close to where we need the stuff, and we've got good friends here."

Jojo turns to my escort: "Got the cargo?"

"It's all there."

"Let's get it unloaded and put in the truck; we're late."

"Well, whose fault is that?"

The man is in a foul mood. I assume someone is putting pressure on him too.

"Never mind," Jojo tells him, "just get your blacks cracking; it's almost light."

What the man mutters in return is lost to posterity as he turns back to the boat. In a minute his crew of five dark shadows start unloading crates off the boat and stacking them on the dock. When it is all piled on the creaking planks, they start loading it into the truck, which in the meantime has turned around and backed up to the edge of the pier. The rest of us, Jojo and his two helpers, my escort and I, watch the blacks sweat in silence.

In fifteen minutes the operation is finished and the boat with my foul-tempered companion is purring its way back out into the river. Jojo turns to me.

"Hop in the back, Roberto."

Without a word, one of his companions climbs up into the back of the truck ahead of me.

"What's in those crates?" I ask.

"The usual—plastique, carbines, ammunition."

"Where're we taking it?"

"The airport. I'll tell you more on the plane; we're running late."

I hoist my suitcase into the back and find a berth among the crates, where my new companion is already parked. Jojo and the driver pull the tarp over and secure it. In the total darkness that envelops us, I sit and sway as the truck starts, lurches slowly off the dock and then accelerates, bouncing and swaying and swishing its way through the quiet predawn. After a while I doze off.

The engine is straining loudly as the metal frame of the aging Dakota groans and rattles. Four of us are in front, with the crates—many more now—filling the rest of the stripped-down hull behind us. It is twenty minutes or so since we have taken off; the plane has settled into a surprisingly low cruising altitude. From my metal seat next to the window I can see the thick, low clouds, floating like puffed lumps of cotton just below us. Occasionally, when a hole opens, the lush green canopy underneath is revealed. Jojo is sitting next to me, the other two guys are across the aisle. There is something familiar about the whole scene, except that none of us are in uniform.

I turn to Jojo: "*Dis*, Jojo."

We have to lean into each other when we talk, to be heard over the din.

"*Oui?*"

"It's time you told me what this is all about."

"Oh that," he says, "sure."

"Where are we heading now?"

"Eville. Elizabethville."

"Where's that?"

"Katanga, all the way on the east side."

"And once we get there?"

"Well, there's that little war I told you about in Marseilles."

"Who's fighting who?"

Jojo sighs.

"It's a bit complicated," he says.

"Take your time," I tell him. "I expect you to level with me. The whole story."

"Might as well."

But he doesn't sound enthusiastic.

"The place used to be part of the Belgian Congo," he says. "Then, when the Belgians decided to quit, a black government set up business in Leo, changed the name to Kinshasa, changed the name of the whole country to Zaire. That's when the guys in Katanga decided to cut loose and set up their own little state. Declared themselves independent, set up one of the local big-wigs as president, name of Tchombé."

"A Belgian?"

"No, local black, youngest son of a big chief, Lunda I think. Officially the Belgians are out, though of course someone had to set up the whole deal, keep the bureaucracy running, recruit people to train the local gendarmerie, set up supply lines . . . The place is unreachable from the coast, except by plane. Whoever controls the strips controls access. So now the black guy sits on top, shakes his spear and rattles his zebra-tail crop, but doesn't really run the show."

"Who does?"

"I was just getting to that. When they started their secession two years ago, the place was controlled by the mining companies and Bruxelles. The companies with their money, Bruxelles with unofficial advisers. Then things got messy—"

"Don't they always."

"Right . . . Well, there was a pious stink at the U.N., the blacks and browns and yellows started screaming, got the Americans to lean on the Belgians. Before you know it, the Belgians got scared and started playing both sides, Eville and Leo, just to hedge their investments, you know, in case the other guy turned out the winner."

"Who's the other side?"

"Leo. It used to be controlled by the ANC, *Armée Nationale Congolaise*. But those guys stopped being an army the day they went on a rampage and butchered their Belgian advisers . . . some of them anyway, the rest left the country on orders from Bruxelles. Next thing you know the U.N. steps in, first with an ultimatum, then with actual troops—Indians, Ethiopians, Irish, Swedes, some Italians—to prop up the black government in Leo. That changes the picture a bit, especially after the Belgians pulled out and quit helping Tchombé. In the meantime the black government in Leo splits into three more factions, with the president firing the prime minister, who then left and set up shop upriver in Stanleyville, which is now Kisangani. . . . Well, to make a long story short, it turned into a free-for-all. Before you know it, some Italian Unies got zapped, an unfortunate misunderstanding really. So now the U.N. is hopping mad, the Security Council is screaming, the General Secretary, a Swede, is pushing for more troops . . . "

Jojo pauses. But there is more. I wait.

"Then," he says, "there are the Ultras—"

"You mean, ours? From back home?"

"No, theirs, the local Belgians. Same thing as ours though, been here for ages and don't feel like leaving. Some of them were born here; it's their home. They want to keep it just the way it is. And they don't like Bruxelles and all those dark foreign Unies to tell them how to run the place. And, these local Belgians are the only ones around here who really care. Well, the mining companies are backing them up with money, all hush-hush, but who knows till when? They're here to protect their investment, so if they see the wind blowing the other way, who knows, they might switch sides. Or the Americans may lean on them the way they leaned on Bruxelles. Right now of course, Tchombé is holding the gun to their ear back in Katanga: got the mine-shafts wired up, threatens to blow them sky high if the guys quit on him. An old trick."

"Who's he again, exactly?"

"Top man there, president, or thinks he is. He's okay though, for a black. Fast with his mouth, a real con artist. The companies like him; he's been their boy all along. They think they can control him."

"What do you think?"

Jojo ponders. I expect he knows it's no use prevaricating, we are both in this together, for the duration, however we got in. He needs me as a comrade, not a prisoner.

"Me?" he says, "I don't know. The guy seems unpredictable to me.

And the Ultras hate his black guts, but they've got nobody else to bet on. It's wide open, anything can happen."

He pauses and takes a deep breath. The long story does not seem to leave him all that cheerful. He looks tired and has lost weight, and there are shadows under his eyes. He is not looking at me as he talks, and I have a distinct feeling he is uncomfortable. The story he has just told me is confused and confusing, this couldn't have escaped him.

"What do you think?" he says.

"Quite a setup," I tell him.

"Isn't it?"

"Sure is. Tell me the rest, Jojo."

"Like what?"

"Like how do *we* plug into this mess?"

"Well . . . When Tchombé declared his secession two years ago, the Ultras got together and set up their own military support group, mostly young settlers from around here or foot-loose Belgians from the Métropole—some ex–*Force Publique* on loan from Bruxelles. It worked out fine for a while. The Katanga Gendarmerie would follow them into battle, so long as they walked in front, way out front, and as long as the other guys were the ANC from Leo. Then the Unie troops started showing up and some of them are well trained. At that point Bruxelles caved in and recalled its military experts, or at least disowned them officially. Before you know it, the Unies start arresting people as mercenaries and shipping them back home. First they'd go on sheer guesswork, then someone gave them a list and they went after everybody on it, which really hurt. That's when recruitment started back home, with big money . . . anybody with military experience. Lots of people around here don't like the U.N. pushing them around. Some of them are from south of here, Angola, Mozambique, Rhodesia, South Africa. With big enough pay, volunteers started coming in. That's when the Fourth, Fifth, and Sixth Commandos were formed, and that's when our own people started coming in on contracts, first the ones already out in Belgium and Spain, then since June directly from Algiers and Marseilles."

I try to digest Jojo's story but it sticks in my craw. I have been listening to the words, but also to his inflection, and what I hear is a surprising note of discomfort, downright uncertainty, this in the in-your-face Jojo I thought I knew in and out.

I suppose he is expecting a response, and the growl of the engine forces me to lean closer and raise my voice.

"A bloody mess," I tell him.

"Isn't it?"

"You don't trust any of them, do you?"

"The Ultras are okay, pretty much like us."

"Like who, Jojo? Like the crazies you've been trying to keep on a leash?"

Jojo sneaks a quick look in the direction of the two companions across the aisle.

"Pipe down, Roberto, we make do with what we've got. You got a better idea?"

"Yes, let's get out of here while we still can."

"We can't right now. We're under contract."

"Fuck the contract."

"Not right now, we can't."

"In other words, we're stuck. For how long?"

"It depends."

"On what?"

"The situation."

"The one you've just described?"

"Give it a chance, Roberto, that's all I'm asking. There isn't all that much work, and the pay is tops."

"Who cares?"

"Wait till you see your contract."

"Who signs it?"

"Officially, a local Belgian working for Tchombé. Company money, eventually."

"They seem to be calling the shots here."

"They own the place. Or used to."

I am not likely to get any further with Jojo right now. I look out the window at the lush green hills. The cloud cover has broken up into occasional white gobs floating just under the plane's belly and casting their dark shadows on the undulating wooden terrain below.

The canopy is less dense now, and is punctuated by open clearings. Some of those are covered with green grass that reflects the bright sun. Others are reddish brown and seem recently plowed. Some of the clearings are fringed with thatched roofs.

As we rattle through a brief rainstorm, the plane lurches and both Jojo and I grab for our seats. It rights itself in a few minutes. I would feel more comfortable if they had given us parachutes, just in case.

I turn to Jojo.

"Not much like home," I tell him.

"No," he agrees.

"And *l'Algérie Française?*"

"What about her?"

"Getting a bit far, don't you think?"

"She's still there where we left her, ain't going to run away. This is just temporary, Roberto, the guys we're working with are friends, Belgian *pieds noirs* who don't like to turn their homes over to the blacks. It's the same deal, same fight. So we come down here and help them out, then they come back and help us, when we're ready to roll back."

"If we ever do."

Jojo ignores my comment, perhaps he doesn't find much there to disagree with. There is an issue we have been dancing around gingerly ever since he met me in Brazzaville. I've been expecting him to bring it up, but so far he has been curiously reluctant. I decide to meet him halfway.

"Jojo," I say, "how do you expect me to handle this? I am still your prisoner, you know."

"Well, that depends."

"On what?"

"On you. You can give me your word."

"To do what?"

"Not to run away. If you agree, it all stays between us. The others don't need to know. As far as they are concerned, you're one of the gang."

"You'd be a fool to take my word for this, Jojo."

"You'd be a bigger fool not to give it to me, Roberto."

We are both smiling and, at the same time, dead serious.

"I don't think I can," I tell him. "For one thing, you don't need my word right now, seeing as how you haven't left me much of a choice. But as for later, no promises. Neither you nor I have the foggiest idea where this is heading."

Jojo sighs.

"I'm not dumb, Roberto. If we must leave, we will. But together."

"Sorry. I can't promise that."

"This will make things messy."

"I know."

"Damn it, Roberto, you're a pain."

"Likewise."

We land on a bumpy, grass-covered strip in the middle of a wide oval clearing, after buzzing over twice with engines screaming at open throttle to scare away the grazing pigs and foraging black-and-brown fowl.

The strip turns out to be the central commons of a native village whose thatched brown huts are tucked away under the canopy's edge all around the clearing. We come to a final rest at the far end of the field near what appears to be, on first inspection, a long shed with thatched roof and rough-hewn sidings.

A boisterous welcoming committee is racing across the grass in the wake of the plane, made up of the village's screaming, arm-waving youth corps. Having chased their pigs and fowl off our landing path, they are now assembling to inspect us, although at a cautious remove. No adults are in sight, though lively voices flow out of the huts and smoke and food smells emanate from cooking fires, all suggesting a communal life that goes on undisturbed, perhaps ignoring us.

In front of the long shed, toward which we are now headed, a small party is slowly assembling. Their assorted fatigue uniforms are interspersed with all manner of custom-assembled tropical garb, bearded faces impenetrable in the shade of the wide-brimmed hats. In the deafening silence that has now replaced the engines' roar, this motley crew is watching us as we slowly clamber down the extended stairwell. Jojo is leading the way; I follow him, our two companions are close behind. The pilot is nowhere to be seen.

As Jojo hits the ground, a tall figure comes out into the clearing from behind the shed, racing toward him. His long gray-streaked beard seems to sprout directly from the deep shadows under the black clerical hat. His incongruous white robes are flapping in the breeze that is generated by his rapid, loping stride. Without formal greeting, he addresses Jojo: "Monsieur Georges."

"Hello, Father."

"Monsieur Georges, we need to talk, I must insist—"

"Later, Father, later."

"This is intolerable, Monsieur Georges. The church is being—"

"Later."

The priest as well as the rest of us are trailing behind Jojo as he whirls into action, rushing to meet the group near the shed. From this point on, our short visit becomes a compressed blur of unloading and reloading cargo. Half of the load is consigned to the shed, the rest reloaded onto the back of a truck that has just roared into life from somewhere under the canopy.

The wooden cross nailed to the shed's roof beam, as well as the white-robed priest who continues to hover about, make it clear that the shed is in fact the local parish church.

Since no one seems to expect much of me, I hang about and observe the proceedings. I am struck by the fact that no local blacks have been pressed into service, and by the watchful, silent demeanor of our youthful audience, who seem to follow our every move with curiosity but volunteer nothing. There is something decidedly odd, even strained, about the whole scene. It doesn't add up.

In an hour, the plane is emptied and gone. Before we depart, I manage to corner Jojo.

"What's with the padre?"

"Mad as a hornet."

"That's obvious. Any reason?"

"We had to borrow his parish hall for storage, temporarily. He isn't all that enthused about our landing in his village either."

"Why?"

"There might be repercussions, later."

"Why do we do it then?"

"The Unies have grabbed control over the airport in Eville, we can't land there. This strip is the closest we could find that's long enough for the Dakota."

"What if they find out?"

"The Unies? They can't do much, haven't got enough troops in Eville, just the skeleton inspection team at the airport. We work around them; we're sending the truck back for the rest of the stuff later tonight. That ought to pacify the padre."

I doubt that, but elect to keep my doubts to myself. Four of us are squeezed into the back of the truck behind the crates, and the tarp cover is pulled tightly over us by the two guys who are left behind to guard. I am the only one who doesn't carry a gun, and in the dark I cannot tell much about my bearded companions. I assume Jojo has filled them in about my status.

The truck takes four hours of slow crawl to make it to a bamboo-fenced compound on the outskirts of town, where the crates are unloaded in the dark. On its way back to the landing strip, the truck ferries us to Hotel Leopold II in the center, where we are put up in what must have surely been, long ago, grand colonial style. Except that the place has fallen into a sad state of disrepair, and is virtually denuded of staff. Once here, I am deposited in a bright upstairs room, sandwiched between Jojo and a bearded Rhodesian who is introduced to me briefly as Mad Mike and appears to be nonverbal.

It doesn't take long to discover that my surprisingly large room must be shared with a horde of giant roaches who crawl out to welcome me aboard, their antennae twirling quizzically. I do my best to ignore them and open the window, pulling the shades aside in hope of a breeze that then fails to materialize. It is pitch dark outside and I make no attempt to investigate the setting, except for noting the creepers of a climbing ficus poised to interject themselves over the windowsill.

The fulcrum of our reconstituted universe soon turns out to be the downstairs bar of the Leo II, which never closes and where booze, choice fuel of the mercenary craft, is being dispensed by the bucket as new commandos form and reform over toasts to the *ancien régime*, here to stay. Whiskey is the lubricant of cultural preference, transmitted this far north by the roaring blond-bearded giants, beefy Boers and Anglos that tower over us like a species of hyper-tree. Together with the whiskey, a comforting lore of good-old-days on the Kraal has filtered up north as well. Golden *belle époque* when a white man could carve his destiny out of the bush on the sweat-drenched backs of the compliant darkies, before the bloody Kaffirs got their wooly heads set on independence. Or rather, before they got their fuzzy brains stuffed up with wild notions of *liberté, égalité, fraternité* by the treasonous liberals from Bruxelles. The few blacks in the bar, petty officers of the Katanga Gendarmerie, huddle at a corner table, drinking their milky cassava-and-millet brew in blank silence.

Eventually, late at night, we are summoned to a room upstairs to sign our contracts. A pair of local Ultras preside, seated at the bare table in a makeshift office, stuffed money envelopes stacked in front of them. Jojo acts as our guide, ushering in the French-speaking contingent one by one. The pay is indeed extravagant, which makes you wonder what you are expected to do for the off-scale largess. The sign-up bonus, the equivalent of one month's pay, sends everybody back to the bar for a fresh round of determined alcoholic oblivion.

As the night spills over into the wee hours of predawn, the crowd becomes increasingly delirious. The cumulative detritus of wrecked furniture and glassware spreads slowly across the room, in the wake of the passionless fist-fights that keep erupting all over the floor. The wreckage is swept up stoically by the lone proprietor, a gaunt, graying Belgian ex-paratrooper who has seen it all and then some. The damage is immediately paid for in crisp Belgian hundred-franc bills. The Southern Africa contingent of hairy blond behemoths, in particular, seem bent on all-consuming mayhem.

In total disgust, I withdraw to my room upstairs, though not before observing Mad Mike, tanked-out as he must be, rouse himself up and stagger up the stairs behind me. Fair enough, I tell myself, let Jojo play his game while I bide my time.

*T*he wake-up call is sudden and jarring. Things change almost overnight. The brash talk in the bar simmers down to a low rumble as many of the self-declared commandos shrink or deconstitute. The word making the rounds now is that the Unies have been reinforced and are slowly extending their control over the province and the town. In preparation for an impending confrontation, those of us who are still here are pressed into service erecting barricades at major intersections. The barricades soon define the perimeter of our shrinking dominion, which we crisscross at breakneck speed astride our commandeered Land Rovers, intent on creating the illusion of simultaneous multipresence. The Katanga Gendarmerie, our trusted allies, melt into the bush when the first shells land near the center of town. Much of the arms and ammunition we ferried in for them from the airstrip follows suit.

After a week of chaotic maneuvers but no real fighting, a truce is declared between the Unies and Tchombé's government. Our presence in the midst of the conflict, an open secret hotly denied, has now become an embarrassment to the secessionist government. We are whisked off back to the bamboo-circled compound on the southern outskirts, where we landed two weeks earlier.

The ten of us now make out a reconstituted commando—five Belgian Ultras, three diehard Rhodesians including Mad Mike, Jojo, and myself. We are camped in reduced circumstances over heaps of equipment strewn about the house. Our three Land Rovers are stashed in the shed behind. Nobody knows what is going on, everybody is on edge, nerves are frayed.

Jojo is still in charge, and is the only one of us to go outside the compound, presumably to maintain liaison with our assorted hosts. Our fresh food supplies are handled by the African cook-cum-butler, whose large family dwells in the thatched hut behind the main house. The three women of his crowded household, whose precise relationship to him remains opaque, cook over the open fires and do our laundry. The multitude of half-naked kids swarm all over the backyard, following us with wide curious eyes whenever we venture outdoors.

A week of confinement is enough for my patience to have worn thin. As much as I have tried to stay out of everybody's way, I find both the Anglos and the local Ultras hard to take, they are beginning to get on my nerves. Nothing they do, just the cumulative grind of enforced shared confinement.

When Jojo comes back one early evening, I stop him on the rotting steps of the front porch whose supporting poles are choked in a purple tangle of bougainvillea.

"What's happening on the outside, Jojo?"

"Nothing much."

"The Unies still there?"

"Digging in."

"The airport?"

"There... the post office too, the radio transmitters, the Gendarmerie, Hotel Leo II, the—"

"Never mind," I tell him, "I'd rather not hear the rest. Sounds like they've got everything."

"Not quite."

"Let's hope they leave us a door we can crawl out of, before this hell hole blows up on us."

"I'm working on it."

"What are we supposed to do in the meantime?"

"Nothing. Wait."

"Till when?"

"Till the guys who pay us say otherwise."

"And how long are *they* going to last?"

I am being unfair to Jojo, since by now it has become clear he has few answers. I am hardly surprised when he loses his patience: "You ask too many questions, Roberto," he snaps. "Why don't you just relax."

"*Merde.*"

But we soon find an opportunity to quarrel again. This time it almost turns ugly. Jojo has been avoiding me, while I, whenever I get the chance, have been goading him. Now I track him down to the dining room facing the backyard veranda, in days gone by the hub of gracious colonial living. I find him there, resting on a dilapidated wicker chair, stripped to the waist and nursing a glass of whiskey, with the half-full bottle on the floor next to him. His wide-brimmed safari hat is tilted low over his eyes, so that I cannot tell whether he is awake or snoozing. I approach gingerly, noting the tight bulge of his jaw muscles that seem to be chewing silently.

"Jojo," I say.

"Huh . . . oh, it's you. Come have a swig."

He is pointing to the bottle.

"Thanks."

I pull a stool and sit next to him.

"You better put a shirt on," I tell him. "The mosquitoes are going to suck you alive."

"Shit, let them."

Together we observe the doings of the black children who swarm the back end of the compound. They are stoking the fire under the blackened laundry kettle with a steady supply of twigs. As they dance about their chores, we can hear their sweet incomprehensible conversation, where alliterating syllables keep recurring at rhythmic intervals.

"You understand their lingo, Jojo?"

"Not a word."

"Ever thought what a zoo we must seem to them?"

He ponders.

"No," he says, "I haven't."

"I suppose you're not around to see enough of it," I tell him.

"I suppose."

We watch the older girl, who must be all of twelve, kneading the steaming wash with a long wooden paddle. Her thin cotton dress is twisting around her waist as she manipulates the paddle rhythmically. It is a quiet scene at which we are the intruders.

"Any chance of us getting out of this dump soon, Jojo?" I ask him.

"What's the rush?" he says.

He seems detached, almost disconnected, as he takes a fresh sip out of his glass.

"I'm getting cabin fever," I tell him. "You keep me here much longer, I'm liable to do something stupid."

"Such as?"

"Take a walk. Make a run for it."

"You better not."

"It's not only me, Jojo. The Anglos are climbing the walls."

"Remind me to get them more booze."

"They're tanked twenty-four hours a day already," I remind him, in case he hasn't noticed. "You keep them in here another week, you've got yourself a clutch of raving lunatics."

"Not much I can do about it right now. The Unie patrols are hunting for us."

"So much the more reason for pulling the plug and going home."

"Home . . ." Jojo echoes, "sounds divine. Where's that, Roberto?"

"I don't know about you, Jojo, not any more. But Marie's waiting for me back in Marseilles."

"Not unless I say so."

"Watch out, Jojo."

"Oh?"

He has not bothered to check whether I've got a gun ever since we have arrived. I could have easily picked one off the open crates stacked all over the house.

"How are you going to stop me?" I ask him.

"I don't have to. The Unie patrols will."

"I might decide to take my chances with them."

"Better be wearing a gun before you walk out of here."

"How do you know I don't?"

In response Jojo whirls around. His half-empty glass crashes to the floor. He is pointing a gun at me. His eyes are red and feverish.

"Don't push me, Roberto."

His voice is strained.

"Go ahead," I goad him.

"I just might."

We are saved by the bell in the person of one of the local Ultras, the thin one named Jean-Louis, our interpreter and emissary to the Anglos, who at this point walks out onto the veranda and sees us facing each other.

"Hey you guys, cut it out! Jojo, what's got into you?"

Jojo says nothing. His hand is shaking as he slowly lowers the gun and plops back into his chair. Jean-Louis turns to me. I shrug, gesturing at Jojo. Jean-Louis keeps looking from Jojo to me.

I give up and walk back into the house, where I take refuge in my room and lock the door. I assume Jojo will come up with an explanation but it is all the same to me, I've had it. Through the window I can hear the drunken Anglos bickering amiably among themselves on the front porch.

In the fast-spreading twilight, the loud buzz of a zillion strange bugs is slowly abating. The critters of the green canopy, feathered or furred, are all intermingled in my non-native ear as they conclude their predusk cacophony. The piercing night howls will commence soon. I am sweating profusely, naked on top of my damp bedding, and the likelihood of getting a decent night's sleep is slowly descending toward zero. I am as determined as ever to break out and take a look at the strange world around me.

It turns out to be ridiculously easy. I wait in my room past three o'clock until I don't hear any more drunk voices rising from the back veranda. I peek out just in case, making sure my comrades in arms have all bunked down for their afternoon snooze. As I tip-toe past their rooms on the way down, I can hear them snoring. Their steady boozing combined with the midday heat makes for a potent narcotic. I stroll out gingerly into the backyard under the watchful eyes of the black kids; I open the wooden gate and walk out. I keep advancing leisurely in the shade of the plane trees, through the back alleys that divide the large compounds to which the local Belgians have staked their claim, fenced with tall barbed wire. Their dogs are raging at the sound of my steps as I pass by. Otherwise, the sweltering heat and saturation humidity seem to have driven everybody indoors.

In a while I alight upon a paved road. I am far enough from the villa, so I follow the asphalt until, a few minutes later, I arrive at what must be the main drag, or at least its southern tail end. I stop and scan to both left and right. The broad avenue is lined with low two-story houses, all fronted with wide patios supported by wooden columns. And it is crowded with natives of all sizes and shapes. Most of them seem to just be there, standing and chatting in small clumps, some leaning on the walls in the deep shade, many squatting on the graveled sidewalk or right in the middle of the pavement.

I turn right and proceed slowly in the shade of the patios, taking care to step around whoever is stationed in my way. My trajectory, however incongruous in the sea of black bodies, elicits only mild curiosity. Many of the seated figures turn out to have small mounds of fruits and vegetables stacked on the ground in front of them, I assume for sale. I recognize the bananas and mangoes and papayas as well as the standard vegetables you find back home. The produce on other mounds is unrecognizable. As I amble past the seated vendors, some of them seem to be singing at me softly in a lingo I don't understand, something sounding like: *"Hapa hapa, muzungu... kununulia kwa bibi kubwa, muzungu... kwa mimi, muzungu..."*

I assume they are offering me their wares, since I could swear some of them sing to the very same music in barely recognizable French: *"Venci musiye, venci musiye... chete pour dame, musiye, ti cadeau cote moi musiye..."*

As I go on, I begin to see an occasional European plowing determinedly through the crowd. They are the only ones who seem to be in a hurry. The black women carry their babies strapped to their backs in colorful bandannas, stopping at leisure to pull their breasts out, twist the bandanna around, and suckle their charges right there, as they chat away and go about their business. The scene is incredibly peaceful, which makes me all the more conscious of how obtrusive I must be as I tip-toe gingerly, apologetically among them.

When I cross the busy intersection in front of the Leo II, I see a squad of Unies clustered around a jeep, wearing their light-blue helmets. Their dark complexion bespeaks India. They hold their carbines at the ready, bayonets unsheathed and gleaming in the afternoon sun. I can see more of them stationed in front of the post office, down the street. They seem tense and I have no way of gauging their training. I keep an even pace, looking ahead purposefully as I pass the hotel and follow the avenue going north.

Half a mile further the stores and patios end abruptly, as does the graveled sidewalk. The road I follow now is shaded under the canopy. The residential compounds on both sides are more modest than those on the south side. In spite of the heat, which refuses to abate, I am enjoying my walk more and more.

The paved road is just about to veer off to the left, where in the distance I can see smokestacks. It must be one of the ubiquitous companies Jojo mentioned. At the spot where the road bends, a weed-grown dirt track is branching out at a sharp diagonal, running along a tall brown stone wall on the right. I follow and soon reach an open gate topped by an aged wood sign, barely legible, proclaiming the place *Jardin Zoologique*.

I haven't been to the zoo in years, I cannot even remember the last time. The big famous ones, I understand, are good to get lost in, like the Metro. The Eville zoo turns out to be different—although for my money just as serviceable—quiet as a ghost-town cemetery.

The toll booth is unmanned; the turnstile gate is missing its swing bar. I walk in and press onward cautiously between thick rows of acacias blazing their intense yellow flowers at no one in particular. In a while I reach a little log house with a signpost declaring "Administration." I peek in through the screen door. It is locked up, and when I knock nobody answers. After a while I give up and launch my tour.

The place is desolate and in shocking disrepair. I pass along rows and rows of empty cages with torn wire-mesh and doors ajar. In a while I come upon a cluster of bird cages that are still occupied, most by birds of prey. I watch the scruffy sad denizens with morbid curiosity, wondering whether there has been anything deliberate in the selection. They seem considerably less ominous than the ones I remember from the Algiers zoo, perhaps because they are scrawny to the point of emaciation and, manifestly, at the tail end of less-than-natural selection.

Next I walk further down the road to visit with the monkeys, who seem subdued and listless. I spend long minutes communing with the lone chimpanzee who, training his doleful, wise eyes right back at me, is having a hard time deciding whether I am worth the trouble of attending to. His musings are still in progress when I bid him a curt farewell. His sad eyes follow me with their implicit *Why?* as I beat my shamed retreat.

More deserted cages follow, at the end of which I find myself face-to-face with a huge owl confined in a disproportionately small cage. As I approach, he opens both eyes and we stare at each other squarely for what seems a short eternity. Our eyeballing challenge finally ends when the owl blinks first one eye, then the other, and then closes both. I wait a while longer, hoping to see him open his eyes again. He remains oblivious, frozen, a stuffed ghost.

I am about to move on when it occurs to me that I am in a position to do this bird a favor. I step back and turn the latch on his cage door. As an afterthought, to give him a hint, I pull the wooden door slightly ajar. Whether the thin squeak of the rusted hinge did the trick or my furtive motion, the owl opens his left eye.

"There," I tell him, "it's a cinch, just push and you're out. *Tu comprends?*"

I wait to see what he will do, but then it occurs to me that he might prefer to do it in private.

"Good luck," I tell him and move on.

I follow the fence along a dry meadow where a small herd of ghostly antelopes scavenge stalks of dry straw. I must be nearing the end of the wide arch that traces the complete tour when I see the elephant. The faded sign pointing in its direction also lists lions and other felines, but as far as I can see the large compound behind the intervening dry moat has nothing to show except for this one visible resident.

As I approach the tall steel-mesh fence, I hear the light tattoo of an impending rainstorm strumming its preliminary staccato on the broad-leaf banana clumps along my path. To the left I spy a small thatched hut with a wooden bench underneath. The two young blacks seated next to each other under the thatch don't seem to notice me. I veer toward them, accelerating just as the drizzle changes into rain and then into a blinding torrent. Neither thunder nor lightning have preceded the downpour, and by the time I make it under the thatch I am soaked. I take my shirt off and twist-drain as much of the warm water out of it as I can, then put it back on. Nodding an acknowledgment at the two blacks, I join them at the other end of the bench. The one nearer me smiles a shy acknowledgment. I smile back and then turn to look at the elephant.

It is a small elephant and, to my inexpert eye, old, with craggy wrinkled flanks of nondescript color, somewhere between brown and gray. Standing as close to the moat as it can without actually keeling over, it is munching its way through an entire tree—trunk, branches, leaves and all—lying on the ground right in front of it. Steam is rising off the rubbery hide, the rain cascading down its deep crevices. The ancient tusks are deeply discolored, rutted by a crisscross of finely etched lines. Now and then, the elephant flaps its incongruously small ears, as it plucks large boughs methodically off the prostrated tree. The trunk, seemingly endowed with a life of its own, snakes and slides as it grabs the greenery and stuffs it into the delicate pouting mouth. In spite of the prodigious quantity, the ongoing feeding orgy is surprisingly dainty, almost self-effacing.

I look at the two blacks sitting next to me. Thus far, they haven't uttered a word. They sit there next to each other, slim bodies in full repose, eyes glued to the elephant. On closer inspection they may well be brothers, although my eyes are not yet habituated to make the determination. What I can perceive, and am strangely touched by, is the overpowering aura of unison they evince. Their unison with each other seems just as compelling as their unison with the elephant. I turn to watch the elephant again.

The rain is beating down harder now; the thatch above us is slowly getting drenched and stray drops begin to filter down to us. The sky is dark; the bright daylight has almost departed, as has the oppressive heat. All of a sudden a zigzag bolt of a lightning, sharply etched upon the dark sky, strikes from across the compound, followed by a distant rumble. Another bolt follows, then another, with the thunders cascading in well-orchestrated response. The elephant stands impervious, munching unhurriedly through its tree.

The three of us watch the elephant in silence, in our dry island under the thatched roof in the middle of the soaking pandemonium. Time goes by. And slowly, as I watch the elephant, my visual field begins to narrow down, so that in a while the periphery all around me has turned dark. Not even dark, just invisible, so that the elephant now hovers in dusky haze. I see it with incredible clarity, matted against nothing but itself, at the same time improbably large and minutely small. Its trunk is moving deliberately, though whether fast or slow I cannot tell, as it plucks fresh boughs from the fallen tree and stuffs them into its shy mouth. I watch, and time seems to stop. The elephant is eating away.

When I finally prise my eyes off the elephant, the rain has turned back into light drizzle. The two blacks next to me are still there, sitting, looking on. I can hear the snorts of what must be water buffalo from somewhere behind us. I can also hear the sharp protective grunt of a mother boar. The world is alive with sounds that have not been there before. I get up and stretch. My clothes are almost dry and I am pleasantly warm if a bit groggy. I nod at the two blacks, who don't seem to notice. I thread my way slowly back toward the entrance, retracing my path. The two blacks remain behind me, watching the elephant munching through its tree.

When I pass the owl's abode, the door is ajar and the cage is empty.

"Good for you, old buddy," I say audibly, suppressing the urge to look around. "Good luck."

I walk past the deserted office and through the broken turnstile, then begin my trek back toward town.

I am back in the center, and it is almost dark. When I get to where the commercial buildings start again, I slip under the protective cover of the wide patio. The crowd is just as thick now as earlier in the afternoon: vendors, shoppers, hangers on crouching in front of open stores, leaning on the walls, clustered in small circles. They avoid my gaze as I come upon them, making way at the last moment with near imperceptible undulations of their agile bodies, all the while maintaining a dignified silence.

God only knows what they are waiting for, now that the sun is down and the only light is coming from the occasional wood-fed fire in sawed-off oil drums. To my untrained eye, they are there in anticipation of something imponderable that is yet to occur, an elusive cataclysm that would demand their witness. I think again of the two young blacks sitting out the rain under the thatch, looking at the elephant. For all I know they are still there, sitting with that deceptive passivity that I can neither interpret at face value nor fathom otherwise.

As I near the Leo II, a discordant sound penetrates the evening, the harsh clang of marching boots. I stop next to a roof post and peer out into the dark. A squad of soldiers is coming up the road. Their light-blue U.N. hats bob and weave like fireflies as they pick up the occasional flash from the fires under the patios. I retreat all the way to the wall and flatten myself near the door of an ill-lit store whose precise business is impossible to gauge from the outside. A voice from behind me calls out: "*Muzungu, ven ci musiye, kujeni hapa muzungu . . .*"

I turn around to find a tall man clad in the Gendarmerie uniform standing at the open door. His face is shaded; all I can see are the huge whites of his eyes and the carbine in his hand, pointed casually at my chest. He gestures with the barrel of his gun toward the door, then pulls back to make way.

"*Ven ci muzungu, hapa nyumbani.*"

"Why sure, thank you," I say and walk gingerly past the pointing barrel.

I almost stumble on the low step leading down in. The gendarme follows me, his carbine pointing the way. We proceed to the back of the low-ceilinged room where, in the flickering light of two kerosene lamps, I can see a primitive bar. A few low tables and an assortment of ill-matched stools are dispersed around the back.

A large black woman draped in black-and-brown cloth and sporting a rainbow head wrap presides over the bar. My companion waves for her and rattles out a few words in quick succession. She nods silently and he motions me to a table in the back.

As we move to take our seats, my companion stumbles over a stool and nearly falls down, at the last moment rescuing himself with the gun, which he manages to turn into a crutch.

"You pardon, *muzungu*," he says, "*venci, tukaleni hapa.*"

"Thanks," I say.

We both sit down, my host with considerable difficulty, almost managing to miss his stool.

"Bit-bit tired," he volunteers. "You drink side me, *muzungu?*"

"I guess so."

The woman is now approaching us, each hand carrying a huge earthen mug. She plops them in front of us without a word and retreats back behind her counter, from where she keeps an apprehensive eye over us. My host shoves one of the mugs in my direction.

"You drink, *muzungu*," he says. "*Chibuku* good, you drink side me."

"Thank you."

The mug I now take in both my hands is filled with a milky gray suspension. My host gets hold of his own mug and raises it in salutation: "Your health, *muzungu*, you-I drink *chibuku* good."

"Yours too," I respond.

I watch him over my raised mug as he proceeds to drain his. His wide open blood-shot eyes are glued to mine over the earthenware rim.

"You drink, *muzungu*," he urges me.

I take a cautious sip. The warm liquid is thick with floury matter;

it tastes sour and fermented, unmistakably alcoholic. I take another sip and lower my mug. My host examines me with undisguised interest: "*Chibuku* good, eh?"

"Terrific," I reassure him.

"You like, *muzungu*?"

"I like."

"Good. You-I drink mo-mo."

Under my host's watchful gaze, I follow his example with another sip.

"Eh . . . " he says approvingly.

He slaps his mug back on the table, which vibrates precariously. We both lean back and eye each other in the semi-dark.

"Good," my host observes, "you *muzungu* good. I like you *muzungu*. You drink this side me, *muzungu*."

"Yes," I say.

His carbine is propped casually across his knees, his left hand caressing the wooden stock, occasionally bringing the stubby barrel up for punctuation. His smiling mouth reveals even rows of gleaming teeth.

"*Muzungu*," he says, "why you come this side my country, why, *muzungu*?"

"Just to visit," I tell him.

"Other *bazungu* they come carry gun. You come no carry gun. Why you come no carry gun, *muzungu*?"

"I'm just visiting," I tell him. "No need for gun."

"Aha," he observes. "This side Katanga, all come carry gun. All *bazungu* come carry gun."

"Well I don't," I tell him.

"Why, *muzungu*, why?"

"Oh, I don't know."

"Me like, *muzungu*," he says, "like be friend. Now worry, see *muzungu* come no carry gun. Me say why, say maybe *muzungu* something special, maybe play trick Old Christophe. You hear, *muzungu*?"

"I hear," I assure him. "No trick."

"But how know?"

As if to emphasize his dilemma, my host's carbine describes a wide arch, at the end resting on the table and pointing directly at my chest.

"This side Katanga," he says, eyeing me earnestly over the pointed gun, "longtime *bazungu* officer come carry real gun, shoot. Katanga gendarme carry stick gun, no shoot . . . Now *bazungu* officer all gone. Now Old Christophe officer, now carry real gun, shoot. See?"

"I see," I tell him.

"Now see why Old Christophe worry *muzungu* come no carry gun?"

"Good point."

"Maybe we drink side point?"

My mug is still more than half full while my host's is almost empty. He raises it, swirls toward the bar and calls to the woman, who is still stationed there: "*Mukazi, tuletee chibuku kupita!*"

The woman looks at him coolly and remains at her station. My host watches her briefly. A submerged tug-of-war seems to be going on between them, at the end of which my host demands, now more emphatically: "*Tuletee chibuku kupita, Mukazi!*"

He is halfway out of his seat when the woman relents and ambles over to our table to retrieve his mug.

"My woman," he informs me proudly, "*bibi wande.*"

He slaps her ample behind with considerable force, producing a resounding explosion that makes me wince.

The woman remains impassive, looking neither at him nor at me. I expect her self-control comes with a price tag. I rise slightly: "Pleased to meet you," I tell her.

Her eyes scan me briefly. Her husband hands her his mug.

"My friend *muzungu* this side thirsty," he tells her. "You bring too."

"No thanks," I tell him, "nothing for me, I've still got this one."

My host ignores me.

"*Muzungu* friend good," he tells his wife, "like drink *chibuku*, like drink this side Old Christophe. *Basi tuletee* fast-fast!"

We wait, the woman seems to be moving about in deliberate slow motion. My host turns back again and again to watch her, I can tell he is about to lose his patience. I suspect a certain amount of lost face is accruing, and I try to smile my reassurance, but his face has turned opaque. Finally, he gets up and walks toward the bar. The woman's back is turned to him as she goes about her business, ignoring the rapidly accruing promise of violence implicit in his tense shoulders.

When he reaches the bar, I see my chance. I rise slowly and start tip-toeing, ever so gingerly, toward the back door midway between our table and the bar. I am almost there when my host turns around sharply. Too late. I freeze. His large doleful eyes are trained on me, his brow now furrowed quizzically. I look at him and wait.

"*Muzungu,*" he says, "*muzungu,* why? . . ."

His gun is rising slowly until it is pointing at me.

"It's getting late, my friend," I tell him.

"*Muzungu* come no carry gun," he says. "Now *muzungu* no like drink this side Old Christophe, go leave."

"Oh, it's not that," I hasten to assure him, "it's just that I'm late. I've got to head back."

But my words make little dent in his disappointment.

"Why, *muzungu,* why?" he implores. "Old Christophe friend good, like drink this side *muzungu.* Why *muzungu* sneak go leave Old Christophe, why?"

I wait. The woman behind the bar has turned and is watching us. Perhaps she has a better idea what to expect.

"*Muzungu* come no carry gun," the man plaintive voice resumes, "make Old Christophe worry. Now *muzungu* no friend this side Old Christophe, no drink. Why? Old Christophe think maybe *muzungu* bad thought inside, maybe bring bad luck this side Old Christophe. Why, *muzungu,* why?"

I hold my tongue but my heart is pounding. Old Christophe's mournful question reverberates in the air between us. The woman is the one who finally breaks the silence, as she places her husband's replenished mug on the bar behind him with a loud bang. He turns and grabs it, take a long sip, then turns back to me. He is swaying on his feet.

"Think you-I walk, *muzungu,*" he tells me, "think we go walk, look see."

With the mug in one hand, he gestures with his gun toward the open door.

It is pitch dark outside. The best I can count on so far is that he is holding the gun in his left hand, the right occupied with the mug. He lumbers out behind me and stumbles, and for a moment I think I see an opening. But then he rights his step and remains ambulatory. He catches up with me as I proceed along the back wall of the bar, delivering an emphatic prod to the small of my back with the muzzle of his gun.

"You-I walk, *muzungu*," he says, "you-I walk."

We are approaching the back corner and are about to step across the narrow walking space between the two buildings when the pressure of the gun barrel at my back is suddenly withdrawn. I hear the sounds of a violent scuffle coming from right behind me, punctuated almost immediately by the unmistakable thud of a body hitting the ground. I turn back in time to see a dark silhouette bent over a heap that must be the prostrated body of my drinking companion. The silhouette rises and walks over toward me, revealing itself to be Jojo, who is standing next to me holding the Old Christophe's carbine.

"Just in time," I observe.

"Shit, Roberto, can't you take care of yourself?"

Jojo is seething with rage as he pitches the carbine into the dense bush across the back alley.

"No big deal," I tell him, "we were just taking a walk, me and Old Christophe."

"With his gun in your butt?"

"A little misunderstanding."

"Shit! Oh, never mind, let's get out of here."

"Wasn't he one of your friendlies?"

"*Merde*. Another one you owe me, Roberto."

This is the first time Jojo has broached the subject in years. We have, by tacit agreement, both managed to give it a wide berth, so much so that it has become somewhat of a taboo. I am surprised at Jojo's bad form, but keeping scores is not something either of us should go into right now, when we need, urgently, to clear out before some real trouble latches onto us.

With Jojo in the lead, we creep slowly between two buildings, hugging the damp wall. As we approach the street side, Jojo raises his hand. We watch and wait. Finally he says: "I don't know why I bother with you, Roberto. You're a fucking pain."

"I suppose it's not too late to remind you I didn't ask to be here? Why don't you just let me go?"

"Not yet."

"When?"

"When we're done. Together."

"How do you expect to keep me?"

Jojo ponders, his eyes scanning the dark street.

"Well," he says presently, "there's always your woman."

I look at him.

"You know, Jojo," I tell him, "that one's getting stale. And in case you haven't noticed, we're both stuck here, in the middle of a bloody hell hole where neither you nor I can get to her. So let's just drop the charade."

Jojo takes a deep breath, fumbles for a smoke, and curses. I wait.

"Shit," he says, "I'll just have to keep a better eye on you, Roberto."

"How? With Mad Mike? Half the time he's too drunk to keep his eyes open."

"Never mind him. Besides, you'll be busy."

"Oh?"

We flatten ourselves to the wall, waiting for the Unie patrol that is now marching up the street. In a minute they round the corner and disappear behind the Leo II. It is long past curfew time and the center of town is now deserted, what with the electricity cut off last week. As an afterthought, I ask Jojo: "By the way, what did you do with Old Christophe?"

"Who?"

"The black gendarme."

"Is that what he was? I carved him some."

"Bad?"

"Let's say he might recover if someone got him to a doctor real quick."

Knowing Jojo and the way we used to do things in the Legion, it is clear Old Christophe has met his final demise in the back alley behind his wife's bar. I wonder how long it will take for her to find his corpse.

"Was that necessary?" I ask Jojo.

"Would you rather I'd let him kill you?"

I am not convinced these were the only options, but am not about to argue the point. After the patrol's steps recede into the night, we make our way in silence back to the compound, each immersed in his own thoughts. I expect Jojo is still seething, but there is nothing much I can do about that. Once again, he has come through. Once again, I owe him one.

Jojo's pledge to keep me busy is redeemed only too soon when, the following morning at the crack of dawn, I am sent out with one of the Belgians back to the airstrip to retrieve a new arms shipment. My companion is driving the truck, and our progress through the gleaming wet countryside is slowed down by the mud-filled potholes in the road that no one has bothered to maintain in years. At times, we must slow down to a crawl, navigating through a stagnant brown pool or crossing a swollen river on a bridge whose existence we hope we can still take on faith.

The roadside is alive with the local peasantry walking toward their garden plots. The men carry their machetes over their shoulders; the women's heads are loaded with large bundles of firewood or produce. More often than not, their babies are swaddled behind their backs in bright-colored cotton shawls. As they dart off the road at the last minute before we pass, some wave to us solemnly. Most ignore us, whether scared or sullen I cannot tell. They seem impervious to the mud we splash at them as we roar by.

By the time we reach the airstrip, the sun is halfway up the sky. Steam is rising off the canopy all around us as we roll on to the clearing. No reception committee is out on the common grass this time. Only two figures are standing in front of the church. The tall one is the old priest, unmistakable with his gray beard and white robe. It is the one next to him that gets me worried. And, as we come closer, my worry turns into disgusted certainty: "*Merde alors.*"

"What was that?" says the Belgian.

"Never mind."

Of all the people on earth, I say to myself. Though somehow I know I have no reason to be surprised. The squat figure standing next to the priest is Jojo's old satrap Martel, who is now stepping forward as my Belgian companion alights off the truck and walks over.

I bide my time; I am not all that anxious to face Martel, this being one time when delay is welcome.

While Martel and the Belgian are engaged in a hushed exchange, the priest steps over to my side of the cab.

"*Bonjour.*"

"*Bonjour, Monsieur le Curé.*"

He squints into my face before recognizing me.

"Ah, *c'est toi.*"

He sounds disappointed.

"I was hoping to see Monsieur Georges."

The old priest's insistence on this honorific reference to Jojo is endearing.

"He was busy, Father," I tell him. "Sends his regards though."

"He does, does he? Well, I wonder if you could pass a message to him?"

"Be delighted, Father."

"Tell him I've lost my flock. They've been spooked by all these big planes and have taken off to the bush. God only knows what they are up to there, but I fear the worst. Tell him I hold him directly responsible. Tell him God will too."

"I'm sure he'd like to know that, Father."

The priest levels a fierce pair of blue eyes at me from under an equally improbably pair of snow-white brows. I lower my gaze, finding it disconcerting to face the intensity of his scrutiny.

"What's your name, son?"

"Robert Aron."

He gestures toward the other two: "You are one of them?"

"I guess, maybe, after a fashion."

"Well, whatever you are, don't be sarcastic with me, son."

"I'm sorry," I tell him, knowing I must be blushing under the brown grime. "Didn't mean to. It's just that Jojo, that's Monsieur Georges, is not exactly disposed at the moment to worry about your flock."

"Well, he better start, because it seems they are beginning to worry about him."

This last one sounds suspiciously like a warning, but the priest stops short of amplifying. I shrug.

"I'll tell him," I say, "though I don't know what you could expect."

"I expect him to stop landing on my strip. I expect him to give me back my church."

"I'll tell him that too."

"I'd be much obliged, son. I tried to tell your new guy over there," he gestures toward Martel, who is still talking to the Belgian.

We both watch them for a spell. I don't expect it took the priest too long to get Martel's measure.

"When did he show up?" I ask.

"Flew in this morning, brought some more of your 'baggage.' I had to help him haul it in, nobody else around. Somehow I don't think he was listening."

"I'm not surprised."

"You know him?"

"Some."

"I see. Well, you better tell Monsieur Georges I can't vouch for what my flock will do next."

"That bad?"

The old priest fixes me with his eyes: "Listen, I've been here for twenty-three years and they're still a mystery to me. I try my best. I think I must be stupid. One day they're the best Christians I've ever seen, the next a bunch of the most depraved heathen. And this is without your gang adding your infernal business to God's. You tell him that too. Tell him he can't use my village any more."

"I will, next time I see him."

"I'd be much obliged, son."

The Belgian is coming over now. He opens the door on the driver's side.

"Let's load her up," he says.

I step out and stretch, then follow behind the truck as he brings it slowly around the left flank of the church. Which is when I cannot any longer delay facing Martel, who seems to be relishing our reunion. He looks smaller than I remember but well fed and neatly groomed.

"Surprised?" he says.

"Hardly."

"I am. Didn't think Jojo would let you come down."

"You should have talked him out of it."

"I tried. I don't know what he sees in shit like you."

"Likewise."

"Still precious, I see."

"Fuck off, Martel, if you know what's good for you."

"Up yours."

His hand slides casually toward the webbing holster on his right hip.

"I don't see a gun."

"Your lucky day."

"Hardly," he says. "I had more luck with your girlfriend, though. Quite a piece, you know. Didn't want to let me go."

It takes all the self-control I can muster to check myself from going straight for his throat. Not close enough. The incongruous image of Marie in Martel's thick paws goads my blood to the boiling point. Fortunately for him, he is too dumb to appreciate the consequences of what he's just done. Fortunately for me, I manage to hold back. Later, I tell myself as my vision slowly clears, plenty of time.

So I say nothing as we proceed to the back of the truck. The shipment is spread on the dirt floor behind the rough wooden pews, and is surprisingly sparse—three wooden crates and a couple of canvas bags. Martel and I throw them into the back of the truck in silence, after which Martel points: "Hop in there before I tie her up."

He is packing his revolver in plain view, and I get the hint.

I climb in and let Martel batten the tarp over the back. What he doesn't know won't hurt him, I remind myself in the dark, feeling the comforting smoothness of the hunting knife in my pocket. We are barely five minutes into our lurching trek when I make my move. I cut a vertical slit through the tarp, extricate myself, then slowly slide down the tailgate and feel with my feet for the back bumper. A narrow nook in the road is approaching us, where the bush crowds in all the way on both sides, shading the now-dry clay under a low hang. I have noticed the spot on the way in. When the truck is directly under the dark ceiling, I push myself off, hit the ground, and dash for cover into the bush. I doubt if they heard me, but even if they did there is nothing much they can do. I plunge into the dense growth and keep running.

My breath is short and I have stumbled and crashed a few times down onto the dense jungle floor that keeps throwing prehensile limbs and thick creepers across my path. The last crash is the one that decks me for good. I am in no hurry to come up this time.

I lie back on the damp undergrowth, trying to catch my breath.

My ankle is hurting like the devil, and when I finally try to rise, the sharp pain is too much to bear. I wince and almost pass out before crashing back to the jungle floor. I know I should try to orient myself, sooner than later if I am to make it back to the church. But for the moment, as things stand, I am just relieved to lie down and rest. Gingerly, I reach down for my foot, trying to assess the damage.

*B*y the time the kids find me, early next morning, my ankle is swollen to the size of a small watermelon. My skin is ripe red with the day's worth of insect bites, an allergic reaction which has blocked my nasal cavities so thoroughly that I am panting through my mouth in short heaves and my throat is as parched as the desert south of the Rif.

I hear their voices from far away, gentle melodies that waft into the midst of my losing battle against the creepy-crawly critters that have been keeping me awake all night. I have crammed myself into a receptive recess in the bosom of a giant creeper-hung baobab tree, where I am at the very least protected from the worst of the downpour. When the kids finally stumble upon my serendipitous nest, I am in the throes of fitful sleep, and for a moment cannot tell whether I am still dreaming.

I have been their captive now—or is it their guest—for seven days, long enough for time to have begun to relax its rigid boundaries. The village's daily existence is woven into simple recurring rhythms, sunrise to sunset punctuated by frequent riverine ablutions and whatever else may pass for routine, by enigmatic comings and goings, by the rhythmic ebb and flow.

Into this elusive daily matrix I have now been pitched rudely, an emaciated light-skinned giant turned sickly purple, lacerated by the fury of insect bites and sporting several weeks growth of facial hair. Erstwhile denizen of the master race, I am now a prostrated, helpless supplicant at their uncertain mercy.

They must have seen my kind before, charging through the bush on tall wheels, sporting dark metal rods that spew loud, instant death. As they slowly pull me out of my makeshift shelter at the base of the baobab tree, where I lie moaning in my anguished demi-dream, they must surely know of how utterly stripped I am of my former powers.

With gentle words of encouragement which I don't understand, they fashion a litter out of supple tree limbs, then transport me on it to the village.

There, the adults—mostly women—that have lingered around through the morning, or those who are done with their early chores in time for midday's trek to the river, cluster around me, watching me gravely and consulting among themselves. With no reticence whatever the women strip and bathe me, then dress my erupting skin with strange salves and cool leaves.

They must be disputing among themselves, all the while, about whether everybody would have been better off if I had just been left to rot right where the kids found me, been consigned to the certain mercies of the bush scavengers whose ominous cacophony had punctuated my sleepless night.

They have never left me alone, not once. I lie there under their thatch, defunct supplicant, taking my time recuperating. The women take turns feeding me. The wizened old man comes to inspect my ankle. He first probes and pokes at the swelling, muttering under his breath. Under his tutelage, the kids then cool my ankle periodically with water out of their calabash jugs.

The children, always the children. They line up around the circumference of my hut, watching me in my discomfort, commenting and nudging each other and, more often than not, laughing uproariously.

Toward the late afternoon, the adults begin to drift back in from their chores, the women from their garden plots strung in small slash-and-burned clearings along the river, the men from whatever mysterious doings that seem to consume their day.

At night the hut is crowded, with a carpet of sleek bodies and intertwined limbs spread around the floor in clumps and heaps. I lie there in their midst on a raised bamboo-frame they have fashioned for me, cushioned by a thin padding of dry banana leaves, an incompetent who cannot be trusted to fend for himself.

When they babble among themselves before drifting in seeming unison into sleep, I listen without comprehension. Soon after dark they all quiet down, lying there clumped together, not a stir to betray anything but oblivion to the blood-curdling calls that emanate, all night long, from the darkness around. Still, when I stir, or rise in my litter, someone will instantly awaken and rise silently, to offer me a jug of water or walk me outside and wait patiently as I relieve myself behind the shrubbery.

The first word I have managed to make out is *umusungu*, which the kids chant to one another whenever they come around to inspect me. Now that I am again ambulatory, if still slowed down with my makeshift crutch, a whole swarm of them hover around me wherever I go, simultaneously following and leading, pointing out to things and naming them and laughing at my manifest ignorance.

The oldest and brashest, and apparently the one in charge, is a girl of about thirteen whose sprouting breasts proclaim themselves proudly, and whose inquisitive eyes are locked upon me, tracking me wherever I go. Her name must be *Mulenga*, which is what she says as she points at herself, having first pointed at me and pronounced me *umusungu*.

That much is simple. As is the next, when she hands me water in a hollowed wooden jug and urges me to drink. *Amaansi, amaansi* she says and gestures. One time, having become impatient with her young cohorts, she pointed to them and pronounced them, with manifest scorn, *abaana abaso*. And, pointing out to the huts and to the clearing we have just regained, back from our afternoon meanderings, she sweeps her arms to include the whole kraal—*abaluba*.

This last one rings a bell, if what she means to tell me is that they are all Baluba. According to one of the Belgian Ultras in our suburban compound, the Baluba were once the dominant tribe in Katanga, claiming for themselves a wide swath of the high veld north of Eville. During their brief, some say brutal, imperial heydays in the sixteenth century, the Baluba had interpolated themselves to the south, planting colonies whose presence in the midst of erstwhile Lunda grounds remains a sore point.

At first sympathetic to the secession, the Baluba—never known for graceful submission—soon became disenchanted with Tchombé. Much of their disaffection is traced back to the mysterious mid-flight dematerialization of Patrice Lumumba, heir to the paramount chiefdom's leopard throne. The charismatic firebrand and ex–prime minister came upon his martyrdom at 20,000 feet somewhere between Leo and Eville. The general consensus among the people who should know, said the Ultra, is that Lumumba was eased off the plane on orders of Tchombé, himself a Lunda prince.

They feed me like they feed themselves, continuously, all day long, plucking down what is there in seeming endless abundance: greens and fruits I have never encountered, off trees and bushes and climbers, munching along the trail as I hobble in their carefree company; grubs pried out of tree trunks, sickly looking soft larvae, delicacies they press upon me and giggle at my reticence; fish they pull out bare-handed diving along the muddy riverbank, roasting them on small fires right there and then.

I tag along contentedly, eager to take their strange offerings in stride. And it must agree with me; it's been ages since I have felt such a mixture of wakefulness and repose, energy and elation.

The evening meal they all take together, myself in their midst. The men, almost entirely absent during the day, reappear and join in to be served first and then cluster by themselves, apart from the women and children.

With the exception of the old shaman who treats my wounds in inscrutable silence, the men have so far shunned me, even when I stumble upon them in the bush, trailing behind the kids on our daily trek. Although in the evening I can see them casting dark looks in my direction, probing, assessing—perhaps wondering? Their avoidance of me is studied and deliberate, in contrast with the women's and children's easy welcome.

Today our meanderings have spread out in a wider arch, due, I suspect, to my ankle having finally mended enough so that I have, for the first time since the injury, left my crutch behind. I limp after the kids along the barely discernible trail, egged on by Mulenga, who is still my self-appointed guide and constant companion.

Early in the afternoon, at the height of the stifling heat and just before the warm sheet of rainwater is due to crash down on our heads, we chance upon the men in a remote clearing. This time they are not slashing and burning the bush. Fifty or so of them are gathered at the center of the clearing, swaying in a wide hoop to the slow beat of a tall kettle drum. Instead of the usual machetes, they are all sporting long dark-wood lances and oval-shaped shields of painted stretched hide.

We lean out cautiously at the edge of the clearing and watch them, the children for once utterly silent. Then one of the men notices us and dashes over angrily. After a brief exchange between him and my guardian, Mulenga, we retreat back to the river, with the kids subdued and Mulenga for once silent.

Their idyllic existence is apparently not the entire story. Tonight, with the women and children and myself retired to the huts, I am kept awake long into the wee hours by the men's deliberations around the fire. Voices are raised; one speaker jumps up to challenge another. I have no clue what they are up to, but the contentious tone harbors conflict. I can only hope it is not about me, I have no way of knowing.

It takes no great feat of divination to conclude that Mulenga harbors designs on me. She has been keeping me constantly within her sight, and even when not right there next to me, her eyes are glued to my face, following my every move, probing, assessing, or is it planning, imagining, scheming?

She is not easy to ignore, what with her lush-lithe body, her lively yet dignified demeanor, and the incredibly unselfconscious yet infinitely aware way with which she bears her grace. If I am to be honest with myself, I must admit I too am taken with her. Having been mired in enforced celibacy for the past few months does not help either.

Not that anything untoward has passed between us thus far, not that there has been much opportunity. We are surrounded day and night by watchful, cheerful chaperons of all manner. But the slowly gathering live tension is unmistakably there, leastwise to my overheated imagination. As is the feel of her expert hands as she ministers to my scarred flesh when she changes my dressings.

Among the kids, she is a natural leader. And even the women, having ceded her the care of her younger siblings, treat her almost like an equal.

When the old shaman visits me the next morning for what turns out to be the last time, one of the older women fetches Mulenga for a lengthy palaver out of earshot. The other kids have departed without us this morning, which is unusual. When the shaman is done with me, I put my boots on and come outside. The old woman is just leaving, and Mulenga now comes and stands next to me.

Her face suggests something unusual is going on, but all she says is something that sounds like an exhortation: *"Muiseni fye!"*

Which she accompanies with a hand gesture pointing out and away from the river.

As I hike behind her through the bush, she is uncharacteristically silent, wending her way just ahead of me through the maze of faint trails they all seem to know as if they were well-rutted highways. We duck and weave to avoid the creepers, stopping occasionally for her to forage. I munch on some more unfamiliar fruit she offers me, as we proceed on our seemingly circuitous route.

The bush under the canopy is freshly doused with last night's rain, and deeply scented. Sudden shafts of light reach down to the floor at syncopated intervals, shooting through the dense green darkness like probing lances. I am following her and cannot tell whether the scents are hers or the jungle's.

When at last we stop to rest, we are inexplicably standing near the baobab tree where the kids found me ten days ago. Startled by the recognition, I look at her for a hint, a confirmation. The issue is laid to rest when she takes hold of my hand and leads me after her under the protective low-slung canopy. Whereby she pulls me down with her on the musty, matted carpet of decayed vegetation, in the snug hollow of the smooth bole where I spent that desperate night swatting at the creepy crawlers and shivering to the howling, screeching accompaniment of the night stalkers.

And for once, I act without thinking, without knowing, without regret, not even an afterthought. I follow her lead and partake of her youth, of her joy, of her utter certainty in the lush treasures she now offers me. It never occurs to me to wonder why, with all her seeming youth and freshness and unbounded joy for the business at hand, she turns out to be, at the same hot breath, such an expert, thoughtful, methodical lover.

She guides me firmly if urgently, and I plunge into her with relish. And for a short eternity there is only the two of us under the merciful dark halo of the old tree.

Nor do I wonder, nor really know, why, when we are pleasantly exhausted a while later, she takes me by the hand again and leads me on to within striking distance of the rutted dirt road the rolls into the large oval clearing. Once there, she stops, points in the direction of the church and urges me on. She seems to know.

"*Ingaanda ya Mpapa Yezu,*" she says, pointing toward where the thatched church should be just beyond the trees. "*Mpapa Yezu! Kuyeni! Kuyeni! . . .*"

Then she takes her leave of me in a rather abrupt fashion, looking back briefly for the last time, her bright eyes dancing. And I watch on as she gracefully swings her heavenly ass down the trail till she plunges back under the canopy and is gone.

I look, and I look again, and again, but it is not there. I come closer, and that is when I see the old priest sitting on a wooden bench in front of the pile of smoldering cinder and burned-down thatch that used to be his church. His cassock is torn and smeared with ashes, his gray hair and beard are singed. If he has observed me coming across the village clearing, he gives no sign. Until I stop just in front of him, when he says by way of welcome: "I told them you'll come back."

"You told who?"

"Your friends. They came looking for you."

"When was that?"

"A while back . . . Who knows?"

"What did you tell them?"

"Nothing . . . Just that you'll be back."

"Thanks, Father."

I settle down to wait across from him on a rotting log. It is early in the afternoon and the heat is still gathering.

"Not much I can offer you," he says.

"What happened?"

The priest gestures with a tired hand toward the burned rubble and partially erect blackened timbers behind him. The charred cross is still nailed to the upright center post.

"All gone," he says. "The virgin, the patron saint, chasuble, font, chalice . . . the missals, prayer books, registry. All gone."

His voice is level, his face blank, his eyes scan the distance beyond as we talk. I wonder if this is how he manifests shock.

"How did it happen?" I ask.

He eyes me slowly through the reddened slits burrowed under his singed brows, then shrugs.

"*Je n'en sais rien*," he says. "I was asleep . . . woke up in the residence, in the back . . . smoke all over . . . choking, blinding . . . barely got out with what I've got on—"

"But how?"

"Who knows? It was bound to happen. First your gang of thugs taking over, desecrating His house. Then my flock running off to the bush. It was just a matter of time."

"But who?"

My question is left pending, to ring and echo in his despairing, mournful, uncomprehending silence. He contemplates the charred heap in front of us. I wait.

"Does it matter?" he says at last. "To Him, ultimately, I suppose . . . I've failed him, utterly. Lost His flock, burned His church. He's got plenty of reasons, don't you think?"

We sit there in silence as the heat of the afternoon grows oppressive, listening to the rising cacophony of the bugs, the piercing cries of birds, the monkeys' chatter in the canopy. We are both hatless and the sun is beating down on us mercilessly.

"We could go into one of the huts," I venture.

"Later," he says. "You go ahead . . . I need to think."

And in spite of my concern for him I am about to follow his advice when I hear the distant rumble of a car's engine.

Five minutes later the Land Rover comes to a stop in front of us and Jojo jumps out of the driver's side. Martel remains seated in the shotgun seat. I rise and wait. Jojo comes closer, and I am startled by the transformation my short ten-day absence has wrought. His beard is speckled with gray, his cheeks are sunken, and his eyes are wild and fevered, as are his wobbly steps.

"It figures," he says, stopping in front of me. "Been here all along? I knew the old fart was holding back on me."

"He wasn't," I say, "I've just arrived."

"Where've you been?"

I wave a wide arc in no particular direction, sweeping the entire countryside in a wobbly half-crescent: "There."

Jojo moves closer to inspect me, and I like what I see in his eyes even less.

"You look too well-fed," he says. "The bush blacks, right? Saw their village from the air, should have burned them down while we were at it."

"Leave them out of it, Jojo."

"Get fucked, Roberto. Let's go. I don't have all day."

I turn and look back toward the old priest, who has not left his perch since Jojo has arrived. His eyes are still fixed at the distance.

"Aren't you going to offer him a ride?" I ask Jojo, gesturing toward the old priest.

"He hasn't asked."

"Don't be a boor, Jojo. He's in shock, can't you tell? Half mad, hardly makes sense. You can't leave him here."

"Who says I can't?"

I don't consider it prudent to respond. Judging by Jojo's voice, he is under considerable strain. The fever is not exactly helping. He seems at loss.

"I can ask him for you," I volunteer.

"Never mind."

Abruptly, Jojo tears himself off from where we stand next to the Land Rover and walks over to the priest, who ignores him until Jojo is practically looming over him. I follow cautiously behind. A silent tug of wills ensues, at the end of which Jojo concedes.

"Monsieur le Curé?"

No response.

"Father Donatus?"

Again, silence.

"Father, would you like a ride back to town?"

The priest turns his gaze slowly, sweeping in a wide arch that takes in the burned church, the lifeless village, the car with Martel sitting silent inside. When his gaze finally lands on Jojo, there is no mistaking the raging fury, the vehemence behind his hoarse voice: "Out of my sight, devil!" he croaks, fairly spitting the words out.

Jojo looks at him, for once speechless. The priest's eyes are boring into him with intense fury.

"Haven't you had enough?" He hisses at him, "Haven't I told you?

I begged, didn't I? I beseeched . . . tried to bribe you, didn't I? Can you imagine how long it took for the Church to plant its tender seed on this thankless continent? To get these people half civilized, just enough to come and sing the mass after we set it to their wild tribal chants and evil drums? Just enough to have their unholy fornicatory bush-alliances consecrated in front of God's altar? Just enough to have their young ones baptized in God's font? Just enough to give modern medicine a tiny bit of elbow-room alongside their heathen foul-smelling shamans? Has it ever occurred to you how many of my brethren have given their life to plant God's Holy Cross in the middle of this infernal snake-infested, mosquito-bitten nowhere? We were barely hanging by a thread when you and your goon-squad showed up, desecrating the house of God with your foul instruments of death and despoliation, spooking these poor wild souls to run back to their barbarous jungle—"

"We didn't—"

"Silence!" the priest bellows. "Off God's consecrated soil! Off with you, Devil! Out, Demon, out! Out, Antichrist, out! Out!"

The old priest stretches his frail body, lost in his soiled cassock. His eyes pierce into Jojo, who finally cannot take it any longer and turns and walks back toward the car. I fall in behind him in silence.

When we reach the Land Rover, Jojo gestures to Martel to move to the back, where Martel makes a big show of cradling his automatic carbine, pointing it at the back of the seat I now occupy, having just displaced him there. As we circle around in a wide arch onto the airstrip and back to the road, I look back. The priest is still sitting there, a small gray figurine in front of the charred pile of masonry, growing smaller and smaller until, as we pull into the road, he disappears behind the dense vegetation.

Sometime later, as we are bumping along the rutted road, I ask Jojo, who is steering in fevered silence: "Who did it?"

"What?"

"Burned his church. And don't tell me you don't know."

"I'll tell you what I goddamn please," he flares at me.

"Which is?"

"That we had nothing to do with it."

"But you knew."

Jojo is silent for a while, concentrating on a raised wooden bridge that is caked over with thick brown mud. As the car lumbers down back to road, he says: "Yes."

"When?"

"What does it matter? Too late to get a word through to him . . . or to do anything about it. Local politics, nothing to do with him or his church. He was just caught up in the middle of someone else's rumble. Something to do with his Baluba mixing up with the wrong crowd in this miserable war we're supposed help win—"

"Swell," I say, "just swell. And why does it sound so goddamn familiar, Jojo?"

"Lay off, Roberto."

"Don't count on it, Jojo. Not any more."

From behind my seat, Martel chimes in: "Why don't we dump him right here, Jojo? Hasn't he given you enough pain?"

"Oh you shut the fuck up, you too!"

The rest of the trip back to town we make in strained silence. We make it back to the compound just in time for the downpour to unleash itself with ominous thunder and bolts of lighting.

*M*artel's carbine, once again leveled casually at me, is a pointed reminder that I am the only one in the packed Land Rover who is not carrying a gun. We left the villa long before dawn, and have just arrived at the fork in the road after a one-hour gut-wrenching drive to the south. We scamper in silence off the two vehicles, after which the drivers park them on both sides of the road, hidden in the bush with only the muzzles of the heavy machine guns protruding. We scatter across the intersection and into the surrounding countryside, clearing up the fields of fire on both sides as best as we can. When we are done, the guns can brace the intersection itself and about a hundred yards of both branches. There is nothing more to do but sit and wait.

We have been told next to nothing about the operation, short of this—a hostile mob of renegade Baluba is said to be coming through sometime this morning in an attempt to reach Eville. Word has been rushed to us that they had broken out of the U.N.-run refugee camp in Kilogo, twenty miles further to the south. We are supposed to intercept and drive them back.

We sit in silence, smoking and marking time, as the sky gradually lights up. The predawn bird calls are gradually giving way to the more even chorus of daytime displays. We must have been lying in wait for more than an hour when a new sound finally intrudes—wailing, piercing clamor, accompanied by the rhythmic boom of kettle drums. They must be just around the bend, on the right-hand side of the fork.

We finally get our first glimpse, from about five hundred yards. The men are marching ten abreast across the road, spilling over to the grassy strips on both sides. From that distance, it is impossible yet to tell how well armed they are, or how many they are. We have been told only a few, at best, will be carrying guns. Still, we are crouched under cover, wondering.

"Let them come real close," Jojo has told us, "all the way into the intersection. Nobody fires till I say so, or till you hear me shooting. Put the first round low over their heads. If they keep coming, let them have it."

The Land Rover where Jojo is crouched next to the gunner is on my left. I am bracketed by Martel to the right. We wait as the marching phalanx slowly closes the gap between us. We can see their polished hardwood spears now, carried upright to give the advancing party the appearance of a bristling porcupine. The men are carrying their painted rawhide shields, the kind I saw that day in the clearing. The drum beat is reverberating louder, one could see the painted black-and-ocher stripes on their glistening faces now.

When the marching column is a hundred yards away and almost at the fork, I scramble over to Jojo's side near the Land Rover.

"Let's give them a couple of warning shots, Jojo," I tell him.

"Not yet."

"Why?"

"If we chased them away now, they'd regroup and take another route. Let them come closer, put the fear of God in them, scatter them good and they'll think twice before trying again."

I dart back to my spot. The column is filing into the intersection now without breaking pace. The war-painted men are marching in front, the drummers at their flanks. But there are more coming behind them, and as far as I can tell they are not men, nor are they armed. I can see the bright rainbow headwraps of the women, and if they are there the children must be with them. That is where Jojo opens fire and the others join in.

The war phalanx in front halts briefly, but the human tide behind them is pressing on. They don't seem to know where the fire is coming from. In a flash, the whole column breaks rank and proceeds in a wild run, straight forward, toward us. On my left, Jojo is shouting: "Get them!"

As I run to join him, I can see black bodies mowed down in the road, caught in the crossfire. Jojo is firing short bursts from his carbine, propped on the hood of the Land Rover.

"Stop!" I scream at him. "There're women and children there!"

I am standing practically over him as he fires. Without pausing, Jojo kicks hard, catching my shin above the barely recovered ankle.

I scream and crash to the ground but get up almost immediately. I am standing in the open between Jojo and Martel, both of whom are still firing. That is when I see the priest at the very back of the melee, in the midst of the flailing women and children. He is standing there motionless in mid-carnage, his soiled cassock now splattered with fresh blood. An erect, silent witness.

Next to me I hear Jojo mutter: "The old idiot!"

"Call it off, Jojo!" I scream at him.

Too late. I watch the old priest teeter like a timber about to be felled, then crumple down slowly in a heap at the crossroads. To my left I hear Jojo's belated lament: "Shit . . . "

Somehow, with nobody giving the command, the shooting peters out. The intersection is littered with prostrate bodies—warriors, women, children. The wounded are moaning quietly, abandoned babies are screaming. We stand and watch in unison, having, by some tacit imperative, come out of our assigned stations along the road. The carnage must have lasted no more than three minutes.

In the silence that has descended upon us, even the jungle creatures have ceased their chatter. I limp over to where the priest's body lies prostrated. His wide-open eyes stare at the sky from deep under his singed brows. His left hand is clamped tight over a tarnished silver cross. A small red stain at chest level of his torn cassock suggests his agony may have been short. From what seems a great distance, I hear Jojo's voice: "Everybody back to the cars! Robert!"

I take my leave of the priest and turn to fall in, an automaton on cue. Then I stop. The body of a small woman-child is lying directly in my path, sprawled in the grass. The side of her head is torn open, the white brain-stuff exposed. She is holding on to a dead child, barely three years old. She may be Mulenga, she may not—it is hard to tell with half her face blown off.

I am about to lean down and take a closer look when Martel's gun prods at my back. I rise and follow in silence. The group is assembled on the two vehicles, waiting, ready to roll. I limp up and cram myself in behind Jojo. We race back toward town in total silence. The sun is rising over the canopy on the right as we drive north. By the time we are back at the compound, the heat is pressing upon the earth mercilessly.

I close my eyes and I see them. The spear-wielding men marching to the rhythm of their long drums, the screaming panicked multitude, the dying priest with his unseeing pale eyes, Mulenga—if it was her—hugging the dead baby, her skull split like a ripe melon. I have been sequestered in my upstairs room for two days now, ever since we came back. My door is locked from the inside; I have refused Jojo's emissaries. I know someone is posted right in front of the door, most likely Martel. They shouldn't bother, need not worry about my whereabouts. I am going nowhere.

At dusk I finally step out and make my way down to the back yard, ignoring Martel, who follows me. The air is fragrant; the bush calls are undergoing their daily transmutation, from the optimistic chatter of the multitude of daytime prey to the blood-curdling howl of the solitary night stalkers.

Under the canopy, this is the time for us to cling and come together, skin to chilled skin, breath to fevered breath, groin to warm groin. We find solace if not safety in the huddle, as hypnotic horrors prey across our faded trails.

Martel, who remains discreetly on the porch, settles down to smoking, his carbine resting on his lap. The yard has not been tended for weeks, the caretaker family having absconded while I was gone. Empty bottles, trash, assorted debris of our existence, are strewn about in haphazard mounds. This detritus, through which I gingerly pick my way, is rising testament to our current state of mind.

I am at loss whether to circle right or left when I hear Jojo's voice, faint yet unmistakable. It is coming out of the window of one of the ground-floor rooms, the one usually kept locked. A second voice now interrupts, it is unfamiliar. I move closer, casually, then lean back on the dirty stucco next to the shutter and make an elaborate show of rolling a cigarette and lighting up.

Jojo is in the midst of talking, his voice agitated.

"You call this an operation? I call it shit! You tell us nothing about the place, zilch! Are there any friendlies around? Maybe, maybe not. Where's the ANC? In Kongolo? In Albertville? Inside Kabalo already? How're we supposed to pull this up? What about support?"

Jojo's interlocutor sounds apologetic: "The Gendarmerie over in Kabalo will be notified over the radio. They'll give you as much support as—"

Jojo cuts him short: "*Je m'en fous ta Gendarmerie!* If they're still there. When has anybody seen them last?"

"Our report—"

"Stuff your report! And if they're there, what kind of support do you think I'll get from them? We'd be lucky if we don't have to bail them out! They're probably into the bush by now anyway. Christ, you don't expect us to take on the ANC and the Baluba *and* the Unies all at the same time without some support! We're only human, you know."

"Now, Monsieur Georges—"

But Jojo's rage is not yet extinguished: "Shit, you take what's happening here in town! The minute the Unies shows up, the whole *Force Publique* disappears. You gave them guns, you gave them ammo, you gave them training! Where is it all now? Where are the white officers? Might as well pull them out and combine them with us, for all the good they're doing you there!"

"You know we can't do that, they are the only force Tchombé's still got on his side."

"Then God help Tchombé, and let's stop pretending about the

blacks fighting on Tchombé's side! Forget it, it's not their war; it's yours! So you better start fighting it with the men you've got, or in two weeks there ain't gonna be no war left to fight! And while we're at it, this business of locking us up in here for weeks on end—*c'est bête*! The men are in a foul mood, that last one south of here didn't help either. No, don't tell me your information said they were armed! Fuck your information, spears and machetes is all they had! You think these men have no pride? They're not going to sit here much longer and wait for the Unies to come pick them off!"

"They're paid to take orders, Monsieur Georges. So are you."

"Fuck your orders! We're paid to fight, not to hide out and butcher civilians!"

"Well, you've got the bridge now—"

"I said fight, not commit suicide!"

There is a pause. I light another cigarette. Inside, the other speaker now sounds conciliatory: "Let's be reasonable, Monsieur Georges. We'll give you all the support we've got. The Kabalo garrison will be notified, we'll send them more Belgian officers. I promise."

The man's voice trails off. When Jojo speaks again, he sounds tired, almost spent.

"Yes," he says, "yes . . . I've heard that before. Did you bring the money? The men are supposed to be paid tomorrow."

"The money's coming; it'll be here by the time you're back from Kabalo."

"Nothing doing. The money before we leave. These men've got a contract. No money, no bridge."

"What's the rush? You'll get paid. What's the big deal about a day or two? We've just brought the money over to the ministry; I just need to stop by there and get the cash—"

"If it's still there! Listen, you want my guys to fight your dirty little war, you pay them, on time. And if I were you I'd go to the ministry tonight, before they had a chance to transfer the last bit of your cash into their Swiss accounts. Why don't you guys wise up and deal directly with us? It'll save you a bundle and at least you know where your money's gone. Shit . . . "

"We'd love to, but you know we can't."

"You could easily pay us double and still save some."

I have heard enough, and my second cigarette is even more foul-tasting than the first. I detach myself from the wall and stroll back into the center of the yard. Martel rises, prepared to follow me. I climb the steps slowly, pass next to him without acknowledgment and go back upstairs to my room. I've got to think. I also must talk to Jojo.

It is eight in the evening and we are assembled together in the dining hall overlooking the front yard. We have just eaten another cold supper; the men are sullen and have not stopped drinking. The water mains have been turned off; there are no houseboys in sight to fetch our water; the stench rising from the sweaty unwashed bodies is overpowering—the real white man's burden. Desultory small talk erupts and trails off. We were all paid, first thing in the morning, a fact that somehow fails to elicit the usual buzz, given the scant opportunity for spending any of it soon.

Jojo raps the table for attention. His admonition is almost superfluous. His voice sounds strained; his eyes are unnaturally bright; his cheeks are even more hollow. Like the rest of us, he is in bad need of a shave. In the twelve years we've been together, I don't recall ever seeing him this run down. Not even in our worst days in the Delta.

"Cut out the noise, guys," he says. "I've got something to tell you."

Jean-Louis translates for the Anglos, who give no sign of acknowledgment as they go on drinking. Jojo looks at them briefly, then goes on: "Better listen real careful now. We've got a job coming up, tomorrow morning early. It's a single raid deal, north of here, about two hundred miles straight up. There's a bridge on the Lualaba, that's the name of a river . . . We go up there and blow it, then come straight back."

The translation proceeds slowly, everybody is finally paying attention. One of the Belgians asks: "How do we get up there?"

"We fly."

When Jojo's last response is translated, there is commotion among the Anglos, one of whom then engages Jean-Louis in a quick exchange at the end of which Jean-Louis turns back to Jojo: "He says there's no airport up there. They've been all over that area before, during the Stanleyville business."

"Tell him there's supposed to be a *Union Minière* strip near

Kabalo," Jojo instructs him. "Tell him the Katanga Gendarmerie is supposed to be holed up in there, guarding the mine."

Jean-Louis translates, after which there is a further exchange. It is clear the Anglos are not reassured by the news, and Jean-Louis transmits their lack of enthusiasm back to Jojo: "He says why don't those monkeys blow the goddamn bridge themselves?"

"They've got no explosives left there," Jojo says. "Besides, there's nobody up there who knows how to do it."

Jean-Louis transmits the information back to the Anglos, then again turns back to Jojo: "They say they don't know anything about explosives either—never done this kind of a job. Come to think, Jojo, we don't have anybody either."

"We do."

"Who?"

"Robert."

"Him?"

I sit way in the back near the window, apart from the rest of them, and now eyes are slowly settling on me. After an awkward pause Jojo speaks.

"Yes, him. He's the best *plastiqueur* we had back home. Right, Martel?"

"Well . . ."

Martel is clearly unhappy with having to provide a testimonial for me. Jojo turns to me: "You tell them, Roberto."

Everybody is looking at me. This is not the time to tell them what I really think.

"What do we know about the bridge?" I ask.

"Next to nothing," Jojo says. "We've got enough plastique stashed right here. We'll take as much of the stuff as we can carry on foot. Ought to be enough. You can rig up the design when you see the bridge."

"I don't know," I say. "How about cord and stuff?"

"They're bringing everything over tonight, more ammo too. You check it all out; make sure you've got enough plastic for at least four charges. That ought to do it for a lousy bridge."

He turns back to the group at large.

"We've got five miles to haul the stuff in from the strip. We'll fly in early and wait for dark right there. Then we go in and blow it up real quick, high-tail it back to the plane, and fly back here. In and out. Ought to be a cinch. Any questions?"

Jean-Louis translates. Nobody says anything.

"Well," says Jojo, "if not, you all better pack everything tonight. They're bringing the stuff over soon. We drive to the plane before dawn."

As everybody begins to talk at the same time, I go over to Jojo, who now sits alone, brooding.

"I'm tired," I tell him. "I'll be up in the room. Wake me up when the stuff gets here, okay?"

Jojo looks up, our eyes meet briefly before I lower mine.

"No monkey business, Roberto."

"You can post Martel at the door."

"I will."

I shrug, turn, and walk out through the door. My ankle is not yet fully healed, I limp upstairs and close the door behind me.

I first assemble the timer, a delicate operation but still a cinch. I pry the small watch open, probe for the right joints, put the thin wires in place and tape the back securely. I shove it into the boot of my bad leg where a slight limp would look natural. Now I am lying on my bed in the dark, waiting.

Most of my life the past twelve years, it seems, has been spent in this unrewarding fashion. I have endured it without much enthusiasm, but have now come to resent it. Mind you, I am good at it—an expert at deferring decision, waiting for a sign, for the right time.

Here is the rub though: unlike the true opportunist I have always assumed I was, I turn out to also be an accomplished procrastinator. Can I seize the day? On this rickety steel-frame cot in a crumbling villa, in a town rapidly reverting to the surrounding bush, in the company of brutes who have surrendered the last shard of their humanity?

I have come here by way of a festering rubber plantation, now only a dim memory, through the barren rock piles of Kabylia, via the charred back yards of Bab-el-Oued. I have been content to just drift, endure, go along. As I wait now for Jojo, who is due to come up any minute, I am assailed by doubts. The one thing I know for sure is that something's got to give.

Jojo comes in without knocking, carrying a flashlight. He is breathing hard and takes a beeline to my lone chair, turns it around, and plops down. We are both quiet for a while, and awkward. Finally Jojo says: "They're here. Better go and pack the stuff."

"Not before we talk."

"Fine. Talk."

I try to put my thoughts in order but don't get far.

"Why are we doing this, Jojo?" I ask.

"What?"

"The bridge."

"What about it?"

"Cut the crap, *Monsieur Georges*," I tell him. "I heard you talking to the creep from *Union Minière* yesterday. You didn't sound all that happy about it either. Why not just say no?"

Jojo remains silent. In the thin yellow light of his flashlight, which he has put on the floor next to the chair, his face is cast in deep shadow. His labored breath comes over in quick rasps.

"You're sick, Jojo," I tell him. "You need a doctor, not a lousy bridge."

I wait. He says nothing.

"You really don't think these guys've got a chance in hell of winning, do you?"

Still no answer.

I prop myself up on the cot, I wonder if Jojo has fallen asleep, or maybe fainted.

"Jojo?"

"Yes."

"I don't give a fuck about what you do. Just give me a reason why I should come along."

"Because we've got a job. Because I need you."

"Try again," I tell him.

"Get off my back, Roberto. What do you expect me to do?"

"Quit," I tell him. "Let's, right now. Dump this miserable war, go home."

"Not yet."

"Goddamn it, Jojo, can't you just for once admit it's over? No more Legion, no more *Algérie Française*, no Bab-el-Oued, no OAS. It's over, Jojo, finished. We've lost."

In the silence that is Jojo's only response, I go on: "Remember that night you came on the boat with Martel?"

"Shit, yes."

"I told you then. I told you again in Marseilles. I'm telling you now. Won't you just for once listen? Let's get out of here while we still can. Let me get you to a hospital. You're a walking stiff, you wouldn't last a mile in the bush."

"I can take care of myself."

"Then leave me out, Jojo. Go do that lousy bridge without me."

But I doubt he will respond. At least he has said nothing about Marie. This is as close as Jojo has ever come to begging. In his fevered brain, I am the one still owing. For those festering five miles of slow terror in the sniper-infested jungle, five miles so long, so long ago, we hardly remember.

How long does one stay owing? As far as Jojo is concerned, forever. In this, I now see, he is much like the old man, who shared this obsession with time's dead reckonings. Scores are never quite settled, accounts cumulate for eternity, nothing is ever lost nor forgotten; no slight ever forgiven, no debt ever left unpaid.

When the chips are down, this Catholic heathen *copain* of mine, hardy sprig of the back alleys of Bab-el-Oued, is just as tenacious a *Judío* as my old *abuelico*. I shall keep owing them both, forever, alive or dead.

It has finally dawned on me, clear as a bell, how Jojo was dead right back there in the dark cul-de-sac in Marseilles. They are all *Judíos*, my French-Alsatian-Corsican-Italian brethren *pieds noirs*. Jews to the core each and every one, obstinate and obsessed, plagued by their compounded histories, their ancient lore and convoluted identity, driven by treasured old grievances, ever-bleeding stigmata. Wherever I turn, I am doomed to be trumped, co-opted by this tribe that insists on owning me body and soul.

As before, the game is up, and once again I give in despite my premonition of doom.

"This is for the last time, Jojo, you understand?" I tell him.

"I hear you."

"No more owing, not a damn thing after this one, remember."

"Okay."

I get off the bed, lean down next to the chair, pick up the flashlight and flash the yellow beam on Jojo's face. He is slumped in the chair, eyes closed.

"Better grab some sleep," I tell him.

He grunts, and I go down to sort out the tools of my trade.

The plane is the same slow Dakota we arrived in. This time it is almost empty except for the eight of us and our packs, arms, and ammunition. And the five drums of aviation fuel we carry with us, our insurance, lifeline, ticket home.

We have taken off before dawn and nobody's had enough sleep. We spend most of the flight time dozing off in the infernal rattle of the old aluminum frame that is in bad need of fresh rivets.

A Dakota will land on the skimpiest of strips, but there is a downside to this—flights that take forever.

Some of the men are smoking in spite of the explosives in their backpacks. When I tell Jojo, he shrugs: "Let them."

He is huddled across from me and seems more frail than ever. Next to him the squat Martel, who somehow thrives in the tropics, is a veritable giant.

Shortly before noon the pilot starts circling. He is a local Ultra who used to work for the mines and thus knows the place. Jojo drags himself up and goes forward to talk to him. The cockpit is open but you can't hear much above the din. After a while Jojo comes back and goes from one man to the other, waking them up.

"Hold on to your packs," he tells us. "The strip is kind of rough. Roberto?"

"Yes?"

"Hang on to your stuff."

"Sure."

I have the drum of electrical cord, the primers and detos and the rest of the delicate implements of my trade, all packed in one large canvas sack. I grab it and plant it on my lap. In the dark, I lean down, pull the small contraption out of my left boot, and place it carefully in the pack.

As the plane makes its final turn and banks sharply for a landing, we brace ourselves and wait in silence. When the wheels finally touch down, we get a taste of what Jojo must have meant. A nasty jolt shakes the old crate, after which it pitches violently, briefly goes airborne again, then lands back and goes hopping and skipping over the rough terrain before finally settling down to rolling speed. You can almost hear the guys letting out their breath.

We are two hundred yards from what looks like a clump of deserted Quonset sheds. Jojo goes back to the cockpit, where the pilot is looking back at him.

"Wait here," Jojo tells him. "Don't shut her off yet."

He then takes two of the Belgians and the three of them climb down to the grass through the bottom hatch.

We wait, listening to the engines' occasional misfire. Once the plane is on the ground, its steep stance makes it almost impossible to see much of the outside, except for the sky. Nobody seems curious; some of the men have gone back to sleep.

I get up and go to visit the pilot, but from his perch all you can see is the bush surrounding the strip.

"Might as well turn her around," I tell him. "We might have to take off in a hurry."

"Better wait for the boss," he says.

He is slumped in his seat, sipping coffee out of a gray plastic Thermos. I nod, and notice his finely lined face, which seems too old for the rest of him, or maybe he is just dog tired.

"Aren't you going to refuel?" I ask.

"We can do it while flying."

He offers me his Thermos and I take a sip.

"Thanks." I pass it back to him.

Ten minutes later Jojo and the Belgians are back. We look up as they pull themselves in through the hatch.

"Turn her around and roll over to the hangar," Jojo tells the pilot, pointing through the window. The plane turns and pulls back down the strip. Jojo turns to face us.

"The place is deserted," he says. "No Gendarmerie, no mine personnel... We're going to stash the plane and unload our stuff, then stay in the shack until dark. We don't know who's around or how far they might be, so please keep quiet and stay put. For all we know, nobody has seen us yet." Nobody bothers to laugh.

When the plane stops for good, we haul our stuff down the ladder and follow Jojo. Behind us, the pilot is maneuvering the plane under a low corrugated-metal roof that must be the hangar. Once in the shed, Jojo assigns guard duty and takes the first two men to show them their posts. It is taken for granted that I am exempt, seeing as how I carry no weapon.

We munch on tinned corned beef and stale crackers. When Jojo comes back, he lowers himself down next to me.

"Better get some rest," he tells us.

In the stifling heat of the shed, nobody talks.

I prop my head on my pack and close my eyes, trying not to think. I should be dog tired, but I still can't fall asleep. The cicadas in the plane trees are buzzing at the top of their register. Otherwise, the place is eerily quiet. I hope this is not a trap, but there's no use raising the issue with Jojo. I wonder whether the bridge is really there, I am anxious to get going and be done. Anything but this interminable waiting. I finally fall asleep.

We are following Jojo in a single file, having been trekking for over two hours. My pack, small as it is, is proving to be more of a nuisance than I have expected; the sharp rim of the electric-cord drum is boring into my shoulder. My ankle is also making its displeasure felt. To spare it, I ease into a slight limp. I am still luckier than the others, whose packs are loaded with plastique and ammunition. I am also the only one not carrying a gun, though I carry an ammunition belt.

The nine of us are wrapped in silence, with Jojo leading the way and Martel bringing up the rear behind me. We left right after sunset and a hurried cold meal, and, if we are not lost, we should be there about now. The night is warm and the bush is much sparser than the rain forest around Eville. The altitude must be much higher, though nobody has mentioned that. Wide open patches of veld—tall clumps of rough-bladed grass—stretch between groves of plane trees. While we have less cover in such a terrain, our progress is considerably

Running Through the Tall Grass

smoother. Especially this time of the evening, with the clipped moon still with us low above the treetops on the left.

We pause on the edge of a small grove, where Jojo waits for all of us to gather around him in the shade. He's got the map in his hand and is scanning it in the beam of a flashlight.

"Now listen," he says, "we're just about there. The bridge is two hundred yards further that-a-way . . . "

He nods, pointing in the direction we have been heading. His voice is a hoarse whisper. I am still surprised at the brisk pace he has set.

On the fringe of the huddle, Jean-Louis translates.

"All right," Jojo continues, "from here on we move in a spread line . . . all of us except Charles, who's going to stay and guard the rear. Here, I'll take your pack . . . "

Charles, one of the Belgians, transfers his pack to Jojo, who hoists it slowly. He scans around for me.

"Robert, you got your stuff all ready?"

"Yes."

"Good. Stay in the back with Martel. The rest of you, hold your guns at the ready; we don't know if anybody's at the bridge. All right, Jean-Louis."

Jojo's orders are quickly rendered into English, after which we again lapse into silence.

"*Bon*," says Jojo, "let's get going . . . spread out . . . further . . . "

Jojo is at the center of the spread line now, I follow a few yards behind and cannot but notice the way he is swaying under his pack. We cut our trail slowly through the rustle of the grass. In a few minutes we emerge on the other side of the grove. Just in front of us looms the elevated railroad ramp. Further to the right, it curves into a dark mass that must be the bridge. Jojo has signaled for everybody to stop. We freeze in place, listening intently, but except for the normal night noises we can make out nothing.

On signal we move again, and soon the tall metal skeleton emerges out of the dark. It is a fair-size structure, and we are now at the point where the rails mount it. Everybody is crouched. I close in behind Jojo, doing my best to ignore Martel right behind me. Two of the Anglos with Jean-Louis drop their pack and move on to secure the other end. We all watch them as they thread their way across the bridge. If anybody is there guarding, this is when they are most likely to hit. Jojo turns to me: "Robert?"

"Yes?"

"Leave your stuff here, let's go take a look. Martel, spread the rest of them on both sides and watch the rear."

I leave my pack behind and follow Jojo along the embankment. We climb down under the bridge to the edge of the water. Small wavelets lap at our feet, but from where we stand we cannot see much in the dark. The metal span is propped on a pair of supporting concrete posts about ten yards out. There is at least another pair further in, maybe more. The exact distance to the other bank is impossible to gauge.

"What do you think?" Jojo says.

"Hard to say from down here. Might as well go up there, take a look."

"Think we have enough plastique?"

"Yeah, for four spots, ought to do it."

"Let's go set it up then, we're running late. All four at the same time?"

"I suppose."

I follow Jojo back to where the others are spread along the embankment.

"Come on," Jojo tells them, "move the stuff up on the bridge. Robert'll tell you where to drop it."

We grab our packs and I follow Jojo slowly across the sleepers between the two rails and onto the bridge span itself. The rest of the guys follow. In a minute I am right above the first pair of columns.

"They can dump half of it here," I tell Jojo, then proceed along the span, scanning for the spot where the second pair locks underneath. The guys are right behind me.

"The rest of it right here," I tell them.

I crouch and peer into the dark between the sleepers, at the point where they bolt on top of the metal cross beams. The top of the concrete posts is barely visible three feet below. It is a simpler design than I have anticipated, child's play. I will be hard pressed to come up with a credible excuse, and Jojo is right there next to me, watching.

I get up and stretch.

"We can lower the packs right on top of the concrete," I tell Jojo, "right at the point where the metal cross spans bolt in. Two here, the other two back there. I'll set the fuse on this side, then patch the rest together with black cord. Ought to do it."

Not surprisingly, Jojo is not buying my plan.

"Why not set each one with its own fuse?" he says. "You've got plenty of wire."

"Sure, whatever," I hasten to agree. "I thought we were in a hurry."

On the inside, I am cussing.

"Not that much of a hurry," he says.

While Jojo supervises the lowering of the bricks at the four spots; I walk back and retrieve my pack and the ammo belt. When the others are done, they clear off the bridge and I go back and rejoin Jojo. He has already selected four bricks for me. I insert a primer in each one, then the smooth metal fuse. My fingers remember. Under Jojo's scrutiny I lower the bricks at each spot, burying each one in a tightly packed mound of oily blocks, leaving the yellow wires dangling free. Then, with Jojo still tracking me like a bloodhound, I attach the edge of the spooled wire to one of the loads, then cross over and splice in its twin. Jojo is holding up the spool, reeling it out for me as we retreat back toward the bank, while I lay the wire neatly next to the rail. We stop, I repeat the wiring scheme.

In a few more minutes we are done and, now in tandem, are rolling the wire off the bridge.

"Better go get Jean-Louis and the Anglos," I tell Jojo. "I want to go and check the fuses again, just to be safe."

"You do that, Roberto," he tells me.

We drop the spool on the bank and walk back to the bridge.

"Just remember," Jojo says, "I'll be checking them again after you."

"You're the boss," I tell him.

I have placed the fuses snug and tight the first time around, there is really no reason to check them again. I will go through the motions, but I know Jojo will check them after me.

I climb down to the nearest post. In the dark, I reach into the bottom of my pack and pull out the rigged timer. I pull out a detonator next and attach it to the dangling wires. The metal tube is resting in my palm, cold and smooth. Next I pull out the spare brick I kept, then push the deto tube snugly into the primer. I try not to think about the hospital, but my fingers remember.

I tape the timer securely to the brick, then empty a pouch in the ammo belt and put the brick inside. It is timed for fifteen minutes, once I press the button.

I go through the motion of kneeling next to the other three spots, then walk off the bridge to where I left the spool near my pack. I wait for the four silhouettes gliding across to join me, noting the one who interrupts his progress twice, crouching briefly at each point, before rejoining me.

"Where do you want it set?" I ask him.

"Do we have enough wire to run it back to the grove?"

"I suppose."

"Good."

He turns back to Jean-Louis and the two Anglos.

"Watch here for five minutes, no more," he tells them. "Then join us at the grove. Grab your pack, Roberto, let's reel her out."

We play the wire out, with me walking the spool and Jojo laying the wire. The rest of squad rushes ahead of us, Martel in the lead. The spool is almost spent when we hit the edge of the grove. We wait for the other three to join us, then Jojo pulls Martel over: "Take everybody back to the other side, where we left Charles. Then go on back to the plane. Set up watch around it; make sure the pilot's got her refueled and ready to take off."

"I don't know, Jojo," says Martel, "just the two of you, one gun . . . Why don't we all wait here?"

"Never mind, just go on. Jean-Louis, give Robert your gun."

In the uneasy silence that ensues, I interject my unwelcome perspective: "I don't need it."

"Who asked you? Jean-Louis!"

Jean-Louis shrugs and offers me his carbine, which I refuse. Everybody is watching the tug of war between me and Jojo. I can feel their palpable hostility, and am expecting Martel to cut in any minute.

"Oh hell, do it your own way," Jojo says in exasperation.

As the rest of them turn to leave I say: "Hold it."

I am unstrapping my ammo belt.

"What's the matter?" says Jojo.
"Better let them take this," I tell him, "won't be any use for me."
He looks at me; I look back. He shrugs.
"Martel."
In the dark I press the button. I hand the belt to Martel, who straps it on. He leans in close to me.
"Better pray they get you, *Juif*," he says. "If they don't, I will."
"I'll remember," I tell him.
"You two cut it out," says Jojo behind me.
The two of us watch the others gliding into the grove like silent ghosts.

$\mathcal{W}$e sit in silence near the empty spool, listening to the receding sound of swishing steps. In a moment we are alone.
"Better hook up the generator," Jojo says.
I lean over and drag my canvas pack closer and pull out the metal hand-cranked generator. I test the crank mechanism twice; I listen to the humming gears and watch for the spark. Everything is in perfect working order. I place the metal box down, pick up the loose end of the electric wire we reeled in from the bridge, slide it into its receptacle, and tighten up the screw.
"Do we need to test it first?" Jojo asks.
"Test it on what?" I ask him.
"Whatever."
"Nay, it sparks just fine. You can come and take a look."
"Never mind."
I kick the empty canvas aside and join Jojo next to the clump of trees, where he is sitting and smoking.
"Want one?" he offers.
"Sure."
I sit down next to him and he lights a cigarette and passes it to me.
"Thanks."
Jojo nods.
We sit and smoke in silence. The quarter moon has gone down, but the stars are real bright. The light, once our eyes are accustomed to it, is enough to navigate back to the strip, while still giving us decent cover. In the country we traverse on our way back to the strip,

this mix of light and dark is just right. In this the high veld is like the Kabylia Mountains but unlike Indochina, where the dark under the canopy afforded indiscriminate cover, for you, for them.

"Better get it done with," Jojo says.

"Let the guys get further away."

"We're both a bit slowed down, Roberto."

"You telling me?"

"That leg of yours looks real gimpy."

"You're not a picture of ruddy health yourself."

"If I had to pull you out again, I don't think I'd last a mile."

"If I had to pull you out again, this lousy ankle wouldn't last a hundred yards."

I wasn't going to bring it up, but am nevertheless relieved Jojo did. We hardly ever talk about what has transpired between us, not since Indochina, not much even then. Our twin misadventures still bind us together though. Like a submerged volcano, the still-smoldering symmetry of our near-identical exploits among the rubber trees keeps sustaining us.

Still, Jojo needs to be reminded, however gently, that we are now even, have been even ever since I pulled him out of that lousy minefield near Duc Tho with the damp green world exploding around us in the burning plantation lifetimes ago.

Put more bluntly, I don't owe Jojo a thing, certainly not any more than he owes me. Our accounts are balanced; it is time he conceded that. What is more, we are not fused together. Each of us is now on his own.

"Did you really have to pull that last caper?" Jojo asks.

My breath catches before I realize he couldn't possibly know about Martel, and must therefore be referring to my week with the Baluba.

"It wasn't planned," I tell him, "seeing Martel there did it. Couldn't be helped. You should have warned me. Or him."

"He wanted to go back and kill you, you know."

"Not for the first time," I remind him.

"You really hurt his pride."

I don't tell him what Martel said, nor what Martel is carrying around his belt. No need to. As we sit there together in silence, the crack of a small explosion wafts our way.

"What was that?" says Jojo.

"Beats me."

"I hope the guys are okay."

"Let's hope."

"I wouldn't bait Martel anymore if I were you," he says. "He's close to cracking."

"We all are."

"Still."

"All right," I tell him, "I won't. The little shit is all yours. Keep him off my back though—I'm not about to put up with him anymore."

A bit disingenuous, that.

"He just talks," says Jojo.

"Talk can kill."

"Forget it. It's almost over."

It is time to be done and get going, but it feels good to just sit there and rest. Our cigarettes are spent; we have said all we are going to say. I have been racking my brain all evening for some way of not going on with this, but Jojo has trumped me at every point; I can't think of a good excuse. What the hell, I think, it is just a stupid bridge. Let's be done with it and go home.

Just when I am about to get up and go for the generator, we hear the approaching rumble of the train from across the river. We are both startled; we haven't counted on a train.

"I guess we better blow her before they get there," I tell Jojo.

"Hold it, let's wait," he says.

"What do you mean?"

But I know exactly what he means.

"Might as well get them together with the bridge," he says. "Go ahead, grab your gizmo and get ready."

"I don't think so, Jojo."

"I don't have time to argue, Roberto, just do it."

"Not this time."

Jojo gets up and limps slowly toward the crank generator.

"Jojo," I call after him, "either you blow it now or we turn around and split."

He keeps walking. I notice, to my great surprise and greater relief, that his gun is still propped against the tree trunk where he has left it. I grab the gun, crank the bolt, and release the safety. I know there is no way he has not heard the loud metal click.

"Jojo," I tell him, "you're not going to blow those guys on the bridge. That's all there is to it."

Jojo ignores me and crouches next to the generator, and I cuss myself for not having somehow disabled it.

"Jojo," I plead with him, "it's either now or never, you hear?"

I move closer to him and raise the gun. The train is now visible, a dark mass chugging its way slowly toward the bridge. As it executes the final wide curve on its slow ascent toward the bridge, I can see the lights in the row of cars it is pulling. There is little doubt about it being a troop transport. I watch it in growing horror as it approaches the bridge. Then the locomotive is beginning to pull across. The rumble of the rolling stock carries over in the vast stillness of the star-bathed veld.

"Jojo!" I scream at the top of my voice. "Get up or I'll have to shoot you!"

I am watching Jojo's back from ten yards away. He is crouched there next to the empty spool, my marker. In the bright expanse of grass under the stars, Jojo is but a small figure huddled down there in total resolve. I watch the locomotive creeping across to our side. And I know what is about to happen and am powerless to stop it.

"Jojo—*nom de Dieu*—don't!" I scream at him for the last time.

I am shivering and sweating and my face is wet with tears. Almost simultaneously I hear the crank of the generator's gears, followed by a deafening roar as the entire bridge—locomotive, troops, cars, and all—rises up in an erupting red and yellow flash, crashes slowly into the river below. Which is when I notice, though I cannot hear it, the exploding staccato rattle of the carbine in my hands.

After a while my arms stop shaking; the magazine is empty. There must be screaming and moaning from the survivors under the bridge, but I can hear nothing except a high-pitched wail in my ears that blocks out everything.

I loosen my cramped fingers out of the trigger guard and pitch the gun to the ground. Jojo lies crumpled where he has fallen, a small heap blending with its surroundings. No use checking, from where I was standing I couldn't have missed.

I turn around and start running. I crash into the grove at full tilt, stumble, roll down, then get up again immediately. I will have to be careful with my ankle if I want it to last me to the plane. I start running again, more slowly now, aiming in the general direction of the strip. When I have traversed the grove, I slow down as the elephant grass comes up to engulf to me. I pause to look for the track we carved out on our single-filed way in, then plunge in, and resume running as fast as my poor ankle will let me.

I have been running now for what seems like hours and am nearing exhaustion. I am woefully out of shape, huffing like an overheated truck. What is more, my ankle is sending me sharp signals. I slow down to a gait somewhere between a walk and a trot, trying to catch my breath. It is impossible to see more than a few yards ahead on the narrow trail. To the right and left, the elephant grass rises above my head, making progress an act of blind faith.

I still cannot hear much except for the high-pitched whine that is boring into my skull. After a while I start running again, though at a slower pace. I need to catch up with the squad, though there's no knowing what kind of welcome I can expect. Gradually, I am beginning to hear the hiss and crackle of the grass as I punch through it.

I have no idea what will happen at the strip. What can I tell the guys about Jojo? Or about Martel, if they press? What can I tell myself about what happened at the bridge? I am numb and exhausted, aching and near deaf. But as long as I keep running, I am all right.

When I slow down to catch my breath again, I hear the first muffled report of the gunshots. The fact I can hardly hear them may or may not tell much about the distance. They are not aimed my way, though, the whiplash crack of bullets above my head is missing.

I keep walking. I try to concentrate. After a while it becomes clear I am getting closer to where the shooting is taking place. It still seems far away though.

I try a slow trot for a while. The grass around me is as endless as the sea under the moonless sky. Somewhere along the way, a while back, I must have strayed from the trail. I am shoving my way through the tall grass now, blindly fending off the sharp blades with my hands and elbows which, together with my face, must be getting bruised.

I crash into a small bush and spill headlong into the grass. I lie there for a long moment, panting, then get up to resume my trot. The shooting is coming from much closer now, some stray bullets are passing over my head.

Now I can hear the voices, coming from all around me, loud and piercing, like the Balubas at the fork. As I plow my way through the slashing, blinding grass, the voices roll my way like angry breakers, crashing over my head accompanied by the boom of the kettle drums.

For all I know I may be nearing the airstrip, the likely fulcrum of the charge. If they are Baluba, we shouldn't count on their mercy. I may just as well sit down right where I am, or turn and run back the other way. Except, in the moonless grass all around me I have no idea what the other way is.

My legs are pumping away on their own as I hurtle myself through the grass, but my mind is elsewhere. I get to thinking about Marie and how horrendously unlikely it is I'll ever see her again. I get to thinking about Mulenga under the baobab tree. About Mulenga at the fork, her head cleaved open.

I do my best not to, but still think about Jojo's malaria-ravaged body crumpled near the bridge, the crank generator still clutched in his desperate hands. I get to thinking about my father, about our now-ancient good-bye to which no face is attached anymore.

But mostly, my mind veers, inexorably, toward the old man. I remember, with fresh remorse, how I had never got to visit his tomb nor read the *Cadísh* over him. I hope he has found eternal rest in spite of my never-to-be-rectified omission. I suspect he will forgive me, especially if he sees me trapped as I am so far from his own resting place. I can only hope his chance of rising with the righteous on the day of the second coming—in his reckoning the first—won't be compromised by the skipped ritual. I can only hope he will find his way—together with the rest of the faithful, a great incorporeal host swooshing through the balmy salted air—back to his beloved *Jerusalén*.

I wonder if he could ever find it in his heart to forgive me for being who I am rather than who he had intended me to be. I wonder why he never told me, never in so many words, who it was he wanted me to be. If I had only been a bit more like him, maybe I would have understood what I am doing here on this moonless night in the middle of this miserable continent, running in the tall grass. I wish I understood why he told me, so secure in his knowledge, eons ago, "Mijico, you'll never have a country." I wish I knew what he meant.

While I am at it, I also regret I never had his patience, nor his perseverance, nor his blind faith, that immutable rock on which his life had rested, in his sweet *Diosito*, God of *Abrahán*, *Isaqué*, and *Jacques* always watching over him from way up there, but never over me.

As I slow down again, I also remember, rather improbably, a song he used to sing to me during those early years after my father left for the war, remember his reedy voice tossing out the *cante jondo*:

En la mar hay una tura,
En la tura una donzella,
En la tura una donzella
Que a los marineros ama.

Dame la mano o tu donzella,
Pá subir a tu nido,
Maldicha que duermes sola,
Vengo a dormir con tí.

I must be getting closer to where all the shooting and the shouting is coming from. It's getting louder. I know I should just sit down, better still, lie down. But here I am, with the last drop of energy in my depleted body, running in the tall grass. I am blind and half deaf and my heart is filled to the brim with infinite, inconsolable regret. But somehow running makes it easier to put up with what's coming. Wherever you are, God, if you are, whenever you're ready, I am all yours now. Come and get me. Go . . .

FOUR

Epilogue

※

Marie

Marseilles, January 1963

*F*or a while, after I got the telegram, there was nobody I could talk to to find out what had happened. For months I had heard nothing, except for the note he left me at the *poste restante*. Then a lacerating long silence. Finally the kind Belgian captain came and found me, and gave me the message from Brazzaville. I was in shock, realizing finally how far away he had gone. The Congo, totally incomprehensible. And nobody here who could tell me why, for how long.

Then no news again. Then finally the telegram. After which I had to run around and pester them for weeks, before someone finally took pity on me and steered me to the right bureau. Whereupon I had to start all over again: cajole, beg, cry, throw hysterics, whatever would do the trick. It was Inspector Mariceau who finally relented and said he would investigate.

They found him, I was finally told, in the grass. He was running back toward the airstrip, they thought. My fallen angel coming back to me. They wanted to spare me the details, bless their hearts, but I insisted. I needed to know how: where the bullets hit him; how long he took to die; whether he suffered untold agonies. I had to know; I think they thought I was mad. Perhaps I was, with grief.

They wanted to leave him there, under the grass. But I insisted; I pestered them, kept calling, threatened to write letters. In the end they capitulated and agreed on cremation. Finally the small package arrived. Even then it took a while to get them to release it. You weren't married to him, they said, his relatives might object. I told them he had no kin, but they said they needed to make sure. After two weeks they gave in and let me have my package. Though not before making me fill out two forms in triplicate.

I went to his people then and explained, the best I could, who he was and how I happened to come by his ashes. I asked for their kind of burial. It turned out he wasn't on their rolls. I explained again, I pointed out, once more I broke down and cried. But nobody would take my word for it since I am not one of them either. I told them the little I knew about his family, the old man. But somehow I couldn't get them to acknowledge ownership.

I finally gave up. I figured, he had bounced around enough; it was time for him to find his final rest, no matter who or what he was. Enough is enough. So the next afternoon, I took the last tourist boat to Château d'If. It was a surprisingly warm day for January, the sea so calm and the boat, mercifully, almost empty. I hugged the plastic-wrapped package to my heart like I would have liked to hug him.

The guide led the few of us around, perfunctorily pointing out the Count's solitary cell, the tunnel the old man had dug through to him, the bunk where the body of the living dead had rested, sown in its burlap sack. Then, while the others were taking their aperitif, I snuck out and made my way to the cliff.

The sun was hanging low over the southwest horizon, the cliff facing directly home. I stood there for an endless moment, longing to have him in my arms just a little longer. It was no use, he was not mine to hold any longer. So I tore the package open and shook his ashes out into the water of our inland sea.

For as much as I knew him, and for as much as he can find rest, let the water of our inland sea be his final repository. The way I reckon it, whether the tides carry him back home to Algiers, or to Cádiz or Modena, or to Istanbul or Athens or Alexandria, or all the way to his people's faraway *Sión*, he may be just as content. This way, I don't see how he could miss.

Yes, I know, they had a chant, *Cadísh* he called it. Someone was supposed to say it over him like our Requiem. But I don't know it, and he didn't either. Besides, they had their chance to claim him, and declined. So let the water claim him if it will.